Hatshepsut's Hideaway

By Fiona Deal

Text copyright 2013

All Rights Reserved

This is a work of fiction.
Names, characters, places and incidents
either are the product of the author's imagination
or are used fictitiously.

Chapter 1

Summertime 2012

The newly discovered ancient Egyptian royal tomb felt ridiculously crowded with nine of us inside it. Actually, it was ten if you included the unconscious Hussein. To be fair, we weren't exactly crammed in. The rock-cut chamber was big enough to hold us all comfortably. The trouble was it was jam-packed with treasure. Every one of the priceless artefacts dated back to the golden age of the pharaohs. We were all edging around these inestimable treasures with as much care as if we were tightrope walking, desperate not to stumble or trip and cause even the slightest bit more damage than I had already disastrously – but unavoidably - inflicted.

Shukura, our friend from the Cairo Museum, had tears streaming down her plump face and was gulping in the stale air in a quite alarming fashion. It seemed to be stuck fast in her windpipe, blocked from making its passage to her lungs. The erratically darting beams from everyone's torches flashed wildly this way and that, trying to take it all in at once. The wonders before us eclipsed any superlative you could possibly dream up confronted with so much gold. Take the word spectacular, for example. It didn't come close. Each and every item was unique, exquisite, and loaded with a historical significance that was quite simply unsurpassable.

Walid Massri, wispy-haired and perpetually dusty-looking curator of the Egyptian Museum of Antiquities, was opening and closing his mouth in a fair imitation of a goldfish. It took him three attempts to speak. When he eventually managed it, his words came out in a kind of strangulated wheeze. 'And you say this tomb belongs to Akhenaten and Nefertiti?' he rasped at me. But he didn't wait for a response. There was no need. He had all the proof he could ever wish for right before his staring eyes. Let's face it; he'd studied Egyptology his whole life. The distinctively distorted statuary of the ancient world's most controversial pharaoh, and the fabled beauty of its most enigmatic queen must be as familiar to him as his own reflection. Both were beamed back at him in the jerking torchlight just about everywhere our flashlights penetrated the darkness. Immortalised in statues, carvings and shrines, Nefertiti and Akhenaten were everywhere. 'It's too incredible for words!' He shook his head as if expecting his vision to clear. When it didn't, he blinked a couple of times. But it was all still there, glittering provocatively back at him. 'Unbelievable!' he whispered faintly.

I brought the fading glow of my own flashlight to rest on a gilded throne with a lifelike image of the royal couple carved onto the backrest. The skill of the ancient artisan who'd created it positively radiated from the piece. Made of wood overlaid with pure beaten gold, with small details like Nefertiti's crown and Akhenaten's pectoral picked out in jasper, carnelian and turquoise, it was more like a portrait than an item of furniture. Impossible to believe it was more than three thousand years old.

I felt an explanation of some sort was in order. 'Their mummies were brought from Ahket-Aten by Tutankhamun for reburial here,' I said. I daresay I had no right to sound as normal as I did, uttering such a mind-blowing statement. But I'd had quite a bit longer than the others to come to terms with it. I had, after all, spent the last couple of days trapped in here.

'You'll find them next door in the burial chamber,' Adam supplied helpfully. 'They're lying next to each other in two huge granite sarcophagi.'

Like me, Adam had a head start on absorbing the wonder and magnitude of it all. Until a few minutes ago, we'd believed ourselves to be entombed in here together for all eternity - and without the benefit of our own pair of sarcophagi to quietly desiccate in.

Walid's throat worked convulsively. Like his colleague Shukura, it looked for a moment as if he was about to be overcome with emotion. But he kept a hold on himself and managed to bring the fishlike opening and closing of his mouth back under control after another moment or two.

'They're here?' he croaked at last. 'By all that's holy, this is beyond imagining.'

Alongside him, Mustafa Mushhawrar, of the Ministry for the Preservation of Ancient Monuments here in Luxor, settled the beam of his torch rather shakily on the gleaming model of the city of Akhet-Aten. Rendered in solid gold and about the size of a table-tennis top, it was a stunning replica of Akhenaten's virgin city, known as the Horizon of the Sun. Complete with temples, palaces, a garrison, and the dwellings of the nobles and peasants alike, it gleamed with the patina of burnished gold. 'This is incredible,' he breathed. 'Look, they've even crafted the Window of Appearances into the model. It's where Akhenaten and Nefertiti dispensed the golden collars of valour and other tokens of their appreciation to loyal subjects. Forget everything else in here, this piece alone is worth a king's ransom.'

I thought it a peculiarly British expression for a thoroughbred Egyptian to come out with. But the awed wonder in his voice transcended all subtleties of language and nationality. Impeccably attired as always in a crisp white shirt, smart coffee-coloured trousers with a razor-edged crease down the front, and crocodile skin shoes polished to a mirror-like shine, and smelling of citrus-fresh cologne, his gaping expression was distinctly at odds with his debonair appearance. Even his narrow moustache was quivering. The fastidiousness I'd sensed about him at first meeting was still there in the pristine white cotton handkerchief he was squeezing between his clasped hands. But in all other ways he was engagingly abandoned in his reaction to the staggering Pharaonic riches laid out before us.

Another voice cut into the breathless disbelief holding everyone spellbound. 'Personally, the chariot's what I'd bid for, should this crazy assortment of antique bling ever come up for auction and I happened to have a spare several million quid lying around.' This was said in a deadpan tone from the dark shadows behind the waving flashlight beams.

I couldn't help but smile. Dan Fletcher, until approximately two, or maybe it was three, days ago my other half … partner … boyfriend … whatever you may choose to call him, and now my ex, has always had a quite remarkable ability to be unfazed by life's unlikeliest scenarios. It was hard to think of one unlikelier than being hemmed in on all sides by vast quantities of treasure in an unknown-to-the-world ancient Egyptian tomb. His torch beam shone on the object of his desire with almost as much brightness as the ironical glint in his eyes.

Akhenaten's golden chariot was indeed a marvel of ancient Egyptian transportation. Fully assembled (unlike the dis-assembled jumble of jigsaw chariot pieces found by Howard Carter in Tutankhamun's tomb), it showed the wear and tear of use but gleamed with a quite excessively vulgar quantity of pure gold; inscribed with the titles of the king, and inlaid with semi-precious stones. It managed to look both sturdy and spindly all at once; strong enough to traverse rough and rocky desert terrain, whilst decorative enough to rate as an exquisite work of art in its own right.

Dan's bone-dry sense of humour is an often endearing, occasionally infuriating but fundamental part of his personality. It has the ability to cut through most things. But it made no impression at all on the gaping stupefaction of the others. Even the lovely Jessica, who seemed to me to have developed a rather serious crush on Dan over the last week or so, appeared not to notice his droll turn-of-phrase. Instead, she added the object of her own desire to his imaginary auction.

'I'd go for the jewels,' she murmured breathlessly, gazing at the golden adornments spilling from Nefertiti's ivory casket with covetous ardour. The delicate box had split apart at some point during its thirty-odd centuries in this arid atmosphere, littering the living rock of the tomb floor with exquisite pieces once worn by Egypt's most famous queen. Under the trembling beam of Jessica's flashlight, the ancient jewellery glittered with a dull fire, bursting with occasional explosions of brilliant colour where the light caught on semi-precious stones set into the gold. 'Look at that necklace…' she said. 'It's magnificent; turquoise, amethyst, carnelian and lapis lazuli, onyx and jasper set in pure gold.'

I had to hand it to her; she knew her Egyptian semi-precious stones. And I had some sympathy with her choice. Really, what woman in her right mind can resist the allure of jewellery?

Jessica lacked the regal beauty of Nefertiti as captured in the famous bust now on display in a museum in Berlin. Cute, elfin and pixie-like are the words that spring more readily to mind looking at Jessica. But jewellery is jewellery. And I daresay some of those ear-hoops; bangles, collars and cuffs would look equally good on a pretty girl with blonde curls, a heart-shaped face and dancing blue eyes as on the stunningly beautiful black-eyed queen they'd been made for. I couldn't help but wonder briefly if they might also look rather fetching on the grubby, lank-haired, sweat-stained individual that was me. I decided a shower and change of clothes might make all the difference.

The shame of it, I suppose, was that in reality Nefertiti's fabulous jewels would spend the rest of their days under bright white lights inside the reinforced plate glass cabinets of a museum. Never handled, never worn, never warmed by the flesh of a living, breathing woman.

I shivered. One woman and one woman alone in the whole of history could lay claim to those dazzling jewels. And, as Adam had just said, she was lying in her stone sarcophagus a short distance away in the burial chamber. It was impossible to imagine how much of her renowned beauty the ancient mummy-maker had succeeded in preserving. But whatever his skill, her skin was no more capable of warming the ancient jewels than the harsh lights of a museum display case. Even so, the jewellery was hers, intended to remain with her through all eternity. I shivered again, reminded of whose silent, immortal company we were keeping.

'So, this is what Pharaoh Ay was banging on about in that crumbling papyrus scrolls you found,' Dan said sagely, swinging his flashlight in wide sweeps across the treasure chamber. 'Well, he promised you "precious jewels", and he wasn't kidding around, was he? There's enough bullion in here to resolve the global debt crisis about five times over.'

Under normal circumstances, Dan's refusal to take things seriously is prone to get under my skin. He's always pooh-poohed all things Egyptological to a quite aggravating degree; possibly just to annoy me. He labelled me an Egypt-freak years ago, perhaps with some justification. I may be an Egyptologist of the strictly amateur variety, courtesy of the Internet, Discovery Channel and National Geographic, but I'm no less ardent for it. Yet despite his wry tone, I could tell he wasn't as unmoved as he pretended to be. There was a definite tremor in his torch-beam arcing back and forth.

Besides, I was feeling particularly kindly disposed towards Dan. If it weren't for him, Adam and I would still be languishing here in the stultifying dead heat of the tomb, without water, in possession of one fading flashlight with almost-spent batteries, and with the lifeblood draining out of us. In Adam's case, the lifeblood was draining out of him quite literally, thanks to the vicious clunk on the head the hideous Hussein had landed on him.

I glanced across at Adam through the shadows. The bandage I'd wrapped lovingly around his head gave him the appearance of a walking mummy bereft of most of his wrappings. He was pale, dust-coated and dishevelled. But, thanks to Dan, he was breathing and walking upright on his own two feet. Whether his renewed vigour was due to the unexpected appearance of our little band of rescuers – all seven of them – or the bottle of water Jessica had thoughtfully thrust at him and which he'd downed in one, I couldn't say. But my relief at seeing him upright again was truly heartfelt. It struck me I must rather like the bruised and battered look. To my eyes, he'd never looked more appealing or more handsome. His blue eyes were shining in his wan and blood-stained face, and his ripped shirt exposed the livid purple bruises on his chest.

I tore my gaze away with a supreme effort and refocused on my erstwhile boyfriend.

I could just about imagine the lengths Dan had gone to in the last few days to launch his rescue mission. When he realised Adam and I were missing he must have hazarded a pretty shrewd guess we'd gone tomb hunting. We'd all come to the conclusion there might be an intact royal tomb lying undiscovered in the cliffs behind Hatshepsut's temple. This was thanks to some ancient papyri we'd found. But Adam and I had been the ones to go off searching for it in the dead of night two … or it might be three … nights ago. We'd failed to anticipate that our nemesis, the deadly Hussein, an antiquities thief and double-dyed villain, would follow us with murderous intent. Thankfully, he'd failed to rob us of any treasure we found, leaving us rotting like sheep carcasses. I think that was the charming turn of phrase he used. But he succeeded quite spectacularly in entombing us – himself included – in among all the gold and royal regalia he'd intended to steal.

How much of this Dan had worked out I had yet to discover. But his appearance a few minutes ago, along with senior members of staff from the Cairo Museum and brandishing a couple of priceless relics originally from Tutankhamun's tomb, spoke volumes. The priceless relics – a pair of solid gold discs – worked a hidden mechanism in the temple wall. This in turn opened a stone entrance passage to reveal the tomb hidden beyond. Adam had fashioned replica discs in our quest to discover the royal burial. But Dan had somehow, unbelievably, persuaded senior antiquities officials from Cairo to fly to Luxor with the real thing stowed in their luggage.

It revealed a side to Dan I'd never even suspected was there. If things turned out as I was beginning to feel they might, then Jessica was a very lucky girl.

It was Jessica's father who responded to Dan's reference to the "precious jewels" Pharaoh Ay had promised us in the crumbling parchment. Ted Kincaid was a professor of Egyptology, retired from the Oriental Institute at Oxford University, where he'd specialised in philology. He'd moved out to Cairo a few years back, and Adam and I had enlisted his help to translate the ancient papyrus scrolls we'd found.

'The "precious jewels" Pharaoh Ay referred to were Akhenaten and Nefertiti themselves,' he said hoarsely. 'Good Heavens! I dared to hope we might find a reburial. But I never dared imagine anything like this. It's a discovery beyond words. All this puts Tutankhamun's tomb in the shade.' He indicated the bewildering quantities of golden artefacts with a vague wave of one hand.

The gulp alongside him betrayed Shukura's attempts to bring her overwrought emotions under control. Ted stepped forward and put a comforting arm around her. They looked faintly incongruous standing together like that. Ted was a dapper silver-haired gentleman in his seventies, with wire-framed glasses precariously perched on the end of his nose; small and slightly built. Shukura was a pleasantly plump woman in her mid-fifties; squeezed into a too-small navy suit, with black ballet pumps on her feet and a patterned headscarf wound around her head and shoulders. She wore several chunky gold rings on every finger of both hands. I knew she and Ted had enjoyed a romantic dalliance once, briefly, many years ago on an archaeological dig in Syria after Ted's wife died and before Shukura met her husband. The bond of affection was still strong between them.

We'd made a friend of Shukura (a professor specialising in the study of ancient coins at the Cairo Museum), and an enemy of the villainous Hussein, in one fell swoop. We'd helped her to expose his gang of antiquities thieves, and to seize back priceless artefacts he'd stolen from the museum during the revolution in early 2011.

So, here we all were. A rather unlikely little band of people to be breathing the stale air of this ancient sepulchre for the first time in more than three thousand years. Shukura, Walid and Mustafa, native and professional Egyptians whom Dan had somehow persuaded to help him save Adam and me from a slow and tortuous death among this mind-numbing collection of grave goods. And Ted, Jessica and Dan; our friends, who'd shared the translation of Pharaoh Ay's papyrus scrolls with Adam and me, and guessed at a hidden tomb, but never dared to imagine a find like this.

The only person showing no reaction whatsoever to the startling collection of golden objects glinting darkly at us was Ahmed, our chum from the local tourist police here in Luxor. Considering he's descended from the most notorious family of tomb robbers in the area, this was quite possibly deeply suspicious. In his defence, he was gleefully occupied resting his impressive bulk on the supine form of our nemesis, the dastardly Hussein; a man he'd been yearning to arrest for almost as long as we'd been on this incredible treasure hunt.

'And you say Tutankhamun himself brought these treasures here from Ahket-Aten?' Walid asked, still struggling to come to terms with the evidence of his eyes.

'Yes,' Adam nodded, tucking an end of his bandage that had come loose securely back into place behind his ear. 'General Horemheb was leading a campaign to topple Akhenaten's Atenist religious cult. Tutankhamun took drastic action to prevent Horemheb desecrating the original tomb Akhenaten had prepared for himself and his great royal wife Nefertiti, and where they were originally buried. He moved their bodies here in secret. It was Tutankhamun's great triumph.'

Walid continued to shake his head as if trying to clear it of tomb dust. 'Astonishing,' he said. 'Everything seems so carefully positioned, almost as if it's on display. Not at all like the jumbled assortment of grave goods in Tutankhamun's tomb. His treasures were piled higgledy-piggledy and with a quite shocking disregard for their fragility.'

I was somewhat heartened to hear him say this. It was the self-same thing that had struck me, gazing into this treasure chamber for the first time. Everything was carefully and lovingly positioned to show it off to best effect. The trouble was, now I wasn't in imminent danger of perishing in here, all I could see as I looked about in the torchlight was the damage I'd wrought. It brought me out in a cold sweat and made me feel quite sick. A casket containing once glorious ceremonial robes was hopelessly smashed, its contents reduced to a pile of glittering powder. I'd knocked over a golden shrine, now lying with one panel unhinged on the floor. And a wooden game box, beautifully carved and inlaid with exquisite hunting scenes was in bits where I'd tripped and fallen on it. My only excuse for this unforgivable sacrilege was that I'd been trying to save Adam's life at the time. He'd been only semi-conscious for a frightening number of our hours trapped in here. Whilst I'd tried to be careful, I'd searched through baskets, caskets and boxes, growing ever more desperate in my search for something I might use to fashion a rope. I needed this to lower myself into the pit where the evil Hussein had dropped the Aten discs that would free us. I couldn't just sit about in the hope of being rescued. I had to take some action while there was still breath left in my body and enough spirit to fight the helplessness of our situation. I'd failed of course; hence my eternal gratitude to Dan for setting us free. But the wanton destruction that seemed so justifiable when our lives were hanging in the balance didn't seem half so forgivable now we were fairly certain of seeing another sunrise.

Thankfully, the others seemed to accept these breakages as the inevitable consequence of the artefacts' thirty-odd-centuries of storage in this stagnant-aired sepulchre. Nobody seemed to be looking for a more recent explanation for the less than perfect state of preservation of some of the priceless relics from ancient Egypt's glorious 18th Dynasty.

I decided I could breathe again and allowed the awesome solemnity of the tomb to cast its spell on me once more.

'To think the last person who breathed this air might be Tutankhamun himself,' Ted said in a sanctified tone of voice.

'Along with Pharaoh Ay, who succeeded him to the throne, and helped him conceive of this hideaway,' Adam said, in no less awe-filled tones. Now he'd recovered from his frightening bout of dizziness, he seemed as boyishly determined as ever to enjoy the moment.

'I've got this strange sensation of time collapsing,' Shukura murmured alongside him, pressing a tissue against her damp cheeks. 'It doesn't seem possible that more than three thousand years have passed since someone was last in here. I keep thinking I might turn around and see Tutankhamun himself standing there.'

'I feel quite giddy,' Walid admitted. 'I've spent years of my life at the museum preserving antiquities. But some of these artefacts look as if they were used only yesterday. It brings the past crashing against us in a quite shockingly immediate way.'

'I know exactly what you mean,' Jessica breathed. 'It makes time seem so insubstantial, doesn't it? As if more than three thousand years is just the blink of an eye.'

'Does anyone else have the feeling we're being watched?' Mustafa asked a bit chillingly.

'Oh please! Let's not start imagining ghosts,' Dan said, hanging onto his dry asperity for all he was worth.

But I knew what the fastidious Egyptian meant. I, too, had experienced the unnerving sensation of ancient eyes watching and judging our trespass on their eternal rest. And there was a distinct moment about halfway through our entrapment when I'd started to believe in the pharaoh's curse. Perhaps it was more than just a load of superstitious baloney designed to scare off tomb robbers. It had seemed all too terrifyingly possible that death would come on swift wings to claim us for daring to disturb the peace of the king and his queen. Always having prided myself on being free of superstitious dogma, this was a definite low point.

'It's easy to get carried away with all the treasure and forget we're standing inside a grave, complete with dead bodies,' Jessica shuddered.

Adam and I exchanged a look. We'd come perilously close to doubling the number of corpses this tomb was designed to hold.

'We're intruding on a sacred burial place,' Shukura whispered. 'I wonder if we should make an offering to pacify their spirits.'

I rushed into speech before Dan could make the comment I knew must be scalding his tongue. 'I think it might be a bit late for that now. But Adam and I were sort of paying our respects when our heinous friend over there turned up and started throwing his weight around.'

'I've got to see the burial chamber,' Walid murmured.

'And me,' Mustafa agreed, lifting his flashlight to the far wall where a narrow opening betrayed the entrance to Akhenaten and Nefertiti's final resting place. 'I can't believe we're inside the living rock behind Hatshepsut's temple. I've worked at this site for years. In all that time I never imagined something like this! I keep thinking I'm going to wake up and find I've been dreaming.'

Adam fingered the bandage covering the wound on the back of his head. 'It's real alright.'

Leaving Ahmed on police duty guarding the still-unconscious Hussein, we edged through the close-packed chamber in single file. The dead air of centuries clogged our throats as we held our collective breath. We skirted around priceless relics from Egypt's ancient past as if they might be trip wired. None of us dared brush against anything for fear of sending one of these irreplaceable artefacts sprawling. I might add I was especially careful. Our flashlights illuminated ornate tables, ritual couches and ivory game boxes. There were carved wooden linen caskets, chests of writing implements, clay jars filled with oils and unguents, decorative cosmetic boxes, tightly woven reed baskets, and almost translucent alabaster vases. Each was an item drawn from daily life in the royal court intended to serve in the afterlife. These day-to-day pieces held an intimacy somehow more poignant than the glittering golden objects like the throne and chariot. They spoke of private moments away from the rituals of royalty and religion.

Reaching the narrow opening carved into the rock at the back of the chamber, we squeezed through one-by-one. It was a tight fit for us all inside the burial chamber as the two huge granite sarcophagi filled the small room.

'My word! Look at the wall relief!' Ted gaped.

'Unbelievable!' Walid shone his flashlight in a slow sweep on the portion of the walls visible above our heads. Bug-eyed, he stared unblinking at the exquisitely carved and painted relief. Unlike the treasure chamber, whose walls were simply chipped away from the living rock, still bearing the marks of the ancient workmen's tools, here in the burial chamber the walls were plastered and decorated; the ceiling painted with multitudes of yellow stars against a cobalt blue background.

The upper section of the wall was completely filled with a huge golden sun disc. It seemed to glow, radiating with life-giving energy, light and heat. This was Aten; the one true God elevated by Akhenaten. The traditional mortuary deities drawn from the ancient Egyptian pantheon of gods and goddesses were notable by their absence. Instead, the sun disc cast its loving rays on images of the pharaoh and his great royal wife carved into the walls. Akhenaten and Nefertiti were depicted with their arms raised in worship, hands outstretched, palms upwards, towards the reaching rays of the sun. Each sunray ended in a little hand, some holding the ancient symbol of life the Ankh. These reached down to bless the royal couple, whose upraised palms seemed designed to channel the radiance of the sun. It looked uncannily as if the ancient sun god and his representatives on Earth were reaching out to touch each other.

'The colours are incredible,' Shukura said. 'So fresh and bright one might easily believe the ancient artisans laid down their paint pots just yesterday.'

This same thought had struck me, entering this sacred sepulchre for the first time. It brought the past crashing into the present again in a quite head-spinning way.

'So, here they lie.' Mustafa said solemnly, gazing at the polished granite surface of the sarcophagus he was squeezed up against. It stood taller than he did, an immense chunk of crafted stone with a thick granite lid. 'Akhenaten and Nefertiti, preserved for all eternity.'

I'd swear the same chill passed through us all at his words. We stared sombrely at the pair of great granite sarcophagi containing the earthly remains of ancient Egypt's most notorious pharaoh and his queen. I felt the full weight of history pressing down on me. Goose bumps prickled along my flesh, and I shivered despite the dense suffocating heat.

'What's this?' Dan asked, edging around the smaller sarcophagus with Nefertiti's throne names carved around its upper rim.

Adam and I followed him until we were all three of us pressed against the back wall of the burial chamber. Jessica squeezed in behind us. But there wasn't enough room for her to see the long niche carved into the living rock. It formed a kind of raised platform along the back wall. I knew exactly what we'd find resting on that chiselled dais. I'd divested it of its golden coverlet during the long hours of Adam's and my entombment. My plan had been to rip it into strips to knot together into a rope.

This hope had proved frustratingly futile. The ancient blanket was made of pure gold thread. It had been woven into a fine chainmail-like fabric; impervious to the knife I'd taken to it. It was huge, originally draped all the way across the long rectangular box it covered. I'd left it back in the entrance corridor where Adam and I had been using it a bit like a duvet in the long hours after we'd given up trying to rip it apart and before we'd been rescued.

In truth, it wasn't a blanket. It was a shroud.

'This,' Adam said with a distinct thrill in his voice,' 'is an anthropoid coffin. See this rectangular box? Well, if you look inside, you can see a human-shaped coffin resting inside a bit like a Russian doll. See? Look, it's painted with a face and headdress, and these gold bands are meant to represent mummy wrappings.'

Dan frowned at the box illuminated in the darkness. 'So, you're telling me there are three corpses buried in here, not just the mummified king and queen we've been whispering about?' He didn't sound particularly happy about it.

'It certainly looks like it. Although I don't think we're looking at another re-burial from Akhet-Aten. This style of coffin dates from further back. I'd say the early part of the 18th Dynasty at the latest. This was probably made somewhere between one and two hundred years before Akhenaten and Nefertiti's time. How intriguing. If I could just get my head to stop pounding, I might be able to lean over and see if there are any inscriptions.'

'We need my Dad,' Jessica piped up from behind me. 'He'll be able to decipher any texts or hieroglyphs it may contain.'

'What have you found?' Ted was already shining his flashlight around the corner of the massive sarcophagus behind us.

Jessica and Dan performed a little acrobatic number, making space for the professor to come and join us by twisting around each other. I noticed she didn't let go of his hand once their contortionist manoeuvres were finished. I'd thought I might mind, but I didn't. I was much more concerned to notice the way Adam was wiping perspiration from his brow with his shirtsleeve. His eyes looked over-bright and feverish in the reflected beam of the flashlight. This could be down to archaeological fervour or a return of the dizziness that had afflicted him earlier. It was difficult to tell with Adam. His passion for all things Egyptological often put that strange hypnotic glow in his eyes.

'Good Lord!' Ted exclaimed as the beam of his flashlight further lit up the anthropoid coffin. 'What a strange thing to find in a tomb of the Amarnan period.'

'It makes me wonder if this wasn't here first,' Adam said in a hushed undertone, rubbing his eyes as if his vision was blurred. 'Maybe Tutankhamun and Ay simply remodelled this sepulchre for their own purposes, rather than go to all the effort of carving it out from scratch.'

'You know what, my boy? I think you may be right.' Ted leaned forward, peering closely at the ancient coffin with his flashlight held about an inch away from the surface. His glasses slipped in their habitual fashion to the tip of his nose and perched there precariously. I was quite distracted, waiting to see if they'd fall off. He was very quiet for a long moment, his brow wrinkled in concentration. Then he straightened and gazed back at the coffin. He highlighted a small, inscribed section with his torch. 'See here, it says, *'Neferure, everlasting beauty of Re; may she be justified; beloved of Maatkare Hatshepsut and Akheperenre Thutmosis."* He looked around at our staring faces. 'We're in a hidden chamber carved into the mountainside behind Hatshepsut's mortuary temple. And if I'm not very much mistaken, this is the anthropoid coffin of her daughter.'

It was at this point that Adam passed out.

Chapter 2

'So, let me get this straight, Merry,' Shukura said, with a small frown wrinkling her brow beneath her turquoise headscarf. 'You found a secret message and a set of hidden hieroglyphics left by Howard Carter inside the picture frame of one of his watercolour paintings? This happened when you got locked in the Howard Carter Museum and accidentally smashed the picture frame trying to escape…? And that's what led to your discovery of the tomb…?'

We were sitting in a small waiting room at Luxor hospital, kicking our heels while the medical team came up with a diagnosis on both Adam and the loathsome Hussein. Personally, I'd have been happy to leave Hussein shut up inside the tomb to expire and slowly desiccate in the hot, moistureless air. But my companions seemed better endowed with the noble spirit of humanity than I was. Adam, having blanked out on us and stayed that way, didn't have any say in the matter.

We were all here, minus the two wounded men and Ahmed, who was standing guard over our nemesis with the intention of slapping a pair of handcuffs on him the moment he opened his eyes. Luckily the presence of a bona fide police officer deterred the medical team from asking too many uncomfortable questions. I'm not sure we could have delivered a satisfactory explanation about where we'd been or how the two unconscious men had come by their injuries. I was beyond the point of fabricating a plausible story to explain the bloodied gashes in their heads or the amount of dust they were both coated in. We said Adam and Hussein had been in a fight and left it at that. In its simplest form it was true. The fact that I'd been the one to inflict the grievous injury on the abominable Hussein by whacking him with a solid gold statuette of Nefertiti seemed a bit beside the point and not worth mentioning.

    I caught myself in the act of biting my nails and sat on my hands instead. It was a bad habit I'd managed to crack aged about twelve. My relapse into nibbling betrayed just how anxious I was feeling. Until I knew if Adam was going to be ok it was impossible to concentrate on much. We'd been sitting here keeping vigil for almost an hour now, and nobody from the medical team had come anywhere near any one of the seven of us.

    I looked around at the faces of the others, illuminated in the stark white light of the single bulb dangling above us in the dreary waiting room. While I'm sure they all shared my concern for Adam to a greater or lesser extent, I wasn't convinced it could wholly account for the way everyone was sitting as if glued to their plastic seats. It seemed we were sticking together for one simple reason. We'd discovered an intact royal tomb packed with treasure. And we hadn't had a solitary moment to figure out what we were going to do or say about it.

    I must say my companions had all managed to stay looking remarkably respectable despite having crawled across a couple of grubby scaffolding planks to gain access to the tomb. Adam and I had instructed them how to rig up this makeshift bridge to successfully conclude their rescue of us. It was the only way of getting to the tomb without falling into the deadly pit shaft halfway along the entrance corridor designed to ensnare the unwary. It was also the only way of getting out again. To be fair to Dan, Ahmed and Mustafa, they'd done an impressive job of shuffling back across those narrow wooden boards with the inert forms of first one unconscious man and then another hoisted between them. And they didn't look any the worse for wear.

    Sadly, I wasn't looking half so presentable. I was wrapped in a voluminous Egyptian robe, borrowed from Shukura's overnight bag. It was the only way of hiding the fact that underneath it I was covered from head to toe in glimmering gold dust. This was courtesy of the ceremonial robe that had disintegrated into a puff of sparkles when I'd tried to lift it from its casket looking for a rope. It's fair to say the Egyptian kaftan didn't suit me nearly so well as it did Shukura. I suspect I looked as if I was decked out in fancy dress. The look wasn't helped by my generally unkempt appearance beneath the swathes of patterned fabric. My usually bobbed hair was plastered greasily against my head. I had panda eyes where what was once mascara had decided to go exploring. And the general stickiness of sweat and dust clogged into my pores disinclined me to want to get too close to anyone.

'Merry...?' Shukura prompted.

'What? Oh, sorry. I drifted off for a moment.'

'I'm not surprised. You must be shattered, you poor thing. And worried about dear Adam, of course.' Shukura's Home Counties accent still took a bit of getting used to. She'd been educated at Oxford and spoke English with no trace of an Arabic accent, and usually at a rate of knots. 'It's just I'm trying to piece together the whole story. You see it was difficult to get too much sense out of Dan when he was demanding our immediate co-operation in flying from Cairo to Luxor with some of Tutankhamun's treasure.'

'You should have seen him Merry,' Jessica said breathily, her eyes shining. 'He was so commanding and masterful.'

I realised that, though unspoken, it was now completely understood and accepted that Jessica was with Dan, and I was with Adam. At least I sincerely hoped I was with Adam. I didn't doubt he loved me, and I returned the sentiment with every fibre of my being. But it would help my peace of mind no end to know he was alive and well.

'It was fortunate Ted was able to vouch for him,' Shukura said, waggling one pudgy and be-ringed finger at Dan in an affectionate but rather school-mistressy way. 'Otherwise, Walid and I may have had him arrested. Honestly! Storming into the museum like that, ranting and raving about Mehet-Weret and Hatshepsut. I thought he was stark staring mad and was about to run for cover. Luckily Ted and Jessica caught up with him at that point and managed to explain that they needed the Aten sun discs from Tutankhamun's Mehet-Weret ritual couch to perform some mysterious rescue operation in Hatshepsut's temple.'

I daresay it was Ted's influence that swung it. Dan might be masterful and commanding, but Professor Edward Kincaid was a renowned Egyptologist with impeccable academic credentials. Shukura, of course, had once known him romantically. Museum curator Walid – the one who really needed convincing – had attended many of Ted's lectures as a younger man and held him in the highest professional esteem.

So, between Dan's sheer force of will and physical stature (Dan's quite a big bloke), and Ted's unimpeachable scholarly reputation, I could well imagine how Shukura and Walid had been bullied, bamboozled and beguiled into making the trip.

Dan and Ted exchanged a bashful glance, as if neither one of them could quite believe how they'd pulled off such a remarkable feat. Jessica, sitting happily between them looking more pixie-like than ever, took hold of one each of their hands and squeezed them to show her pride in their achievement.

'We're lucky that visitors to the museum are so few and far between in these troubled times while we elect our new government,' Shukura added. 'In these last few days since the verdict of Mubarak's trial, and with the renewed demonstrations in Tahrir Square, tourists are staying away. It made it a relatively straightforward task for Walid and me to borrow the Aten discs. Walid put screening up inside the glass display case containing the Mehet-Weret couch, with a sign saying it was undergoing preservation. Hopefully it will be some time before anyone notices the gold discs are missing from between the cow horns, and we'll be able to return them before the alarm is raised.'

'It wasn't quite such a straightforward endeavour bringing the discs through the airport security controls,' Walid put in, sounding a trifle sheepish about his part in all the subterfuge, and scratching at his wispy hair as he recalled his daring. 'I was carrying them inside one of the museum's metal safeguard cases; chained to my wrist in the way we're required to when transporting any ancient artefacts outside the museum. I was obliged to show every single official document, accreditation and certificate I possess to prove my identity and my authority to carry such priceless relics on my person, and not submit to them being taken into the aeroplane hold. I concocted some story about bringing them for an exhibition in the Luxor Museum.' He brushed a sheen of perspiration from his top lip, obviously quite overcome at the memory of his audacity. 'I've never done anything like that before in my life. And I pray I never have to do so again. I don't doubt it took years off my life.'

I felt an apology was warranted and said so. 'I'm sorry, Walid. Adam and I never intended for you to put your career on the line, or your lifespan for that matter. We've taken unforgivable advantage of your position at the museum. When we turned up in Cairo last week, name-dropping Ted and asking you to weigh and measure the Aten discs, we had no idea we could land you in so much trouble. You see Adam was intent on making replica discs so we could see if there was indeed anything to be discovered behind the walls of the Hathor Chapel in Hatshepsut's temple. We'd figured out if there was a hidden tomb anywhere, it had to be there. And we were working on a hunch that the Aten discs acted as some sort of key. We were horribly economical with the truth when we came to see you. And I'm truly sorry for it. That goes for you too, Shukura. I feel thoroughly ashamed. It's just, at that point, we didn't really know if there was anything to be found. We were caught up in the Boy's Own adventure of it all, and we wanted to keep it secret until we knew what we'd found.'

Shukura blinked a bit owlishly at me. Then her face broke out in wreaths of smiles. 'Ashamed?' she squeaked. 'Don't be ashamed, Merry. I'm having the time of my life!'

Walid smiled at me a bit less exuberantly and brushed at the dusty circles on the knees of his trousers, looking embarrassed. 'Please don't mention it. It was worth it to see such sights as we have all beheld in these last few hours. Never in my life did I dream of seeing such wonders outside the sterile confines of my museum.'

We all took a moment to ponder them. But Shukura was impatient to get back to the story and fill in the gaps.

'Your friend Ahmed, the police officer, was waiting for us when we touched down in Luxor,' she said. 'He was jabbering in a quite excitable manner, switching from Arabic to rather broken English so it was impossible to follow what he was saying. There was something about you disappearing into the temple in the dead of night and vanishing. He kept on wailing about not having given you enough water. I deduced from this he'd been aware of your original intentions. But then he got quite confusingly muddled and agitated trying to explain that he'd found an empty makeshift campsite in the hills behind the temple. He kept going on and on about a thief who pushed Dan off a cliff.' She darted a glance at Dan, obviously trying to reconcile the fit and healthy look of him with someone who'd been shoved off a clifftop and ought by rights to be dead. 'I couldn't make head nor tail of it at the time. But I gather this was the devilish scoundrel who followed you into the tomb, was it? Hussein, is he called? The one who put Adam in his current predicament?'

It was Dan who answered, invited into the conversation by Shukura's searching glance. He failed to satisfy her curiosity about the clifftop incident. It was true there was no visible sign of any bumps or bruises on him now that he'd removed his sling. But I was pretty sure his torso was still bandaged up like a mummy underneath his shirt. 'Yes. It seems Hussein was staking out the temple, waiting and watching. He sensed we were onto something because he was spying on us when Mustafa showed us the Hathor Chapel, which is usually off-limits to tourists. Hussein knew about the ancient papyrus Merry and Adam found because he stole it from us. I'm pleased to say I managed to get it back.' He puffed out his chest a bit, and I smiled, remembering his athletic prowess and the rugby tackle he'd executed so faultlessly. 'Anyway, he obviously guessed at buried treasure, or something of the sort, and decided to move in to strike when he saw Merry and Adam turn up on their own in the middle of the night.' He shot me a rather accusatory glance to accompany his words. I daresay he'd have something quite colourful and not particularly complimentary to say about the impulsive decision Adam and I had made to go off tomb hunting, just the two of us. But for now, he was holding it. For such small mercies I suppose I had to be grateful.

'You didn't mention these papyri to me,' Mustafa said in gently aggrieved tones, absently flicking his handkerchief at the dust clinging to his crocodile skin shoes while fixing me with a reproachful look from his soulful dark eyes.

'No, I'm sorry Mustafa. We're guilty of the same lack of candour with you, as with Shukura and Walid here. It's true we had a hidden agenda when you treated us to a private tour of the out-of-bounds parts of the temple that day. You see we had some clues we were trying to fit together. We were trying to figure out what relevance the sun god Aten might have in Hatshepsut's temple, dedicated so ostentatiously to the rival god Amun. Of course, when you showed us the Hathor Chapel and we saw the numerous depictions of the sun disc carved into the walls between her cow-horns, we started to get an inkling that we might be onto something. I'm sorry you've been dragged into this. I imagine Ahmed had to rouse you from your bed to gain access to the Hathor Chapel, since Adam and I had the key Ahmed had "borrowed" from you.' I added an ironic inflection to the word since I was quite sure Ahmed had been less than scrupulously honest when taking custody of said key. It struck me just what a perfidious trio we were,

Adam, Ahmed and me. The only excuse was that we'd set out on our adventure much in the spirit of the three musketeers. Our lack of scruples and occasional law bending (I persuaded myself we hadn't exactly broken it) had far more to do with the thrill of solving a puzzle, each clue leading to the next, than any malice aforethought or inherent dishonesty in our characters. Or so I told myself.

'It is of no importance,' Mustafa said with a gracious inclination of his head. It might almost have been a bow had he been standing. I was coming to learn the formality of the Arabic culture, especially among men over forty. 'Like Walid, I consider myself honoured to have shared in such a magnificent experience. I hope one day I may be privileged to study the papyri that led you to the discovery. Of all things, I find the ancient texts most fascinating. I have been learning to read hieratic script at night school. I hope some day to become a true Egyptologist, not just a bureaucrat assigned to the preservation of our country's ancient monuments.'

'Ah yes, the papyri,' Shukura said with a bright note of anticipation in her voice. 'Now, am I right in thinking the clues in Howard Carter's hidden hieroglyphics led you to discover them? And the clues in the scrolls led you to discover the tomb?'

I sighed and nodded, feeling unutterably weary. The adrenaline that had fuelled me through the last few days was definitely starting to wear off.

'How thrilling! Now, I want to hear the whole story. You must tell me all about how you came to be locked up in Howard Carter's house overnight. It is now a museum, I understand, and a very good one. I must make the time to visit while I am here in Luxor. And I want to know how his picture got smashed, and what it was that made you realise you might have found something of significance hidden inside the frame. Did you already know Adam at this point, or did you meet him after your fateful discovery? I feel I have had a very garbled version of events from Dan and Ted here, and I have not yet got it straight in my head exactly what happened.' She looked at me with the flush of expectancy staining her rounded cheeks.

I opened my mouth to tell her about Howard Carter's unauthorised nocturnal visit to Tutankhamun's tomb on the eve of its official opening in November 1922 when he and Lord Carnarvon sneaked into the tomb in the dead of night. They were desperate to know exactly what it was they'd found without a load of officials and bureaucrats breathing down their necks and dogging every step, whether it was an intact royal burial, as they were daring to hope, or just a magnificent cache. During that clandestine visit, they found not only Tutankhamun, still resting in the burial chamber where he'd been placed more than three thousand years previously; but also, the papyri. Swept up in the unimaginable thrill of their discovery, they took the ancient scrolls with them when they crept back out of the tomb. They meant to return them in due course, but only after they'd had a chance to have a good look at them. Carnarvon took them home with him to Highclere Castle in England, intending to study them over Christmas. He came back to Egypt in the New Year without them, thinking he had all the time in the world to bring them back. The clearance of the tomb had barely begun. The trouble was he promptly succumbed to an infected mosquito bite – or the pharaoh's curse, depending on your point of view – and inconveniently died. Carnarvon's widow inexplicably refused to give the papyri back to Carter until the last possible moment, ten years later, after he'd finished clearing Tutankhamun's tomb. By then it was impossible for Carter to return the scrolls to the tomb, or account for them. So, rather than own up to the covert night-time visit when he and Carnarvon misappropriated them, thereby sullying both their reputations, he bricked them up inside an abandoned tomb shaft in the Valley. He left a mysterious message inside the frame of one of his watercolour paintings, which I stumbled across when I got locked inside his house overnight and inadvertently smashed it trying to escape. The tragedy for Carter was that - while I suspect he may have translated the papyri; in the same way we'd done - he'd not been able to act on the new knowledge it had furnished him with. So, the discovery of the most sought-after tomb in all of ancient Egyptian history had fallen to us.

Shukura's tragedy, on the other hand, was that she wasn't destined to hear the whole story just yet. While I was ordering my thoughts, trying to decide where to begin, how to describe the madcap treasure hunt I'd found myself on because of finding Carter's hidden cryptogram, a movement in the doorway distracted me.

Adam stood there, with his head swathed in bandages, grinning goofily at me.

Careless of any sense of modesty or decorum, I leapt up and flung myself at him. 'Oh, thank God! Are you alright? What did the doctors say?' I peppered him alternately with questions and kisses, swiping ineffectually at the tears spilling freely down my cheeks, in a riotous confusion of emotion and relief.

'Hey, go easy,' he laughed, hugging me close. 'There's just the small matter of a mild concussion to contend with. The doctors order complete rest and relaxation, and no excitement. So, you need to stop kissing me, Merry; or I'll fail in the starting blocks.'

The others all jumped out of their seats at his unexpected appearance. They gathered around, patting him on the various parts of his upper body within reach, in the way of nice people wanting to express their pleasure at seeing him compos mentis again.

Dan grasped him in a firm and fervent handshake. 'Good to have you back in the land of the living, mate.'

'Good to be here,' Adam grinned. 'I'd hate to miss all the fun of what we're going to do with our find. I can't wait to see the press headlines!'

I frowned at him in my best impression of a nursemaid. 'So, the ban on excitement doesn't extend so far as our discovery of an intact royal tomb complete with shedloads of treasure.'

He smiled at me, his lovely blue eyes twinkling with devilment. 'Well, I figure the brain-taxing part is over. We've decoded the hieroglyphs, solved the puzzle they posed us, found and translated the papyri, and worked out how Aten is key. I reckon the next part should be a breeze in comparison.'

We moved away from the doorway, and all subsided onto our seats. I drew Adam down on the chair alongside me, keeping a tight hold of his hand. There was every chance I might never let it go. The feel of him returning my grip with a tight squeeze of his own sent a spreading warmth through me, and I completely forgot to be tired. Instead, I was filled with a supreme sense of gladness and well-being. Adam was ok. And right down on the deepest level of things that really mattered, it was all I cared about.

But the tomb was uppermost in the minds of everyone else.

'So, what exactly *is* the next part?' Dan enquired mildly.

I darted a quick glance at his face, my suspicions immediately aroused by his studiedly neutral tone of voice. Dan had been begging us to go to the Egyptian authorities right from the start, literally from the moment I found Carter's hidden message. For one very good reason or another, Adam and I had always managed to resist his pleas. His expression was carefully bland, but he avoided making eye contact with me even though I'm sure he knew I was looking at him. This served only to deepen my misgivings. I had no doubt getting high-ranking staff from the Cairo Antiquities Service in on the act had been part of his plan all along. I'll bet he was secretly delighted when he learned that Adam and I were missing. It gifted him the opportunity to take matters into his own hands. I almost growled, but just about managed to bite it back, and stepped into the breach before anyone else could.

'So, have we decided we definitely do have to go public with the tomb?' I challenged. 'It's just, you see, Adam and I had pretty much decided to lock it up behind us and do our best to forget about it.'

Everyone but Adam gaped at me as if I'd flipped. Walid was imitating a goldfish again. Mustafa realised his mouth had fallen open and shut it with an audible click of his teeth, his moustache quivering. Shukura's eyes bulged in an almost cartoon-like manner, which actually quite suited her since they were darkly rimmed with kohl. She looked particularly striking, staring back at me like that, dazed, wide-eyed and unblinking. Even Dan, Ted and Jessica shared a slack-jawed moment. Before any of them could regain their composure, I hurried to explain.

'I mean, I know it's like the most awesome discovery. Ever!' I babbled, sounding frighteningly like a teenager as I struggled to put what I wanted to say into words. 'But part of me thinks Akhenaten and Nefertiti were meant to lie there, at peace for eternity. Who are we to disturb them? I'm sure it sounds crazy, when I was as eager as anyone to see if there really was a hidden tomb carved into the cliffs behind Hatshepsut's temple. But now we've found it I feel differently. It's stopped being a game, a treasure hunt; a puzzle that needs solving. It's become real. We've stumbled across an ancient burial with the remains of the dead still in situ. Surely, we have to respect it for what it is. I, for one, am not at all sure it can't still be classed as grave robbery to make off with the grave goods, even if their destination is a state-of-the-art museum. Though more than three thousand years have passed, and our thirst is for historical knowledge, not riches or gold, it still feels like sacrilege to me.'

Adam squeezed my hand again, giving me the courage to go on.

'So while I can completely understand that many people would say the beautiful objects we've all seen should be on show to the whole world – protected behind plate glass as an everlasting tribute to the most remarkable period in ancient Egyptian history and the larger-than-life characters who inhabited it, a bigger part of me thinks they deserve peace and enduring escape from the indignities of DNA testing, CAT scanning and the mawkish gaze of the masses. It's a total accident that I stumbled across the clues that led to the discovery of the papyrus. I'm not sure I want the responsibility of plundering their tomb.'

My impassioned speech was met with silence.

Ted was the first to regain his critical faculties. 'I applaud the sentiment, Merry. Very well said, indeed! The trouble is we might not have any choice in the matter. Ahmed may succeed in putting the despicable Hussein behind bars where he belongs – always assuming he hasn't expired through there in the emergency room - which might be the best outcome we can hope for. But if he survives there's nothing to stop him shouting the odds from his prison cell. The authorities would have no choice but to investigate his claims.'

It was almost as if he'd called up a member of the medical team by osmosis, or telepathy, or some other form of psychic power. Literally as he finished speaking a doctor appeared in the doorway.

'I thought you might like to know that the other injured gentleman is regaining consciousness,' he said in careful English. 'I am pleased to report his condition is no longer believed to be life threatening.'

We all smiled with varying degrees of faked sincerity and listened to his footsteps retreating along the corridor and out of hearing range.

'Well, I suppose to have dispatched all three of the despicable Said brothers to the Afterlife within a couple of weeks of each other was a bit much to hope for,' I said bleakly.

To be fair I wasn't quite as bloodthirsty as I sounded. And it wasn't wholly accurate to count ourselves responsible for their dispatch. The first of the villainous triad of brothers had suffered an accidental death when he tripped and fell trying to scale a sheer cliff-face in the Valley of the Kings in the dark. The fact that both Adam and Dan were in hot pursuit at the time was quite possibly beside the point. Ahmed would have us believe a divine cobra was to blame, rearing up in front of him on the slope. The second brother took his own life, jumping from the tenth-floor window of a tenement block in Cairo. Again, our being on the scene at the time was purely circumstantial. We'd tipped off the military police that a gang of antiquities thieves was selling stolen artefacts onto the black market from a dingy apartment in Cairo. That the police raid took place just as the second brother was disposing of the evidence by flinging priceless objets d'art out of the window was just a matter of bad (from his point of view) timing. His decision to follow the artefacts through the open window, cracking his head open on the concrete paving ten storeys below, must, I'm sure, have seemed preferable to a life sentence in an Egyptian prison.

Hussein's brush with death was different. I was rather thankful Osiris – or his modern equivalent – hadn't accepted our contemptible foe into his fond embrace in the underworld. Whilst I'd whacked Hussein on the head with the Nefertiti statuette entirely in self-defence, it was a solemn fact that I'd been the one to administer the killer blow. Never having perpetrated any sort of violence against another living being in my life, to achieve murder at the first attempt seemed overly ambitious. Even downgraded to manslaughter, my prowess seemed horribly over-played. So, all things considered, I was glad the blow wasn't of the killer variety after all. But it did leave a rather dangerous loose end hanging.

At this point in the conversation, again almost as if drawn by an unseen hand, our friend Ahmed joined us. His bulky frame filled the doorway. He looked really quite impressive in his white tourist police uniform, complete with black boots, black belt and black beret – not to mention the black gun. He gazed around at us with all the imperiousness of the Angel Gabriel (or the Muslim equivalent) sent to deliver the Word of God (or Allah, as it may be).

'Dat man who imprisoned you in de tomb...' he declared importantly. 'Well, he is suffering from a kind of brain damage known an am.. amnos... amnas...'

'Amnesia,' Adam supplied helpfully.

'Yes!' Ahmed said, pouncing on the word with alacrity. 'Dis man, he has lost his memory. It is a good thing, no? *Inshallah*, he will not be able to blow de flute...'

'...Whistle... ' Adam offered.

'Yes, whistle. He will not be able to blow de whistle on de tomb!' Ahmed finished triumphantly.

Chapter 3

Ahmed's new mission in life was to put the abominable Hussein under lock and key where he so richly deserved to be. Despite Hussein's memory loss, Ahmed was able to prove his identity as a wanted man. He'd been on the run for days, since we exposed his villainous gang of antiquities thieves. It might be some time before he was in a fit state to stand trial. But in the meantime, there was no danger of him being set free. So, while Ahmed maintained custodial watch, the rest of us returned to the sanctuary of the Jolie Ville Hotel, where, for one reason or another, all the non-Egyptians among our little party were staying.

The hotel was an oasis of tranquillity away from the hustle and bustle of downtown Luxor, situated on an island hugging the eastern bank of the Nile, with great views of the Theban hills on the west bank and a lovely botanical vibe thanks to a veritable army of gardeners who kept the lawns neatly trimmed and the flower borders constantly watered.

We trooped in just as breakfast service was starting and made our way straight for the outside terrace overlooking the Nile. The sun was just lifting above the eastern horizon behind us, staining the surface of the mighty river soft-pink and making the rocky outcrop of distant hills shimmer with the mauve and purple heat haze of early morning. It promised to be another fearsomely hot day. Egypt in June swelters with fierce, unyielding heat and merciless sunlight. There's a majestic quality to the soaring temperature. It demands awe, respect and submission in much the same way I imagine the pharaohs once did.

We pulled two tables together and grouped our chairs under the wide awning of a canvas patio umbrella, subsiding into the shade and requesting coffee of the hovering waiters. For a long moment no one spoke. All gazes were drawn irrevocably across the shifting dark waters of the Nile to those distant glimmering hills turning from pink and purple to buff and bronze as the sun rose. I knew we were all thinking the same thing. We'd seen with our own eyes the unimaginable treasure hidden inside a rock-cut chamber carved into those craggy far-off hills. We were all picturing the secret royal burial that had lain silent and undisturbed for more than thirty centuries. It was an almost inconceivable passage of time. I found it quite head-spinning to think of Nefertiti and Akhenaten lying there in that darkened chamber during the multiple millennia spanning the rise and fall of the Greek and Roman empires and the emergence of Christianity and Islam. They'd been entombed there throughout the days of the Mayan civilisation of the pre-Columbian Americas, the Ming dynasty in China and the Sultans of the Ottoman Empire. Tudors and Stuarts had come to march briefly across the world stage. American presidents had been variously elected, assassinated and impeached. We'd fought two World Wars, emerged blearily from the swinging sixties, and entered a new millennium dedicated to the joint worship of technology and celebrity. History had unfolded across the centuries. They'd lain there throughout, preserved inside their granite sarcophagi, surrounded by their spectacular treasures. I remembered the promise Pharaoh Ay made in the papyrus scroll he buried with Tutankhamun … *"Our precious jewels shall persevere throughout all eternity."* I shuddered as a chill rippled through me. He wasn't wrong.

The waiters brought tall silver pots of steaming coffee. Jessica scampered off to bring a selection of rolls, croissants and pastries from the breakfast buffet. I realised I was ravenous and tucked in greedily, draping a napkin across the colourful folds of Shukura's kaftan, which swamped me from head to toe. Adam nibbled on a currant bun beside me. I knew he was still suffering bouts of dizziness, and he'd confessed in the taxi that had brought us back to the hotel that his head was still pounding like a kettledrum. But he was determined not to miss out on a moment of the council of war we'd decided on to agree our course of action.

I noticed the raised eyebrows and exchange of questioning glances that passed between the waiters as they poured our coffee. But they were used to seeing us battered and bruised, sporting all manner of injuries and ailments. Jessica's black eye was healing up nicely, I was pleased to see; and Dan's arm was out of a sling, although he was still moving a bit stiffly. So, seeing Adam's head swathed in bandages was really nothing new. And the dust clinging to our clothes could have come from just about anywhere. Egypt is one of the dustiest places on earth. So, our friendly serving staff refrained from comment, contenting themselves with expressive little shrugs and infinitesimal shakes of their heads, which still managed to eloquently convey their consternation at the scrapes we kept getting into.

They welcomed the three newcomers to our group politely but showed no signs of recognition. I was a bit surprised at this considering Shukura's face had been plastered all over the Egyptian newspapers in recent days. She'd become a darling of the media as the one instrumental in recovering artefacts stolen from the Cairo Museum during the rioting days of the revolution. That she'd simultaneously routed the nefarious gang of antiquities thieves responsible only added to her press appeal, momentarily diverting the country's readership from coverage of the verdict of Hosni Mubarak's trial and the renewed demonstrations in Tahrir Square.

But the waiters didn't even blink at her magical appearance among us. As for our other two new companions, Mustafa was a local man, but obviously not notable outside of the Ministry for the Preservation of Ancient Monuments in Luxor. Walid, senior in the Cairo Museum hierarchy, had yet to appear in a Discovery Channel documentary in the way of his famous former colleague Zahi Hawass, so failed to be instantly recognisable. The waiters dispensed coffee, waggled their eyebrows at the sorry state Adam had returned in, and left us alone.

'What I don't understand, Merry,' Jessica said with a tiny wrinkle furrowing her forehead, 'is how you and Adam ever thought you could see something like that … that…' She darted a glance behind her to check she couldn't be overheard, and then spun back towards me, looking all pink-cheeked and perplexed. '…that *tomb*,' she whispered thrillingly, 'and then walk away from it and pretend it never existed. Surely it would've driven you nuts in the end! I don't see how you could ever hope to live a normal life with a secret like that weighing you down.'

It was a fair point and one I'd struggled with myself. 'You heard what I said back at the hospital,' I said with a small shrug, wiping a few stray crumbs from my lips with my napkin. 'I think I'd find it harder to carry on as normal knowing myself responsible for so-called scientists perpetrating the kind of indignities on Nefertiti and

Akhenaten that poor old Tutankhamun's mummy has suffered since he was first unwrapped.'

Ted sat forward and rested his empty coffee cup back in its saucer. 'It's a valid point you make Merry, and you're right to lay the ethical dilemma before us. But I can't help thinking if it adds to our historical knowledge then perhaps it's justifiable to disturb the dead. Scientific methods have come a long way since the early twentieth century. The recent DNA testing on Tutankhamun added volumes to what we knew before about his family tree and what may have caused him to die so young. Just imagine how much more we could learn from this discovery. I've been a student of Egyptology for my whole life. Most of what we know comes from years and years of fieldwork thanks to archaeologists who've dedicated their lives to sifting through centuries' worth of sand and silt with little more than a trowel and a paintbrush. It's painstaking, backbreaking work, and all it usually harvests are a few broken potsherds and ostraca. The temple walls have yielded all their knowledge to us. And most people believe the Valley of the Kings to be exhausted of its secrets. A find like this one is unique. It opens up the opportunity to answer all sorts of questions. As we saw for ourselves, Tutankhamun's tomb resembles a rather tawdry prop room by comparison. A study of the artefacts in that chamber and, yes, of the remains of Akhenaten and Nefertiti themselves could spill new light across the most hotly debated and contested period of all ancient Egyptian history. Who are we to withhold that kind of knowledge from the world?'

I fiddled with the braiding on my chair-cushion feeling horribly torn. The others were listening intently, keeping their own counsel for now. But I'm sure they all had an opinion. Reaching a consensus among eight people on the best thing to do was likely to be nigh on impossible. And it was slowly dawning on me that my chances of holding the casting vote were practically zilch. I may have been the one to start out on the quest leading to this awesome discovery, but it was out of my hands now. I didn't know whether to feel sick to my stomach about it or heartily relieved.

'It just feels like a betrayal of Howard Carter,' I murmured unhappily.

'What on earth do you mean?' Shukura asked.

'Well, the reason he bricked up the papyri in that tomb shaft and didn't go off and discover our tomb for himself was because he wasn't able to admit how he came into possession of the scrolls without sullying his own reputation and that of Lord Carnarvon. He'd have had to admit they misappropriated them from Tutankhamun's tomb on an unauthorised dead-of-night visit. It was tantamount to stealing. We might know he intended to put them back and was only prevented from doing so because Carnarvon's widow was such an old witch. But I'm not sure that would've cut much mustard with the authorities back then - or now for that matter. So, if we start shouting from the rooftops about this amazing royal tomb we've discovered, we'll have no choice but to reveal the papyrus that led to us finding it. That, in turn, will drop Howard Carter right in the soup; and I'm not sure that seems at all fair to his memory. I guess I feel a bit protective of him, that's all. I mean I know it probably sounds stupid, since he's dead, but I feel he's kind of accompanied us on this madcap treasure hunt we've found ourselves on. I don't want to be the one who ends up ratting on him.'

I admit I got a bit emotional towards the end of this speech. The others stared at me in a deep and uncomfortable silence while I bit down on my wobbling bottom lip and blinked back the sudden unbidden tears. I'm not usually one given to overwrought outbursts. I think all the drama of the last few days was definitely catching up with me. That, and the lack of sleep. Adam put his arm around me and drew me close, gently bushing a stray tear from my cheek with his forefinger. 'I adore you, Meredith Pink,' he whispered meltingly in my ear. 'And I'll bet Howard Carter does too, wherever he may be now.'

Amazing how much better that made me feel.

Ted cleared his throat and looked at me rather mistily from behind his glasses. 'Your sentiments are a great credit to you Merry,' he said, sounding more professor-like than ever, although I knew he was being kind. His voice was very gentle as he went on, as if he was afraid of upsetting me further. 'But, as you say, Howard Carter is dead. He's been dead for more than seventy years. And I don't think he has any family left whose reputation can be damaged by association.'

'Besides which, the unauthorised nocturnal visit he and Carnarvon made to Tutankhamun's tomb is an open secret now, isn't it?' Dan asked, reaching for another croissant. 'The world may not know about the papyrus they filched, but they've been accused over the years of pocketing all sorts of other bits and pieces, which have turned up in museums all over the world.' He tore off a corner of croissant and dipped it in the knob of rapidly liquefying butter on his plate. 'Didn't you once say that despite being our most renowned excavator, responsible for arguably the most spectacular archaeological discovery of all time, he never received any public plaudits or accolades during his lifetime or after his death. No knighthood or OBE, as he might reasonably have expected. It does rather make you wonder whether the powers that be already had an inkling that he might not have been entirely on the straight and narrow.'

Adam and I received this in a rather mutinous silence – Howard Carter being something of a hero of ours. Adam had dropped his arm from around my shoulders, since it wasn't the most comfortable of positions to be sitting in at the breakfast table, but he was still holding my hand. He squeezed it to stop me arguing as Dan went on.

'So, Merry, I don't think you need to take the full weight of his reputation onto your own shoulders.'

'Besides which,' Ted interjected, 'there must be some doubt as to whether Carter would have shown the same scruples as you if Carnarvon's widow had handed the papyri back sooner than she did. As you said earlier, if she hadn't hung onto the scrolls for more than ten years, there's every chance Carter would have discovered the hidden tomb behind Hatshepsut's temple nearly ninety years ago. I doubt he'd have shared your qualms about encroaching on Akhenaten and Nefertiti's eternal rest.'

I had to acknowledge this was true. And Howard Carter had laid claim to our new discovery in a manner of speaking, since he'd left the trail of clues behind that had led us to find it. Maybe I should stop worrying about his posthumous reputation, and just sit back and let him take the credit.

Jessica had been following the debate with bright interest while she sipped at her coffee. 'I simply don't understand what you're so concerned about, Merry,' she chirped up. 'These people are all dead. Whether it's Howard Carter, who's been gone for less than a century, or some crusty old pharaoh and his wife, who vanished off the face of the earth more than three millennia ago, they're none of them in any position to argue today.'

Yup, I thought. She and Dan were a match made in heaven. He showed a notable lack of reverence for all things historical too. But it wasn't quite so easy to see Ted's paternal and Egyptological influence on her. She was gazing at me with wide, sparkling eyes.

'I mean surely this is your opportunity to achieve fame and fortune beyond your wildest dreams,' she went on. 'The world media is going to be clamouring for your story. You never know, Hollywood might even come calling. If you think about it, everything that's happened to you over the last few weeks has all the hallmarks of a movie. You could be a celebrity, Merry; the toast of the town wherever you go.'

'It's far more likely I'll be dumped in a flea-ridden Egyptian jail, and they'll throw away the key,' I muttered darkly.

'Yes. And quite right, too,' Dan cut in with a decisive nod. 'You've played fast and loose with the law and order in this country for long enough.' And he proceeded to list my misdemeanours with as much enthusiasm as if he was entering them to win a criminal of the year contest. 'First you brazenly pinched those hieroglyphics from Howard Carter's house when the right and proper thing to do would have been to hand them over to the police on the spot.

Then, once you'd sleuthed your way through the little set of conundrums they posed you, you wilfully tampered with private property in the world-famous Winter Palace Hotel and helped yourself to another little coded message from our dear old Mr Carter. Not content with that, you persuaded your police chum to break you into a locked tomb so you could discover the walled-up papyrus scrolls. And all that's without even mentioning the shenanigans that led to you "borrowing" Mustafa here's key so you and Adam could get inside the off-limits part of Hatshepsut's temple in the dead of night to go tomb hunting.'

I glared at him, no longer feeling anywhere near as kindly disposed towards him as I had when he'd turned up with the Aten discs from the Mehet-Weret couch to set us free. 'Thank you for spelling out the case against me so articulately. Please be sure to put yourself forward as lead witness for the prosecution at my trial.'

He sat there looking as smug and stony faced as the Sphinx. I could tell he was enjoying himself immensely.

Jessica, on the other hand, looked quite alarmed. 'Surely, they won't give you a custodial sentence, will they, Merry? You'll be acquitted or paroled; or made to serve a suspended sentence at the very worst, won't you?'

I helped myself to a refill of coffee, thinking it preferable to dumping the remaining contents of the pot all over her pretty head.

Shukura, Mustafa and Walid all exchanged mildly agitated glances. Walid, as the one in highest-ranking authority around the table, decided it was time to take charge. 'Let's not have any more talk about Merry going to prison,' he said firmly, brushing his wispy hair back from his perspiring brow, and nudging his chair more fully into the shade. 'I'm quite sure we can all overlook a few little transgressions from the straight and narrow considering the exciting set of circumstances she's been caught up in.'

I nearly leapt up and kissed him. I contented myself with an evil-eyed glance at Dan and a squeeze of Adam's hand as Walid went on.

'Merry, I have followed most closely your ethical concerns about bringing the tomb to the attention of the world. I will take it as a matter for my own conscience, and I will relieve you of the responsibility. Having seen those chambers with my own eyes and bearing the position I do in the Ministry for Antiquities; I consider we have no choice but to reveal this amazing find for the enlightenment of future generations. I agree with Ted. Its importance to the historical record, and to our quest for a better understanding of ancient times cannot be overstated. We can credit you for your part in the discovery, finding a way to gloss over your - what shall we call them, peccadilloes? - if you wish. Or you can choose to remain anonymous, and we will concoct a story to account for the discovery. Perhaps we can get creative and "stage" the discovery from scratch. These are matters we can debate in slower time. So, my decision is that we must go public with this remarkable find.' He gazed solemnly around at our faces. 'But I determine that the time to do so is not now.'

'What do you mean?' Shukura spluttered.

'We must wait,' he said calmly. He spoke with a quiet authority that brooked no argument and I saw at once how such an unassuming, some might even say meek and mousy man, had risen to such a position of responsibility in the upper echelons of the Cairo Museum. He evidently reserved his assertiveness for the moments when it really mattered.

We all stared at him. I couldn't help but wonder if the one resembling a goldfish right now might be me and clamped my lips together awaiting his explanation.

'These are the most turbulent times Egypt has known in recent years,' Walid said slowly, enunciating each word slowly and in his precise English overlain with its distinct Egyptian accent. 'Only last year our country experienced the violent revolution of the Arab Spring. Cairo was described as a "war zone" in the international press.' He made speech marks with two fingers of each hand to emphasise the words. 'We have been under martial law since then. Just over a week ago we witnessed the demonstrations in Tahrir Square over the verdict of Hosni Mubarak's trial.'

'We know,' Adam said with a small nod. 'We were there. Although Mubarak was jailed for life, the demonstrators were furious about the acquittal of key security officials who were accused of killing protesters in the 2011 riots. From the look of things when we were at the museum, the demonstrators were settling in for a lengthy bout of banner waving.'

'That is correct,' Walid said. 'Many of them are still there. And I predict over the forthcoming weeks things may escalate further. In less than two weeks time Egypt goes to the polls for the final round of the presidential election. Remember this is only the second election in Egypt's history with more than one candidate. And many believe the first, which returned Hosni Mubarak to power in 2005, was rigged. It is our first democratic election since the revolution last year. It is a landmark occasion. Egypt's future hangs in the balance.'

I was starting to see where he was going with his argument. Shameful to admit, I'd been far more interested in Egypt's ancient past than its modern concerns since arriving here on holiday last month on my post-redundancy trip to Luxor. I knew candidates for the presidential election had to be born in Egypt to Egyptian parents and were not allowed to hold dual nationality or be married to a foreigner.

But that was about it. My interest in the election process itself had so far extended only to a fervent hope that the tourism industry wouldn't be affected for long. This was a great time to visit Egypt since so many tourists were staying away, so the major tourist sites were delightfully uncrowded, and it was brilliantly affordable. But looking at it from the Egyptian perspective the impact on the economy was potentially catastrophic. If the Foreign Offices of the UK and other nations deemed it unsafe for tourists to travel to Egypt, as they had during the revolution itself, repatriating those who were already here – it could spell disaster. I'd been told tourism counted for one in seven jobs in Egypt. Walid was right. There was a lot hanging on the upcoming presidential elections.

'The process has been fraught with difficulty so far,' Walid continued. 'In mid-April the Supreme Presidential Electoral Commission announced the disqualification of ten candidates. Reasons for the disqualifications were not given. The disqualified candidates were given forty-eight hours to appeal. But all appeals were rejected.'

'Doesn't sound much like a democracy to me,' Dan muttered archly.

'No,' Walid agreed. 'And it led to more disturbances in the streets. Then, in late April, the Commission ratified the new Corruption of Political Life law. This excluded two more candidates from the presidential race who had served under

Hosni Mubarak in the ten years leading to his resignation. One of them, a former general under Mubarak, appealed. The Commission caved in and overturned its original decision, allowing him to stand.'

'An interesting about-turn,' Shukura put in. 'It meant that although twelve candidates stood for the first round of the election last month, it effectively became a two-man show.'

'Yes,' Walid nodded. 'As Shukura rightly says, the first round in May produced a runoff between Mohammed Morsi, the Islamist candidate backed by the powerful Muslim Brotherhood; and Ahmed Shafik, fresh from winning his appeal, the last president to serve under Mubarak, and seen by many as a hangover from the previous regime. So, this is where we find ourselves today… in the midst of a power struggle between these two men. I fear it could lead to a polarised and possibly violent second round in a couple of weeks. This is a tense and uncertain time for Egypt.'

'And you're saying this hotbed of political unrest is not the right setting for the explosive announcement of an intact royal tomb discovered in ancient Thebes,' Ted said, nodding comprehendingly.

'Not just any royal tomb,' Adam qualified. 'But the joint burial of Akhenaten and Nefertiti.'

'Possibly the most fabled and sought after royal burial of all time.' I added.

'Pure dynamite,' Shukura breathed, her kohl-rimmed eyes wide as she registered the implications of it all.

'Pure gold,' Jessica amended. 'And lots of it.'

Mustafa fingered his narrow moustache, looking troubled. 'It is correct what you say,' he addressed Walid respectfully. 'It is a sad fact that during the tumultuous days of the revolution, law and order broke down. Vandals broke into some of the ancient monuments and museums before the military managed to secure them again. It is not a good thing to see tanks on our streets and armed militia guarding our precious heritage. You are right to point out the risk to the tomb if the military is not able to adequately protect it. But I do not understand what alternative you are proposing. There are eight of us…' he gestured around the table, indicating each of us in turn with an expansive sweep of his hand; '…ten if you include the police officer and the injured man we left at the hospital. How do you propose to keep it a secret?'

Walid gazed around at our faces with all the sombre solemnity of a priest weighing up the faithfulness of his flock. 'I will trust you,' he said simply.

Mustafa looked decidedly unhappy. His gaze came to rest heavily on each of us one by one. I noticed it lingered first on Jessica and then on me. I doubt it was our womanly charms he was assessing. Instead, I was pretty sure it was our blabbermouth potential. He confirmed it with his next words. 'In these days of social networking and instant messaging any one of us could have the news posted around the globe in seconds. As Jessica has already pointed out, there is money to be made if we choose to be unscrupulous. And I am sorry to sound disrespectful ...' Again, it was Jessica and me he was eyeing, I noticed. '...But how can we be sure these people are who they say they are? I mean, I know Meredith claims she came to Egypt as a casual tourist, and stumbled across a set of hieroglyphics in Howard Carter's house by accident, but...'

'Now just hang on a minute,' Adam cut in angrily.

I laid a soothing hand on his forearm, forestalling him. 'It's alright,' I said. 'Mustafa's right to want to check us out. I mean we're not just talking about the random discovery of a bit of broken pottery, are we?'

To be fair, I could understand why Mustafa might feel a bit resentful of us considering we'd found the tomb on his patch. I was still suffering pangs of guilt that we'd allowed him to show us around the off-limits chapel carved into the rock behind Hatshepsut's temple under false pretences. If I were him, I daresay I might feel a bit aggrieved at our duplicity too, despite his fine words back at the hospital in response to my apology. It was to his credit that he cared so much about protecting our find and was willing to challenge us so openly. I was perfectly willing not to take offence.

Walid met my eyes and smiled. 'I will trust you,' he repeated. 'And I will have faith that you will all prove worthy of my trust.' He turned his head to look at Mustafa. 'Please be assured, I do not take this decision lightly. It is my responsibility to preserve our nation's ancient history for the enlightenment of all future generations.' He said this with a soft sincerity that sent a chill down my spine. 'And I do not just mean the future generations of Egypt, but of the world. The wonders of our ancient civilisation belong to the international community. I have a duty to the League of Nations not just to the Egyptian Ministry of State for Antiquities. Our country is under military rule and does not yet have a democratically elected government. What you describe as a hotbed of political unrest, Ted' – he turned his head and gazed sadly at the professor – 'is actually a country in crisis. I cannot even contemplate announcing the discovery of the tomb at a time like this. I would hold no jurisdiction over what might happen to it. And I cannot, I simply cannot...' He paused and wiped beads of perspiration from his brow with his napkin, then folded it back onto his lap with slightly shaking hands. 'I simply cannot allow that magnificent tomb to become a pawn in a political or nationalistic power struggle. It needs a team of the best archaeologists drawn from around the world to work on it. We simply don't have sufficient expertise or facilities here in Egypt to ensure everything is properly documented and conserved, and I count myself in that deficit. And we must allow for the international press to descend on Luxor, clamouring for coverage. I just don't think Egypt is equipped for it right now. If we disclose this now, we run the risk of the military closing our borders and erecting a huge "Keep Out" sign to the rest of the world. And, if that were to happen, then the United Nations in New York might decide to take matters into its own hands and try to wrest control away from us.' He paused for a long moment, his gaze drawn back across the inky Nile to the distant Theban hills where our tomb lay hidden, dark and silent once more. One by one we all followed the direction of his stare, until we were all gazing at the craggy mountainous outcrop on the horizon. The hills glowed deep terracotta in the searing morning sunlight, protecting their secret occupants between layers of sunburnt and wind-grazed rock.

Slowly, we all tore our gazes away and came back to look at each other again. Walid let his pause draw out a few moments more, then, judging he had our full and wrapt attention, he spoke into it. 'No. Now is not the time to make rash and irresponsible announcements about this wonderful tomb. We are going to have to make a solemn and binding pact of silence.'

Chapter 4

It was a straightforward matter in the end. Walid composed a carefully worded letter. We each signed it, and dispatched Dan to the hospital to gain Ahmed's signature. The dreaded Hussein was still blissfully bereft of his memory, with no foreseeable prospect of its recovery, so there was no danger of a loose end on his account. Walid produced a duplicate letter for each of us on the hotel photocopier. In simple terms it told the story of the discovery, naming each of us in turn and the part we'd played. If any one of us broke ranks without the agreement of the rest – or if any one of us should suffer an inexplicable accident – the letter authorised any or all of us to lay the whole matter before whatever authority we deemed appropriate. There were raised eyebrows all around at the inclusion of the "accident" clause. But Walid wasn't taking any chances. He said it was an awesome burden of trust we were individually taking on and placing in each other. It was only fair that he should make some allowance for Mustafa's earlier qualms. In this way he felt our British and Egyptian interests were jointly and severally protected. If need be, we may call on assistance from an embassy, the judiciary, or members of the Egyptological community of either nation - or any other as we saw fit. Our signature was our commitment that we would not disclose the secret beyond our band of nine holders. We stopped short of signing in blood. But I could tell we all felt the full weight of the promise we were making, and a sober duty to uphold it. We sealed the letters up in crisp white envelopes and each took possession of one, agreeing to lock our copy in a safe or bank vault away from prying eyes and where nobody could stumble across it by accident. We agreed to wait six months. Walid suggested this as a reasonable amount to time to allow the dust to settle on the outcome of the elections. Then we would reconvene to review our pact of silence and decide what to do next. It would be nearly Christmas, I realised. It felt like a lifetime away.

Walid and Shukura left for Cairo that afternoon. Walid was desperate to get back to the museum. There was the small matter of returning the Aten discs to Tutankhamun's ritual couch before anyone noticed they were missing and raised the alarm. And Shukura had a husband and three children at home waiting for her. Poor Shukura: I think our pact was hardest on her, not able to take her family into her confidence, and as a woman who so loved to talk. I hoped Selim, her husband, would accept the scanty version of the truth we'd agreed on, and not press her for more. Walid was taking the crumbling papyrus scrolls Howard Carter misappropriated from Tutankhamun's tomb back to Cairo with him. In all conscience we couldn't hang onto them any longer. Ted had picked them up and brought them back out of the tomb with us almost without thinking while the others wrestled with the inert forms of first Adam, then Hussein. The scrolls were still carefully stored inside the silken lining of Carter's battered 1930's style suitcase, as they'd been for the last eighty years or so. We'd decided Shukura could tell her husband about the papyri without letting on that we'd already translated them. The story was simply that we'd discovered them – Ted was a renowned Egyptologist after all, so it wasn't beyond the bounds of possibility that he'd been conducting some fieldwork and found them - and alerted the museum. So, she and Walid had come to Luxor on a mission to collect them. They'd be stored in the museum until time could be found to study them properly. Walid planned to lock them safely inside the museum vault, so it wasn't so far from the truth.

Shukura clasped each of us against her in an agony of goodbye. I didn't mind this now I'd had the luxury of a shower, washed my hair and was dressed once more in a clean set of my own clothes.

'I'll return your kaftan once I've washed the gold dust off it,' I promised her. 'I don't dare ask the hotel laundry to do it.'

She kissed my cheek with a sound smack of her lips. 'There is no hurry, Merry. Keep it as a souvenir if you wish. I have several. I am going to miss you. But I will think often of you and of your remarkable luck at getting locked inside Howard Carter's house. What a terrific adventure it set you out on! You are not going to know what to do with yourself now it is at an end.'

I wished she hadn't said this. It mirrored my own feelings a bit too closely.

She turned and hugged Adam against her ample frame. 'Now Adam, you must take plenty of rest as the doctors ordered. A few days by the pool for you, young man, allowing all those bumps and bruises to heal. I'm sure Merry will be a very attentive nursemaid.' And she winked cheekily at me over his shoulder.

She reserved a special embrace for Ted, looking a bit mistily into his eyes, and patting his back with all the tenderness of the deep and enduring affection they shared. 'Keep safe and well, my dear,' she said softly; then waved around at us, and squeezed herself alongside Walid and Mustafa on the back seat of the waiting taxi parked at the kerbside. They planned to drop Mustafa in downtown Luxor on their way to the airport.

We stood on the steps of the reception building waving them off, then turned and looked at each other with rather bemused and vacant expressions.

'Now what?' Adam said uncertainly, stepping back into the shade.

'Now nothing,' Dan declared decisively. 'Now we follow the good lady's advice and spend a couple of days getting burnt to a frazzle around the pool. Then I, for one, am going to forget all about this crazy crusade we've all been on and go home. I do have a job to go to, you know, even if the rest of you are footloose and fancy-free. I don't hold out much hope of this nation sorting out its political situation any time soon. So, I think it's a pretty safe bet we can forget about announcing that blingsome tomb to the world for a good many years to come. It can stay hidden away in the hillside behind Hatshepsut's temple forever for all I care. In actual fact, that would suit me just fine. And like you've said all along Merry, it's probably the best outcome its unlikely pair of fossilized occupants can hope for. As for me, I'm for a swift return to whatever passes for a normal life in this day and age. Beer anyone?'

I was rather taken aback at this unexpected endorsement of my opinion coming from my erstwhile boyfriend. I'm not sure I could remember a time when he'd ever agreed with me on anything even vaguely Egyptological before.

'Maybe later,' I said weakly, lost for a more fulsome response in the wake of his onslaught.

He shrugged and took Jessica's hand. 'We'll be at the pool bar if your change your minds.' And swinging her hand in his, he disappeared back through the reception block with a definite spring in his step while she jogged along jauntily beside him.

We watched them go. It was amazing how quickly we'd all become accustomed to the switch-about in relationships.

'It's going to take a bit of getting used to not having any sleuthing to do,' Adam said regretfully, taking my hand and moving to follow.

'There is one little puzzle you might like to turn your minds to,' Ted remarked from the marble steps.

We both turned to stare at him.

He gazed back at us with wide innocent eyes behind his glasses. 'It's just that in amongst all the excitement, everyone seems to have forgotten there are not two fossilized occupants in that tomb,' he said in a fair parody of Dan, 'but three.'

'Neferure,' Adam breathed eagerly. I could almost feel him perking up beside me.

'Yes, Neferure; Hatshepsut's daughter. She seems to have died young since it appears she vanishes from the historical record during Hatshepsut's reign. I still think it's decidedly odd that Nefertiti and Akhenaten are sharing their final resting place with her. Now, come with me. I have something to show you.'

He drew us into the spreading shade of a sycamore tree in the hotel gardens. We sat on a thoughtfully positioned bench decorated with dried bird droppings and looked at him expectantly.

He smiled enigmatically and undid the flap of the canvas satchel he was wearing strapped across his body from shoulder to hip. He couldn't have been any more mysterious about it had he been a magician about to pull the proverbial rabbit out of a hat. We stared while he reached under the flap. What he drew out was a stone tablet exquisitely carved with hieroglyphics.

'What's that?' Adam gaped. 'It looks like a small stele.'

'Well done, my boy. That's exactly what it is.'

'But where did you get it?'

Ted's expression was more inscrutable than ever. With his features all craggy and closed up like that he resembled nothing so much as one of the stone statues of the pharaohs that littered the monuments and museums of Egypt. Although it must be said his narrow, wire-rimmed glasses were something of an impediment to the overall impression.

'You didn't …?' Adam breathed.

'Don't tell me …' I murmured, dumbfounded.

'Yes, well, like our dear old friend Howard Carter, I have every intention of putting it back,' Ted said blithely. 'But I hope to make a little study of it first.'

Adam and I gawked in open astonishment.

'While the rest of us were fully occupied getting Adam and the vile Hussein out of the tomb in one piece, you slipped a priceless ancient artefact into your satchel? Ted! I'm shocked to the core!'

He smiled benignly at me. 'Yes, well all I can say is it was one of those heat-of-the-moment things. I spotted the stele just as Adam passed out. It was resting against the footboard of the anthropoid coffin. In all the kerfuffle I just sort of picked it up. I'm not one generally given to kleptomania, but this little piece of granite exerted an almost magnetic pull on me. I couldn't resist it, and I can't say I'm sorry, my dear. Over the last few weeks, you two have helped me realise there's life in these old bones yet. I'm not ready to hang up my Egyptological boots and go gaga. Our adventures have given me a new lease of life. So, all things considered, I don't feel too guilty about my skulduggery. I have not stolen the stele for some shady private collector or to sell onto the black market. As a faithful student of Egyptology, I will treat it with all the reverence it deserves. I will be its temporary custodian only. When the time comes, I can assure you I will pass it into the tender loving care of Walid Massri at the museum.'

I opened my mouth, feeling I really ought to express a bit more in the way of shock and horror. But then I realised Ted's hasty bit of pilfering was really no different to me walking out of Howard Carter's house with his secret message stuffed into my pocket. And, not only that, I believed every word he said. I was quite sure Ted would guard that ancient bit of rock with his life if it should ever prove necessary. There was really no one better to keep it safe all the time it was out of the tomb. I grinned conspiratorially at him instead. 'So, what exactly is a stele?' I asked, really perfectly happy to have another little Egyptological enigma to consider.

Adam sat forward. 'It's a stone or slab, like this one, with an inscribed or sculptured surface, usually used as a monument or as a commemorative tablet. Quite often a stele stands upright. Akhenaten used them as boundary markers around his new city of Akhet-Aten to dedicate the city to the worship of the Aten. If you think of the Rosetta stone in the British Museum, that's also a stele; although much bigger than this one, of course.' He took the stele from Ted and rested it on his lap, tracing the hieroglyphs with the tips of his fingers. 'Wow, it's beautifully carved, isn't it? Have you been able to figure out what it says?'

'Not all of it just yet; we've been rather preoccupied with other things since leaving the tomb,' Ted reminded him gently. 'But some of it is instantly recognisable and stands out quite clearly.'

He took the stele back from Adam and rested it on its own lap. Although only about the size of an iPad, I could tell it was heavy. Ted had reached his seventies without developing any sort of a stoop. He was really amazingly fit and sprightly. But I didn't think the lack of stoop would last much longer if he persisted in carrying a solid slab of granite slung over his shoulder.

The stele was made of polished, almost shiny, black granite. The hieroglyphics were deeply carved into its surface, suffering none if the centuries-worth of wear and tear I'd seen in other examples on display in the museums of the world. It was in such perfect condition I felt we might almost be able to see ancient fingerprints on the gleaming rock.

'See this column of hieroglyphs here,' Ted pointed out, gently underscoring the one he meant with one fingernail. 'Well, it replicates the inscription on the coffin. It reads, *'Neferure, everlasting beauty of Re; may she be justified; beloved of Maatkare Hatshepsut and Akheperenre Thutmosis.'"*

Adam nodded. 'We know Neferure was born when Hatshepsut was still great royal wife to her half-brother Thutmosis II, long before she had herself declared pharaoh. Neferure was their only child. It seems Thutmosis II may have been a sickly individual and died young.'

Ted was bobbing his head impatiently. He knew all this. His glasses slipped to the end of his nose in their habitual fashion as he pointed to another inscription carved into the polished granite. 'So, tell me what you make of this.

I know you don't read hieroglyphs in the normal course of things. But surely, you'll recognise…'

'…The titles of Nefertiti,' Adam finished excitedly, gazing in rapt wonder at the stele. ' *"Hereditary princess, Lady of all Women, Mistress of Upper and Lower Egypt, Neferneferuaten Nefertiti."* They're similar to the inscriptions carved around the rim of Nefertiti's granite sarcophagi in the burial chamber.'

'So, this stele links Nefertiti to Neferure even more explicitly than sharing the tomb with her,' I said, stating the obvious to make sure I hadn't got the wrong end of the stick.

'That's right,' Ted confirmed. 'What we need to work out is why. This stele was made during Akhenaten's reign, that's clear enough. It's carved in the distinctive Amarna style; and look, there's a dedication to Aten, the sun god here. So, I'm guessing Nefertiti and Akhenaten didn't end up buried with Neferure by accident. I think there must be some link between Nefertiti and Neferure. And I think Ay and Tutankhamun must have known about it, which is why they chose that particular burial spot when they brought the remains of Akhenaten and Nefertiti from Akhet-Aten for reburial.'

'Well, there's the obvious similarity in their names,' I suggested tentatively. I had to remind myself I was with one bona fide Egyptologist, and one would-be Egyptologist. Adam had studied under Ted at the Oriental Institute,

Oxford years ago. He'd been forced to drop out of university due to tragic family circumstances. But he'd never given up his avid interest in the subject. I was trailing by some considerable distance in the knowledge stakes since much of what I knew had been picked up reading novels set in ancient Egypt. But I was no less enthusiastic for it.

Ted smiled at me in that rather grandfatherly way of his. 'True,' he said. '"Nefer" means "beautiful" in ancient Egyptian. Literally translated, Nefertiti means, "the beautiful one has come". Neferure means, "the beauty of Re". There's another famous queen of the later 19th Dynasty, who was consort to the famous Ramses II. Her name was Nefertari, which translates as "beautiful companion".'

'So, you're saying the similarity in names is likely to be coincidental.'

Ted tilted his head, 'I'd never dismiss the possibility out of hand. But I think we must look for something more substantial.'

Adam inserted his forefinger underneath the little halo of bandages he was wearing and scratched his head. 'There must be more than a hundred years separating Neferure from Nefertiti. Would that be right?'

'Yes, give or take,' Ted said with a small shrug. 'If we allow for Neferure being broadly contemporary with Thutmosis III, who succeeded Hatshepsut to the throne, then there are four generations between Neferure and Nefertiti; with Nefertiti belonging to the fifth.'

'Didn't Neferure have another tomb cut high into the cliff-face in the Theban hills?' Adam asked with a frown as he concentrated on dredging up from his memory every small detail he could remember about the ancient princess.

'Yes, our friend Howard Carter found it, although it was empty. He felt the tomb had been used, since traces of ochre and yellow paints could be discerned. But there was no sign of a body.'

'So, I wonder if, like Akhenaten and Nefertiti, she was moved from her original tomb to that secret burial chamber behind Hatshepsut's temple. And, if so, I wonder why, and by whom?'

'These are intriguing questions indeed,' Ted agreed. 'So, we must see what other revelations this stele may offer us. Now, I will leave you two young people to ponder these mysteries while you join the others by the pool. I intend to spend the rest of the afternoon in the air-conditioned sanctuary of my room with my reference books.'

As it turned out, Adam and I didn't spend anywhere near as much time pondering these intriguing questions and ancient mysteries as Ted may fondly have imagined. Nor did we join Jessica and Dan by the pool. This was the first moment alone we'd shared since our dramatic rescue from the tomb. It was far too precious to waste.

His eyes met mine and issued a silent invitation, his irises deepening from pure blue to intense violet in the way they always did when he was in the grip of some fierce emotion. Drawn irresistibly by their mesmerising pull, I leaned forward and kissed him.

'It's very *very* good to be alive,' he murmured against my lips.

'When I think what would have happened if Dan hadn't found us...' I murmured back, shuddering at the thought of it.

He took my face between his hands and gazed deeply into my eyes. 'So long as when the time comes, I can still die in your arms, Merry; then I'll die a happy man. But let's hope that's a few decades in the future. For now, I'm perfectly content to enjoy the here and now. So come here.' He held his arms open.

I flung myself against him with a bit more enthusiasm than I think he was expecting. He winced and grunted.

I sprang back with a small cry of distress, 'Oh Adam, I'm sorry! I hurt you! I keep forgetting. Your poor bruised chest. And your poor bandaged head!'

He grinned. 'I keep forgetting too. I'm taking it as a good sign. I think it means I'll live. But, even so, it strikes me perhaps I could do with a little lie down. It might do me good to submit to the tender ministrations of someone who cares about my recovery. I'm suffering a mild concussion, after all.' He gazed at me, his eyes firing signals. 'And I'm wondering if the best place may not be a garden bench in full view of all the other hotel guests to have my various ailments tended to. So, lovely Merry, we have two air-conditioned rooms to choose between. Which would you like it to be: yours or mine?'

I daresay I had something of the look of the Cheshire Cat about me when Adam and I went to call for the professor on our way to dinner a few hours later. Adam was also looking decidedly pleased with himself. There was some expression about cats and cream that kept running through my head when I looked at him. I seemed to have felines on the brain. Perhaps it wasn't surprising considering some of the sinuous and supple ways we'd found to work around Adam's assorted cuts and bruises this afternoon.

Ted opened his door to us with a broad smile. 'Adam, Merry; come in, come in. I'm just searching for a tie.'

Ted has never quite got the hang of this modern day and age where the requirement to smarten up for dinner is a matter of choice not etiquette. While some places still require a jacket and tie for dinner, the Jolie Ville isn't one of them.

Adam looked clean-cut and handsome in chinos and a loose cotton shirt. The shirt hid the livid purple bruises on his chest. I was intimately acquainted with those bruises, having pressed a gentle kiss against every one of them. I felt heat surge in my cheeks, and forced my traitorous thoughts away before the tell-tale colour betrayed me. The bandages still wreathing his head lent him a raffish, rather daredevil look. I felt quite breathless every time I looked at him. On the basis this was approximately once every three seconds there was some risk that I may need an oxygen mask before the evening was through. A single glance in Ted's wall mounted mirror revealed my flushed cheeks and bright sparkling eyes, as well as the simple cotton dress I'd slipped into for dinner once I'd dragged myself out of Adam's arms.

Needing distraction, I flipped through one of Ted's Egyptological books and asked, 'So, Ted, any progress with the stele?'

'I'm glad you asked, my dear,' he smiled at me while knotting his tie. He secured it with a little golden tiepin in the shape of a sphinx. 'It's got me quite transfixed. There's one title that appears repeatedly.' He picked up the stele from the dressing table, where he'd obviously spent the afternoon studying it, and brought it across to show us. 'See, here. It's one of Nefertiti's titles. We noted it this afternoon. It reads *"hereditary princess"*. The inscription goes on to list more exhortations to Nefertiti. This section translates as *"The leading woman of nobles; great in the palace; perfect of appearance; beautiful in the double plume; united with favour; whose voice people rejoice to hear; great wife of the king; his beloved mistress of the two lands; Neferneferuaten Nefertiti; granted life for ever and eternity".'*

I shivered. There's something about these ancient texts that gets to me every time and brings me out in goose bumps. It must be said Ted's voice is particularly well suited to reading them aloud. It's deep pitched, well modulated and with the sonorous timbre of age running through it. I'm not sure those ancient titles would sound half so evocative spoken in a piping young voice.

'But it's this next bit that's got me intrigued,' Ted continued, running his finger across the exquisitely carved glyphs to highlight the passage he was referring to. 'If I'm interpreting them correctly, then I think these symbols here translate as *"descended from"*. And the passage beneath it reads, *"hereditary princess; beloved mistress of the king's scribe; she who bore the pharaoh's great royal wife; lady of grace; endowed with favours; Neferhetep; granted everlasting happiness in the field of reeds".'*

We stared at each other. 'The stele seems to be describing Nefertiti's mother,' Adam said on a note of enlightenment. 'It's the only possible explanation. *"Beloved mistress of the king's scribe"* would seem to suggest Ay, who was the grand vizier under Akhenaten. We know from reading Ay's papyrus that he was Nefertiti's father. Her

84

mother is not recorded anywhere in the historical record, is she?' He looked to Ted for confirmation.

'That's correct,' Ted nodded. 'Ay's rock-cut tomb in Akhet-Aten, which he never occupied, mentions only someone called Tey as his wife. She's described as the wet nurse to the pharaoh's great royal wife. Most historians who believe Ay was Nefertiti's father have interpreted this as meaning Tey may have been Nefertiti's stepmother. This would mean Ay had a previous wife, who bore Nefertiti, but who was probably dead before he commissioned his tomb.'

"Neferhetep,' I said wonderingly.

Ted smiled at me. 'Yes. And that's not all. Now listen to this next passage. Again, if I'm translating these hieroglyphs correctly, then it reads, *"Neferhetep…who is descended from the hereditary princess; fair of face; great of praises; lady of perfection; Neferneferu; for whom the imperishable stars burn brightly".* So, what do you make of that, hmm?'

Adam cleared his throat. 'You're reading us a family tree that traces the maternal line back from Nefertiti,' he said, sounding a little bit choked.

Ted grinned at him, then turned his gleaming eyes on me, pushing his recalcitrant glasses back up onto the bridge of his nose. 'Shall I carry on?'

We both nodded dumbly, and Adam reached for my hand.

' *"Neferneferu…who is descended from the hereditary princess; sweet of love; mistress of happiness; wise of counsel; Neferkhare; granted peace and prosperity in the Afterlife".'*

'I think I'm getting the gist of this,' Adam said in a rather strangled voice. 'And Neferkhare is descended from…' he prompted.

Ted twinkled at him over the rim of his once-more slip-sliding glasses. *'"… The hereditary princess; lady of joy; mistress of jubilation; for whom Re sails through the sky in his solar boat; Neferamun; resting in eternal bliss among the immortals".'*

'And Neferamun is descended from…' I whispered.

' *"…The hereditary princess; daughter of divinely anointed pharaohs; beautiful one of Re: Lady of Upper and Lower Egypt; Mistress of the Two Lands; God's wife of Amun; Neferure; granted life everlasting with her divine mother Maatkare Hatshepsut".'*

Little hairs stood up on the nape of my neck and along my forearms. 'So Neferure may have died young but not before she gave birth to a daughter,' I breathed. 'And I was right to think the 'Nefer' part of their names was a link. Every subsequent daughter shared it; ending only when Nefertiti had her own daughters.'

'Yes, I've been wondering about that,' Ted said musingly. 'My theory is that maybe she felt she didn't need to perpetuate it any further because she'd re-gained her birthright, sitting as Great Royal Wife on the throne of Egypt.'

'So, none of those other 'Nefers' was married to a pharaoh?' Adam queried. 'None had the status of great royal wife?'

'No, I've checked. There were four pharaohs between Hatshepsut and Akhenaten. They had multiple wives between them, but the only one known to have a 'Nefer' in her name was Nefertiry a consort of Thutmosis IV. She would be broadly contemporary with the Neferneferu of the stele – but it's a completely different name. I don't think we're talking about the same person.'

'And you think the 'Nefers' of the stele including Nefertiti, may have been brought up believing their birthright to have somehow been denied them?' I asked, trying to make some sense of what we'd heard.

'It's impossible to say for sure, although it's a compelling conjecture. Neferure achieved an unprecedented status as a royal princess after her mother declared herself pharaoh. As Hatshepsut took on the role of pharaoh, so Neferure took on a queenly role in public life, serving in high offices in the government and religious administration of ancient Egypt. Some of the titles given to her, such as Lady of Upper and Lower Egypt, Mistress of the Two Lands, and God's Wife were official roles. They had to be filled by a royal woman in order to fulfil the religious and ceremonial duties - normally of the senior queen or great royal wife - in the government and temples.'

'So, I wonder what happened that meant Neferure's daughter was prevented from becoming a great royal wife herself,' Adam mused. 'She obviously lived to maturity, having a daughter of her own. Under normal circumstances we might reasonably expect any royal daughters to turn up among the harem of the next pharaoh. It's a time when siblings were routinely married to each other to keep the royal blood pure. A stray royal princess might serve as a focus for any rival claims to the throne, so the pharaoh couldn't afford to leave her in spinsterhood for long.'

'Exactly right, my boy,' Ted approved. He glanced at his watch, reminding us we were running late for dinner, and Dan and Jessica would be waiting. 'I haven't quite finished studying the stele, so maybe it has more secrets to reveal to us. But it does rather make me wonder who the father of Neferure's daughter might have been.'

Chapter 5

'I'm booked on a flight back home in a couple of days,' Dan said. We were eating pizza in the hotel's Zigolini Italian restaurant. We'd toyed briefly with the option to have dinner al fresco on the terrace overlooking the Nile, serving ourselves from the buffet and listening to the hotel singers crooning their way through popular melodies. But it was a breathlessly hot, still night; and we opted for air conditioning over entertainment and the authenticity of an Egyptian evening in June.

'I'm going back to Cairo to sort out some stuff, then I'm going to join him in a couple of weeks or so,' Jessica said brightly, then shot a quick searching at Ted, as if she hadn't meant to come out with it quite so baldly. 'So long as that's ok with you, Dad?'

'Yes, yes,' he said with a small wave, smiling fondly at her. 'Of course you must do whatever you wish. You're a grown woman with your own life to lead. And after all the unpleasantness you've had to contend with since the revolution, what with Youssef, and all; yes, it's a good idea for you to return home to England. There is really no need for you to stay here as a help-maid to me; much as I've loved having you here in Egypt with me.'

The unpleasantness Ted referred to was Jessica's brief and unhappy marriage to Youssef Said, one of the unholy triad of brothers of whom the rotten Hussein was the last man standing. She'd had no idea she was marrying into a gang of opportunistic and thuggish antiquities thieves. The newly married pair had wound up living with Ted after Youssef was injured in the rioting in Tahrir Square. I'm not sure it's a set of circumstances Ted would have chosen, and it seems it didn't take long for Youssef to start showing his true colours. I don't imagine the last sixteen months had been particularly comfortable. Looking at the gleam in Ted's eyes, I had a sneaking suspicion he was actually rather relishing the thought of having his little flat near the Giza plateau in Cairo to himself again. He could study the stele and his Egyptological reference books in peace and get back to living his own life.

The merry widow smiled happily. 'I might see if I can get a job for one of the theatres, doing costume design. It's what I took my degree in after all.' She squeezed Dan's hand on the tabletop, clearly looking forward to more than just a new career.

'So, what about you, Pinkie?' Dan asked, taking a swig of his beer. 'What are your plans between now and Christmas?'

I think he used my nickname without thinking. Dan's always called me Pinkie, his way of taking delight in my ridiculous surname. But I wasn't sure how appropriate it was now he and I weren't "together" anymore. Still, I suppose old habits die hard. Nobody else seemed to have noticed. Jessica was still squeezing his hand as ardently as ever while smiling expectantly at me. Adam's hand rested on my knee under the table. I concluded I was being overly sensitive to the changed dynamic between us, and let it go.

I shrugged, not really wanting to think about it. I was so happy in the here and now. It was tempting to just drift along for a while and let the future take care of itself. But I knew I couldn't drift indefinitely. 'I suppose I need to find myself a job of some description,' I said with a sigh. 'My redundancy money won't last forever.'

'Here, or back at home?' Dan queried.

I flashed a quick glance sideways at Adam. 'Well, I'm not here on a working visa, just a holiday one. And my flat's been standing empty at home for weeks now.' For all that Dan and I had been together for the last ten years, we'd never actually lived together. I had a flat in leafy Sevenoaks in Kent, while Dan lived a bit further up the commuter line towards London. 'My mum's left a couple of messages on my mobile reminding me it's her birthday at the end of the month. So, I guess I can stay for another week or so...' I trailed off unhappily and brought my hand to rest on top of Adam's, trying to convey without words that given the choice I'd stay here in Egypt with him forever.

'And you, Adam?' Jessica asked. 'Will you check out of the hotel and move back into your flat in Luxor now Ahmed has that awful Hussein locked up? It's safe for you to go back there now without thinking he might turn up any minute to murder you in your sleep.'

It was true Hussein had been dogging our steps in a quite vindictive manner. It was a relief to be rid of him. I was glad I hadn't killed him, but I couldn't regret inflicting the amnesia that rendered him harmless.

Adam turned his hand under mine and clasped it gently. 'I might come back to England with the rest of you for a while,' he said musingly. 'For one thing, it's unmercifully hot here in summertime. Plus, it strikes me there's quite a lot going on back at home this year. London's hosting the Olympics after all.' He smiled sideways into my eyes, and I knew there was a third reason he was transmitting in the same wordless way I'd done a moment ago. He squeezed my hand to confirm it, and my heart skipped a beat knowing he didn't want to be parted from me any more than I did from him. 'You might need to put me up though, Merry, since I sold my house as part of my divorce proceedings.'

I tilted my head to observe him through narrowed eyes, masking the delight bubbling up through me. 'It's a hardship I daresay I'll learn to suffer,' I murmured.

'I'm quite happy to chill out here for a few more days first,' he added. 'The doctors ordered rest and relaxation, remember?' He twinkled at me a little bit provocatively, leaving me in no doubt about what he had in mind. I'm not sure restful or relaxing were necessarily the first words that sprang to mind remembering our afternoon's activities, and always assuming I was reading the signals right, but I certainly wasn't complaining. 'Besides, I don't think I'm supposed to fly with concussion. I'll see about booking us onto a flight next week, Merry; and I'll hand the keys to my flat back to the landlord until the autumn.'

So, it was decided. We were all going home; Ted to Cairo, and the rest of us back to the UK.

'But we've got to be back by December,' I reminded everyone. 'That's when we're meeting up with Walid, Shukura and Mustafa to decide what to do about the tomb.'

It felt a bit strange spending our last few days in Luxor as simple holidaymakers. Something about this mythical and mysterious land of the pharaohs had woven its way so far into the fabric of my being I felt I belonged here. Returning to England didn't feel like going home. It felt like going away. Egypt was in my blood. Whilst it was true I'd come here on a simple holiday – my post redundancy 'time out' trip – with all that had happened to me since, I now felt myself to be part of this dusty, barren, rather inhospitable landscape. I loved everything about it, including its choking Saharan sand, aggressive sunshine and hob-nail-booted flies. Ok maybe I'm stretching it a bit far with the flies. They're the peskiest, most infuriatingly persistent little blighters you can imagine. But Egypt's their home (literally) as much as mine (spiritually), so I put up with them.

I hadn't come here thrill-seeking. If I'd wanted that I'd have gone cage diving with great white sharks in South Africa or white-water rafting over Niagara Falls or something. But without asking for it, and quite by accident, I'd found myself caught up in an adventure beyond my wildest imaginings. In truth, I wasn't quite sure how to settle back into tourist mode. Egypt's haunting history had reached out and grabbed me by the scruff of the neck and I had no desire whatsoever to shake myself free.

'I don't suppose Ted found anything else in that stele that might send us off on another treasure hunt, or on a quest to solve an ancient mystery, or anything like that, did he?' I asked a bit bleakly, turning on my sunbed to look at Adam. He was stretched out in the deep shade alongside me, drying off after a dip in the infinity pool. We were booked on an early flight to Gatwick tomorrow. Ted had returned to Cairo, taking Jessica and the stele with him. Dan was already back home and back at work, no doubt looking forward to Jessica's arrival at the weekend.

Adam pushed his sunglasses up on top of his head, dislodging his bandages, and grinned at me. 'Are you feeling as bereft as I am without a conundrum to crack, a papyrus to translate or a tomb to break into?'

'It seems so,' I admitted. I was pleased to see the bruises decorating his chest had faded from the livid purple of a few days ago to soft lilac bordered by pale yellow. His torso looked a bit like a pastel-painted sunset. He'd been told his bandage wreath could come off tonight. The head wound caused when the venomous Hussein smashed him against the tomb wall was healing up nicely underneath it.

'I've done my best to distract us from the boredom of it all,' he said sadly. 'But it seems I'm not able to compete with Howard Carter or King Tut when it comes to holding your interest, Merry.'

I swiped at the fly that was dive bombing us and smiled wickedly at him. In his attempts to distract us he'd proved himself quite imaginative. 'Oh, I don't know,' I said. 'You've had your moments. If you're willing to pretend to be Indiana Jones again, I daresay you could distract us quite successfully for the rest of the afternoon.'

He reached for his Fedora hat and waved it a bit theatrically at me. He'd had it for years, and I'm sure he'd bought it quite specifically for the purpose of imitating his hero. Suffice it to say he'd invented things to do with that hat in the privacy of our hotel room that sent shivers of anticipation down my spine. Just seeing it on his head was enough to make me go all molten and boneless feeling, remembering what he'd been up to last time he was wearing it. 'Come with me,' he commanded, pulling me up from the sunbed with a firm grip and a dark glint in his eyes.

It was some time later that we returned to the subject of the stele. My head was resting on his shoulder, and we were draped around each other in a loose-limbed sort of way, allowing the air conditioning to cool our bodies.

Adam scratched absently at his temple beneath its wrappings. 'I do think there's a mystery attached to that stele. But I'm not sure the stele on its own is enough to help us solve it. Ted told us the last passage suggested Neferure may have died in childbirth. But there's no mention of who the father of her daughter may have been, or what happened to the daughter after her death. All we have is the knowledge of the unbroken mother-daughter succession from Neferure to Nefertiti. It's tantalising to conjecture on what it might mean, but it's not enough to send us off on another quest to unlock a secret from Egypt's ancient past.'

I sighed and stroked my fingers absently across his chest. 'No one has been able to prove one way or another whether Neferure was ever married to Thutmosis III, have they?'

'No – although it seems pretty certain she must have been meant for him. He was her half-brother, so she was the logical choice. But they were both children when their father the pharaoh died, and Hatshepsut put herself on the throne in his place.'

'I've never quite got my head around all these incestuous marriages,' I mused. 'It must have been a pretty claustrophobic in the early 18th Dynasty, what with all the inter-relationships. Hatshepsut was also married to her half-brother, wasn't she? They were Neferure's parents.'

'Yes, she was the daughter of Thutmosis I and his great royal wife, Queen Ahmes. So, Hatshepsut always saw herself as being of pure royal blood. Her husband and half-brother, Thutmosis II, was born of a harem wife. But as a son it gave him precedence to the kingship when their father died.'

'So, if Neferure *was* married to Thutmosis III, then it was a case of history repeating itself. Neferure was the daughter of Thutmosis II and his great royal wife Hatshepsut, so must have considered herself fully royal; while Thutmosis III was also the son of a harem wife, wasn't he?'

'That's right, and a minor one at that according to some scholars. It's been suggested she was little more than a concubine. But, even so, since Hatshepsut had no son, only a royal daughter, Neferure, it still gave Thutmosis the right of succession when his father died. The reality is he came to the throne as a small boy. Hatshepsut stood regent to him for a couple of years, as the senior ranking queen. She was also in the bizarre position of being both his aunt and stepmother. But then she took matters into her own hands in an unprecedented and quite remarkable manner. She declared herself pharaoh, sitting on the throne of the Two Lands with the crook and flail firmly in her own grasp. While it was a full co-regency with the little boy, the temple carvings leave little doubt that Hatshepsut was the senior pharaoh. She was the one wielding all the power.'

'You have to wonder why she didn't just do away with Thutmosis III altogether,' I said. 'Surely it would have been the easiest thing in the world to arrange for a little accident to befall him or to slip poison into his food.'

'That's a very bloodthirsty way of thinking, Merry,' Adam scolded. 'But yes, many scholars have said the same thing. It's another one of ancient Egypt's little mysteries.' He turned his head to kiss me absently on the temple. 'For all her bravado, perhaps she was a traditionalist at heart. Or maybe she didn't think it would be good for her everlasting *Ka* to have the blood of a divinely anointed king on her hands. She was a great subscriber to *Ma'at*, which loosely translates as truth and justice, the natural order of things. It was the opposite of chaos; something the ancient Egyptians had a great fear and loathing for. Hatshepsut's throne name was *Maatkare*, which means something like *truth is the soul of the sun*. Who knows, perhaps she was simply waiting for him to grow up so she could see him safely married to her daughter Neferure. Then Neferure would be great royal wife in more than just name and ceremonial duties. The fact is, when Hatshepsut died after a twenty-year reign Thutmosis III did succeed her. And some would say it was a good job too. He proved to be Egypt's finest warrior pharaoh, conquering lands as far north and south as Syria and the fourth waterfall of the Nile in ancient Nubia.'

'But it still doesn't answer the question about whether or not he married Neferure, and whether he was the father of her daughter. She was only about sixteen when she died, wasn't she? That's tragically young to die in childbirth.'

'It's likely Thutmosis would have wanted to marry her,' Adam said, stroking my hair. 'After all it would have consolidated his right to rule since she was a pure-blooded royal heiress. From what I've read, it seems there are some inscriptions to one of his later wives, Satiah, that appear to have been carved across the top of original text that may have read Neferure. But it's inconclusive at best.'

'How frustrating that the stele is silent on the subject of the father of Neferure's daughter.'

'There's just one symbol Ted hasn't been able to decipher, right at the end of the stele,' Adam said. 'But he doesn't think it's a name. In fact, he can't seem to figure out what it's supposed to be. It's a hieroglyph he's never seen before. He said it looks a bit like the double plume of a feather; rather like the image of the god Amun wearing the two vertical plumes on his head. But Ted hasn't been able to translate it in any way that makes sense.'

'So, it's not some cryptic pictogram we can puzzle our way through,' I said with disappointment.

'Sadly for us, it doesn't appear so.'

'And there's nothing else on the stele that might send us off on a quest for the next clue to help us solve any of its mysteries?'

'I'm sorry to say not.'

'So, we really do have to go home tomorrow?'

'I'm afraid so Merry.'

I turned grumpily into his arms. 'Then I think I might just need a bit more distraction before Ahmed comes to wave us off at the airport.'

* * *

England was suffering a soggy summer. After the vigorous blue skies of Egypt, the endless rain was a dampener on more than just the gardens of Great Britain. My spirits sagged, saturated by the deluge.

I'd been so swept up in the mystique of the ancient Egyptian royals that I'd completely forgotten about – and missed – the momentous milestone in the British monarchy's history: the Queen's Diamond Jubilee celebrations.

Union Jack flags defied the dismal weather, hanging rather limply from flagpoles and draped as bunting between streetlamps, dripping with rainwater. But they injected a welcome colour into the grey drizzle of the great British summertime. I admired their ability to remain perky looking despite the oppressive grey clouds.

Nobody was in any hurry to take them down since the Olympics were only a few weeks away. But, obsessed as ever by the weather, people gazed at their rain-soaked surroundings and exchanged prophesies of doom about the washout the greatest sporting event on earth would prove to be if the weather didn't follow the fine example being set by the flags and perk up a bit.

It was chilly too. Disinclined to expose my skin in skimpy tops and little skirts, my tan was fading as fast as Adam's bruises.

We kept a close eye on the News, our ears pricking up at any mention of the Egyptian elections. The outcome of the main election was delayed by a week. But towards the end of June Egypt's election commission announced the Muslim Brotherhood candidate Mohammed Morsi had won the nation's presidential run-off. Morsi claimed victory by a narrow margin over Ahmed Shafik, the last prime minister under deposed leader Hosni Mubarak. The commission declared 51.7% of the vote for Morsi versus 48.3% for Shafik. So it was a close run thing. Field Marshal Hussein Tantawi, Head of the Supreme Military Council in Egypt congratulated Morsi on the victory. But it was still pretty clear from all the news reports that the military was holding onto all the levers of power. Morsi's win came after widespread reports and speculation about a possible deal between the Brotherhood and the military council.

I watched and listened to all this with a heavy heart. Things in Egypt seemed as unsettled as ever. Call me prejudiced, but I'd come to the conclusion anyone with the name Hussein wasn't wholly to be trusted. I wasn't sure the Field Marshal's congratulations boded well for Egypt's future or our prospects of announcing the royal tomb any time soon.

Morsi's victory was greeted with scenes of wild celebrations by tens of thousands of his supporters in Tahrir Square. The Muslim Brotherhood vowed to stay in the square to protest at the Military Council's power grab; and good luck to them too, I thought. I wondered what our friends Shukura and Walid were making of Egypt's modern history as it unfolded around them. They had a birds-eye view of things from the Egyptian Museum, which was situated on the northern edge of Tahrir Square. Even during the final week of the electoral process, while the votes were still being counted, constitutional amendments were being announced. Anyone with half a brain could see the new presidency held very little power compared to the military. It was the military that had dissolved parliament and held the final say on the drafting of a new constitution. As Dan might have said, 'Some democracy!'

My mother's birthday fell on the last day of the month. She'd organised a garden party for family and friends out at the quaint cottage my parents share in deepest, darkest rural Kent. It was the finest day of the year since Adam and I had returned to England; cool, but with a brave attempt by the sun to stay shining for at least an hour or two between the cloudbursts.

I think my mum was secretly relieved to find I was no longer with Dan. It's fair to say the rot set in a few years ago when she accidentally overheard him referring to her as Puff the Magic Dragon. In the normal way of things my mum has a pretty decent sense of humour. But I'm not sure she was inclined to see the funny side on that particular occasion. The wedding ring still notably absent from the third finger of my left hand after ten years and scant prospect of grandchildren didn't help. My mum's pretty broad-minded but I think she was privately of the view that Dan was stringing me along until something better hove into view. She never voiced any opinion on the matter, so I was never able to refute it. (After all, as things worked out, Dan and I could have levelled the same accusation at each other). But I always felt it was hanging there, unspoken. Thankfully my brother did the decent thing a year or two back when he and his wife produced as delightful a pair of cherubic offspring as anyone could possibly wish for. I was eternally grateful to him, relieving me as it did of the obligation to feel too guilty. That I dote on my little niece and nephew goes without saying.

The look my mother subjected Adam to as we walked down the garden path was coolly appraising. I'm not sure what she'd been expecting since I'd informed her on the phone that I was bringing along the new man in my life; someone I'd met in Egypt. But she bucked up visibly to find he wasn't a native of that middle eastern country. (I feel compelled to point out; my mother is not racist. But she is a teensy bit "old school". Whilst she embraces people of other cultures, she doesn't necessarily want me, her only daughter, "hooked up" [her words] in a cross-cultural relationship.) She brightened even further when she learned Adam had been educated at Oxford. He didn't add that it was at the Oriental Institute rather than one of the prestigious business faculties. Nor that he'd been forced to drop out before completing his studies. But he was compelled to tell the whole truth when she looked him squarely in the eye and asked what he did for a living. His lack of current employment was a definite black mark, and his desire to be an Egyptologist blacklisted him even further. That he'd spent the years leading up to the credit crunch in banking just added insult to injury. My mother judges bankers little better than criminals and thinks they should all be locked up for the evils they've perpetrated on our economy.

All that said they got on like a house on fire. Adam unleashed his smile, accepted third helpings of her homemade strawberry shortcake and allowed her cream Burmese cat to shed hairs all over his brand new trousers. She called him "dear" and invited him to call her Audrey, saying Mrs Pink was far too formal and made her sound like something out of Enid Blyton. I'm not sure she's ever forgiven my poor father for foisting such a ridiculous name on her; or the world at large for letting her be born a generation before it was routinely acceptable not to take on one's husband's surname.

All things considered; it was a very encouraging first meeting.

The London Olympics were upon us before we knew it. They were billed to inspire a nation, and they certainly inspired me. We hooked up with Dan and Jessica to watch the events of Super Saturday unfold in front of us on a big screen in Hyde Park. Thankfully the weather thumbed its nose at all those who'd prophesied disaster, turning warm and muggy if not exactly bright. The din and ecstasy of that night will stay imprinted on me forever. We munched our way through the picnic we'd brought with us, screaming ourselves hoarse as we watched Jessica Ennis, Mo Farah and Greg Rutherford storm to gold for Team GB. We did it all over again on Terrific Thursday in early September, sharing a Chinese takeaway at my flat in Sevenoaks and yelling our lungs out as Jonnie Peacock and David Weir, our astonishing Paralympians stormed to victory.

It was heart-warming to see the way we Brits let go of our cynicism and embraced the spirit of the games. It made me feel there was hope for us yet, despite our world-famous reserve and general world-weariness. Britain emerged from the games a better place, and I was glad I'd seen it for myself.

We all settled into a semblance of normality. Considering Dan and I had never shared a place to live, Jessica made herself right at home in his bachelor pad. Adam, by the same token, settled into my little flat in Sevenoaks as if he'd been born there. I found myself a job temping in the communications team for a local housing association, and Adam returned to his online Egyptology studies. But as the weeks dragged by, I could feel myself growing more and more restless.

'What's wrong Merry?' Adam said one night in late September, tossing his Indiana Jones hat into the corner of the room when it became clear it wasn't working its usual magic.

'I'm sorry,' I whispered, turning my face against his chest, unmarked now by the bruises and abrasions that had eventually healed and faded away. 'It's just I find myself longing for Egypt. Especially since the nights are starting to draw in. I'm not sure I can face the onslaught of winter after our notable lack of a summer.'

He pulled me close and tucked the covers up around our ears. 'Our adventures in Egypt have taken on something of a dreamlike quality, haven't they?' he remarked.

'Too much so! You know, given the choice, I'd go back and sleuth my way through Carter's conundrums to find the tomb that was Tutankhamun's triumph all over again. I miss Ahmed and Ted, and I'm not sure I want to wait until December to see Shukura again. She may be Mrs Motormouth, but I love her to bits. I need to face up to it and get myself a proper job. But I keep wishing the job could be in Egypt rather than here in good old GB. I've been putting it off and putting it off, but the fact is, Adam, I can't do temping forever. I need to earn a living. I'm just at a bit of a loss about were to start, because my head says it's here, but my heart is in Egypt.'

He cupped my face in his hands and stared deeply into my eyes. The dark shadows alleviated only by the yellow glow of the streetlight positioned directly outside my bedroom window played a game of darkness and light on his face. 'Are you sure, Merry? Because there's nothing I want more than to return to Egypt. But I'll stay here if this is where you think your future lies.'

I wondered why it had taken us so long to have this conversation. 'You once said we should write novels together, or devise treasure hunts for tourists, or write guidebooks to all the famous sites setting out the personality profiles of all the major players of ancient Egypt. You said we could devise murder mystery games, or…'

'…I remember,' he smiled. 'But, you know, there's another option, if you're up for it…?'

'What is it…?' I breathed, feeling anticipation take hold of me.

'I've been looking online at the prospect of owning a dahabeeyah.'

'A what?'

'Well, we'd probably think of it as a kind of sailing yacht. Dahabeeyahs were the original Nile River cruise boats. Thomas Cook pioneered them in Victorian times when he introduced wealthy travellers to the delights of tourism along the Nile. Before the advent of steam ships, they were the only way to sail up and down the Nile. But they gradually lost out to the modern cruise boats as tourism became available to the masses.'

He had my full attention. I sat up in bed so I could look at him properly.

'I think there might be a bit of a niche in the market that we could turn to our advantage, Merry. I think there's a genuine appeal in these vintage sailboats for people drawn to Egypt by the lure of nostalgia as well as by the wonders of antiquity. These restored old boats offer antique passage in an antique land. They only accommodate eight or ten passengers at a time, so they're pretty intimate. They're small enough to be completely booked by families or a group of friends. And they have the advantage of not having to stick to the rigid schedules of the large cruise boats when it comes to sightseeing. They can berth at the less visited sites, and it's possible to entirely customise each itinerary.'

'And you're suggesting we should buy one and offer intimate cruises?'

He sat up and drew his knees up against his chest under the sheet. His eyes sparkled in the dull lamplight. He really was irresistibly good looking, with his hair all pillow-tousled and his features animated with enthusiasm. 'Yes! I've got enough money put by to make the initial investment. I think we could offer "authentic" tours of Egypt.' He made the speech marks in the air with his fingers. 'But with an additional twist. I thought we could specialise in educational tours. Without wishing to sound conceited, I think I know enough about Egypt's ancient history and monuments to put together an interesting schedule for the discerning traveller. Perhaps we could even invite Ted along to offer proper lectures. He's a renowned Egyptologist and likely to be quite a draw for those keen to experience Egypt properly, not just rush in and out of the major sites with their cameras clicking. I was thinking with your marketing skills, you could perhaps design a brochure for us and create a website to manage bookings.' He broke off suddenly. 'What is it, Merry? Are you cross? Oh please, you're not going to cry, are you?'

I cleared my blocked throat and swiped at my brimming eyes. 'Adam, I think you need to rescue your Indiana Jones hat from the corner of the room where you flung it. I feel it may come in handy for something I have in mind to show you just how much I love you; and adore your idea.'

Chapter 6

We arrived back in Luxor in late-October. Ahmed greeted us joyously before our feet even hit the tarmac at Luxor airport. He was waving at us from the bottom of the wheeled-up aeroplane steps, decked out in his full tourist police regalia of gleaming white freshly starched shirt and trousers with scissor-sharp creases in all the right places, teamed with a black beret, thick black belt (holding in his ample middle), finished off with shiny black boots and a highly polished big black gun. He was grinning from ear to ear, treating us to an eyeful of his truly appalling dentistry.

'Dat man who mislaid his memory,' he yelled ecstatically when we were still only halfway down the steps. 'Well, still he searches for it in vain. Dis is good news, yes?'

'Its very good news,' Adam called back, reaching the bottom step and disappearing into a manly bear hug.

'*Inshallah*, it is hidden somewhere he will never find it!' Ahmed prayed.

'God willing,' I agreed, reaching up on tiptoes to kiss his cheek.

'At last, you are come home,' he announced.

'Amen to that,' I said; and grinned at him. 'By which of course I mean Allah be praised.'

'It is good,' he said. And that was that. The verdict was pronounced. Egypt and Ahmed welcomed us back with equal warmth, almost as if we'd never been away.

I'd spent the last few weeks in England registering my flat with a lettings agency to arrange for it to be rented out on a rolling six-month lease. I'd put my personal items in storage. For the first time in my adult life, I was experiencing the heady feeling of being relatively free and unencumbered. I didn't have enough money in the bank to keep me going indefinitely; but I had my redundancy money and some savings, and I'd done a careful budget. I figured I could see myself through a year or so without an income if I was sensible. Adam, who had more of a financial cushion behind him than I did, was minded to be generous. But I was determined to be independent and pay my way.

We were back in Egypt under multiple-entry business visas. These entitled us to a ninety-day stay and six-month visa validity. While we were here, we'd need to approach the local authorities under jurisdiction of the Labour Ministry with details of our business plan to apply for our work permits. These had to be issued on Egyptian soil, so we still had some way to go before the future we'd spent the last few weeks dreaming – and talking incessantly – about could start to become a reality.

Adam had arranged for us to view two dahabeeyahs, both of which were undergoing renovation work in a small boatyard a little way south of Luxor.

We wasted no time, making the trip on our first full day back. We parked our hired scooters in the shade of a sycamore tree and approached the little dockyard with some trepidation. It looked more like a boat graveyard than a boat repair yard. The coating of wind-blown sand covering everything in sight probably didn't help. Even the palm trees were sagging under a summer's worth of dust. The boatyard contained an odd assortment of feluccas and little motorised water taxis as well as a couple of the large cruise boats, looking like nothing so much as giant metal biscuit tins. We were met at the quayside by Khaled, a half Egyptian (father), half Scottish (mother) engineer. He explained he'd taken up the restoration of old boats as a hobby, then made a career out of it as demand for an alternative to the modern Nile cruise boats experienced a bit of a resurgence prior to the revolution.

'Of course, business is much slower nowadays,' he said sadly. His Scottish accent was a bit of a surprise. It was so unexpected coming from someone in a galabeya, turban and open-toed sandals. The blue eyes in his nut-brown face were a bit startling, too. 'It's a risky time for you to be venturing into business in Egypt, particularly in tourism.'

Adam and I had talked about this endlessly. We'd ended up tossing aphorisms about and decided the one we most subscribed to was "Nothing ventured nothing gained". 'Let's face it,' Adam had said. 'We can make all our mistakes while tourist numbers are down and then ride the crest of the wave when things pick up again.'

I had to admire his optimism. But I also felt myself duty-bound to point out that if we made all our mistakes when business was slack, we ran the risk of finding ourselves without any business at all when - *if* - things picked up. He'd grinned at me and accused me of being 'ever the pragmatist.'

On such little differences are the best of relationships formed. So, I smiled to myself and decided Adam and I would work out well enough in business given a fair wind. His romanticism and my practicality ought to make for a fine combination. And that was before you added our joint passion for Egypt – and for each other, of course.

Khaled wiped his oily hands on a cloth and led us towards where the two dahabeeyahs were moored in a kind of semi-dry dock, resting half in and half out of the Nile. I have to say they didn't look much from a distance, nor indeed close up. Both still awaited their outer paintwork, and the larger one entirely lacked windows, with just a series of square holes along its beam. The massive sails that make dahabeeyahs such an impressive sight on water were nowhere to be seen, probably unstrung somewhere below deck. To reach the boats we had to negotiate a series of ramps and steps, then pick our way along a cluttered, rusting pier, stepping over coils of rope and various other health-and-safety-defying debris.

'You need to mind your step here,' Khaled warned us as he put out the gangplank to give us access to the first dahabeeyah. By 'gangplank' I mean a strip of wood about eight inches across, with a few strips of wood nailed across it to form little steps, and rusty nails protruding to inflict tetanus on the unwary. Khaled levered the plank into place at a rather jaunty angle and secured it precariously by butting a rusting petrol carton against the near end at our feet. He offered me his hand, accompanied by a rather wicked gleam in his eye. Recognising a challenge when I saw one, I hopped up onto the tightrope (I mean gangplank) and did my best impression of a gymnast, hopping along it unaided. I'm pleased to report I did not fall headfirst into the Nile.

'Things have come a long way since the Victorians used to travel along the Nile by dahabeeyah,' he informed us conversationally as we all made it safely onboard. 'In those days a round trip from Cairo to Luxor took about forty days. A Victorian traveller wishing to sail the Nile not only had to hire the boat for the duration but also provision it, debug it and de-rat it. And that was before hiring the crew and overseeing the boatmen.'

I shuddered at the thought of bugs and rats.

Khaled grinned at my reaction. 'Nowadays you need to make sure you keep it regularly sprayed to keep the mosquitoes at bay in spring and autumn. But I can promise you no bugs and no rats if you keep up a bit of basic maintenance.'

'But we still need to think about a crew,' I said to Adam.

'You'll need a captain to sail the boat, a chef and a housekeeper-cum-serving assistant as a minimum,' Khaled advised us. 'Assuming the two of you will take over the management of the boat and organise the tours.'

I could see Adam's blue eyes were snapping with excitement. 'How long would it take for a boat like this one to make the round-trip from Luxor to Aswan?'

'You'll need at least a week. These aren't the fastest boats on the Nile, but they're the most picturesque by far and they give you the opportunity to go to some places off the beaten track.'

I looked about me, trying to envisage this rather unlovely husk of a boat as our home. Dahabeeyahs are shallow-bottomed barge-like vessels, usually with at least two sails, one at the bow and one at the helm. The basic design has been around since the time of the pharaohs, with similar craft being depicted on tomb and temple walls.

Khaled saw my uncertain glance at the little reception area we were in. 'It's a long way from finished, he said. 'You're just seeing the basic shell. All the major restoration work is done. Structurally she's sound as a pound. But I need to put in a proper kitchen with all mod cons – you must have water purification in Egypt – and then the whole thing needs varnishing, painting and furnishing. I'm probably looking at another four weeks of work on this one, and perhaps a couple of months on the other.'

'That probably suits us,' Adam said. 'We figure we need to go on a couple of Nile cruises to see what the competition's like. Can you show us around?'

The dahabeeyah was basically on two levels. From the little entranceway where the gangplank deposited us at the front end of the boat, we entered a narrow passageway with three cabins on either side. One of these would be ours if we chose to make this our new career choice. They were all en-suite. Khaled showed his true talent in the way the luxurious little bathrooms had been added into the bedroom space without seeming to encroach upon it. At the end of the passage a door opened into a semi-circular space, following the shape of the stern. Khaled explained half of this would be set out as a dining room for the cooler winter nights when meals would need to be served inside, not up on deck as in the hot summer months. The other half would be fitted as a luxurious lounge-bar, where guests could come to read or relax, play games or hear lectures about the various sites making up the itinerary.

A doorway at the end of the lounge led out onto a small open deck. Below deck down a steep, narrow stairway was the space for the kitchen, ample in size, well lit and airy. Beyond it were tiny cabins for the crew. Each had its own bathroom facilities, which Khaled assured us was a luxury for those working on the cruise boats. That these were minute, without space to swing a mouse let alone a cat, didn't seem to be the point. Khaled was fiercely proud of this feature.

The little open deck also contained a quaint spiral staircase leading to the upper deck. This was the pièce de résistance. True, it didn't have space for a plunge pool or a jacuzzi, as I'm sure some of the modern boats must have. But it was charming, a real throwback to a more leisurely and bygone era. It was half-covered with a canvas awning to protect passengers from the sun, with lovingly restored wooden floorboards and an antique polished wooden railing, finished with ornate brass fittings. I imagined it resplendent with potted plants, rattan furniture and antique steamer-style recliners; maybe even a few Turkish rugs scattered hither and thither. Yes, this was the nod to Victorian nostalgia I felt some travellers might be looking for; and there was plenty of space up here for starlit nights eating al fresco watching the moon cast its sliver of light across the dark waters of the Nile.

'I love it,' I breathed, captivated. In my head I was already furnishing the cabins and the lounge area. Lots of teak, I decided, with pure Egyptian cotton sheets in neutral colours, and fluffy white towels in abundance.

'You haven't seen the other one yet,' Khaled said, hearing me. But though I pride myself on my pragmatism, this dahabeeyah had reached into my soul and taken up residence.

We toured the other one, of course. It was bigger, with more cabins and room for a separate dining room and lounge. But it didn't speak to me in the same way the first one did.

'Do they have names?' I asked.

'This large one's the *Philae*,' Khaled said. 'The smaller one's called the *Queen Ahmes*. Bit of an obscure name, I'll grant you. I understand she was an elusive ancient Egyptian queen. Can't say I've ever heard of her myself. You'll probably want to think about re-naming her if you decide to go ahead.'

At the mention of Queen Ahmes, I stopped breathing. Adam reached for my hand, and I knew he was feeling the same crazy sense of destiny I was. All goose-bumpy I gazed up at him. 'Did Fate just take you by the shoulder and give you a damned good shake?' I asked with a tremor.

'Yes,' he said, his blue eyes deepening to violet. 'Not half.'

Khaled was looking at us as if we'd switched to a foreign language. And maybe in a sense we had. He wasn't to know that it was inside the frame of Howard Carter's portrait of Queen Ahmes that I'd found the secret message and hieroglyphic cryptograms that had started me out on this whole Egyptian adventure. But Adam knew it, and so did I; and this boat having the same name was just too spooky a coincidence for words.

'Queen Ahmes was Hatshepsut's mother,' Adam said.

Khaled nodded sagely, but in all honesty I'm not sure he was any the wiser. Not all Egyptians are avid students of their country's ancient heritage. I guess being half-Scottish and evidently brought up in those northern climes if his accent was anything to go by, he had more of an excuse than most not to know more than the popular headlines about Egypt's fabulous past.

Adam explained, 'In a roundabout way she's kind of wrapped up in how Merry and I met, so she has a special place in our hearts.'

Khaled nodded again, taking the oily cloth out of his pocket and wiping his hands on it again.

'It's meant to be,' I whispered to Adam, squeezing his hand.

'So, I take it you won't be changing her name,' Khaled said in a down-to-earth manner; cutting right through the treacly way Adam and I were gazing at each other. 'I can paint *Queen Ahmes* down the side in big bold italics and you'll be happy.'

'Yes,' Adam confirmed emphatically. 'We will.'

'Okey dokey,' Khaled said, and I suppressed the crazy urge to giggle at his turn of phrase. I really was feeling quite ridiculously euphoric.

While the men talked numbers and timescales, I wandered a short distance away and propped myself against a dusty anchor, gazing at the *Queen Ahmes* in her semi-dry dock. I was experiencing one of those weird moments of displacement, feeling a sudden jolt of recognition for this nearly restored boat, almost as if I'd bumped into someone I recognised as an old friend; but then couldn't place in terms of how I knew them or why I felt such an overwhelming sense of familiarity.

There was no answer to it. But looking at the more-than-a-hundred-year-old dahabeeyah I felt an affinity and an odd sense of certainty. We were destined to have good times I thought, this boat and Adam and me.

'If you're planning on doing some research by taking a Nile cruise of your own...' Khaled said as we shook his hand ready to leave, '...you could do worse than the *SS Misr*. She's a deluxe steam ship originally built in 1918, and later purchased by King Farouk. I did some work on her when she was in dry dock for maintenance a couple of years back. She's a propeller steamer, lovingly restored, with all the charm and fashion of the early twentieth century. She's contemporary with Howard Carter's discovery of King Tut's tomb, so she's got some history attached to her. My guess is if you go ahead with this dahabeeyah venture she's the type of vessel that'll be your main competition. She's a whole lot bigger, catering for a still-intimate forty-or-so guests. She boasts all modern conveniences, international cuisine and top-class service. You should check her out. She's your competition for the discerning traveller wanting a slice of nostalgia.'

'Thanks,' Adam said, shaking his hand warmly. 'We might just do that.'

The *SS Misr* was due to leave Luxor to travel to Aswan in a few days' time. We booked ourselves a cabin with no difficulty at all. Sadly, tourist numbers were still badly in decline despite the election of the Muslim Brotherhood's popular candidate Mohammed Morsi. Egypt's new constitution was still a work in progress, so potential visitors remained circumspect.

Adam and I had checked back into the Jolie Ville Hotel until we could crystallise our plans. Adam's tiny flat near the Souk in Luxor wasn't big enough to accommodate us both so he'd handed back the keys. We figured it couldn't hurt to have the choice of three swimming pools, multiple restaurants, plus the bonus of the hotel's star attraction, Ramses the camel who offered rides on a daily basis.

The weather remained aggressively hot in daytime, the brazen sun blistering down from a hard, hot sky. But the stifling night-time temperatures we'd experienced in June had softened to a much more amenable warmth. Evenings were pleasant, balmy and starlit. I'd forgotten the magnificence of the Egyptian nights, but it didn't take long for us to become re-acquainted.

With a little bit of time to kill before we could check out our competition, we gave into the irresistible magnet-like pull of the west bank. As the sun blazed high in the vast blue sky, we climbed the footpath skirting the northern boundary of Hatshepsut's temple. It led to the top of the bay of cliffs. These surrounded the temple as a kind of bronze-coloured amphitheatre. The cliffs were patterned with creases and crevices and deep vertical fissures, the product of centuries of windblown sand, occasional torrential rain and the baking heat of the sun. The path was steep in places and strewn with scree and loose rocks. We concentrated on watching our step and left conversation for later. But it was impossible not to pause every so often to admire the dramatic beauty of the temple rising on slopes on our left-hand side. It was set into the cliffside like a natural extension of the strong, severe amphitheatre of rock surrounding it. Rising on three terraces and cut with graceful porticoes and long sloping ramps, it made full use of the terrain and brilliant Egyptian climate, deliberately incorporating the contrast of strong shadow and sharp sunlight into its design. The temple was an ancient work of art that had hugged these cliffs for nearly three-and-a-half thousand years. As always when confronted with such an unimaginable passage of time my mind tried to perform mental gymnastics to help me comprehend it. As always, I failed.

Finally, puffing a bit, we reached the top. If we kept going along the ancient pathway worn into the rock by millennia's-worth of footfalls we'd reach the Valley of the Kings. We'd trodden the path before, the night we made the fateful discovery of the papyri Howard Carter walled up in an abandoned tomb shaft. The Valley literally backs Hatshepsut's temple, on the opposite side of the cliffs. Today we didn't keep going. We passed the spot where the appalling Hussein pushed Dan off the cliff, both suppressing a shudder and wordlessly joining hands as we remembered how close a call it had been. Curving left, we came to a spot where we could descend with relative ease through a series of shallow switchbacks onto a narrow shelf, giving us a birds-eye view of Hatshepsut's temple and the dusty Nile plain laid out before it.

It was a spectacular view. The temple was directly beneath us to our left, laid out like a child's model. Across the dustbowl that was the desert plain in front of it lay the ruins of centuries old temples rising from the sand and rock. It was a hazy day. The Nile and the suburbs of New Gurna on this side of the Nile and modern Luxor on the far bank were lost in the smog. On a fine day it was possible to see as far as the Red Sea hills on the horizon; but not today. Today we contented ourselves with the close-up view, which was what we'd come for.

I stared at the architecture of this finest of ancient Egyptian temples below me, leaned against Adam's broad and bruise-free chest and whispered, 'Did I dream it?'

He knew at once what I meant and wrapped his arms around me, hugging me close against him. 'It's hard to imagine them lying there among all that golden treasure while tourists traipse about the place oblivious within a few hundred metres of them, isn't it? But no, Merry, you didn't dream it. What Dan describes as *'that blingsome tomb'* is down there beneath our feet, hard though that is to believe now.'

I tried to picture Akhenaten's golden chariot, Nefertiti's jewel casket; the two stone sarcophagi and the older anthropoid coffin containing Neferure's earthly remains. But it was like recalling something I'd once seen in a movie; exaggerated and unreal. Instead, I found myself focusing on the restored statues of Hatshepsut. They stood against a number of the columns on the upper level of her temple. I was seeing them in profile and from above, but I knew each one stood over eight feet high; Hatshepsut in the Osiride pose, with her arms crossed across her chest, hands against her shoulders, holding the crook and flail of royalty.

'I wonder if Hatshepsut knew there was a secret chamber behind her temple, or whether it was carved later,' I mused, settling into the comfort of Adam's arms and stretching my legs out in front of me. 'It seems a bit strange that Neferure ended up there, considering she was probably originally interred in that cliff tomb you were telling me about.'

'A hideaway behind Hatshepsut's temple,' Adam murmured. 'It does seem likely it was excavated earlier, and Tutankhamun and Ay made use of it when they decided to bring Akhenaten and Nefertiti to Thebes for reburial. But I think they were the ones who devised the hidden doorway and hit upon the idea of using the Aten discs as keys to work the mechanism to open it. Remember, one of the papyrus scrolls we found was an architect's drawing of this temple. Senenmut, Hatshepsut's famed architect and possible lover must have drawn it. He's credited with building the temple. The papyrus didn't show the hidden chamber, but Ay highlighted the Hathor Chapel and added the inscription *Aten is key*. Considering Ay was Nefertiti's father, married to Neferhetep who was one of the 'Nefers' descended from Neferure; I'm guessing that's how he came into possession of the architect's drawing. I'll bet the drawing was handed down from mother to daughter in the same way the title *"hereditary princess Nefer-whatever"* was.'

'So, the drawing would have been given into Neferamun's care, since she was Neferure's daughter. But who by? Senenmut? Are you suggesting he may have been the one to move Neferure from her cliff-cut tomb and relocate her to the secret hideaway behind Hatshepsut's temple?'

I felt Adam's shrug. 'I don't know, but it seems likely. He was probably the only one who knew about the secret chamber since he oversaw all the temple building works. Remember that little sketch of him – the little self-portrait - on the wall inside the Hathor Chapel? I wonder if it was meant to be a kind of marker, pointing to the location of the chamber for those privy to the secret. And Senenmut and Neferure may have been especially close. He was more than just Hatshepsut's architect and possible lover. One of the most prestigious roles Hatshepsut gave him when she had herself declared pharaoh was personal steward to her small daughter. Countless statues have survived showing Senenmut with the young Neferure on his lap. Hatshepsut appears to have given him sole charge of her daughter's upbringing. I'm guessing he must have been pretty fond of Neferure.'

I drifted in a kind of haze for a while, gazing at the temple. 'Do you believe Hatshepsut and Senenmut were lovers?' I asked at last.

Adam thought about it for a moment. 'Yes, I think I probably do. I don't think she'd have handed her daughter into his care if there weren't a pretty special bond between them. He was granted unprecedented privileges and rose to become one of the most powerful men in the country. Yet he was a commoner with humble origins. Evidence suggests he was a bachelor for his whole life. That was unusual for a high-ranking statesman. Perhaps it suggests his affections were engaged with someone it was impossible for him to marry. And he had a majestic tomb carved for himself in the precincts of the temple down there.' He waved towards the far-off parking lot to show me roughly where it was. 'That was unheard of for a non-royal; although it seems he never occupied it. But the most compelling evidence is an ancient graffiti-type sketch found on the wall of a cave near here, which historians believe dates back to Hatshepsut's reign. It was probably dashed off in an idle hour by one of the men working on the temple.

It's a kind of stick drawing showing two people *in-the-act*, so to speak.'

I grinned at his quaint turn of phrase, 'An intimate act...?' I queried.

'Quite,' he said. 'And it's quite explicit. What's interesting is the female figure is wearing a headdress with long lappets that fall over her shoulders, like the royal *nemes* headdress. She's not wearing anything else; I should point out. The male figure is also unmistakeably naked apart from a close-fitting skullcap, which some scholars think was worn by officials of rank.'

'So, the couple in the sketch also enjoyed wearing hats to add a certain *je-ne-sais-quoi* to a particular activity,' I giggled wickedly.

Adam chuckled and squeezed me. 'It would seem so, Merry. We don't appear to have hit upon anything new! Anyway, before you distract me from the point, it seems whatever the true nature of their relationship contemporary gossipmongers clearly had them down as lovers.'

I smiled, twisted around in his arms, and gave in to the overwhelming desire to distract him from the point, reaching up to kiss him.

Despite his fine words, he gave in without a moment's hesitation. We were happily absorbed in our kiss when I felt an odd shifting sensation beneath me.

I snapped open my eyes and stared into his, less than an inch away and registering the same shock. 'I know you have a powerful affect on me,' I murmured against his lips. 'But I didn't know you could literally make the earth move.'

No sooner were the words out of my mouth than there was a deep rumbling noise. Something bounced off down the cliff beside us, bringing a shower of dust and loose debris with it.

'Rock fall,' Adam said urgently, hauling me to my feet and shoving me roughly backwards. He flattened me hard up against the cliff-face with his body pressed against mine. His arms encased me like steel bands; protecting me from the avalanche of rock I could hear crashing around us.

I clung to him in terror, with my head pressed into his shoulder, praying the whole cliff-face wasn't about to crumble away, taking us with it, plunging hundreds of feet onto the jagged rocks below.

The noise of the tumbling rocks was deafening. I felt the impact as a falling stone glanced off Adam's shoulder and heard his grunt. Another one ricocheted like a gunshot off the cliff next to us sending a cloud of dust and pin-sharp chippings raining over us.

Suddenly the noise ceased. There was a moment of deathly calm. I was just daring to take a breath, thinking the worst was over, when I heard a sickening crack. Before my scalp had even had time to prickle as I registered what this meant, the ledge on which we were standing came sheer away from the cliff-face and we started to fall.

Chapter 7

The narrow shelf we were standing on broke apart and slid down the cliff-face, taking us with it. Thankfully we didn't fall far. It was only a mini subsidence. We came to a spine-jarring halt on a ridge of rock jutting from the cliff-face only a few metres below where we'd been sitting earlier. We could have reached it by following another switchback in the cliffside if we'd decided to descend further. We landed in an ungainly heap of arms and legs amid stones and boulders, some of them the size of small cars. We were coated in orange rock dust.

I sat up and disentangled my limbs from Adam's. 'Are you alright?'

His shirt was torn at the shoulder and blood oozed from a gash at the top of his arm where the falling rock struck him. He spat out a mouthful of dust and peered at me, gritty-eyed. 'Pah! Apart from swallowing half the Theban mountainside, I'm fine. What about you? All in one piece?'

I got gingerly to my feet, testing for bruises. 'Surprisingly, yes.' My relief was fulsome and heartfelt at finding myself intact and with everything still in working order. I held out my hand to help him up.

He took it and clambered upright, picking loose chippings from his hair. Shading his eyes he peered up the cliff-face. 'Thank God that's over,' he said with feeling once he'd assured himself there were no more rocks waiting to hurl themselves down the cliff-side at us. 'All things considered I'd say we're lucky to have got off so lightly. That could've been a whole lot worse.' He swiped at the dust on his clothes, sending little terracotta clouds swirling in the air around him, and picked his way across the debris of scattered rocks to the edge of the little shelf we were standing on. He gazed downwards at the fallen rocks far below and shuddered.

My canvas bag was strapped crossways across my body. Luckily, I hadn't removed it when Adam and I were sitting gazing at the view of the temple. I pulled out a bottle of water as Adam re-joined me. While he took a couple of swigs I burrowed about and gave a triumphant little shout as I found a packet of antiseptic wipes lurking at the bottom among the biscuit crumbs, old train tickets and sticky sweet wrappers. I cleaned him up as best I could, but I didn't have anything to use as a bandage. 'It's only a surface wound,' I said, wiping away the last bits of grime from the gash. 'So, although it might keep bleeding for a while it's probably best to let the air get to it.'

He grinned at me. 'It's quite nice to have you playing nursemaid again, Merry. It's been a while. I didn't realise how much I missed it.'

I swiped playfully at him then went to sit on a convenient boulder while I used the remaining antiseptic wipes to clean my own face and hands. I looked up. 'So, is it time to go?'

'I think we may have a small problem on that score,' Adam said. He was standing a few feet away. Fallen rocks and stones of varying shape and size littered the ledge around him, and he'd scrambled across a couple of the larger ones so he could get a better view back up the cliff-face. 'I'm not sure we can get back up to the path from here. There are a couple of huge boulders blocking the space. One of them looks particularly precarious. I don't think we can risk trying to climb across it. It's likely to go tumbling into the ravine down there, taking us with it.'

I looked around. The cliff-face rose sheer and forbidding in front of me. While it was full of cracks and crevices, most of them were vertical, gouged into the rock over the centuries by windblown sand and the scorching heat of the sun. Hand and footholds were in short supply. I didn't fancy scaling the cliff-face in any case. I picked my way across the rock-strewn space and peered down. It was a long drop to the foothills below. I could still see Hatshepsut's temple slightly off to the left of us. 'What are you suggesting? That we go down instead of up?' I called back over my shoulder. Neither option was especially appealing. I wondered if we could shout for help to the tourists visiting the temple. But they were too far off to hear us. And even if they could, a rescue would need ropes and other mysterious mountaineering tackle. Whichever way I looked at it, I didn't fancy the idea of climbing up the sheer cliff-face, aided or not.

Adam clambered back across the fallen rocks and came to join me. 'I think going down is our only option,' he said, taking my hand. 'There's no way back up without risking another rock fall. So, we either attempt to go down, or take up residence on this narrow ledge for the rest of our natural born days.'

'I've never been the out-door type,' I murmured. 'Let's go.'

We found a place on the ridge of rock where the drop to the shelving slope below was fairly shallow. Adam went first, crouching down and jumping, then turning to help me down. Higher up, we'd been able to walk down a series of gently descending switchbacks. Here, the descent was steep, and we didn't dare stay upright. Sometimes crouching and clinging to the jagged cliff-face, sometimes crawling on our hands and knees, and keeping a weather eye out for snakes and scorpions, we inched our way downward, descending by a series of narrow ledges and disintegrating fissures in the rock. Loose scree and chippings crumbled away and tumbled down the cliff-face as we went. My heart was in my throat the whole time. One slip or wrong move, one rock that couldn't bear our weight, and we'd go hurtling forward onto the fallen boulders below.

I lost track of time. My hands and knees were scraped and bleeding. I knew the sun was starting to go down by the fiery rays dazzling my eyes. Sweat dripped down my face and my aching muscles burned and cramped, protesting the unaccustomed activity.

Finally, we reached a wider shelf about half way down the cliff-side and I collapsed onto my back. 'I have to rest,' I groaned.

Adam slumped alongside me. We lay there for a long time, catching our breath and letting the heat of the sun dry the perspiration on our bodies.

'Come on, Merry,' he said at last. 'We must keep going. The sun goes down quickly here.' He glanced at his watch. 'It'll be getting dark in another hour. I'm not for spending the night out here unless we absolutely have to.' He passed me the water bottle and I took two long swallows.

As I was handing it back so he could finish it off something caught my eye. It was a splash of colour where colour didn't ought to be. I blinked a couple of times, thinking the flaming sunlight was painting dots before my eyes. The only colour I'd been aware of for the last couple of hours was the burnished bronze of the cliff-face set aglow by the equally burnished radiance of the sun. The colours I'd glimpsed just now were red, green and blue. I blinked a couple more times; just to be sure my eyes weren't playing tricks on me. 'Adam, what's that?'

'Huh?' he asked, capping the empty water bottle and putting it back in my canvas holdall, which he was helpfully carrying.

'Over there,' I pointed. 'See that little gap in the rocks? I can see flashes of colour inside.'

He scrambled to his feet and pulled me up with him. Stiff muscles momentarily forgotten we picked our way across the rubble strewn ledge.

'My God Merry, you're right! I think the rock fall has dislodged this boulder here and it's rolled away to reveal a sort of entrance.' The thread of excitement in his voice was unmistakeable.

'Entrance to what?' I asked.

'That's what we're about to find out,' he said, squeezing behind the boulder.

I was a bit fearful of creepy crawlies, so I didn't follow him immediately. But his voice echoing from inside the rock-face soon changed my mind.

'Crikey Merry, come and take a look at this!'

I squeezed behind the boulder and though the small gap in the rock and caught my breath. The sun came with me through the narrow entranceway, lighting the space beyond with dazzling golden beams in which dust motes floated. The light revealed a rectangular chamber about the size of a single garage carved into the living rock. The walls and ceiling were plastered and brightly painted with images so fresh they looked like the brushstrokes were made just yesterday. But I knew we were looking at an ancient sanctuary dating back to the days of the pharaohs. The walls were painted the dull ochre of warm Sahara sand. Columns of exquisitely drawn and colourfully painted hieroglyphics filled the upper registers of the wall reliefs. But it was the life-size images of a man and a woman, one wearing the royal regalia, which caught and held my attention.

'Well, we have our answer,' Adam breathed.

The pharaoh depicted here was clearly a woman, wearing a long, patterned sheath dress, with a regal headdress with the divine cobra Wadjit rising from her forehead. In image after image, she was shown facing a man wearing a cape over his shoulders, with a linen kilt folded around his hips. The intimacy between the two figures was obvious. Their right hands were clasped, while their left hands were raised palm to palm in front of their faces almost as a sign of worship of each other.

'Hatshepsut and Senenmut,' I said unnecessarily.

Adam leaned forward to look at the oval cartouche painted above the pharaoh's image. ' "*Maatkare*,"' he translated.

'And this?' I asked, pointing to the column of text behind the male figure. Adam had been using his online studies to brush up on his knowledge of hieroglyphics in the months we'd spent at home. I was confident he could have a go at translating it.

'I think that says, "*Steward of Amun*",' he said, studying it. 'It was one of Senenmut's official titles.'

'So here we have a hidden shrine dedicated to what? Their love for each other?'

'That's certainly the way I'm reading it,' Adam ventured. 'Look. Some of these scenes are reminiscent of the wall scenes at Deir el-Bahri. This one shows Senenmut's mission to Aswan to cut Hatshepsut's famous obelisks out of the granite quarry. And here we have the expedition to the fabled land of Punt. Some scholars believe Senenmut led the expedition to bring back shipfuls of precious commodities for his queen, the pharaoh.'

'The one thing they couldn't record openly was their relationship. So, they carved it onto the walls of this little sanctuary high up in the hills behind the temple. Another of Hatshepsut's hideaways, this time an everlasting memorial to their love for each other.' I was forced to swallow the lump in my throat as I said this. It was unbearably touching to gaze at the images. They managed to be joyous and poignant at the same time. I was pretty sure, given the need for secrecy, that Senenmut himself must have painted these images. He and Hatshepsut probably came here often. I could imagine him unveiling each new wall relief to her as he finished it; with the queen-pharaoh standing back to admire and congratulate him on his handiwork. The feeling of walking in their ancient footsteps was overwhelming and made me a bit dizzy. There was a fierce intimacy to this place. There was a damp patch in one corner where rainwater had penetrated over the centuries and the plaster had flaked, making the scenes difficult to discern. But with everything else so fresh and new-looking, I could almost convince myself they'd walked out of here just yesterday, only for Adam and me to return today. Time was a distorted concept and suddenly three-and-a-half thousand years seemed but the blink of an eye.

Adam pulled his iPhone from his pocket – miraculously undamaged considering the rock fall and our subsequent perilous descent of the cliff-face – and started taking careful photographs of the images and hieroglyphics. 'Ted's going to have a fit when he learns of this,' he said.

I made a slow study of the closest wall reliefs, admiring the lifelike skill with which they were drawn. The scenes of the expedition to Punt were especially compelling. They showed a series of great ships setting out, with sailors hanging like monkeys from the rigging. The land of Punt itself was depicted as a kind of botanical paradise, full of exotic trees and flowers. The houses of Punt were beehive-shaped grass huts, mounted on stilts, with ladders giving access to little platforms. Several such huts were shown scattered throughout a date-palm grove full of birds and butterflies. The next series of reliefs showed the Egyptian sailors loading their ships with all manner of weird and wonderful goods to bring back to the Theban court including spices, ebony and ivory, fresh myrrh trees and assorted animals including apes, monkeys and a sleek-looking panther. The final sections showed the triumphant return home. Senenmut was depicted prostrating himself before the female pharaoh, arms outstretched in worship, clearly dedicating the entire cargo for her pleasure.

As I was admiring this last scene the glowing light inside the little shrine faded, almost as if someone had turned down a dimmer switch. Shadows filled the sanctuary. The sun had slipped silently over the horizon, taking its golden rays of light with it. 'It's getting dark,' I said in dismay. We'd been so caught up in our remarkable find we'd forgotten the urgent need to complete our descent of the cliff face.

Adam stared at me in consternation through the sudden gloom. 'There's no way we'll make it to the bottom before nightfall,' he said. 'And I don't much fancy our chances in the dark.'

I looked around me at the uneven floor strewn with small pebbles and loose scree. 'But the only alternative is...'

'...Yup, to hole up here for the night,' he nodded.

We stared at each other as the dark shadows thickened, both contemplating our lack of food and water and the complete absence of anything comfortable to curl up on.

'It's only for one night,' he said brightly. 'We'll last out until morning without any trouble. The sun comes up early. We can be out of here at dawn and back at the hotel for breakfast.'

I tried not to look as unhappy about the idea as I was feeling. After all, we'd spent the night in worse places. The stifling, dead-aired interior of a certain tomb came to mind. At least here the air was fresh; we knew we were free to leave any time we chose, and we weren't being pursued by a double-dyed villain intent on murdering us. 'But what about nocturnal visitors?' I asked before I could stop myself. 'Cobras and the like.'

'Good point,' he conceded.

We spent the last few minutes of twilight out on the shallow ledge gathering a collection of the biggest rocks we could carry and squeezing with them back through the gap in the rock into the chamber. We brought plenty of small stones too. Then we literally bricked ourselves inside, piling up the rocks in the doorway until they completely filled it, and plugging the gaps with the stones, leaving no little holes where a long slithery thing might take it into its head to attempt to join us.

I was hot by the time we'd finished, and it was impenetrably dark. So successful was our rock-wall not even starlight could filter through the cracks.

'Come here,' Adam invited, pulling me into what I imagined was a corner and then down onto the floor alongside him so I could put my head against his chest. 'We might as well try to make ourselves comfortable.'

I picked a few prodding stones out from underneath me and settled against him. 'How's your shoulder?'

'It's fine,' he reassured me. 'You know Merry, I'm not quite sure what it is about you, but you seem to have a quite remarkable talent for discovering hidden Egyptian treasures. Most archaeologists spend a lifetime scrabbling about in the dust and don't have even a whisper of the success you've had. The best they can hope for is the odd broken statue or pot. You've found an earth-shattering papyrus, the most sought-after tomb ever, and now this: a little sanctuary that proves the relationship between Hatshepsut and Senenmut once and for all.'

I ruminated on this for a while. It was true ancient Egypt seemed willing to offer up her secrets to me. I was pretty sure that Adam and I must be the first people to step inside this chamber since Hatshepsut and Senenmut left it for the last time, levering that giant boulder in place so it would remain hidden. And we'd seen inside her other hideaway where her daughter was laid to rest. I wondered if she minded us camping out in what she must once have viewed as her most private, sacred places.

'I wonder what sort of woman she was,' I mused.

'Hatshepsut?'

'Mm. I mean she must have had the most incredibly forceful personality to have the audacity to put herself on the throne like that; and to be accepted, ruling unchallenged for twenty years while the boy king whose kingdom she usurped grew up and became a man. In some ways I still feel her charisma crackling down the centuries at us.'

'Many scholars have called her the first great woman in history,' Adam murmured. 'She undoubtedly had the support of powerful men. Many of her father Thutmosis I's favoured ministers swore allegiance to her when she seized power including Ineni, another architect, and Ahmose Pen-Nekhbet who was an old soldier who'd fought alongside the old warrior king. And she must have had the backing of the powerful priesthood of Amun. The most influential of her adherents when she took the throne was a man called

Hapuseneb. He was both a vizier and the High Priest of the temple of Amun at Karnak. Even so, it was an astonishing achievement to wrest the throne for herself – even if she did condescend to allow her co-ruler, the boy Thutmosis III, to play second fiddle to her in major ceremonial events.'

'Thutmosis III exacted his revenge though, didn't he?' I yawned, pillowing my head against Adam's chest more comfortably. 'I wonder how many years he spent smouldering with suppressed fury, thwarted ambition and resentment while his aunt-stepmother usurped his throne and presided over a lengthy period of peace and prosperity in Egypt.' I was aware that, when she died, and Thutmosis became sole pharaoh, he'd wasted no time in seeking to erase her from history. He had his henchmen chisel out her name on the monuments, and her images from the temple walls, often leaving conspicuous Hatshepsut-shaped gaps in the reliefs. Here at Deir el Bahri the temple must have echoed to the blows of the sledgehammers smashing her statues to smithereens. I'd read about excavators finding dozens of statues of Hatshepsut smashed to bits and dumped in a quarry near the temple. So, Thutmosis had been careful to ensure she would die the second and final death, by obliterating her name and carved image from every spot he could get at. As well as having titles and portraits erased and her statues smashed, he'd ordered her famed obelisks to be walled up to ensure her cartouche and proud inscriptions were hidden.

'Hatshepsut wasn't the only one to suffer,' Adam murmured against my hair. 'The campaign of destruction went after Senenmut too. While it doesn't seem that he was ever interred in the magnificent, almost royal tomb he carved for himself in the precincts of Hatshepsut's temple, he had another tomb, more suited to his official rank, on the slopes of a hill not far from Deir el Bahri. No one has been able to prove one way or the other whether he was ever actually buried there, but his sarcophagus certainly was. It was strikingly like Hatshepsut's sarcophagus, and probably made at the same time. Hatshepsut's kingly sarcophagus was left intact, but Senenmut's was literally broken to bits. Over twelve hundred fragments of it were found, scattered over the ground near his tomb, and these pieces only made-up half of the original sarcophagus.'

'So Thutmosis III exacted his revenge,' I repeated. 'He obliterated all memory of Hatshepsut and her lover Senenmut and re-wrote the king-list to expunge Hatshepsut from the royal record. He went on to become Egypt's finest warrior pharaoh. Only the levelling forces of time and the brilliance of modern archaeology foiled his designs on Hatshepsut's name and her place in history.'

I could feel Adam grinning even though I couldn't see him. He loves it when I confidently expound my own knowledge of ancient Egypt as if I learned it from the studious pages of history books instead of popular fiction or Discovery Channel documentaries, as is actually the case. 'There's just one little fly in the ointment,' he said.

'What's that?' I sat up and tried to look at him. But the blackness was thick and oppressive, closing in on all sides. All things considered I actually preferred being where I could feel him since it was a simple fact that I couldn't see him. I rested my head against his chest again and waited for him to answer.

'Just that it seems that the entire dramatic scenario of resentment and revenge, female throne-robber and seething, bitter king might be a highly fictionalised version of events.'

'Why? What do you mean?'

'The latest evidence suggests the campaign by Thutmosis III to destroy Hatshepsut's memory didn't begin until late in his own reign – twenty years after he became sole ruler, in fact.'

I sat up again. But the pitch blackness hadn't miraculously changed, so I subsided once more against Adam's broad chest. I picked a few more pricking stones out from underneath me and tried to find a comfortable position to relax in.

'The theory is that Thutmosis III didn't feel any need to act against the memory of his aunt-stepmother until he was an old man and felt his son's succession to the throne needed to be secured. But the trouble with this line of reasoning is there's no evidence of rivals to the throne, legitimate or not. And there was no question of his son's legitimacy. He was born of Thutmosis III and a lesser royal wife. All the recent evidence points to a belated attack on Hatshepsut's monuments, somewhat haphazard but decidedly vengeful.'

I could feel my eyelids drooping, and my muscles were definitely seizing up after all the unaccustomed wear and tear. 'It does rather make you wonder about Neferure and her *hereditary princess*,' I said, stifling a yawn. 'I can't help thinking there might be a link there somewhere.'

Despite the early hour the darkness was complete and cloak-like in its warmth – perhaps because we'd bricked ourselves in so the fresh air I'd waxed lyrical about earlier was having trouble circulating. I was tired from the exertion of our perilous scramble down the cliff-face. Somehow Adam's warm chest made up for the lack of any other physical comfort. Whatever, I felt myself drifting towards sleep and made no attempt to divert myself from arrival.

I opened my eyes to the first luminous glow of dawn. Even our little brick wall couldn't prevent the early light from penetrating the gloom of the ancient sanctuary that had been ours for the night. My entire body felt as if I'd been steamrollered. There was no part of me that didn't ache. Even my eyelashes felt heavy, coated in dust and sticky from wiping yesterday's perspiration out of them. My first response was to the urgent call of nature. So, I levered myself ever so gently out of Adam's protective arms, got up, wincing at the stiffness of my protesting limbs, and crossed the chamber, starting to dismantle our rock-and-stone barrier from the entranceway.

'You're up bright and early Merry,' he murmured from behind me.

'Need to find a large rock to disappear behind,' I muttered, knowing he'd catch my meaning.

He grinned. ' "*Merry and bright*" now that's got to be a title for something worth writing. I'll give it some thought. Rustle me up some bacon and eggs while you're out there, will you?'

I poked my tongue out at him and escaped among a small shower of rocks into the pink-tinged early morning light. The air had a pure crystalline quality to it, and I breathed in deeply before going in search of my own private rock.

Much relieved, I made my way back to the little hideaway in the hills to find Adam minutely studying one of the wall reliefs in the gentle light of dawn.

'Now this is an interesting scene,' he said, smiling at me as I squeezed back into the small chamber. 'Come here and tell me what you make of this.'

I peered at the wall reliefs exquisitely painted against the ochre background. 'It appears to be some kind of feast or festivity,' I said. 'Look, there are musicians here with little cones of perfume on their heads, and this looks like a troop of dancers.'

He nodded. 'So, tell me how you interpret this.' He pointed a little further along the section of wall.

I gazed at it for a while. The image looked a bit like a pastiche of a historical drama. Hatshepsut was there, brilliant in her gorgeous regalia, with the cobra and vulture rising on her brow from the double crown of the Two Lands and wearing a robe of the sheerest pleated linen. No less impressive a figure stood close to her side, equally bedecked in gold and precious stones and resplendent in a long kilt and with an ornate wig on his head. This was Senenmut, taking pride of place alongside the queen-pharaoh. But two other figures were central to the little melodrama. They stood before the towering statue of the god Amun, which was painted wreathed in blue incense.

'I recognise that inscription,' I said, pointing to the hieroglyphs above the central female character's head. 'It's the same as the one on Ted's tablet of stone.'

Adam grinned an acknowledgement at me and intoned ' *"...The hereditary princess; daughter of divinely anointed pharaohs; beautiful one of Re: Lady of Upper and Lower Egypt; Mistress of the Two Lands; God's wife of Amun; Neferure".'*

'And the man at her side?' I asked. 'Who's he? He's decked out in the royal regalia, so I'm daring to guess; and his name is inside a cartouche, so the evidence is mounting up, but I need you to confirm it for me.'

Adam's gaze rested on my face for a moment, acknowledging the simple logic of my deductions, but was drawn irresistibly back to the wall relief, given another opportunity to study the painted hieroglyphs and practise his translation skills. 'This says '*Horus, Mighty Bull, Enduring in Kingship, powerful of strength, sacred of appearance, Menkheperre, Thutmosis Neferkheperu; son of Re, beautiful of forms".'*

'Thutmosis III,' I interpreted.

'Yes,' Adam breathed. 'She was married to him after all. This scene must be depicting the wedding celebration.'

I agreed with him. There was no other way of interpreting it. But something about it bothered me. It was a formal scene, painted in the stiffly posed style of traditional ancient Egyptian artwork. Yet the stiffness in the pose of the young princess went beyond rigid. She looked positively plank-like. 'Why do I have a sneaking suspicion he may not have been the father of her daughter, despite the 'nefer' in his throne names, too?'

Adam stared at me. 'You're daring to suggest she got herself pregnant by someone else?'

I shrugged. 'Call it female intuition. I just can't help thinking she doesn't look too happy on the wall up there. Thutmosis was her half-brother after all. Hard to blame her if she didn't exactly fancy him.'

'My God Merry; that would have been a betrayal of unimaginable proportions!'

Chapter 8

The *SS Misr* lived up to Khaled's billing as a lovingly restored deluxe steamship boasting all modern conveniences, international cuisine and top-class service. We were welcomed on board and offered cold flannels and a glass of *kerkedah* (a deep red, sweet, ice-cold drink made from stewed hibiscus blossoms) by a smiling crewmember resplendent in a floor-length black galabeya with gold braid at his collar and cuffs, and a neat black *fez* on his head.

I gazed around the impressive, panelled reception area complete with a sweeping central staircase, velvet upholstered chaises in pastel shades and ornate glass and gilt side tables loaded with Egyptological picture books; and felt myself gripped by very mixed emotions. 'Adam, it's *beautiful*,' I breathed. 'How on *earth* can we ever hope to compete?'

Adam replaced his cold flannel on the silver dish placed there for the purpose and squeezed my hand. 'We don't attempt to compete. We simply offer an equally luxurious alternative for the discerning traveller who wants to travel in authentic style while visiting the ancient sites. The *Queen Ahmes* has sails, remember? The *Misr* can't offer that.'

That's what I love about Adam. He always finds the positive angle.

'We must look and learn Merry, and then go away and figure out how to do it even better. This is research, remember? But I see no reason why we can't enjoy it to the full while we're on board.'

While Adam saw to our checking in procedures, I flicked through the *Misr's* promotional brochure, getting ideas for how I might go about marketing our dahabeeyah. Packed with top quality photographs and printed on glossy card, the brochure informed me: *The Nile steamer as a leisure pursuit was pioneered by British tourists in the late 19th century looking for a comfortable way to visit Egypt's ancient sites. Originally constructed in 1918 by the Royal Navy the SS Misr was converted into a luxury Nile cruiser for King Farouk in the 1930s. Lovingly restored by Voyages Jules Verne in cooperation with the Egyptian Ministry of Tourism, the addition of every possible modern comfort now allows today's traveller to enjoy luxurious surroundings and a historic ambiance in the wake of the last reigning king of Egypt.*

'I wonder if anyone famous ever travelled on the *Queen Ahmes*,' I murmured to myself, looking for an angle. I made a mental note to check it out.

'The boat's only going to be half full for the trip,' Adam informed me, returning with our room key. 'Tourists are still staying away. Lucky for us; we've been upgraded to the Panoramic Suite on the upper deck. Before the other passengers arrive – most of them are flying in from Gatwick and Manchester this afternoon – Honi here has offered to give us a tour.' He beamed at the galabeya-bedecked attendant alongside him, who bowed rather theatrically at me.

'It will be my pleasure, sir and madam. I am very proud to work on this very lovely boat.' And he started leading us up the staircase, talking as he went. '*Misr* means 'the Kingdom of Egypt' and the décor reflects the fashion of the period with cabins decorated in styles linked both to the history of the vessel and Egypt: Ottoman, Empire, English, Art Deco, Louis XV and Louis XVI. You will see. I will show you these cabins with pleasure.'

The staircase curved back on itself. As we reached the top Honi led us into the dining room. 'This is the Marasem Restaurant,' he informed us proudly. 'As you see this period-style restaurant accommodates all guests at table windows to enhance one's perspective while cruising. We invite all our guests to dine at one sitting for dinner and share their wonderful experiences of the unique and magnificent treasures they encounter on the banks of our glorious Nile.'

I found myself liking Honi very much. His effusive style reminded me of Ahmed, although his English was better and he was approximately half the size of our tourist police chum; an energetic and wiry little man with a ready smile and bright, snapping eyes. With his brown creased up face and twinkling eyes he reminded me of nothing so much as a very cute monkey. I wondered how easy it would be to find our own version of Honi for the *Queen Ahmes*.

The restaurant was panelled in a rich, dark wood that might have been mahogany; I'm no judge. The walls were painted deep red and covered with black and white photographs of famous Egyptian dignitaries in neat black frames. Long windows extended down both sides of the room, but I wasn't sure I could wholly agree with Honi about the unimpeded cruising perspective. The windows were all draped with luxurious curtains trimmed with brocade. I'd say they were a distinct distraction from the view. I wondered if white slatted blinds might be better on the *Queen Ahmes*, or maybe sheer muslin drapes to let in as much light as possible. This restaurant was glorious, but considering it wasn't yet lunchtime, it was very dark.

Honi led us back out to the gallery surrounding the central staircase. 'Here you see we have a beautiful shop.' His eyes snapped at Adam with wicked humour. 'You can buy lots of gold jewellery for the so lovely lady, yes? Our Egyptian gold, it is of very good quality; all eighteen carats, very pure.'

I blinked at the quantity of gold on display in the window. It looked like Aladdin's cave.

'Now follow me,' Honi said, leading us up a narrow staircase set against the wall at the side of the shop. It curved back on itself, bringing us up into a beautifully decorated lobby area, oriental in style, hung with what looked like huge Chinese lanterns.

'This is the Dahabia Bar decorated with a nostalgic nod to the Ottoman Empire. And through here is the Saraya Lounge.' He led us through the bar into a gracious lounge that wouldn't have looked out of place in Versailles.

'Ah, this is the influence of Louis XV and XVI,' I said. I much preferred this lighter, almost feminine style of décor to the dark heavy panelling of the restaurant. It was a big room, scattered with exquisitely upholstered sofas, elegant chairs and pretty little footstools set around low occasional tables.

He nodded at me, nut-brown eyes twinkling. 'Yes, and you see we have the grand piano set up over here. We like to provide our guests with the piano entertainment while they sip an aperitif or after-dinner cocktail.'

There was no way I could imagine us squeezing a grand piano on board the *Queen Ahmes*. Our guests would have to make do with a quiet game of cards and the best atmosphere I could create with an iPod and wireless speakers.

'Unlike most modern cruise boats, we have our public lounges on the upper decks. We find this enhances the cruising experience for those who wish to observe the journey in air-conditioned luxury rather than outside in the hot sunshine.'

Honi led us though the lounge and out through French doors at the back onto a lower sundeck with deeply cushioned wicker chairs grouped around coffee tables.

'It's lovely,' I said, as he looked at me for approval. We were moored not far from Luxor Bridge, and it was true the sundeck gave an uninterrupted view of the Nile stretching away behind the boat, both banks lined by palm trees nodding dozily in the breeze.

A spiral staircase led to an upper sundeck with luxurious sunbeds set under canvas awnings and a sizeable splash pool. I started to feel a bit depressed again. I'd fallen in love with the authentic Victorian viewing platform on our dahabeeyah with its stripped and varnished wooden decks and gracious aspect, but this was in a different league.

'Don't forget, we have sails,' Adam whispered in my ear.

Honi completed his tour by showing us a selection of the bedrooms. Each had its own unique décor and style drawing inspiration as he'd said from the fashions prevalent in the first half of the twentieth century or from Egypt's post-

Ottoman past. They were the last word in luxury, each with an exquisite marble bathroom and plenty of wardrobe space.

'We have just twenty-four passenger cabins and suites,' Honi told us. 'We are very unusual among cruise boats as each of our bedrooms offers a small outside balcony, see?' And he swept back the netting to reveal a neat little outside space with an intricate latticework railing. 'With a crew of sixty-three we are dedicated to providing the highest possible level of service for our honoured guests. We aim to achieve a truly intimate experience.'

Well, our dahabeeyah could beat the *Misr* hands down for intimacy. With just five bookable cabins we'd be catering for a maximum of ten travellers. But I didn't see any way of us rivalling the *Misr's* staff-to-customer ratio by squeezing fifteen crewmembers on board.

'Would you like to view the original steam engines?' Honi asked as he locked the door behind us on a rather delightful twin-bedded room. 'A tour of our engine rooms is offered to all guests during the cruise.'

'We'll wait to join the others then,' Adam said. 'We don't want to seem unsociable to our fellow travellers, and we've taken up enough of your time, Honi. You've been more than generous showing us around like this.'

He insisted on accompanying us to our suite. It was on the same level as the restaurant and took up half of the front of the boat.

'It's stunning,' I reassured him as he looked at me and raised a questioning eyebrow. I didn't mind the wood panelling in here as it was lighter than in the restaurant and the red paint was also a shade paler. The bed looked deeply comfortable, covered with a richly pattered quilt that picked up the pattern in the Oriental rug covering the polished floorboards. A pretty display of flowers and an ornate silver terrine piled with fresh fruit completed the effect of no-expense-spared luxury.

Adam showed his appreciation of Honi's service in the time-honoured way. Honi bowed himself out of the room, earnestly promising us the trip of a lifetime on this most beautiful of boats. 'Our customers in the last two years have voted it the best vessel in the whole of the world,' he assured us and quietly closed the door behind him.

'The dahabeeyah has sails,' Adam reminded me for the third time, seeing my downcast expression. 'And we can offer our guests a genuine houseboat experience. Ours will be an equally luxurious but slightly more under-stated offering, that's all.'

Brightening, I perched on the edge of the vast bed and scratched at the scabs forming on my kneecaps where the grazes were starting to heal. 'I'm thinking white and light and airy with rattan furniture, cotton bed linen and muslin drapes.'

'Sounds wonderful,' he said. 'There's only so much wood panelling and red paint a man can take. Now move over, I'm coming to join you. You look particularly fetching sitting on that impossibly extravagant silken quilt. Sadly, I think this is no place for the Indiana Jones hat. I wonder if I could buy a black *fez* in the gift shop. I fancy one with a jaunty little tassel.'

We had a light lunch sent to our room and spent the afternoon up on the sundeck luxuriating on the cushioned recliners in our swimsuits while we awaited the arrival of the other passengers.

'Ted is beside himself with excitement,' Adam said, looking up from scanning the Inbox on his iPad. 'I don't think he knows quite where to start, given the number of photographs we emailed him. He says your propensity for stumbling across miraculous finds from Egypt's ancient past is truly astonishing. I think he's a bit in awe of you, Merry.'

I looked at the purple bruise and scraped skin on Adam's shoulder and the assortment of encrusted scabs on my knees and shins and decided these miraculous finds were not without their drawbacks.

Adam had photographed every square inch of the little sanctuary in the Deir el Bahri hills. We'd done our best to block up the entrance with rocks. The little shrine had endured in secret for millennia. We felt Hatshepsut and Senenmut might thank us for our care in seeking to secure them another few centuries undisturbed. While we thought it unlikely intrepid holidaymakers would include a spot of mountaineering in their itineraries and stumble across the small shrine the way we had, we didn't want to take any chances. Then we'd slithered and slip-slided our way down the remaining cliff-face, emerging among the boulders in the foothills alongside Hatshepsut's temple. As Adam had promised, we were back at the Jolie Ville for breakfast.

He'd spent an age electronically zipping up the images and protecting them with the most obscure passwords he could think of. Then, brimming with excitement and impatient to share the news with his old mentor, he'd made a lengthy phone call to Ted while I took a long soaky bath and picked tiny chippings of rock out of the bloody abrasions on my hands and knees. I listened to their conversation through the open doorway and thought our little adventure on the cliff-face sounded quite dramatic in the re-telling. Adam's good at telling stories. He has quite a poetic turn of phrase. I decided I could enjoy it in retrospect, now we were safely installed back at the hotel, far more than I'd enjoyed it at the time.

I heard Ted's voice rise in a shout of scholarly triumph when Adam confirmed Hatshepsut and Senenmut were lovers, and Neferure was indeed married to Thutmosis. I didn't need to be able to hear what he was saying to grasp his impatience to take receipt of the photographs Adam was about to email him. He took every care taking down the passwords, getting Adam to repeat them several times.

'He's still trying to decipher that unusual double-plumed symbol on the stele,' Adam said when he came off the 'phone. 'He's hoping there'll be something in the photos of the rock-shrine that might be able to help him.'

Now, he flipped over onto his stomach on his sun lounger and grinned at me. 'I think it's fair to say you've given my old university lecturer a whole new lease of life, Merry. I'm not the only one whose life has burst into Technicolor since you came on the scene.'

I was quite moved by this little speech and let the kiss I offered him express just how much it affected me.

The *Misr* was a dress-up-for-dinner sort of place. Adam donned a light jacket over his shirt, and I put on a pretty dress with a hemline that fell below my unattractively crusty-looking knees.

We were a little late arriving in the dining room. I'd been a bit flummoxed by how to work the quaint antique shower in our marble bathroom and Adam had come to help. Suffice it to say he figured out the Victorian-looking mechanism with no trouble at all once he'd joined me behind the glass screen.

Three tables were set for dinner, each set for six people. It was clear the *Misr* would be steaming along the Nile half-full. Two of the tables were already occupied by travel-weary new arrivals. We joined the third where a couple I'd guess were in their mid-forties were already sitting. They smiled politely up at us as we arrived, and we returned the greeting, introducing ourselves as we sat down. We spent a few minutes exchanging small talk over the welcome glass of sparkling wine the immaculately attired waiters handed round, while we waited for the final couple to join us.

Francesca had an important-sounding job in property development and Doug was an ambulance driver. Although older, after a few minutes in their company they reminded me so much of Dan and me as a couple I didn't know whether to laugh or cry.

'I've always been fascinated with ancient Egypt,' Francesca confided. 'There's something so vast and grandiose about it. Nowhere else has ever captured my imagination in quite the same way.'

Doug rolled his eyes in a comical display of long sufferance. 'It has great weather; I'll give it that. But the lack of decent golf courses is a bit of a drawback. As for all those tomb-and-temple thingies, I can't help thinking once you've seen one, you've seen them all.'

'We're planning to travel down Lake Nasser to see Abu Simbel,' Francesca smiled, letting her husband's comment roll off her in a way that suggested many years of practise. 'I'm hoping it will be the one to change his mind. After all, it's a marvel of modern engineering as much as ancient, having been moved up to higher ground by UNESCO to save it from the rising water when the Aswan High Dam was built.'

Doug rolled his eyes again and grinned at us. 'She sounds like a walking guidebook when she gets going.' But I noticed he squeezed her hand to take the sting out of his words. 'You know I'm not convinced all the 'thousands-of-years-old-this' and 'centuries-old-that' isn't some clever scam that's got us all fooled. Some of the paintings in the tombs look suspiciously fresh to me. It wouldn't surprise me to learn some enterprising man-on-the-make struck on the idea of a kind of country-wide theme park back in the good old days and has been sitting back coining it and laughing up his sleeve ever since.'

Adam and I stared at him in stupefied silence. Then Adam let out a shout of laughter. 'What a novel idea! You mean he created the tombs and temples out of fibreglass and polystyrene rather in the way Walt Disney conceived Disneyland!'

"Exactly!' Doug grinned. 'Perhaps Howard Carter was in on the act when he 'discovered' Tutankhamun's tomb. You know, there's a replica of it in the Luxor Hotel in Las Vegas. We've probably all been taken in for years thinking the real thing is any more genuine. You'll probably find those tacky things in display on the Cairo Museum are made of paste.'

Adam laughed again and I could tell Doug's sense of humour appealed to him. 'You know, I'm not sure you're so wide of the mark. When Zahi Hawass was the Minister for Antiquities here in Egypt, he was planning to build life-size replicas of the magnificent tombs of Seti I and Nefertari. They've been closed to the public for years to protect them from the damaging effects of condensation caused by the thousands of visitors who trooped through them every year. Hawass's belief was tourists would be willing to pay to see replicas as a substitute for the real thing, rather than be denied the opportunity to experience the tombs at all.'

'Sounds a bit Steven Spielberg to me,' I murmured and decided to steer the conversation onto more normal territory. 'So, you've clearly been to Egypt before?'

'Yes,' Francesca said, eyes shining. 'This is our third trip. But we've never done a Nile cruise before. We're celebrating a special anniversary, so we decided to splash out. This looked such a lovely historical boat, and the idea of travelling on a restored steamer appealed, so here we are.'

Adam leaned forward, 'Have you ever considered a dahabeeyah...?' he started, but he was curtailed by a sudden commotion in the doorway.

'Yes, I am most certainly alone,' a strident female voice cut across the low hum of conversation in the restaurant. It immediately ceased as all eyes turned towards the voice. 'My travelling companion was struck down by a nasty dose of the pharaoh's revenge on our first day in Luxor. That's your quaint expression for a gippy tummy, yes? And then when she was well enough to go out for a little walk, she was set upon by a swarm of trinket sellers trying to palm her off with all manner of tacky-looking souvenirs. They followed her from one end of the Corniche to the other, jabbering away at the top of their lungs and waving their wares in her face. She suffers with her nerves at the best of times. Well! It was all too much for her and she caught the evening flight home. I think she'll stick to weekends enjoying cream teas in the Cotswolds from now on. But I, myself, am made of sterner stuff. Oh yes. A trip to Egypt is what I promised myself. And a trip to Egypt is what I shall have. So, I'm sorry you've gone to the trouble of setting an extra place at the table young man, but I shall do my best to make up for the absence of my friend.'

I think we'd all followed this marvellous bit of theatre with a somewhat embarrassed curiosity. We didn't want to make it obvious we were staring but it was impossible not to. Here was someone who might best be described as a CHARACTER. And it seemed evident she would be joining us at our table.

I turned to exchange a *this-should-be-interesting* look with Adam, only to catch sight of the appalled expression on his face.

'Adam, what's the matter? You look quite sick.'

He attempted to clear his throat but choked and spluttered on a sip of sparkling wine. 'Oh God,' he gasped in asphyxiated tones. 'It's Eleanor.'

'Eleanor?' I looked at him blankly.

'My ex-sister-in-law,' he groaned.

The penny dropped. He'd told me about her, I recalled, early on in our acquaintance when we were getting to know each other over dinner at The Winter Palace. If I remembered rightly, he said she'd taken a dim view of him marrying her sister, and he hadn't exactly warmed to her either. I wondered if she felt any more kindly disposed to him now that he'd divorced her sister (since she'd left him for another man). I revised my earlier judgement and decided perhaps *interesting* wasn't the word for it after all. But I couldn't think of a better one, so it seemed the only thing to do was sit back and let the scenario unfold.

'Good evening,' she said as the waiter pulled out a chair for her at our table and she sat down. 'I am Eleanor Hayes. Please accept my apologies for my lateness. I was delayed coming on board due to the excessive length of time I was kept haggling in one of the shops in the Souk for a necklace I'd taken a fancy to. These local shopkeepers all try to hoodwink one into believing it's a genuine artefact one's purchasing, but they don't fool *me*. I decided on the price I was willing to pay, and I was quite prepared to stand there all night if necessary to get the excitable little man to accept it. I could have caught the boat up by taking a taxi to Edfu if required, and that's what I told him. Really, this haggling lark is quite tiresome, but I do pride myself on being rather good at it. You see, the trick is to...' Her gaze snagged on Adam's face, and she came to a screeching halt. To be fair, it was more of a gasp than a screech, but the general effect was the same. I was a bit disappointed to be denied insight into the trick of haggling, never having been much good at it myself. Oh,' she said. 'Adam. Yes, I remember Tabitha saying you'd scurried off to Egypt before the ink was dry on the divorce papers. I wondered if I'd run into you. And here you are.'

That she managed to convey her low opinion of Adam in these bland few sentences said much for the subtlety of the English language when it was accompanied by a deadpan tone of voice and an expressionless face.

'Hello, Eleanor.' Adam matched her perfectly in transmitting volumes-of-vocabulary with two short words and a level tone.

I stared in open fascination at the cyclone of a woman who'd just blown in among us. I guessed her to be about the same age as Francesca, so perhaps mid-forties. But the contrast couldn't be starker. Francesca was a slim, attractive redhead with shoulder length hair and a keen eye for fashion if her emerald silk top and chunky jewellery were anything to judge by.

Eleanor, though equally attractive in terms of raw material when you looked closely (and, believe me, I was forced to look closely), seemed to have no interest whatsoever in the feminine arts of hair, clothes and make-up. And she was quite possibly colour-blind. Her lavender blouse and the jaunty red waistcoat she was wearing over the top positively screamed at each other; although both reeked quality, Betty Barclay at the very least. And they clashed violently with the gold-and-blue patterned scarf she'd tied through her hair. The hair itself, poking out here and there was of the sort I think is usually described as salt-and-pepper, only with perhaps an extra helping of salt. Glasses of the milk-bottle-bottom variety made her eyes seem oddly distorted. And she'd allowed herself to grow rather thick around the middle. Consequently, she seemed at least ten years older than her probable years. Never in my life have I met someone who seems to rejoice quite so enthusiastically in looking as unattractive as possible.

I remembered Adam telling me she was a headmistress in an upper crust boarding school and just about as prim as you might expect. I wondered if the school might be St Trinians; or maybe this was just a look she reserved for holidays. Perhaps she was more of a twinset-and-pearls type back home.

'Eleanor, this is Merry,' Adam said, falling back on his manners in the age-old way of most Englishmen in times of adversity.

Eleanor glanced at our joined hands and treated me to the kind of look most people reserve for slugs. 'Merry?' she queried, as if she might not have heard him correctly. 'What? As in Christmas?'

'Meredith,' I said weakly; unequal to her and conceding it at our first encounter.

'Ah, Meredith,' she said as if pronouncing a verdict - although I wasn't at all sure whether I'd been sentenced or released. 'Yes, that's a name I've heard of.' I wondered if perhaps nicknames or abbreviations weren't allowed at her upper crust boarding school. I also wondered briefly what a school headmistress was doing on holiday as October gave way to November. I discovered later her upper crust boarding school awarded students a generous two-week autumn half term break.

Sensing the undercurrents crackling away like an underwater eruption about to set a tsunami in motion, Doug stepped bravely into the breach. 'And we're Doug and Francesca,' he beamed, over-doing the affability a bit, but I could completely see where he was coming from. 'So I gather you've been in Egypt for a while already, Eleanor? You've spent some time in Luxor?'

I could have kissed him. What a lovely man! I decided there and then we'd invite Doug and Francesca onto our dahabeeyah whether they'd ever considered it or not.

Eleanor seemed equally relieved to be diverted from the unwelcome distraction Adam and I posed and given the opportunity to hold court once more. 'Yes, that's right. I arrived a week ago with a friend who, as you may have heard, failed to acclimatise and decided to return home *post haste.*'

'Yes,' Doug said mildly. 'I think we may have caught a little of the tale. So, have you had an enjoyable time so far?'

Eleanor accepted the glass of sparkling wine the waiter offered her. The rest of us nodded our assent to top-ups with perhaps a shade more than our usual alacrity. 'Yes; indeed, I found the hot air balloon trip over the west bank particularly exhilarating.'

'I'd love to do that,' Francesca said, looking a bit wistful. 'But Doug doesn't like heights so…'

'You must do it,' Eleanor proclaimed, interrupting her. 'The whole experience is quite uplifting.' (I don't think she saw any pun in this statement) 'It's a pre-dawn start, of course. One finds oneself taken to what appears to be a giant car park on the edge of Luxor. I don't mind telling you I thought I'd taken leave of my senses as I watched a dozen-or-so balloons being prepared for flight. Feisal, the captain of my balloon instructed me to leave the piloting to him and not seek to tamper with the controls. I daresay he imagined himself impossibly droll; especially when he pointed out he was the only one with a parachute and he alone could send the great plumes of fire into the balloon to give us ascent. I find one must place one's trust in one's pilot; and I was perfectly happy to do so. As the first streaks of dawn lightened the eastern skies we lifted off, and by the time the sun poked its face above the horizon we were skimming along over the Theban hills towards the Valley of the Kings. The whole of modern and ancient Egypt was laid out below us. I will never forget the spectacle of the other brightly painted balloons defying the forces of gravity to ride the airwaves over the temples of the west bank. I took a good few photographs to remind me, just in case. I have to confide though; the landing was a bit harum-scarum. The basket was dragged along on its side for some time before the ground crew got hold of it.'

'Weren't you frightened?' Francesca asked a bit breathlessly.

'Not a bit of it,' said the game old bird that was Eleanor. 'I clung on grimly, trying to look unconcerned and pretending I'd known all along this would happen. I'm British after all.'

I was perfectly happy not to like Eleanor if that's what Adam's past experience deemed appropriate; but I have to say she was entertaining. She was here alone and seemed determined to make the best of it.

'Do you have a favourite sight-seeing destination?' Francesca asked.

Eleanor took a sip of her sparkling wine, considering. 'Well, Karnak is magnificent, of course; but I can't help thinking Hatshepsut's temple steals a march on it.'

'Oh yes,' Francesca breathed passionately. 'I love Hatshepsut's temple. It's so beautiful and somehow gracious in its proportions.'

'Of course, it's made more fascinating by the intriguing inter-relationships of the people who had a hand in creating it,' Eleanor said. 'You know, Hatshepsut was an egomaniac, a power-crazed individual who chewed men up and spat then out when they'd served their purpose. It's possible she was the first feminist in history. I have the utmost respect for her.'

I felt Adam stiffen beside me, but he kept a hold on his tongue. I think since we'd spent the night in her rock-cut sanctuary we both felt a special affinity with Hatshepsut.

'Her great love was supposed to have been a man named Senenmut,' Eleanor informed us. 'He was her chief architect and the man responsible for designing and building her magnificent temple at Deir el Bahri. She granted him unrivalled privileges. He was allowed to carve a tomb of royal proportions for himself in the temple precincts; and Hatshepsut gave him responsibility for the upbringing of her only child, the princess Neferure. Yet something happened before the end of her reign that made her drop him like a stone. In my view Hell hath no fury like a woman scorned. He must have done something cataclysmic to incur her wrath. He certainly never occupied his magnificent tomb in sight of Hatshepsut's temple; and it seems unlikely his body ever rested inside the sarcophagus in his secondary tomb that was smashed to pieces as part of Thutmosis III's campaign to obliterate all traces of Hatshepsut's reign. I've made a study of it, and I think I can consider myself an authority on the matter. Believe me when I say Senenmut either served his purpose or perpetrated some crime she was unable to forgive. There's no other explanation for his disappearance from the historical record before Hatshepsut's death or for his apparent failure to occupy either of the tombs he'd had built for himself.'

I'm sure she could have gone on with her lecture indefinitely. But the waiter came to invite us to make our selections from the dinner buffet now available at the serving station in the centre of the restaurant.

Adam took my hand as we approached the buffet. 'Sorry Merry; I'm not sure this Nile cruise is going to turn out to be the quiet holiday-cum-research experience we were hoping for.'

Chapter 9

We were up at the crack of dawn for the first scheduled excursion of our sightseeing itinerary. We joined the other guests in the lobby area at the foot of the grand staircase at the pre-determined time. Eleanor was conspicuous by her absence. If my assessment of her character was right this meant she was either planning a morning queening it with the *Misr* all to herself, or she was up and about already and had been out for a morning constitutional. Last night, she had held court for the rest of the dinner service, bestowing upon us in stentorian tones her opinion of Egypt; everything from its ferocious climate to its unsettled economy, its unpredictable political situation and the conditions in which its food must be prepared to avoid the gastric fate that had befallen her erstwhile travel companion. I think we were all exhausted by the time she declared herself ready for bed and left us to breathe a collective sigh of relief and enjoy an after-dinner cocktail with Francesca and Doug in the lounge.

Now, our Egyptian tour guide stepped forward to introduce himself. 'My name is Tariq. It will be my pleasure to introduce to you our magnificent ancient monuments,' he assured us with a bright smile.

'He doesn't look old enough to be a qualified Egyptologist,' Adam murmured in my ear, sounding a trifle envious. Adam considers himself a "thwarted" Egyptologist having been forced to drop out of university before completing his degree at the Oriental Institute, Oxford. There's nothing he'd love more than a set of graduation papers with his name on them. Although he'd picked up the threads of his online study course, I don't think he felt it had quite the same kudos.

'I'm not complaining,' I murmured back. 'He may be young for an Egyptologist, but he's quite easy on the eye.'

'And here was me thinking you had eyes only for me,' he said mournfully.

I reached up and kissed his cheek, 'Always.'

'This morning, we will visit one of the best preserved of all the ancient Egyptian temples. Edfu,' Tariq informed us happily. He was smooth-featured and long-limbed; neatly attired in cotton trousers and a Ralph Lauren polo shirt. 'We will travel to the temple in a convoy of horse drawn carriages. This mode of transport is known as a caleche. It is very popular with the tourists. You will see the horses are well looked after, which has not always been the case here in Egypt. We are thankful to you, our British guests, for teaching our people much about the care of these animals. There is still much to do to protect the welfare of the horses, but I am pleased to say there are many charities at work in Egypt ensuring they are rested regularly in the shade and get plenty of water and fresh greenery to eat. For our tours we will not use any driver who shows any negligence towards his animal. Now follow me please.'

Adam took my hand as we hopped down onto the quayside from the gangplank. 'I'm not sure I'll be allowed to accompany our guests from the *Queen Ahmes* on their visits to the sites – at least not as an official guide,' he said sadly. 'I believe the Egyptian tourist authorities are pretty strict about the tours being given by Egyptian Egyptologists. It's fair enough, I suppose, since it's their country. But it might be a bit of a drawback to our plans.' He looked a bit crestfallen about it.

I'm not so sure,' I said. 'Not all tourists like traipsing about in groups, being led here, there and everywhere by a guide carrying a flag or whatever. Some people prefer to be more independent and do things under their own steam and at a pace they set for themselves. You could give them the best of both worlds: a talk on the dahabeeyah, which they can listen to in air-conditioned comfort with a drink in their hand, then set them free to tour the sites at their leisure. We'll make the travel arrangements to get them there and back; and provide them with little foldout maps showing where all the key points of interest are located. I never think there's enough "free" time on organised excursions. It's all a bit of a route march. We can offer an appealing alternative to that.'

'That's what I love about you, Merry,' he said, lifting me up and spinning me around. 'You always look for the positive angle.'

Dan once told me Adam and I are like two peas in a pod. I figured he might be right. Yesterday it was Adam giving the positive assurances while I felt a bit downcast touring the *Misr* wondering how we could possibly compete. Today I was the one bolstering his spirits while he looked at Tariq and felt himself lacking in comparison.

'Now now, isn't it a bit early in the morning for all that?' Doug called, waving to us from the steps leading up to the boardwalk where the horse-and-carriages were lined up and waiting for us.

'Little does he know,' Adam said with a wicked gleam in his eye, recalling our energetic start to the day.

We waved back and watched him help Francesca climb up into the caleche, then lever himself in alongside her.

'This one's ours, I think,' Adam said as we reached the top of the steps. 'Yes, a nice-looking animal; very glossy coat.' He smiled at the galabeya-clad driver who stepped forward to help us up into the carriage.

'I cannot condone this!' A strident, immediately recognisable female voice cut through the still morning air. 'This is animal cruelty and must be stopped.'

Eleanor had missed Tariq's little speech about the care of the horses and was making her feelings known with her typical forthrightness. I have to say I applauded her sentiment in general. I can't stand any form of cruelty to animals. But it was clear these specimens were well cared for. And let's face it; the local people needed all the work they could get in these difficult times. It was in their best interests to look after their horses. Personally, I'm all for anything that supports the Egyptian economy. Besides, a horse-drawn carriage is a whole lot greener than a taxi.

'Eleanor making a spectacle as always,' Adam muttered, seeing me safely on board and climbing up behind me. 'You know, I wonder if she makes a habit of being late just so she can make a grand entrance.'

Tariq rushed across to her. 'No no, dear lady, please let me assure you, the best care is taken of these horses…'

We didn't hear how the exchange ended as our driver gave a whisper-light flick of his whip and with bells jingling merrily we pulled away from the kerb and started our short trip to the temple. But we saw how it ultimately turned out as Tariq himself helped Eleanor descend regally from her own personal caleche when it arrived in the temple precinct.

'He won her over,' I said, staggered.

'If I read Tariq right, he's a young man who knows how to use his masculine wiles on ladies of a certain age.'

'You should know,' I accused. 'You've not been above employing the same wicked tactics yourself.'

He grinned at me unapologetic. 'It's just a question of knowing that a smile gets you a whole lot further than a frown.'

We waited while Tariq bought our tickets and handed them out to everyone in our little party of eighteen guests from the *Misr*. Then he led us past the modern tourist kiosk, along a paved pathway and onto the temple forecourt. Its imposing façade was impressive to say the least; a towering pylon of stone deeply carved with gigantic images of the gods.

Tariq led us into the shade and started his tour. 'Many of the temples you will see nowadays in Egypt are in a poor state of preservation and you will need a finely developed imagination to picture what they must have looked like in ancient times. But Edfu is the exception. While the paint has gone from the walls, the temple itself is in a near-perfect state of preservation. True, it is not as old as some of the most famous temples. Karnak and Luxor temples were already over a thousand years old when the first foundation stones were laid here. This temple is from the Ptolemaic period, often known as the Graeco-Roman period. Work on Edfu started in 237 BC and was completed 167 years later.'

He went on in similar vein, leading us through the pylon with its huge granite statues of Horus the falcon god standing sentinel on either side of the gateway. We toured the forecourt, hypostyle hall and inner vestibules. I listened to everything he said with avid interest. Tariq was a good guide, but I couldn't help but think Adam would be better. He has an ability to bring history to life in a way Tariq hadn't mastered yet.

The temple was quiet with visitor numbers so far down. Walking through its dark, silent chambers I felt myself transported more than two thousand years into the past.

'It's really very evocative, isn't it?' Francesca said as our paths crossed in the dark interior of the sanctuary where once the divine barque of the god rested on a low platform.

'Quite frankly it gives me the heebie-jeebies,' Eleanor said loudly. 'I keep thinking I'm going to turn a corner and stumble across an ancient priest performing some mysterious religious rite. It's decidedly unnerving. I prefer the wide-open spaces of Karnak and Luxor where one can look up and see blue sky.'

'But it wouldn't always have been like that,' I said. 'In ancient times the temples were mostly enclosed like this one. It's only because they're so much older than this one that we don't see them like that today.'

'Yes, thank you, Meredith,' Eleanor said. 'I think I grasped the subtlety of that point when Tariq explained it earlier. But it's nice of you to repeat it just in case I might be hard of hearing.'

I was so taken aback I didn't know what to say. Adam squeezed my hand. 'Ignore her,' he whispered. 'You're worth ten of her.'

'I'm going outside,' Eleanor announced. 'I will sit in the forecourt and contemplate the impressive reliefs while you all troop about in the darkness.'

'I don't think she means to be rude,' Francesca said softly, smiling at me. 'I think she's just so used to holding court in her school-mistressy way she doesn't know how to leave it behind.'

I smiled back, liking Francesca and determined not to let Eleanor put a dampener on this Nile cruise for me.

Tariq gave us half-an-hour of free time. As I said, it's never enough. Adam and I made a slow study of the inner chambers. 'We need to cover all the usual stuff, but also find something a bit different to help bring it to life,' he said. 'By my reckoning people are far more interested in people than they are in places. I need to find a human angle to enliven it. This is where the god Horus is supposed to have a deadly battle with his evil uncle Set. Maybe I can make something of that.'

The words had barely left his mouth when a loud scream echoed through the temple.

'What the...? Adam and I snapped a look at each other.

'Stop thief!'

It was unmistakeably Eleanor.

We ran back through the temple, dodging between the towering columns in the hypostyle hall and emerged at a sprint into the bright sunlight of the forecourt.

Eleanor stood by the row of columns lining the outer wall, waving her arms in the air; still shouting 'Stop thief' at the top of her lungs.

'My handbag,' she screeched. 'A young ruffian snatched my handbag from the floor beside me. Of all the audacious, criminal, downright despicable things to do.'

'Couldn't have happened to a nicer person,' I muttered under my breath.

Adam proved himself a whole lot nobler of spirit than me. 'Which way did he go?' he demanded.

'Over there, through that birthing chamber type place, or whatever Tariq said it's supposed to be,' she waved wildly.

Adam didn't wait for her to finish. At the first wave he was off. As other members of our party from the *Misr* joined us, clamouring to know what had happened, Adam sprinted off in pursuit of the audacious ruffian.

While I debated whether I should go after him, Eleanor regaled us all with her opinions on the lack of law and order in Egypt, the Military's patent inability to keep tourists safe and the pitiable state of the nation in general since the revolution. I was trying to find the words to ask her why she'd come at all when she clearly had such a dim view of the place when Adam returned. I let out a hearty sigh of relief at the sight of him. I figured I knew the answer to my question in any case. I was quite sure it must have something to do with price. Egypt is an affordable destination at the moment, and I was fast forming the view that Eleanor was a cheapskate.

'Is this it?' Adam called as he jogged towards us holding aloft a brown leather handbag resplendent with a row of bright red tassels.

'You got it back!' Eleanor declared. I waited for her to thank him or at least show some pleasure at its return, but she simply took it back from him as he held it out to her.

'It was dumped by the postcard stand near the tourist kiosk,' he said, puffing. 'I can see the zip's open, so I guess the thief rifled through it. Is much missing?'

Eleanor searched through the contents. 'A small amount of cash,' she said with a shrug. 'But really, they picked on the wrong person for their bit of opportunistic daylight robbery. If they're stupid enough to think I'd come out in a place like this with anything of value on me they've got another think coming. Do I look like I was born yesterday?'

No, I thought unkindly, you most definitely do not.

* * *

'Nice family you married into,' I murmured later while Adam and I were sunning ourselves on the upper deck.

He pushed his sunglasses up on top of his head and flipped over on his sun lounger so he could see me properly. 'The trouble is, I think Eleanor's spent so many years lording it over everyone, she doesn't know how to stop. She's ten years older than Tabitha and there's a twelve-year gap between her and Tarquin. Their parents are bohemian types, not great at taking responsibility or living in what we might call the real world. I think Eleanor was forced early on into the surrogate mother role to her younger brother and sister to make up for the deficiencies in their proper parenting.'

'Careful,' I said. 'You'll have me feeling sorry for her.

He shrugged. 'I kind of do in a way. I think there's a spirit of adventure in her somewhere. She's just never had her rough edges smoothed off. She's gone from being the headmistress of her family to the headmistress of her girls' boarding school. If anything, it's solidified the blunt and bossy aspects of her personality, so she doesn't know how to be anything else.'

'Well, she's worth her weight in entertainment value,' I said, searching for something nice to say. 'But I do hope we don't get too many like her when we get the *Queen Ahmes* up and running.'

'Amen to that,' he said with a grin.

I pondered Adam's marriage break-up and the strange character of his sister-in-law for while. But to be honest neither played on my mind for long. I was lucky, secure in my relationship with Adam. I knew from my own past experience with Dan how easy it was to drift on – sometimes for years – in a relationship that was neither horribly wrong nor one hundred percent right. Thankfully Dan and I hadn't needed to extract ourselves from a marriage. But I could well imagine how Adam and Tabitha might have ended up in theirs. I knew about the emotional turmoil of Adam's early twenties after his parents died. And at a guess I'd say Tabitha may have benefited from another few years in the maturing barrel when they met, given her bohemian parenting and spinsterish older sister.

It was to my ultimate advantage that she'd left him. Adam suffered no regrets. The only one who seemed to bear any sort of grudge was Eleanor. Maybe it was natural if she'd always played the mother hen to her baby sister. Whatever, I decided I could live with her disapproval for the few days of this cruise. I had no intention of ever clapping eyes on her again afterwards.

Tariq appeared on deck mid-way through my musings. 'Ladies and gentlemen, I come to draw to your attention to this most interesting part of the Nile. We are passing through a place called Gebel el Silsila. As you can see, the cliffs here come right down to the banks of the Nile without the lush border of greenery in between.'

We scrambled off our sun loungers and joined some of the other guests at the rail where Tariq was standing. He pointed to the west bank, where the tawny coloured rock glowed like the well-brushed mane of a lion. At first it was difficult to see why he might describe this as one of the most interesting sections of the Nile. Earlier I'd sat by the rail quite transfixed by the timeless view either side of the boat. The ancient river surged beneath us, a deep inky blue. On either bank views of Egypt ancient and modern drifted by — mud-brick dwellings adorned with out-of-place satellite dishes, dusty children splashing in the shallows, cattle and donkeys grazing on sandbars, minarets rising from little hamlets of ramshackle homes; swaying palm trees, barking dogs, and countless fishing herons. Right now, the view was nowhere near so picturesque. Actually, it was a trifle forbidding. The cliffs and Sahara sand swept down to the river on both sides. The Nile cut through an inhospitable desert landscape without a shred of greenery to relieve the stark, barren rock. But finally, I discerned the shapes Tariq was pointing towards so excitedly.

'Here, you can see the rock-cut shrines of Horemheb, Seti I, Ramses II and Merenptah.'

We squinted through the glare of the ferocious sun and could see the rather tumbledown and topsy-turvy shrines to which he referred. They looked a bit like ancient rock-cut houses rising among the rocks lining the riverbank.

'Both banks of the Nile here were used as a quarry site from the early 18th Dynasty right up until Graeco-Roman times. A chapel to a vizier who served under Hatshepsut is also located here.'

Adam took a couple of photographs as the *Misr* steamed gently past. Then we subsided back onto our sun loungers in the shade.

'Is what Eleanor said the other night true?' I asked after a while. 'Did Senenmut disappear from the historical record before Hatshepsut's death?'

Adam rolled onto his back and shaded his eyes with his forearm. 'No one knows for sure. The historical record is frustratingly, some might say tantalisingly, silent about Senenmut's last days and death. Eleanor's right when she says he doesn't appear to have been buried in either of his two tombs, although it's clear both were vandalised. Someone wanted to destroy all memory of Senenmut. Eleanor's latched onto the old romantic notion that he betrayed Hatshepsut in some way, and she sought to exact the revenge of a woman scorned. But that theory, although popular once, has been largely discredited. Research suggests the campaign against Senenmut was linked to the one seeking to obliterate all memory of Hatshepsut enacted late in the reign of Thutmosis III.'

'So, I wonder why he disappeared from the historical record, and what happened to him.'

'All we know is he retired abruptly from public life somewhere around the last four to six years of Hatshepsut's reign. Since he wasn't interred in either of his tombs it seems unlikely that he simply died before her. Some researchers have speculated he may have died abroad or drowned in the Nile, hence no body for burial. But it seems unlikely such a tragedy wouldn't have been recorded on any contemporary monument. Hatshepsut recorded just about everything else. What I find intriguing is that his disappearance from the historical record seems to coincide, at least loosely, with the death of the princess Neferure.'

Suddenly my imagination started firing like a rocket launcher. A little conjecture of my own had just occurred to me. I sat up abruptly and stared at him. 'If my hunch is right and Thutmosis III wasn't the father of Neferure's daughter, I wonder if Senenmut was!'

Adam gaped at me as if I'd grown another head. 'I doubt that very much. If that little chamber in the rock told us anything, surely it was that Senenmut was absolutely devoted to Hatshepsut. If Senenmut loved Neferure, and I believe he did, it was as a father-figure or protective guardian, not as a lover.'

Frankly I believed this too. I shrugged off the echo of Eleanor's voice telling us in no certain terms that Senenmut had fallen from Hatshepsut's favour. But my scalp was still prickling. 'Ok then, so maybe he spirited the baby away to get her out of harm's way. Perhaps there was an awful sort of justice in Neferure dying in childbirth. But it still left the loose end of a newborn *hereditary princess* hanging.'

Adam squinted up at me. 'Merry, forget the dahabeeyah. You should write fiction.'

* * *

'Is there any part of our itinerary you're particularly looking forward to?' Francesca asked that evening, making a brave attempt at small talk over the dinner table. She asked her question of all of us in general. But Eleanor's response was prompt and emphatic. She seemed fully recovered from her bag-snatching incident at Edfu.

'Oh yes,' she said waving her fork in the air. 'I'm especially keen to view the unfinished obelisk lying in its granite quarry in Aswan.'

It seemed a strange choice to me when she could select from wonders ancient and modern including various tombs and temples, Kitchener's botanical island, the engineering miracle that was the Aswan High Dam, and the Old Cataract hotel in Aswan where Agatha Christie wrote *Death on the Nile*. The unfinished obelisk, commissioned by Hatshepsut, and still lying in its quarry - abandoned when a fault was discovered in the granite - was certainly peculiar as a 'must-see' destination.

'I find myself quite fascinated by anything Hatshepsut-related,' Eleanor informed us. 'I was at Karnak just the other day, standing in the shadow of the two massive obelisks she had raised there. Let me tell you, they are a marvellous sight to behold.'

She spoke as if none of us had ever seen them for ourselves, although we'd all told her quite plainly that we'd visited Egypt before. In Adam's case he'd made an academic study of it. I found it quite unnerving that Eleanor had latched onto Hatshepsut at about the same time we had. Ah well, great minds! I concentrated on cutting into my rice-stuffed vine leaves, enjoying their spicy flavour.

'Oh yes,' she continued as if we'd commented, although none of us had. 'I find I admire Hatshepsut very much. Perhaps it's because she dared to rule in a man's world. I think the raising of the obelisks was one of her towering achievements.'

Eleanor liked talking in puns, I'd noticed. She also liked holding court. And since she was in full flow none of us had the nerve to interrupt her.

'You know, they had to be cut out of the granite quarry in Aswan, dragged over a rugged landscape strewn with giant boulders, and then manoeuvred onto huge cargo ships designed to transport them down the Nile to Thebes.' She took a mouthful, chewed, swallowed and continued. 'Each obelisk was estimated to weigh just less than 200 tons, and there were two of them. Imagine that! How those boats didn't sink under the weight I will never know. And to this day no one's quite sure how the obelisks were erected once they'd been dragged into position at Karnak. The needles of stone are almost precisely vertical, within one or two millimetres parallel to the sides of the base.'

I wondered if we were supposed to gasp in amazement. But it seemed we weren't required to give a reaction or response of any kind. Eleanor had merely paused for breath and a sip of wine, and swept on,

'If the unfinished obelisk had been completed it would have been the largest ever raised, nearly one third larger than any other. You know, three sides of the shaft were quarried before a flaw was discovered in the stone and it was abandoned, still partly attached to the parent rock.'

'I'm looking forward to seeing it too,' Francesca said staunchly. She had commendable poise. 'It's impossible not to admire Hatshepsut, I agree.'

Eleanor beamed at her. This was a colourful sight given the flushed cheeks she'd acquired after a glass of red wine (Obelisk, as it happened) which clashed with her cerise silk top and the flaming orange scarf she'd wound turban-style around her head. She really did have the most eye-popping dress sense.

Eleanor thanked the waiter as he topped up her wine glass; then swept an imperious glance around the table at us all. 'The tragedy for Hatshepsut was that after all those glory years she had such a sad and sorry end.'

I stared at her. 'I wasn't aware too much was known about her final days.'

She gave me a look both kindly and condescending. Kindly because I'd offered her another chance to lecture; condescending because my own knowledge was so evidently inferior to her own. Adam, wisely, was keeping quiet. Francesca leaned forward slightly, politely interested. Doug seemed to me to be enjoying himself. He didn't give two hoots about the ancient queen who made herself pharaoh. But I think he found the theatrics of the modern schoolmistress who'd descended among us with all the subtlety of a tornado quite entertaining. He sipped on his Sakkara beer and observed us all with a definite twinkle in his eyes.

'She grew incredibly fat, you know. Oh yes,' Eleanor nodded as if to agree with her own proclamation. 'We know this because her mummy was identified just a few years ago. Archaeologists used a missing tooth to positively identify the mummy as Hatshepsut.'

'A missing tooth?' I asked, intrigued despite myself.

'Yes, you heard correctly Meredith. We all know that after her death Thutmosis III took steps to erase all traces of her. In my own opinion this silly man acted on some misguided idea that he needed to remove the female interruption in the male Thutmoside lineage.'

I wondered how ancient Egypt's greatest warrior pharaoh would feel being dismissed as a silly man! Eleanor's feminist principles coming to the fore again.

'He had statues of her torn down, monuments defaced, and her name scratched from the records. In particular, her mummy went missing. The puzzle of what happened to it has troubled Egyptologists for more than a century.'

I glanced at Adam, and he nodded and squeezed my knee under the table as if to say *she's right so far so we may as well let her run with it.*

'Howard Carter discovered Hatshepsut's tomb while excavating in the Valley of the Kings. He found two sarcophagi, one for Hatshepsut and the second for her father, Thutmosis I. But both were empty. The mummy of Thutmosis I turned up among a mummy cache discovered in the hills behind the Valley in Victorian times when a goat fell down a hole.'

I had to hand it to her. She knew her history. I remembered Ahmed telling us this story. He loved to regale anyone and everyone with it since he was descended from the herdsman who'd owned the goat.

'But Hatshepsut wasn't there,' Eleanor said, forking a meatball into her mouth. 'In recent years speculation about the riddle of the missing mummy focused on a separate tomb, also excavated by Howard Carter. Inside he found the partially disturbed and decaying coffins of two women lying side-by-side. One bore the inscriptions of Hatshepsut's wet nurse. The other was anonymous. As the tomb wasn't royal Carter closed it up again. But a few years ago, archaeologists decided to re-investigate. They took the unidentified mummy to Cairo and performed a CT scan on it. The scan revealed the mummy was an obese woman probably in her fifties who had bad teeth.'

To be fair to Eleanor she had us all rapt by this point. There's something quite gruesomely appealing about ancient Egyptian mummies. Even Doug was leaning forward, and Adam gave a small nod to show she'd got her facts straight.

'In search of more clues the archaeologists suggested a CT scanner be used to examine artefacts known to be associated with the queen-pharaoh. One of those was a small wooden box that bore the cartouche of Hatshepsut and contained a liver.'

'A liver?' Doug repeated. 'Ugh! Gross!'

'Oh yes,' Eleanor confirmed briskly. 'Embalmers typically eviscerated the dead before embalming them but preserved the organs in jars and boxes.'

I noticed Francesca quietly put down her knife and fork at this, leaving her dinner half-finished.

'Now here's the remarkable part.' In her enthusiasm, Eleanor even managed to include Adam and me in the baring of her teeth that passed for a smile. 'The CT scan revealed a tooth in the box, along with the liver. A dentist was called in. He concluded that not only was the mummy of the fat lady missing a tooth, but the hole left behind and the type of tooth that was missing were an exact match for the loose one in the box.' She stared around at us triumphantly. 'So, there you have it. Hatshepsut discovered. A fat lady with bad teeth, who died in her fifties and suffered the ignominy of being snatched from her royal tomb and dumped in a non-royal grave as part of the campaign to erase her from history.'

While Adam disappeared into the bathroom for a pre-bedtime shower and to clean his teeth, I powered up my laptop. I wanted to find out about the last days of Hatshepsut. A few minutes later he re-appeared, smelling sweetly of shampoo and toothpaste. He came and kissed my neck, then sat on the bed watching me. 'So, what have you discovered?'

'Nothing,' I said. 'After all the magnificence of the earlier part of her reign, the last few years don't seem to contain any notable building works or major achievements. It makes me wonder if she went into a kind of decline after Senenmut disappeared.' I sat staring off into space for a while, mentally picking up the threads of my earlier conjecture.

'Come to bed Merry,' Adam said after watching me for a while. 'I found a black fez with a rather jaunty yellow tassel for sale in the gift shop. Look, here it is.' He plopped it on top of his head. 'I'm dying to try it out. Enough theorising for one night. Come here!'

Chapter 10

The second sightseeing stop on our Nile cruise was Kom Ombo, another Ptolemaic temple dating from the Graeco-Roman period of dynastic Egypt's dying days.

It was an early start again, but the air was warm and full of birdsong as we left the *Misr* and strolled the short distance along a tree-lined boulevard from our mooring to the stone steps leading up to the temple forecourt.

Tariq gathered us all together and started his tour. 'While more magnificent temples can be found elsewhere in Egypt, no site can rival Kom Ombo for its beautiful setting, perched on the edge of the Nile with a perfect view of the river, emerald fields and golden desert beyond. Kom Ombo is a temple to be savoured.'

There's something about a handsome man, flush with enthusiasm for his subject and gifted with a poetic turn of phrase that's really quite irresistible. I thought so the first time I met Adam. Tariq, though younger, was from the same mould.

'This temple lies at the start of a road leading to desert gold mines. It is said the Roman army trained elephants here. In ancient times the river at this spot was filled with sandbars. These were home to large numbers of Nile crocodiles, some of the biggest and most ferocious on earth.'

'Are crocodiles still in the Nile?' asked one of our fellow travellers. He sounded a bit unnerved. I wondered if like me he was picturing all those grubby children splashing about in the shallows.

'No. They died out after the Aswan dams were constructed. But they thrive still in Lake Nasser. In ancient times the town here was closely associated with Sobek, the crocodile god. This temple is unusual for being dedicated to two gods: Sobek – who was worshipped in the right half of the temple and Horus the elder in the left half. These two halves are mirror images of each other.'

Tariq led us through the hypostyle hall and a series of vestibules and sanctuaries, pointing out the finely carved raised reliefs as we went.

'Now there are four things of particular interest I want to show you,' he said. 'First, we have carvings on the back walls of the temple showing ancient medical instruments. You will notice something that looks very like a modern scalpel, as well as a set of scales and other tools. The ancient Egyptians were skilled surgeons. It has been suggested they even performed brain surgery. Second, there is a calendar carved onto one of the walls. It shows how the ancient Egyptians used a numerical system to record the passage of time. Third, we have a Nilometer here that descended into the river in ancient times. The walls were calibrated to record the height of the annual flood and so indicate the likely crop yield for the next year. And finally, we have a little chapel housing a few mummified crocodiles. These you must see for their curiosity value. Now the temple is not busy today but even so the queues for these points of interest have already built up. They are standard fare on all the tour itineraries. So, I will not be able to pause long before each one. I suggest I show you where they are and then allow you free time to explore them at your leisure. The *Misr* will be moored here until lunchtime, so you may take your time, and we can meet back at the boat.'

We were all happy to agree this plan. As I'd said to Adam, it was a bit atmosphere defying to tramp around these magnificent temples in a party of nearly twenty people, crowding around each point of interest like a load of locusts descending on a crop. We obligingly followed Tariq while he showed us where everything was, then happily disbanded and went our separate ways.

Adam and I sat on a low wall for a long time waiting for the crowds to disperse; then dutifully retraced our steps. We took photographs of the medical reliefs and the carved calendar; then leaned over the circular wall enclosing the Nilometer to peer down into the murky depths far below. It was really quite impressive; the ancient Egyptian form of economic planning.

'I'm struggling to think of something different to say about this place,' Adam said as we made our way back through the temple. 'Although the crocodiles are something of a feature.' We approached the little chapel where their crumbling mummified remains were displayed. 'I wonder if I can find an angle there to give our holidaymakers on the *Queen Ahmes* something more than the standard tour.'

The words had barely died on his lips when a piercing shriek rent the air. It was such a strange action-replay of the scream at Edfu yesterday, we almost put it down to déjà vu and didn't react. But the hesitation was split-second. 'Eleanor,' we both said at once.

We broke into a run, sprinting towards the small, dimly lit chapel just as a galabeya-clad and be-turbaned young man bolted from it with all the explosive speed of a cork fired from a champagne bottle.

Eleanor was the only person inside. The queues had long-since dwindled as the early-morning tours departed. She was sitting on the hard stone floor among the crocodilian display cabinets, breathing heavily and clutching together the collar of her primrose yellow blouse. It was quite clear the buttons on said garment had been ripped open from the collar to just below her ample chest.

203

'My God, Eleanor! Are you alright?' Adam said, dropping down beside her.

'What happened?' I also plopped down onto the flagstone floor.

'I think that young heathen tried to ravish me!' she announced a bit breathlessly.

I don't think either of us meant to gape as rudely as we did. But the thought of Eleanor as the target of any sort of ravishment was a bit hard to swallow to be shamefully honest.

'Did he try to steal anything?' Adam asked.

'No. He made no attempt on my handbag at all. Since yesterday I've had it clamped against me in a vice-like grip at all times. But I don't think it was money he was after.'

'So, what happened?' I asked agog.

She sat up and swiped at the dust on her ankle-length indigo-blue skirt. 'Well, I waited for ages and ages for the chapel here to empty. I wanted to have the place to myself. There's something noble and terrifying about these ancient beasts lying here in state. One needs to experience the full impact without a load of ignorant tourists yapping away incessantly and the constant whir and click of cameras and those silly little telephones everyone uses for recording images these days. I wanted to just stand and feel their ancient presence.'

I wondered if she realised how she sounded, rhapsodising about a bunch of two-thousand-years-dead crocodiles.

'As soon as I saw I could have the place to myself I darted inside so I could commune in peace with the disciples of Sobek. I was just raising my camera to my eyes when the villain struck from behind.'

There was so much in this little speech I wanted to react to. But I knew my instinctive objections were beneath me and suppressed them.

'He crept up on me with all the stealth of a cat burglar,' Eleanor continued breathily. 'I was caught completely unawares and with no means of defending myself. He spun me around, caught me in his strong young arms and peered intently at my heaving bosom.'

Why did I have a sneaking suspicion Eleanor was starting to enjoy herself?

'Oh Adam, you should have seen him!' she declared. 'A native Egyptian clad in flowing robes and with a bolt of fine cloth wound around his head like a sheik. Beneath it his black eyes snapped in a darkly seductive manner...'

'We did see him,' Adam commented blandly. 'He was wearing a grubby galabeya and a dirty turban. He was a kid of about nineteen and galloped out of here as if the hounds of Hell were after him. I don't think he liked your scream, Eleanor.'

She looked annoyed at having her romantic balloon burst. 'Yes, well, clearly, I was shocked and horrified. What's one supposed to do? One can hardly stand by passive, limp and unresponsive whilst one's clothes are ripped from one's body. Of course I had to scream.'

'Yes,' I soothed. 'And you saw him off in fine style.'

Eleanor's gaze rested on mine with calculating precision. I could see she was wondering how to turn the situation to her advantage now the critical moment was past.

'Goodness me; I feel quite faint. Adam, I'm not sure I can make my own way back to the *Misr*. My nerves are shot quite to pieces. You may just have to carry me.' And she flopped back against the flagstones in a rather ungainly heap of primrose-yellow and indigo blue.

As Adam hoisted her to her feet in as gentlemanlike fashion as he could muster, I glared at her and decided there was no better fate I could think of than to have her mummified and entombed in the Valley of the Drama Queens.

***

'There's an email from Ted,' Adam said excitedly as the *Misr* pulled away from its moorings and started to steam gently towards Aswan.

I was wriggling into my swimsuit ready for another afternoon sunbathing on the upper deck. I stopped wriggling and went to peer over his shoulder as he entered the password Ted has used to protect it.

Dear Merry and Adam Ted started rather formally. He hadn't mastered the art of starting an email with "Hi".

One of the biggest mysteries arising from a study of ancient Egypt is why Thutmosis III waited approximately twenty years to carry out his campaign of destruction against the memory of his aunt-stepmother Hatshepsut. Some scholars say he was removing the stain of female rule from the royal lineage, so the Thutmoside line would be preserved for future generations unblemished. Some say he was shoring up the throne for his son, who was born of one of his lesser wives. The truth is no one knows. It is all speculation and conjecture at best. But I feel sure there are clues to what really happened recorded on the walls of the little rock-cut chamber you stumbled across in the Theban hills.

I felt a thrill go through me. Adam glanced up at me and shifted over so I could perch alongside him on the upholstered stool in front to the ornate dressing table to see his iPad better. He put his arm around me, and we read on together.

One question has always been why Thutmosis felt the need to include Senenmut in his frenzy of destruction.

Nobody is sure what happened to Senenmut. But it is hard to see what kind of a threat he could have posed to the finest warrior pharaoh Egypt ever had a generation after Hatshepsut's death.

'He must have been long dead by then,' I murmured. 'Or a very old man indeed.'

Several things about the photographs you took of the rock-cut chamber intrigue me. Principal among these is the fact that I do not believe the hieroglyphic inscriptions packed around the upper registers of the walls are contemporary with the pictorial scenes beneath them. It seems to me they were added later and tell a different story, although I have made only a small start on translating them. I believe Senenmut inscribed them after Hatshepsut's death.

'So, he did out-live her,' I breathed. 'But why then did he disappear from the historical record a few years before she died?'

It looks to me as if the death of her daughter Neferure marked the end of the glory days of Hatshepsut's reign, Ted wrote as if in answer to my question. *It seems to have been a turning point. There is one last pictorial scene in the chamber after the one of the wedding feast for Neferure and Thutmosis. It's where the paint has flaked from the wall of the chamber and the plaster is a bit damaged. If I am interpreting it correctly, it shows Neferure being interred in her cliff-cut tomb. Hatshepsut is shown bent over with grief.*

Senenmut is holding her up. What's interesting is Thutmosis is notable by his absence. There are no depictions of any major events after that. What's clear is Neferure's death seems to coincide with Senenmut's disappearance from the historical record. It is only after Hatshepsut's death that he appears to have started carving the hieroglyphics onto the walls. My feeling is that he added the pictorial funerary scene at the same time, that is, after Hatshepsut's death.

Adam and I glanced at each other, searching each other's eyes for what it might all mean. Finding no answers we turned back to Ted's email.

The section of inscriptions I have transcribed reads something along the lines of, "The Ka of my beloved Maatkare, foremost of noble ladies, has flown to the imperishable stars and her earthly remains rest now in her house of eternity. I am returned here to Waset after an absence of many years; no one hearing, no one seeing. Maatkare can no longer protect her daughter the God's Wife of Amun from the vengeful hands of he who now sits alone on the Horus throne. As once I safeguarded the royal princess in her lifetime, so now shall I do so to preserve her in the Afterlife. I know a secret sanctuary where she can rest for millions of years. Then must I return to my hideaway in the frontier town and keep safe the precious gift that has been passed into my care…" The text ends frustratingly with another depiction of that symbol, Ted wrote. *The same one as on the stele. I still haven't been able to decipher it. As you know, Waset was the ancient name for Thebes. I can only assume Senenmut is telling us he removed Neferure from her cliff-tomb and re-interred her in the secret chamber where we know she rests to this day. Quite what she did to incur the wrath of her husband Thutmosis is not made clear. But it seems obvious Senenmut was given charge of her baby daughter, what he refers to as "the precious gift" and felt the need to hide her out of harm's way somewhere. The most likely frontier town is Aswan. Senenmut was familiar with it since he'd overseen the quarrying of the obelisks from the granite mines there.'*

'I told you so!' I said with a small surge of triumph. 'I'll bet my hunch is right. Thutmosis was no more the father of that baby girl than you are; and he knew it. That's why he was absent from Neferure's funeral. But it seems he was determined not to let her rest in peace once Hatshepsut was safely dead and no longer able to protect her. So Senenmut took it upon himself to spirit her to the safety of the secret chamber behind Hatshepsut's temple. It's clear I was wrong to imagine Senenmut could possibly have been the father of Neferure's daughter. But it's equally clear he took on the role of protector and guardian of the baby as he had been for Neferure herself.'

210

'So, you've been proved right again, Merry,' Adam said with a small smile. 'But it still doesn't answer the question about why Thutmosis left it another twenty years to go after the memory of Hatshepsut and Senenmut.'

'Twenty years is long enough for a baby girl to grow up and become dangerous,' I said darkly. 'I'd love to know who the real father of Neferure's daughter was. And I wonder what that strange symbol is supposed to represent and what kind of threat it posed to Thutmosis so late in his reign.'

Ted signed off his email with love to us both, leaving Adam and I to stare at each other and wonder if we had enough pieces to solve one of the most intriguing puzzles of ancient Egypt.

* * *

'This afternoon we have a special treat for you,' Tariq said with a smile. 'We have been successful in arranging a private sailing on a felucca. What is special about it is we don't have to restrict ourselves to the River Nile, as is the case for most tourists. We have been granted permission to take our cruise on Lake Nasser. This is a rare privilege. You will see the magnificent site of the Aswan High Dam from the water, and we will sail past Kalabasha Temple, one of those re-sited by UNESCO above the rising waters of the lake.'

We were grouped together on the upper deck watching our arrival at the attractive riverside town of Aswan.

'Aswan is situated downriver from the First Nile Cataract,' Tariq informed us. 'It is Egypt's southernmost city. In ancient times its location had strategic importance, at the crossroads of trade routes between Egypt, Africa and India. Exotic goods were traded here. As you can see Aswan is set on the most enchanting part of the Nile, where the Sahara Desert comes right down to the water's edge on the west bank and the river is dotted with islands.' He pointed broadside from the boat. 'You see this large island in the middle of the river here, with the fancy hotel at this end. This is Elephantine Island. It was known as *Yebu* during Pharaonic times, meaning "elephant". It is the oldest inhabited part of Aswan. It is not known whether the island was named after the huge grey granite boulders at the southern end, which resemble bathing elephants, or because it was a major ivory trading post. The ruins of many ancient temples can be seen on the island, one of the oldest being the Temple of Satet built by Queen Hatshepsut. Close to here are the granite quarries where Hatshepsut's famous obelisks were cut from the rock.'

'Aswan is a lovely town,' Francesca said at my elbow, while Doug got busy with his camera. 'Doug and I were here a few years ago. Its laid-back atmosphere makes it one of the most relaxing places in Egypt to visit. The locals here don't hassle you quite as energetically as they do in Luxor.'

'Now it will be a short trip by minibus to the felucca landing platform on Lake Nasser,' Tariq said. 'And then we can commence our cruise as the sun starts to set over our so-beautiful country.'

There's a certain timelessness about sailing on a felucca. The giant triangular sail looks a bit like a huge white feather strung from the rigging above the wide wooden deck. The smiling, barefoot, galabeya-clad crew helped us on board along the rickety gangplank and invited us to mind our heads as we ducked under the rigging. We took our seats on the cushioned benches lining each side of the boat, slung low enough in the water that we could trail our fingers in the sparkling waters of Lake Nasser if we chose. Some of our fellow cruise companions looked a bit askance at the young man from the tourist police who joined us, complete with his big black gun. But I knew this was standard practice and took no notice. He barely looked old enough to know how to use it. But that wasn't the point. It was a nod to security and that was what mattered.

It was a balmy afternoon, with just enough of a breeze to send the felucca zipping across the waves. The fiery sun hovered high in the vast blue sky as if uncertain, hesitant about making its descent towards the western horizon. I let its rays kiss my face, tilting my head back, closing my eyes and enjoying the feel of the warm wind brushing ever so gently against my cheeks.

'Lake Nasser is the largest artificial lake in the world,' Tariq said proudly. 'It stretches more than 500 kilometres from Aswan to the Sudan. When the High Dam was constructed it flooded a huge expanse of land down as far as Abu Simbel in Nubia and beyond. Dozens of ancient temples had to be carefully relocated, moving them stone by stone to higher ground to rescue them from the rising waters.'

'The temples weren't all that was affected,' Eleanor said loudly from a little further down the boat. She was suffering no ill effects from her fainting fit at Kom Ombo, I noticed. Her voice was a strident as ever. 'I understand approximately 800,000 Nubians were displaced from their homes.'

'Yes, that is correct,' Tariq confirmed. 'Many of them settled in Aswan as well as other villages along the shoreline.'

'And I've been told the lake is changing the climate in Egypt. Is that right? The air is more humid due to the huge volume of water.'

Tariq smiled, trying to look as if he welcomed these comments, despite the challenging tone in which they were uttered. 'You are correct again. The dam was built to stop the worst excesses of the annual Nile flood, as well as to provide electricity and irrigation water for Egypt's crops.'

'Yet surely it must pose a terrorist risk,' said the chirpy and ever optimistic Eleanor. 'I've heard it said that if the Dam was bombed or breached it would cause a tsunami-like wave that would devastate most of Egypt.'

Tariq looked uncomfortable; as well he might, beleaguered and bullied like this. 'Dear lady, please believe me when I say the benefits far outweigh…'

He was cut off before he could finish. 'Look! There's a crocodile!' one of our fellow cruise-mates shouted excitedly.

'Let me see! I've never seen a crocodile outside of a zoo!' exclaimed his wife.

'Well now's your chance. See him? Sunning himself on that sandbar over there?'

We all crowded onto the starboard side of the felucca, craning to see. The water level was quite low at this time of year after the long hot summer. The shallows were strewn with grassy sandbars sadly littered with plastic water bottles, coke cans and other modern rubbish. Everyone got busy with cameras and camcorders.

'I don't see him,' Eleanor said loudly, pushing her way towards the little space on the felucca's side where the gangplank was raised and lowered.

'There, see?' Adam said, pointing.

Eleanor let out a gasp that might have been delight or horror, or perhaps a combination of the two.

'Goodness me, he's *enormous*,' Francesca shuddered. I actually felt the shudder, since she was pressed so close alongside me.

She wasn't exaggerating. He looked like a gigantic log felled from some massive tree. Only the scales and his staring eyes betrayed his camouflage. Eleanor leaned forward, peering through the milk-bottle lenses of her glasses and shading her eyes with her hand across her brow. 'Dear me, what a magnificent creature.'

'This is very unusual,' Tariq said. 'Crocodiles are rare in this area. Now be careful everyone, please. Do not lean too far.'

'Look! There's another one! It's moving; see?'

We all craned forward again to look where he was pointing; just in time to see the prehistoric-looking beast open its jaws in a lazy sort of yawn and slide sinuously from the sandbank into the water.

Eleanor raised her camera and managed to shove her elbow into the face of the man standing next to her. He let out a small cry of protest and stepped sharply sideways. I didn't see exactly what happened. Someone jostled someone else. There was a bit of frantic pushing and shoving, then a sudden yelp followed by a loud *splash*.

216

After a moment of horrified silence pandemonium broke loose. Everyone was shouting at once.

'Eleanor!' Adam yelled in horror, realising she had fallen in. 'Lower the sail! Stop the damn boat!' Then before I had any idea what he intended to do, he jumped up on the cushioned benches and dived.

'Adam! *No!*' I screamed. But it was too late. He was already swimming towards the flailing arms and gulping face of Eleanor, thrashing about in the water already some distance behind the felucca. Beyond them the water was broken by a triangular wake, with a long scaly snout at its tip. 'Turn the boat!' I shrieked. 'For God's sake! Someone *do* something!'

But it seemed everyone was transfixed with horror, powerless to do anything but watch. I scrabbled frantically to free the life ring from the side of the boat and flung it desperately into the water. It landed with a splash a few feet from the boat, of no help whatsoever. The crocodile and Adam were both converging on Eleanor. I didn't see who got there first as I was grabbed from behind and shoved backwards landing with a thump on the narrow bulkhead running along the centre of the felucca. I scrambled back to my feet whimpering with fright. There was no sign of Eleanor. Adam dived under the water and so did the crocodile.

'*No!*' I shrieked, only to find myself shoved unceremoniously aside again. It was Doug, pushing past me to climb onto the bench as the crew scrambled to lower the sail. He stood there with his feet braced against the shallow rim of the boat.

'Give me the gun,' he ordered our young tourist police companion. The boy seemed paralysed with fear, clutching the gun against him like a talisman. 'I said give me the gun!' Doug roared, wresting the big black weapon from the boy's trembling hands. He squared his shoulders and took aim at the spot where Adam and Eleanor had disappeared with the crocodile.

The water bubbled and all three reappeared, their heads bobbing back above the surface. Adam seemed to be holding onto Eleanor, who didn't look as if she was conscious. The crocodile had something hanging from its mouth. I nearly fainted with horror. But it wasn't dripping blood. The beast shook it loose then reared up terrifyingly out of the water, jaws open, as if planning to dive down on top of its two victims, swallowing them whole.

I screamed. Doug fired.

The crocodile gave an awful sort of bellow and crashed backwards into the water, sending up a sheet of spray. Adam started swimming but his progress was painfully slow, weighed down by the inert and waterlogged form that was Eleanor. I cast a frantic glance at the sandbar. It would only take the other crocodile a matter of seconds to reach them should he be minded to slide into the lake.

In the water, the wounded crocodile was thrashing and rolling wildly, sending spray in all directions. Doug took careful aim and fired another two shots into the wounded animal. The bullets hit with bull's eye accuracy and with a horrible kind of sigh the crocodile sank beneath the waves in a spreading pool of blood. Under normal circumstances I deplore the killing of any creature but all I could do was sag with relief.

'Good shot!' Tariq shouted.

Doug had the gun trained on the other crocodile. 'Pull in the life ring,' he murmured to me.

I leaned across the side of the felucca groping about in the water for the rope then hauling it wetly towards me. As soon as I had purchase on the ring, I yelled Adam's name and flung it out to him. He grabbed hold of it and all those of us close enough reached forward to pull him and Eleanor towards us and then haul them onboard.

Eleanor was a dead weight, unconscious but breathing. Both streamed water but mercifully not what I feared to see most: blood.

'Are they unharmed? Oh, thank God!' Francesca fell to her knees on the wooden planks, turning Eleanor over as she suddenly spewed across the deck, ridding herself of the water she'd swallowed all over the feet of the people crowding around her. I wondered if she'd still be as keen to commune with the disciples of Sobek now she'd had a dunking with one of them.

Adam was slumped on the floorboards, chest heaving, hair plastered wetly against his head. I wanted to collapse alongside him, but my body wouldn't respond. I was paralysed with relief, torn between the need to fling my arms around him and never let him go and also scream my head off at him for daring to put me through the terror of the last few minutes. All I could do was stand there like a stupid lump drinking in the sight of him and offering up a heartfelt little prayer of thanksgiving to Sobek for sparing him.

Doug jumped down from the bench and handed the gun to Tariq rather than back into the trembling hands of the police child. 'How the hell did you survive that?' he asked Adam roughly, gripping his shoulder. 'When I saw you disappear under the surface, I thought you were done for. I was sure he must have got hold of one of you. Usually, a crocodile takes its victim deep underwater, rolling all the way. How did you escape?'

'I kicked him in the snout,' Adam rasped, still gasping for breath. 'He got hold of my boot and yanked it off my foot. I think the laces got caught in his teeth.'

I noticed his bare right foot for the first time. Those old walking boots had been a feature of Adam's wardrobe since long before I had known him; at least twenty years at a guess. I felt my eyes mist over with ridiculous tears as I thought how much I'd miss them, even given my own much shorter acquaintance with them, and what a wonderful sacrifice they'd made.

'I've heard of being pulled up by your bootstraps, but I'd say you took it to extremes today,' Doug grinned. 'Those boots probably saved your life.'

'That, and you being such a crack shot,' Adam smiled up at him. 'Thanks mate, I owe you one.'

Doug shrugged, 'I knew all that target practise firing at tin cans with my Dad's old rifle would pay off one day.'

'Just don't get too big for your boots,' Adam murmured weakly.

Their Boys Own humour was too much for me. With a strangled choke I leaned across the side of the boat and threw up comprehensively into the lake.

Chapter 11

'I've got a small gift for you,' Doug said to Adam at the dinner table.

Adam opened the small, candy-striped paper bag Doug handed him across the table, and grinned widely. 'A crocodile tooth! Is it a real one?'

'I think so. Francesca found it in the bazaar in Aswan when we went for a stroll before dinner.' He squeezed his wife's hand on the tabletop. 'We thought you could wear it on its little leather bootlace around your neck as a kind of memento of both the crocodile and your old boots. You never know, it might bring you luck.'

Adam's handsome face glowed with pleasure. I knew he'd made a real and lasting friend in Doug.

Eleanor had decided to eschew dinner with the rest of us in the dining room in favour of a solo meal in her cabin. I wasn't sure what to make of this. She'd eked out every last modicum of melodrama on the trip back to the *Misr*, reclining in a kind of semi-swoon at the back of the felucca. I failed to see how she could *still* disapprove of Adam. But to my certain knowledge she'd done nothing to thank him for saving her life. All things considered I was glad she wasn't sitting across the table from me. I'm not sure I could have restrained myself from giving her a hearty slap.

'So, are you making the trip down to Abu Simbel tomorrow?' Francesca asked.

'No,' I said. 'We thought we'd make the most of our time here in Aswan before the boat turns around and heads back to Luxor in a couple of days.' The truth was our dahabeeyah cruises would go no further than Aswan so the magnificent temples of Abu Simbel, two hundred or so kilometres south on Lake Nasser weren't part of our research trip. 'I'm sure you'll have a wonderful time, although it's an early start, I hear.'

'We're flying down rather than coaching it,' Doug said. 'But 5.30am is still early enough considering this is a holiday.' The rolling eyes of long sufferance were back, but we knew him well enough now to know he didn't mean it and laughed. 'So, it's an early night for us, I think.'

We said goodnight after dinner, and Adam and I headed to the upper deck for a nightcap in the balmy night-time breeze. The Nile was particularly beautiful, dancing with golden lights reflected from the floodlit tombs of the nobles on the far bank. They dated from Egypt's Old and Middle Kingdoms and made this one of the most historic views on earth. I gazed at the crocodile tooth on its little leather strap hung proudly around Adam's neck and felt goose bumps rise on my skin. He caught me looking. 'You know what Merry? Forget the Indiana Jones hat and the fez! This crocodile tooth gives me a whole bunch of different ideas…!'

I looked at the dark glint in his eyes and the goose bumps disappeared in an instant, replaced by an altogether different sort of shiver. While I wasn't at all sure I'd forgiven him for the moments of heart-stopping and sickening terror he'd subjected me to on the felucca, I decided his close encounter with a crocodile might have some compensatory factors after all. I was certainly willing to explore the various different options he might be considering for how to make it up to me.

We took our time about it and enjoyed a well-deserved lie in next morning. The *Misr* was unusually quiet, most guests having signed up for the optional excursion to Abu Simbel. We had a leisurely breakfast in the sunshine on the upper deck and debated how to spend the day.

'Call me single-minded,' I said. 'But I want to see the stuff here that Hatshepsut had a hand in. I mean, all the Ptolemaic stuff is great in its own way, but it doesn't hold quite the same appeal. I've got this romantic image of Senenmut holed up here with the baby Neferamun to keep her safe from the vengeance of the cuckolded Thutmosis. I just have a feeling there might be something here that will help us understand what actually happened, and why Thutmosis went after Hatshepsut and Senenmut twenty years after he became pharaoh in his own right.'

'Once you get hold of a mystery,' Adam said, smiling, 'you don't let it go, do you? You're like a terrier with a bone.'

'Well, wouldn't it be great to have a new story to tell the guests on our dahabeeyah?' I asked innocently. 'One the archaeologists and Egyptologists haven't unlocked yet...'

It was while we were gazing in awe at Hatshepsut's unfinished obelisk, its underside still attached to the bedrock, that Adam's iPhone vibrated in his pocket. 'It's Ted,' he said, glancing at the display panel. We moved into a quiet space in the quarry away from the boardwalk all decked out for tourists and put Ted on speakerphone.

'Merry! Adam!' Ted's voice buzzed excitedly into the hot sunshiny air around us from the wonderful electronic device in Adam's hand. 'You won't believe this! Thutmosis was not the father of Neferure's daughter!'

I nearly laughed out loud and whooped in triumph. Only my enormous respect and affection for Ted stopped me. Adam went very still. He shoved his sunglasses up on top of his head and gazed at me in wonder, his eyes deepening from blue to violet in the way I loved so much, and as they always did when he was in the grip of some strong emotion. 'You were right,' he whispered. His quiet endorsement meant more to me than if he'd shouted it from the rooftops. 'Bloody hell Merry, I've heard of feminine intuition, but I hadn't really given you much credence for it on this occasion. I thought it was just a romantic conjecture. But, once again, your instincts are spot on!'

'What? What?' the professor asked, unable to follow Adam's whispered commentary by telephone satellite.

'It's just I had a hunch that might be the case,' I said, grinning for Adam's benefit. 'But you've got some evidence?'

'Senenmut's wall carvings make it clear. I've translated the whole passage now. I don't suppose he had any reason to dissemble in what he recorded. He hasn't carved anything on the walls of that secret sanctuary to give anything away that Thutmosis wouldn't have already known.'

'So, what does it say?' Adam and I both asked together, our words overlapping with our shared Egyptological fervour.

'It names the father of Neferure's daughter. He was her cousin, a young man called Amenmose.'

Adam and I stared at each other blankly. I rather rejoiced in this since Adam's knowledge of all things Egyptological is so far superior to mine. But he was unable to steal a march on me this time.

'Now this gets a bit convoluted,' Ted said. 'So, listen closely. Hatshepsut was the fully royal daughter of her father, the pharaoh Thutmosis I, and her mother, Queen Ahmes, his great royal wife, who was also descended from the Pharaonic line. Thutmosis I and Queen Ahmes had a son called Wadjmose, who was also fully royal. Sadly, Wadjmose died before his father, but not before he had a son of his own, Amenmose. Perhaps because Wadjmose predeceased his father when Hatshepsut was still a child, she was married to her half-brother Thutmosis II, who was her father's son by a lesser wife. He came to the throne as the sole surviving male heir of Thutmosis I. Hatshepsut and Thutmosis II produced only one child, Neferure.'

'And Neferure grew up and fell in love with Amenmose, the son of her mother's full brother.' I deduced.

'Yes!' Ted said excitedly. 'I'm guessing she thought he was of purer royal blood than her younger half-brother Thutmosis III – whom I guess she was forced to marry as he was already Pharaoh, having been born of Thutmosis II.'

'So Neferure would have considered her daughter Neferamun to be a true hereditary princess. But Neferamun was conceived of an adulterous relationship. Because no matter how many wives and concubines a pharaoh was allowed to have, his wives were not granted the same privilege. Oh my God! So, the baby Neferamun arguably had a stronger place in the royal lineage than Thutmosis did!!'

'Yes,' Ted said. 'But she was only a woman. So, I still fail to see what sort of a threat realistically she could have posed to the mighty Thutmosis III, especially twenty years into his solo reign. I feel sure the answer is in this mysterious symbol I have still been unable to decipher. If I could understand what it means I feel we'd have all the answers. Senenmut spent some of the most important years of his life in Aswan. So, it would be lovely to think that there might be some clue there that could help us solve the mystery, even all these centuries later.'

We had lunch at the Old Cataract Hotel, turning it this way and that; but concluded we still didn't have enough pieces to explain the belated decision by Thutmosis III to destroy all references to Hatshepsut and Senenmut after such a long passage of time. Instead, we amused ourselves trying to remember the plot of *Death on the Nile*, including whodunit. This iconic hotel was where Agatha Christie wrote her famous Egypt-based murder mystery. It took no great leap of imagination to picture her sitting in the shade on one of the terraces with her pen poised and her mind working at full throttle.

The hotel had a fabulous view across the Nile to Elephantine Island and some of its ancient ruins. 'Didn't Tariq say Hatshepsut built a temple or a shrine or something over there?' I asked as we sipped our coffee.

'Yes, the temple of Satet,' Adam nodded. 'I don't know much about it. But I agree we should check it out. If there's time we'll go this afternoon. But I promised I'd help Tariq to devise his quiz questions for the galabeya party tonight, so right now we need to get back to the boat pretty sharpish.'

We arrived to find the tour party to Abu Simbel just returned, travel-weary for sure but all brimming with wonder at the staggering sights they'd seen. All, that was, except Eleanor. She may well have found Abu Simbel equally awe-inspiring for all I know but it certainly wasn't the topic uppermost in her mind right now. She was haranguing poor Honi quite mercilessly and at the top of her voice as we stepped from the gangplank into the cool interior of the *Misr*'s reception area and accepted the cold towel and glass of peppermint tea the crew had ready for us.

'It's just not good enough, Honi. I've always lived by the motto that there's a place for everything and everything in its place. It is not acceptable to return from a sightseeing trip and find the housekeeping staff have taken it upon themselves to rearrange my cabin in my absence.'

'I find this very difficult to understand, Miss Hayes,' Honi said, looking perplexed and fingering the ornate ivory braiding on his black galabeya-uniform in agitation. 'What is it that you say has been rearranged?'

'Just about everything!' she complained. 'My toiletries are all lined up in a different order in the bathroom. My clothes are hanging in a different sequence in the wardrobe. I'm very particular about having everything colour co-ordinated, with all the outfits grouped together.' I couldn't help but raise my eyebrows at this, even though I was pretending deafness to what was going on. 'It seems your staff removed everything from my wardrobe only to return it in a completely random order. The same thing has happened with the personal items I keep folded away in the drawers. All seem to have been removed and replaced again – neatly enough I'll grant you – but not in their original locations. I accept and applaud the need for cleaning. Indeed, I wish more hostelries took the trouble to delve into those "beneath the surface" spots. But surely not while a guest is in situ and has everything ordered to his or her satisfaction. I will now have to spend the afternoon re-positioning all my belongings into their original location, so I am able to find what I'm looking for. It's most tiresome.'

'I humbly apologise for any inconvenience,' Honi said, pulling on all the skills he'd no doubt honed from his years of experience and all the excellent customer service training I'm sure he'd had. 'But it is not the usual practice of my housekeeping team to touch wardrobe or drawer space while a guest is in residence. I will investigate to see if there is some reason why it has been necessary to be more thorough than usual in keeping the cabins in tip-top condition. Perhaps they were concerned a mosquito had entered through an open window, or something of that nature.'

I didn't hear Eleanor's response. Adam and I had handed back our cold towels, finished our small glasses of peppermint tea, and climbed to the top of the staircase out of eavesdropping range. I was a bit miffed that she hadn't even registered us, since in my view she still owed Adam her sincere and heartfelt gratitude for rescuing her from the crocodile. But maybe, all things considered, it was best to give her a wide berth as far as possible and not court trouble. Assuming she felt well enough to join us for dinner tonight, there'd be plenty of opportunity to see if she was willing to do the honourable thing.

We met Tariq out in the shade on the lower sundeck behind the Saraya lounge. 'Now today is a very special anniversary,' he said seriously as we sat down. 'It is ninety years to the day since Howard Carter discovered the tomb of Tutankhamun.'

Adam and I took a moment to stare into each other's eyes. We'd already clocked the date. Tariq couldn't imagine the special significance Howard Carter held for us. But we took a moment to acknowledge it.

'We will have a galabeya party for our guests, as is traditional on a Nile cruise. It is a chance for everyone to dress up in traditional Egyptian costume and … what is your English expression… let their hair down?'

We nodded and smiled, 'Yes, that's it.'

'We'll have a whirling dervish and a belly dancer, as our guests have come to expect. But tonight, I want our galabeya night to have an extra twist. I thought an Egyptian quiz with questions based on some of the places we have visited, and some general knowledge about our remarkable ancient Pharaonic history. We will give a lovely prize of a gift from our shop to a generous value for the winner. Now Adam, while you've tried not to let it show, it's obvious you know as much if not more than I do… so your help in devising questions is appreciated!'

While they batted ideas back and forth, I drifted off. Through a whole set of remarkable circumstances, Adam and I were privileged to know more about ancient Egypt than it was possible to read in the history books. We had Howard Carter to thank for it. So, I was fully in support of the plan to celebrate the anniversary of his discovery of Tutankhamun's tomb. The fact it had led to the discovery of another even more astounding tomb almost ninety years later remained our sworn secret. Whether we'd be able to go public with our find any time soon remained to be seen. Egypt was still unsettled and unpredictable. Every day we saw the queues for gasoline and for bottled cooking gas, since the previous regime's deal with the United Arab Emirates had folded and the economic squeeze on the man–and-woman-in-the-street had taken hold. In many ways Egypt was still a nation on a knife-edge. We were immune to it in a sense in our little quasi-tourist bubble. But I wasn't sure if we could stay immune to it forever if we applied for our working visas and tried to make a go of our dahabeeyah dream.

Adam glanced at his watch, 'Enough quiz questions to sort the wheat from the chaff?' he asked.

'Thank you,' Tariq said with a smile; then turned serious. 'I dread to think what would have happened yesterday if your friend had not been so adept with a gun.'

'Please…' Adam said, holding up his hand. 'It was all just spur of the moment stuff; we don't need to do a postmortem.'

I winced at his turn of phrase.

'No; but you must understand a story like that could put us out of business. Perhaps you remember the awful reports of shark attacks on the Red Sea coast last year. Egypt's tourism industry is suffering enough without adding sharks and crocodiles to the list of reasons holidaymakers should stay away. I very much want to add my own appreciation for your reckless and selfless bravery. If that lady had died yesterday in the jaws of a crocodile, I feel our tourist industry may have shut down for good.'

Reckless was right, I thought. Adam didn't seem to know where to look. So, I suggested there was enough time to visit Elephantine Island if we made a start now. After all, the crocodile experience had led me to the certain knowledge I didn't want him growing too big for his boots.

'Ah yes, Elephantine Island is worth a visit,' Tariq nodded. 'And it is not on our schedule. You will do well to make the trip.'

'We really don't know very much about it,' I said. 'Only that you mentioned Hatshepsut had built a temple there.'

'That is correct. In ancient times, the island was the cult centre of the ram-headed god Khnum, creator of humankind and God of the Nile flood. The island contains ruins of the ancient fortress town that once stood at the southern end. The remains of the Graeco-Roman Necropolis of the Sacred Rams can also be found there. Hatshepsut's temple to Satet is interesting for being built over the top of a much older shrine, which can still be reached by an ancient shaft and staircase. Yes, it is well worth a look. Over the last few seasons German archaeologists have excavated the entire area. I believe they are finishing their work there now.'

I felt my heart sink. I'd started to get excited, picturing Elephantine Island as the fortress town where Senenmut may have secreted the baby Neferamun three-and-a-half-thousand years ago, and knowing Hatshepsut erected a temple there. But if German archaeologists had been crawling all over the place for years, I very much doubted any discoveries remained to be made.

We hired one of the little motorised water taxis to take us across the Nile to the little landing platform. It was a beautiful afternoon, and the feluccas were out in force on the river. But I didn't enjoy the trip as much as I should have. I knew for sure no crocodiles survived in the mysterious waters of the Nile these days. Even so, my imagination kept playing tricks on me. I fancied I could see them basking in the afternoon sunshine amid the great grey boulders strewn in the shallows around the island. Every piece of driftwood made me freeze with terror. All in all, I was weak with relief and gratitude by the time we moored at the landing stage. I knew I needed to give myself a severe talking to. If I planned to make a new life here in Egypt offering luxury Nile cruises aboard a lovingly restored dahabeeyah then a fear of the water and a propensity to see deadly crocodiles in every ripple on the surface was a distinct hindrance to success.

We approached the restored temple of Satet along a paved walkway. Its stones glowed warmly in the sunlight. I stood still in admiration. Restored like this, the temple looked curiously modern. No longer a tumbledown ruin, it was a study in straight lines; rectangular pillars holding up rectangular roofing blocks. It was all very impressive, but perhaps not very lovely.

'This is fascinating though,' Adam said when I voiced my thought out loud. 'Look, the German archaeologists have drawn in the missing parts of the wall reliefs so it's possible to discern what the whole image is supposed to represent.' These were fashioned in outline; simple, clean line drawings in outline on the bare plaster to show the missing sections.

The place was deserted. It was just us and a couple of archaeologists studiously bending over a row of stone blocks. They appeared to be gently cleaning the dust of centuries from their surface with soft-bristled brushes. I remembered what Ted had said about archaeology being hard, backbreaking work, and paused to admire their dedication. They didn't even look up, so intent were they on their labour of love.

We left them to it and wandered through the pillared hallway. The temple was small by the standards of those we'd visited so far on this trip. It consisted of several rooms and a surrounding gallery. The entrance on the right-hand side of the temple façade led to a large hall with two columns decorated with Hathor heads. From here a doorway set in the northern rear wall led to a chapel dedicated to Amun, while the door on the left of the rear wall led to the other rooms. A small team of archaeologists was at work in the Amun chapel, although it wasn't clear what they were doing. We turned away, not wishing to disturb them and made a slow study of the rest of the temple.

I couldn't help but feel disappointed. I don't know quite what I'd expected. Maybe some blinding flash of light to illuminate the missing piece of the Hatshepsut puzzle? But I guess it was wishful thinking. We made an intimate study of all the wall reliefs. Nothing stood out as significant.

'Oh well,' Adam said. 'It was worth a look.'

We were turning to leave when a sudden loud crash from the direction of the Amun chapel made us jump. We cast a quick, startled glance at each other. The crash was followed by a moment of silence then a commotion of raised human voices.

'What's going on?' I asked. 'They sound very excitable.'

Adam shrugged and we moved closer. There were perhaps three or four voices raised in agitation. I didn't understand a word, since the rapid exchange was taking place in a language I recognised as German, though I don't speak it.

Adam and I stepped through the doorway to the Amun chapel from the open hall into a billowing cloud of dust.

'What the…?' Adam exclaimed.

The excitable exchange in full-throttled German stopped. Through the dust three faces turned to stare at us.

'Hello,' I said, relying arrogantly on being understood since English was the international language.

'We heard a crash…' Adam said enquiringly, his German clearly as deficient as mine. The dust was starting to clear. Before any of the Germans could respond Adam leaned forward. 'My God! A hidden doorway…?'

All three continued to stare at us, almost as if we were some evil apparitions come to disturb their discovery. Then the tall, sandy-haired man stepped forward. '*Ja. Guten tag*; I mean hello. You are tourists?'

'No,' Adam said promptly. 'I'm an Egyptologist, Adam Tennyson.' He thrust out his hand and the German shook it almost as a reflex. 'I studied under Professor Edward Kincaid at the Oriental Institute, Oxford. This is Meredith Pink. She is a student of Egyptology, and I am her mentor.'

Luckily, I could put my choking fit down to the dust still swirling around us. As a rule, Adam tells the truth. That he was equivocating now told me everything I needed to know about the importance he was attaching to the hidden doorway.

'Professor Kincaid. *Ja, er ist ein guter menschhe;* he is renowned in his field of philology. I have heard of him, although I have not had the privilege to attend a lecture.'

'And you are…?' Adam said boldly assuming the upper hand.

'Dr Hans-Dieter Schneider; and this is my wife and dig-partner Dr Hannelore, and our assistant Erich.'

I realised Adam may have missed a trick by not introducing himself as a Dr of the PhD variety. If he thought so too, he didn't let it show. 'So, what have you found here?'

The excitement flooded back into Hans-Dieter's voice. 'I don't know. It was just a suspicion we formed. We have been excavating here for some time, and we felt the temple layout to be somehow distorted. It seemed there should be a small chamber that was not there to complete the symmetry.' He pronounced is 'w's as 'v's and vice versa, but it was easy enough to understand him. 'Today is the anniversary of Howard Carter's discovery of the tomb of Tutankhamun, you know. So, we hoped it might be a lucky omen. We inserted a little electric charge here in the wall where we imagined a hidden chamber might be; and you are here now to see the result.'

'Just so I'm clear, this temple dates from Hatshepsut's reign?'

'Yes, or shortly afterwards. Thutmosis III also added to this temple. But not in this particular part of it.'

'So, you believe you've electrified a hidden doorway leading to some sort of hideaway from the early 18th Dynasty?'

Hannelore stepped forward. She was a small, buxom woman with a disproportionately small nose. Above it her large eyes snapped impatiently. 'Rather than stand about here debating it, we could sneak a peak,' she said in perfect idiomatic, if rather sarcastic English. I have to say my sympathies lay with her. While the men were establishing their credentials and debating historical timelines, us women would have been through the hidden doorway like rats down a drainpipe.

'Please...' Adam said, motioning Hans-Dieter forward with all the graciousness of a superior officer granting a subaltern a favour. 'After you.' I suppressed another choking fit and fell into line as a good trainee Egyptologist should do behind her mentor. I knew what he was doing. He was acting out a level of command to ensure Hans-Dieter didn't banish us forthwith from his excavation site, as he had every right to do. To be fair, the tactic was working. And frankly I'd have walked over hot coals rather than leave the Satet temple without a look inside the hidden chamber.

Chapter 12

'I thought you said Thutmosis III didn't have a hand in this part of the temple,' I murmured, looking at the scene before me. 'I'd say this has all his hallmarks.' I was only the trainee, so no one took much notice. But Adam flashed a quick glance into my eyes, and I knew he was thinking the same thing.

We'd entered a small square chamber. I had to admire Hans-Dieter and Hannelore their suspicion it was here. While I knew they had survey instruments and suchlike, the chamber was little more than a niche set behind the wall of the Amun chapel. There was no doubt about it though; they'd found another hideaway. Their lucky hunch had paid off. 4 November may prove momentous yet again. This had none of the magnificence of Howard Carter's find, and was in a parlous state; but it was an astonishing discovery, nevertheless.

The walls and ceiling had once been painted. What was left of the reliefs was reminiscent of those in the hidden rock-chamber in the Theban Hills. But here huge chunks were missing. In some places the plaster had flaked, whole sections falling off and littering the stone floor like a carpet of autumn leaves. Elsewhere it seemed a determined effort had been made to take a hammer and chisel to the walls.

Hans-Dieter swung his flashlight in a slow sweep of the chamber. *'Ich verstehe nicht was ich auf der suche,'* he said. 'I don't know what it is that I am looking at.'

We all stood crowded just inside the entrance. We knew the rules. Meticulous recording and preservation of every tiny scrap of fallen plaster and all the smashed masonry were imperative. I didn't envy the German team the hours and hours of painstaking work they had ahead of them.

'I think it's a burial chamber,' Adam said slowly. 'Which is very unusual within temple walls, I'll grant you. But those great big chunks of masonry over there look like the smashed remains of a sarcophagus. And that thing in the corner' – he pointed, and Hans-Dieter lowered the beam of his torch at the spot – 'looks to me like the burnt out shell of an anthropoid coffin.' We all gazed at the charcoaled lump of wood, blackened and distorted but still vaguely discernable in shape.

'One thing's clear,' I said. 'If a burial took place here, someone was determined not to let the body rest in peace. They've hacked the place to bits.'

'Bodies, plural,' Adam corrected softly. 'Look, there's another burned out shell of a coffin over there. And there's too much smashed stone all over the floor for it to come from just one sarcophagus. Plus, the colour of the granite is different. I think we're looking at a joint burial. But I agree with you, with this amount of damage it's going to be nigh on impossible to work out whose it was. As far as I can see there's nothing left of the bodies themselves. My guess is whoever caused this destruction didn't leave until he was good and sure he'd obliterated all traces of them.'

I suppressed a shudder. Watching our step, we all moved slowly and cautiously into the chamber. 'There has got to be a clue,' Hannelore said. 'We just need to find a single inscription, a few lines of preserved text…'

I made a slow study of what little remained of the wall reliefs. I didn't have a flashlight but there was just enough daylight spilling through the doorway from the Amun chamber to illuminate the small space. Almost nothing remained intact. If once these walls told a story, it was no longer possible to read it. Nevertheless, all my instincts were screaming with the significance of this find. We were standing in Hatshepsut's temple; a temple – according to Hans-Dieter – that was later added to by Thutmosis III. That this was part of the same campaign of destruction Thutmosis perpetrated against Hatshepsut seemed obvious. I was turning away from the wall when something caught my eye. I froze and leaned closer, all the little hairs along my forearms and on the nape of my neck standing on end. 'Adam,' I whispered, reaching out for his hand. 'Look…!'

He peered at the wall just above our heads and I heard his breathing stall. He glanced back over his shoulder.

Hans-Dieter and Hannelore were making a similar study of the opposite wall, muttering away to each other in guttural German. Erich had left the chamber in search of his camera and tripod. Adam gripped my hand and stared back at the fragment of wall relief. 'It's the same symbol,' he breathed.

I nodded excitedly. I'd known I wasn't imagining it, but it was good to hear him confirm it. 'The strange double-plume-type image that Ted's not been able to decipher.'

Frustratingly, the sections of wall relief all around it had been hacked away or come loose and fallen to the floor. While Adam took his iPhone from his pocket and unobtrusively took a couple of photographs I succumbed to a bad case of the chills. Ted had said there must be a clue somewhere in Aswan to help us solve the mystery of why Thutmosis sought vengeance against his aunt-stepmother twenty years after her death. I had a strong feeling we were looking at it. Actually, we were standing in it. This whole chamber was a clue.

The volume and pitch of Hannelore and Hans-Dieter's low-toned exchange suddenly changed. Hannelore let out a small whoop.

'What have you found?' I spun round to face them and took a couple of steps across the rubble-strewn floor careful not to crunch anything underfoot.

'There's a small portion of text here,' she said, pointing to the wall. 'It reads *"Steward of the King".*'

'One of Senenmut's titles,' I exclaimed, matching her for excitement.

'It doesn't name the king in question,' she said cautiously. 'But it is highly suggestive.'

'If the wanton destruction hadn't already given the game away,' Adam murmured behind me.

I turned back to face him while Hannelore and Hans-Dieter took up another rapid exchange in their native tongue. 'You think one of the bodies buried here was Senenmut's?' I whispered, shivery with chills and bristling with goose bumps all over again.

'I don't know,' he whispered back. 'But something about this place makes my scalp prickle. It's unnerving, don't you think?' I knew exactly what he meant. The bodies might be long gone but we were standing inside an ancient burial chamber, for all that it was in a niche inside the temple walls rather than cut into the living rock like most ancient tombs. 'It doesn't seem that Senenmut was buried in either of his tombs in Thebes. And we know he holed up here in Aswan with the baby Neferamun for the last years of Hatshepsut's reign. He returned to Thebes after Hatshepsut's death to move Neferure from the cliff-tomb to the secret hideaway behind Hatshepsut's temple. And then he came back. I wouldn't stake my life on it, but I'll echo what Hannelore just said: it's highly suggestive.'

'So, *if* one of these burnt-out coffins was Senenmut's, then whose was the other one – Neferamun? And who performed the burial before Thutmosis, or his henchmen found it and hacked the place to bits?'

He gazed around at the walls, staring at what little was left of the reliefs. I could see he was mentally trying to fill in the blank spaces in much the same way the German team had painted in the outline of the missing sections on the temple walls outside. I watched him, loving the little wrinkle between his dark eyebrows. I could almost hear his brain whirring. This was Adam doing what he loved; what he should've been born to. I was glad he'd dropped the "thwarted" from his introduction of himself as an Egyptologist. Egyptology was in his blood, and he didn't need a doctorate to prove it.

'I think this is a male burial,' he said at last. 'If I'm reading them right, the reliefs originally showed the deceased being introduced to the gods, as was fairly typical certainly in royal burials. If you look around the walls at what's left of the figures, they're dressed in kilts, not sheath dresses. I don't think Neferamun was buried here.'

Erich came back with his camera equipment, so we edged cautiously sideways to give him space to set up his tripod. I picked my way between the stone chippings on the floor, careful not to step on any, to the far wall of the small chamber. I was standing between the remains of the two burnt out anthropoid coffins. Once again, I'd crossed a threshold of more than three-thousand-years. It was a spine-tingling feeling to leave the modern world and enter a space that hadn't seen the light of day for thirty centuries or more. It seemed to echo still with the sound of the hammers wielded to such devastating effect. I felt if I closed my eyes and opened them again, I might find myself transported back in time and could witness the whole event for myself. I even tried it; such was the spooky sense of time warp that settled over me. But when I opened my eyes again Erich was there with his tripod and the space resembled nothing so much as a smashed-up jigsaw; only one that would take years and years to piece together.

I looked at the charcoaled remains of the two coffins and tried to intuit who had once lain within them. Hans-Dieter and Hannelore would probably dedicate months if not years to the study of this small space. But I couldn't see how they could possibly hope to make much sense of it such was the thoroughness of the hatchet job carried out here.

I glanced at my watch and realised Adam and I would soon have to leave them to it and get back to the *Misr*. I just felt there must be *something*. Standing totally still, I let my gaze travel over the walls and floor one more time. And then I saw it. It was a small slab of rock, badly damaged for sure, but covered in tightly packed inscriptions. I drew in a sharp breath and just about stopped myself from pouncing on it. It was rather like the one Ted "borrowed" from Neferure's burial. Adam heard me gasp and spun around. 'There...' I pointed. It was half buried under plaster flakes and pinned under the charcoaled wooden frame of what was once a coffin.

He crouched down and eased it out, slowly and gently, careful not to disturb anything around it.

'What have you found?' Hannelore stepped cautiously between the piles of chippings to join us, and Hans-Dieter followed her. Adam held it flat on both palms so we could all see.

'A stele,' Hans-Dieter breathed on a note of reverence.

'Hallelujah,' Hannelore nearly shouted.

'But its in very poor condition,' Adam noted sadly. 'There are whole sections missing.'

Hans-Dieter shone his flashlight on the surface. One symbol stood out starkly at the top. Adam saw it too and lifted his gaze to look meaningfully into my eyes. We were reading each other's mind again, knowing we had to be careful not to give too much away. We had answers to questions Hans-Dieter and Hannelore couldn't dream of asking. But it would only take a thoughtless word to invoke them. If our promise to Walid was ringing half as loudly in Adam's ears as it was in mine, it was probably enough to deafen him.

'I've never seen that symbol before,' Hannelore said, frowning. 'What's it supposed to be? It looks like two interlocked feathers.'

'The same symbol's carved onto the wall over there,' Adam said, pointing.

'So, it has a significance of some sort. I wonder what it is.' She peered at the wall then back at the stele.

'There's a small section here that's undamaged,' Hans-Dieter said, tracing the hieroglyphs lightly with his fingertip. 'I think it says "...*of my father's father Wadjmose and his father before him....*" And the next bit's too damaged to read.

Hannelore wrinkled her tiny nose in concentration. 'Wadjmose,' she repeated thoughtfully. 'I think Thutmosis I had a son called Wadjmose.'

'That's right,' Adam said. 'But he died before his father so never came to the throne.'

'The whole of the next section's missing,' Hans-Dieter said, raking his long fingers through his sandy hair. 'But there's another line here that's relatively intact.' He frowned over it for a moment. 'I read it as "...*beloved brother and husband of ...*", and then there's a name that seems to start with an N. See the wavy line there,' he pointed. '...that's the hieroglyph for N, but the rest of the name is missing. *Dies ist frustrierend, nein*? Frustrating!'

A small suspicion was forming in my mind sending little bursts of nervous energy zinging through my bloodstream. I was starting to have an inkling what that mysterious symbol might mean.

'Isn't that a name there?' Hannelore pointed, indicating an inscription a little further down.

'The first part is damaged, but the latter portion might say *"something-amun"'* Hans-Dieter said a bit doubtfully. 'I think the next bit reads *"son of Amenmose".'*

'I think Amenmose was also a son of Thutmosis I,' Hannelore said. 'He and Wadjmose were brothers, but they both died before their father, which is why Hatshepsut's half-brother Thutmosis II came to the throne.'

I was sure she was right. But what we knew, and she didn't, courtesy of Ted's translation of rock-shrine hieroglyphs, was that Wadjmose also had a son called Amenmose; a son who'd indulged in an adulterous affair with the princess and God's wife Neferure and fathered her daughter Neferamun.

'You said "son" of Amenmose?' Adam queried quietly. I looked up into his eyes and saw the same suspicion dawning there that was whispering through my own consciousness.

'There's another name alongside it,' Hans-Dieter pointed out. 'It reads *"Djehuty, beloved brother and husband, born on the same day as his beloved sister and wife Neferamun, of Amenmose and Nef..."* ...and again the inscription is too damaged to read.

While Hans-Dieter and Hannelore exchanged a few words in rapid German, no doubt trying to figure out what on earth it might mean, I gazed into Adam's darkly lashed eyes. 'You said the reliefs on the walls here are fairly typical of a royal burial,' I whispered. 'Which suggests at least one of the people buried here was royal or considered himself to be.'

He nodded, squeezing my hand, and whispered back, 'And the symbol means…?'

Every fibre of my being was buzzing with a strange kind of static as I stared into his eyes and knew we'd found the answer to an ancient mystery that had perplexed archaeologists for decades. 'Twins,' I mouthed. 'Neferamun had a twin brother, born of Neferure and her cousin-lover. There was a pretender to the royal throne of Egypt after all.'

* * *

We got back to the *Misr* with scarcely enough time to don our costumes for the much-anticipated galabeya party. Even so, the first thing Adam did was put a call through to Ted. 'I can't wait to tell him! This isn't something I can put in an email. I want to hear his reaction.' But Ted wasn't in, and Adam's call went unanswered. 'Damn,' he said.

Honi greeted us at the entrance to the restaurant. He was resplendent in his long black galabeya with ornate ivory braiding, with a cape-like bolero style jacket over the top, also lavishly trimmed with braid. His fez was perched on top of his head at a jaunty angle. The little black tassel swung cheekily as he bowed to us. 'Tonight, in honour of the occasion of Mr Howard Carter's spectacular discovery of Tutankhamun's tomb, we have a sumptuous Egyptian feast for you!' He grinned at us, little walnut brown eyes twinkling between the monkey-like creases in his face. 'You will sample all our traditional Egyptian delights. Make sure you leave room for dessert. Our pastry chef has excelled himself tonight. The little delicacies made of coconut drenched in honey are particularly good.'

'We're definitely up for a celebration,' Adam's emphatic tone matched Honi's enthusiasm perfectly. 'As you can see, we've dressed up.'

'And very fine you look too,' Honi said, bowing again in honour of the effort we'd made.

Francesca and Doug rose to greet us as we approached our usual table. Doug let out a shout of laughter. 'Adam, in that get-up you look like a dodgy sheik about to ravish some innocent young maiden.'

I could see exactly what he meant, and I must say I had high hopes for a bit of ravishment later tonight. I was more than happy to play the role of innocent young maiden if required. Adam's floor-length galabeya was black, with a stiff upright collar stitched with gold tread. Over it he wore another floor-length black robe, sleeveless, tied loosely at the middle and richly decorated with gold piping. He'd wound an ornate black-and-white headscarf around his head, held in place by a gold-and-black corded head-ring of the type favoured by the sheiks of Saudi Arabia. His blue eyes flashed with dark humour and if his thoughts were running along anything like the same lines as my own – and I'm pretty sure they were – I knew we'd have no need of either his Indiana Jones hat or his new fez tonight.

'And you look the picture of Cleopatra herself,' Francesca smiled at me. 'I love all the kohl.' My own costume was a floor-length white shift dress, with a broad ornate collar in the ancient Egyptian style with a golden sash tied around my waist. I already had roughly the right hairstyle and I'd finished the look with a rather tacky golden headdress I'd found in the gift shop and, as Francesca noted, lots of kohl around my eyes. 'We feel boring in comparison,' she laughed.

It was true they hadn't gone to town in quite the same way we had. Doug was in a plan black galabeya and looked decidedly uncomfortable about it. I wondered how much effort Francesca had put into convincing him to wear it. He reminded me forcibly of Dan. I couldn't imagine any force on Earth persuading Dan to wear a galabeya. He'd asked me once why the locals insisted on parading around in dresses. By comparison if there was one thing you could say for sure about Adam and me it was that we loved the whole dressing up lark. 'You look lovely,' I assured her, and it was true. Her galabeya was a simple long shift dress in green cotton, embroidered with intricate patterns in the same soft green. It looked amazing with her colouring.

Looking around, all the other guests were similarly attired in Egyptian regalia, entering into the party spirit with varying degrees of enthusiasm if the range of costumes was anything to judge by. But entering it, nevertheless.

'I can't wait to see what Eleanor decks herself out in,' Doug said wickedly. 'I'm imagining an overblown version of the Queen of Sheba, shimmering with all the colours of the rainbow.'

We ordered sparkling wine in honour of the occasion (the cost of champagne is astronomical in Egypt) and waited for Eleanor to join us.

'So, I'm dying to know what you made of Abu Simbel,' I said to Doug as we sat down. 'Was it still a case of *once you've seen one temple you've seen them all*?'

'He *loved* it,' Francesca said with a bright smile. 'Don't let him tell you differently.'

'Well, I still thought it was a bit Disney,' Doug qualified, not wanting to appear too enthusiastic. 'I mean, those four great big statues look like they should be at the entrance to a theme park. I was expecting to go inside and find a rollercoaster at the very least. Or if not a theme park, then maybe a film set. One of those big blockbuster types with Harrison Ford in the lead role.'

Adam chuckled and shook his head, 'That's one of the marvels of the ancient world you're talking about so derisively.'

'But I'll admit the whole thing was pretty awe inspiring once I stopped expecting Steven Spielberg to call *"lights, camera, action"* at any moment. I have to say the pictures on the walls helped; all those scenes of the pharaoh riding his chariot into battle and the bloody carnage as he ripped the enemy apart. It was stirring stuff.'

'The battle of Kadesh,' Adam nodded. 'Yes, Ramses II claimed it as a great victory over the Hittites. He plastered it all over the walls of most of his temples. He wasn't a man backward in coming forward about his triumphs.'

We went on in similar vein for some time, each of us keeping half an eye on the door so as not to miss Eleanor's grand entrance. After a while we realised that we were the only table with an empty place setting for dinner. Most of the other guests had served themselves from the buffet of aromatic starters, even if they hadn't quite moved into the main course yet. The wonderful smell alone was making my stomach growl and my mouth water.

'I hope she's alright,' Adam said after a while. 'I don't feel we should start without her, but my stomach's starting to gnaw at my backbone I'm so hungry. Do you think we should check on her?'

'Let's give her another five minutes,' Doug suggested.

'So, what have you two been up to today?' Francesca asked.

We told them about our being on the spot for the momentous discovery of a hidden chamber within the walls of Hatshepsut's Satet temple.

'How exciting!' Francesca breathed. 'So, like Howard Carter, you've actually had the experience of stepping back into the past; the first people to breathe the air in that hidden room in, what, thirty-odd centuries?'

Yes, and not for the first time, I almost said. Taking the little rock-cut tomb in the Theban Hills and the stunning re-burial of Nefertiti and Akhenaten into account, this was our third bit of time travel. I was rather shocked at how blasé I'd become about the whole thing. 'Yes; and quite surreal it was too,' I smiled, giving myself a mental shake. 'But not over-flowing with gold in quite the same way.'

'It may take the German archaeologists years to make sense of what they unearthed today,' Adam said, and I saw his crossed fingers under the table. We'd both felt a guilty sense of dishonesty – or at least that we weren't playing off a completely straight bat – leaving Hans-Dieter and

Hannelore to their remarkable discovery, knowing we, a pair of amateurs, knew a whole lot more about it than they, the professionals, did. But we were sworn to secrecy. I had a feeling the world would come by the knowledge we had in its own good time. It all rested on the decision Walid Massri made when we met up next month. We told Francesca and Doug as much about the little hideaway as we dared until, glancing at my watch, I saw almost fifteen minutes had ticked by.

'I'll go and check on Eleanor,' I offered. 'She's in one of the rooms just opposite, behind the jewellery shop. I saw her lock it up and leave it yesterday.' I left the restaurant in search of our missing dinner companion. Quite frankly, it would be a relief to find she was suffering from what she'd quaintly described on the first night as the "Pharaoh's curse" and decided not to join us. Doug, Francesca, Adam and I got on famously as a foursome, but we tended to allow Eleanor's larger-than-life presence to dominate when she was with us. I was still miffed with her for her failure to prostrate herself in gratitude before Adam for the whole saving-her-from-the-deadly-jaws-of-the-crocodile incident. It sent me into a cold sweat every time I thought of it. So, generally, I tried not to. *She'd* actually been in the water with the fearsome creature. And I wasn't talking about Adam. I daresay it was a combination of these thoughts that made my knock on her cabin door somewhat more peremptory than it might otherwise have been.

There was a moment of stillness and a weird kind of silence behind the cabin door that was noticeable because somehow, I felt it hadn't been there before, although I couldn't have told you why my skin was prickling. I knocked again. 'Eleanor? It's Merry. Are you alright? It's just you're awfully late for dinner. We were getting worried about you.'

The silence magnified tenfold. There was a strange scrabbling sound. Then a scrape – like the rasping sound of a metal lock pulled back – and then a splash. Yes, it was definitely a splash.

'Eleanor?' I called again, more urgently this time.

There was a long pause. I listened to the stretching silence. That splashing noise made no sense. Finally, just when I was about to go to find Honi and ask him to unlock the door, I heard, 'Meredith? Is that you?' Eleanor's voice sounded distant and a bit distorted. I leaned my ear closer against the door and shouted against the doorjamb,

'Eleanor? Yes, it's Merry. Are you ok? Can you hear me?'

'I've locked myself in the bathroom,' was the unusual response.

I paused to exchange a confused look with someone, only to recall I was on my own, standing in the corridor outside Eleanor's cabin decked out in full Cleopatra-like regalia.

'I'm sorry?' I called, feeling a bit ridiculous. 'I didn't quite catch that. Did you say you're trapped in your bathroom?' I suddenly had visions of the antique latch sticking. Poor woman, she'd probably thought she was there for the night – although why she felt the need to lock her bathroom door when she was the sole occupant of her cabin was beyond me.

'Not trapped,' she shouted. 'I locked myself in to get away from the snake!'

The look I turned to exchange with my non-existent companion this time was positively incredulous. I know I'd had a couple of glasses of sparkling wine on an empty stomach, but still... I caught sight of my reflection in an ornate wall-mounted mirror and made a stupid face at myself. 'Did you say snake?' I called, trying to make my voice loud enough for her to hear through the closed door while quiet enough not to make myself too ludicrous to anyone else who might be within hearing range, the housekeeping staff, say. I mean, I was decked out like a tragic Egyptian queen who'd allegedly opted to commit suicide by the rather terrifying means of an asp bite. I had a horrible feeling Eleanor was playing some cruel joke on me. But then my scalp prickled again. I remembered the inexplicable splash. Something rather odd was going on.

'Yes, snake,' she shouted rather hysterically, or was it just impatiently? 'He brought it in and let it loose in the cabin.'

'Who did?' This was getting weirder by the second.

'One of the staff,' she yelled. Yes, definitely impatient. 'He was wearing that ostentatious braided galabeya and the be-tasselled fez that passes for a uniform around here. I imagine he just jumped ship. Literally. I heard the splash. He is no doubt swimming to shore even now. I have no idea whether the snake is still on the loose in my cabin.'

I was trying very hard to get a grip on the situation, but it kept slipping out of my grasp. 'What are you doing locked in the bathroom?' I shouted.

'Well, what the hell would *you* do with a deadly snake rearing up in front of you? Hold out your hand to stroke it?' Even in the extremity of emotion she still had a firm grip on her critical faculties, which is more than I could say for myself right now. 'Meredith, I credit you with a modicum of intelligence. Which is more than can be said for the tormenting little man who set the snake on me. He didn't speak a word of English, so his intentions were not completely plain to me. I daresay he thought I'd swoon on the spot or give in to whatever nefarious plan he'd hatched and was using the snake to threaten me with. I didn't wait long enough to find out. I took one look into the black eyes of that snake and bolted for the bathroom; then bolted the door behind me. I think my action may have taken both the snake and his charmer by surprise. I have been listening to strange sounds of activity in my cabin for a good half-an-hour now. I am grateful for your concern, but I don't suggest you open the cabin door until you have a snake catcher with you. I, myself, am quite content here in the bathroom for the time being.'

Chapter 13

'I don't know if she's finally flipped her lid or whether to believe her,' I whispered to Adam. Two glasses of sparkling wine were still playing havoc with my reasoning ability.

'Well, I don't think we can risk not taking her seriously. If the last laugh is on us, I suggest we accept it graciously. It's an Egyptian party night after all – maybe it's Eleanor's unusual way of entering into the spirit of things.'

We told Francesca and Doug to start their meal without us. 'Small domestic incident,' Adam explained. They knew of the ex-in-law connection and accepted this at face value.

We went in search of Honi and whispered the critical points into his ear. His eyebrows inched upwards until they almost made contact with his fez. 'A snake catcher, you say. No, I don't think we need one of those. I can catch the snake.'

We took a moment to absorb this surprising statement, staring at him open mouthed. 'What, even if it's a cobra?' I squeaked in a silly high-pitched voice that didn't sound like mine. 'Eleanor said it reared up in front of her. That sounds like a snake of the venom-spitting variety.'

'Oh yes,' he said with blithe self-confidence. 'I was a snake charmer in my younger days. I used to put on a show in some of the hotels in Luxor. I can catch it. What troubles me more is what a potentially deadly snake is doing onboard our so-wonderful boat. We did not book a snake charmer as part of tonight's entertainment.'

'Eleanor said one of the staff took it into her room and threatened her with it.'

Honi's frown deepened and grew even more perplexed. 'I know Miss Hayes is not popular with the staff. She is rather loud and complaining and not easily satisfied. But I do not believe a member of our highly trained team would take it upon himself to do such a thing, not even as a practical joke. The consequences would be too severe. Good jobs are scarce in Egypt. Those of us who are lucky enough to have one will not easily be persuaded to do something to jeopardise it. It is not in our interests to frighten tourists. Particularly not those of a disposition to make life difficult for us.' He was leading us towards the kitchen as he spoke. 'I will need a long pole to stand the best chance of success.'

We waited outside the doorway, and he emerged moments later with a long-handled toasting fork. 'This is not ideal. Catching a cobra is about elegance of movement, not force. It is important the snake does not feel threatened. The best way is with a long hook. You slide the hook under the snake and lift it, then put it in a bag. Because its movement is not restricted the snake does not feel threatened. Using that method I can catch a snake in seconds.'

'Could we make a hook out of a coat hanger and find a long pole to attach it to?' Adam asked. He sounded nervous. Indiana Jones-like it was clear he did not like snakes.

'Let us take a look to see what we are dealing with,' Honi suggested. 'I will just collect a linen laundry bag along the way.'

I couldn't rid myself of an overwhelming feeling of ridiculousness as we followed Honi back into the corridor and approached Eleanor's cabin door. Honi looked purposeful, but his black fez and braided galabeya gave him the appearance of a man in fancy dress going into battle armed with a toasting fork. He was brandishing it before him like some sort of talisman. With Adam in his full sheik get-up, and me in my exotic Cleopatra costume it was all too surreal for words. Honi rapped on Eleanor's door. 'Miss Hayes? Can you hear me? This is Honi.'

'Yes Honi, hello. Have you come with a snake catcher?' she called back. 'I am not leaving this bathroom until I know the vile reptilian creature has gone.'

'I am here with Adam and Merry. If there is a snake, I am going to...'

'Are you doubting my word?' she shouted. 'Because if so...'

'No, no...' Honi soothed. 'Of course not, dear lady; but it is possible the individual who brought the snake to your cabin took it away with him when he left.'

'I doubt that very much – ' she snorted – 'since he had the temerity to jump from the balcony into the Nile when Meredith came calling.'

Honi took a key from his pocket. 'With your permission I am coming in, Miss Hayes.'

'Stand back Merry.' Adam drew me away from the doorway. 'Just to be on the safe side...'

Honi unlocked the door, turned the handle, and gently swung it open. I saw him make a slow searching study of the room from the threshold. Then a kind of stillness settled over him. 'Ah yes,' he said. 'There is a snake.' I nearly fainted on the spot. Right up until this point I'd been sure it was all some kind of elaborate charade being played out to add some spice to the evening's proceedings. 'Come here my beauty,' Honi said softly.

He stepped across the threshold very slowly, making as little movement as possible. I couldn't help but follow. I was drawn after him as if magnetised. I needed to see this snake for myself.

It was big and black, about four feet long; coiled on the floor in front of Eleanor's dressing table. As Honi approached it reared up to a height of almost two feet with its big black hood spread and its beady eyes fixed on Honi's face.

'The toasting fork is not big enough,' Honi said softly. 'This is a large snake. I will need to catch him by hand.' He passed the toasting fork back to Adam and moved forward into the room carrying only the linen laundry bag.

I held my breath as Honi and the snake stared hypnotically into each other's eyes. The snake was swaying sinuously, hissing and flicking its tongue. I wondered if it was deciding between spitting venom or just springing forward to sink its fangs into Honi's face.

Adam and I stood mesmerised in the doorway. This was a sluggish kind of fear, very different from the terror of watching Adam in the water with the crocodile. That had been fear of the heart pounding, blood-churning variety. Everything had sped up as if someone had pressed the fast-forward button on a remote control. Now my heart was thumping with a slow steady rhythm that hurt. My lungs felt constricted. I like to think I was breathing but the oxygen didn't seem to be circulating. My blood wasn't so much churning as stuck fast, glued up and congealed in my veins.

'Honi, please be careful,' Adam said in strangled tones.

Honi started waving the laundry bag in front of the cobra's face, edging forwards as he did so. 'I need to be close enough to reach behind his hood,' he murmured. The snake followed the movement of the laundry bag, moving its upper body rhythmically as if swaying in time to some music the rest of us were unable to hear. The movement was frighteningly hypnotic. Honi was crouching down as he approached, until his eyes were level with the cobra's flattened head. My lungs felt as if they might explode with the breath I was holding. There was an almost primeval horror in watching a man and a big black snake pitting their wits against each other.

Honi waved the laundry bag some more. The snake lunged at it. I shrieked and jumped backwards. Honi was equally agile on his feet, leaping out of harms way.

'Meredith?' Eleanor called from the bathroom. 'Are you hurt?'

'No, no, not at all,' I assured her weakly, trembling with fright. 'Honi is a very brave man. I'm sorry Honi. I know I'm a frightful coward.'

Not for a split second did he break eye contact with the snake. 'It is perfectly understandable Merry. Please do not trouble yourself. This powerful creature is testing me out. He is a clever one. Just stay by the doorway and everything will be ok.'

Honi and the cobra resumed their sinuous dance. There was a long moment of drawn-out tension; then things moved pretty quickly. Honi waved the linen bag some more. The cobra leaned forwards but without lunging this time. Honi reached behind its flattened hood and in a lightning strike pinned the cobra's head against the floor. 'Pass me the toasting fork, Adam, would you please?' he asked calmly, while the snake writhed and coiled violently, trying to escape.

Adam sucked in a shaky breath as if bucking up the courage. He crept forward on tiptoe to hand it over, immediately leaping back to re-join me by the door. 'Give me a crocodile any day,' he murmured with a shudder.

Moving with a deft and steady speed, Honi held the cobra's head in place with the fork, while he eased the laundry bag open. 'Now this is the tricky part,' he murmured. 'I need to catch him by the tail so I can feed him headfirst into the bag. I must be quick, so I suggest you stand well back.'

I'm not sure we could get much further back without actually moving outside into the corridor. But we needed no persuading to edge to the other side of the open doorway. I didn't quite see how Honi did it, he moved so fast. One moment he had the cobra by the head, the next by its tail; and a moment after that he was tying the cord of the laundry bag into a tight knot with a self-satisfied air. The deadly snake was heavy inside it.

My knees gave way, and I sank onto the floor, limp with relief. Adam subsided alongside me. 'Phew Honi,' he rasped, letting out the air in his lungs in a great rush. 'That was a few minutes I don't ever want to live through again. You were awesome.'

Honi's little monkey face creased into a happy smile. 'I am always glad to be of service. With a snake it is just a question of showing respect and judging the moment. Now, I have an investigation to perform among the staff; and I must take this magnificent creature somewhere where he can do no harm and equally come to no harm.' He lowered his voice to a whisper. 'If you excuse me, I will allow you to be the first ones to speak to Miss Hayes. I would happily face ten cobras every day rather than just one of her. She is a formidable woman, to be sure.' And with his weighty cargo shifting about in the bottom of the linen laundry bag he bowed himself out of the room. Adam and I stared at each other, speechless.

'Has Honi gone?' Eleanor called from behind the panelled bathroom door.

'Yes, Eleanor.' Adam pushed himself back up off the floor, gave himself a small shake and held out his hand to help me up. 'He's taken the snake with him. It's safe for you to come out now.'

The bolt scraped back, the bathroom door opened and out stepped Eleanor. I'm not sure who did the biggest double take, her or us. It's probably fair to say she wasn't expecting to be greeted by Cleopatra and the Sheik. We were equally unprepared for the vision of loveliness she presented wrapped in a long fluffy white bathrobe; with a white towel wound turban-style around her head and dainty white mules on her feet. The absence of clashing colours and her usual milk-bottle-lens glasses rendered her really quite beautiful. I'd suspected as much on that first night, peering through the layers of hideousness she rejoiced in wearing to glimpse the woman underneath. She had a flawless complexion, and her eyes were an attractive hazel colour.

'Wow, Eleanor, you look amazing!' I blurted before I could stop myself. I was still in shock after all.

She peered suspiciously at me as if searching my face for any lack of sincerity. 'Thank you, Meredith,' she said at last, not finding it. 'I was only just deciding what to wear when that houseboy knocked on the door.' I wondered if she'd developed her garishly flamboyant style as a kind of armour to stop anyone getting too close, but didn't have time to pursue this intriguing line of conjecture as she went on, 'After that, all thoughts of dressing for dinner were rather driven from my mind.'

'What exactly happened?' Adam asked frowning.

Eleanor drew the little cushioned stool out from under the dressing table where a few moments ago the cobra had been writhing. She plopped herself onto it and gazed at us a bit myopically, waving for us to sit down on the bed. Her manner was as regal as ever, but I was still getting used to her new look as the woman in white. 'He simply knocked on the door. When I opened it, he held up a wicker basket. As he was dressed like all the other staff in a long black robe with all that elaborate braiding all over it, I assumed he'd come to change the towels and that it was a laundry basket he was carrying. As soon as he was inside the cabin, he closed the door behind him. Then he snatched the lid off the basket and that filthy flat-headed black snake rose up out of it. The young man jabbered something at me in Arabic pointing at my throat. Discerning that was where he intended the snake to sink its fangs into me, I threw my hairbrush across the room. Luckily it was right next to me on the dressing table so I could snatch it up in an instant. The snake reared towards it, and I used the distraction to fling myself into the bathroom and bolt the door.'

'Quick thinking,' Adam approved. 'I dread to think what would have happened otherwise.'

Eleanor gave a small shrug. 'I think the survival instinct kicked in, that's all. I perched on the lid of the toilet seat listening to the strange sounds emanating from the cabin. I imagine the boy was some kind of snake charmer and knew how to control the hideous creature. I was just wondering if he intended waiting me out when you came knocking on the door Meredith.' She got up and walked across the cabin to the still-open door leading to the balcony. She stepped out onto it, peered down into the dark waters of the Nile, then came back inside, closed the door behind her and locked it, swishing the curtains closed. 'I shall think twice before opening my cabin door another time.'

Adam was gazing around the room. It was one of the *Misr's* best, a fine example of Ottoman styling. There was no sign of anything amiss. 'So, what was he doing?'

A shared thought struck us, and we all swung our eyes towards the wardrobe at the same moment. Eleanor moved across to it and opened the little latch. As she pulled back the door it was immediately obvious the small metal safe had been taken apart with screwdrivers and a hacksaw. 'But nothing's been taken,' she said confusedly. 'My passport's still here, and a whole pile of Egyptian banknotes.'

I stared at her and everything suddenly slotted into place. 'Your handbag was snatched at Edfu temple. At Kom Ombo someone attempted to mug you. Earlier today we overheard you haranguing… I mean politely asking Honi why the housekeeping staff felt it necessary to move your belongings around.'

Adam caught my drift. 'You're saying someone searched her cabin.'

'Exactly. It's obvious.'

Eleanor plunked herself back on the ornate stool, looking perplexed; as well she might. I spoke my thoughts aloud as I attempted to fit it all together in my head. 'Originally they thought Eleanor might be carrying around with her whatever it is they're after, either in her handbag or on her person,' I addressed Adam initially; then turned to Eleanor. 'When it became obvious that wasn't the case they decided to search your cabin, Eleanor, while you were safely out of the way on your excursion to Abu Simbel. But they still couldn't find what they were looking for. So, tonight, a young man brings a deadly snake in here to frighten you into unlocking the safe for him; except that your instincts for self-preservation meant he had to do the job for himself.'

'It's all sounding horribly plausible,' Eleanor said with a small frown wrinkling her brow under the towel. 'But how do you explain the crocodile? You know I always felt I was pushed.'

I shuddered at the thought of it. 'It's possible the crocodile incident was somehow contrived to get you out of the way. One of those friendly felucca boys may not have been quite so friendly after all.'

'Or maybe that *was* just an accident,' Adam said. 'I'd like to think no one's actually setting out to murder you, despite the snake. I agree with Merry; the cobra was probably just meant to frighten you out of your wits, not actually kill you. Besides, I don't see how a potential thief could blag his way on board the felucca *and* onto the *Misr*.'

'Whichever way you look at it,' I said. 'You've got something someone else wants, and they're willing to resort to some pretty nasty methods to get it. Are you sure there's nothing missing from the safe?'

Eleanor shook her head, just as a sharp rat-tat sounded on the door. 'Miss Hayes, Merry and Adam, it is I Honi. May I come in?'

Adam went to open the door to him.

'I regret to inform you we have had a stowaway on board,' Honi said baldly. 'I have made a search of the boat and found a set of grubby old clothes and a pillow stashed behind some machinery in the engine room. It seems this stowaway has stolen one of our uniforms, which is how he was able to move around the boat freely and approach your cabin unchallenged, Miss Hayes. He will not dare to attempt to climb back on board now. My team is alerted to the danger and keeping a vigilant look-out.'

I scratched my earlobe, distracted for a moment by the thought that at least on our dahabeeyah the staff-guest ratio would be small enough that we'd notice a newcomer. In the current circumstances it struck me as a distinct advantage our little sailing boat would have over this luxurious and staff-stuffed steamship. But I wasn't distracted for long. 'So, this same person has been trailing you, stowed away on board possibly all the way from Luxor. Think Eleanor,' I entreated her. 'What have you got that someone would make all that effort for?' Even as the words left my lips and she frowned in open mystification my brain lit up with the answer. 'The necklace!' I practically shouted. 'It must be the necklace! At Kom Ombo the young man you said tried to ravish you actually pulled apart the collar on your blouse – I'll bet it was just far enough to see if you were wearing any jewellery underneath.' I didn't miss the little look of disappointment that swept across her face. She still wanted to believe it was her feminine charms he was hoping to catch sight of. I was sorry to rip the delusion of herself as a fantasy figure away from her, but it was all becoming horribly clear to me, so I swept on, 'And tonight you said the man with the snake was jabbering away in Arabic and pointing to your throat. He was asking you about the necklace!'

'What necklace?' Adam asked in confusion.

Even Eleanor was looking a bit baffled.

'Eleanor, that first night on board you told us you were late for dinner because you were held up in Luxor haggling over a necklace at a shop in the Souk, remember? You said the shopkeeper was trying to hoodwink you into believing it was a genuine artefact you were purchasing but you weren't fooled. You'd determined the price you were willing to pay and wouldn't be budged, telling him you'd stand there all night if necessary and catch up with the cruise boat at Edfu. Is it possible you told him which cruise boat?'

'I may well have done,' Eleanor acknowledged, while Adam stared at me open-mouthed.

'Merry, how do you remember all that?'

'Well, you see, it's just I was rather fascinated by Eleanor when she first joined us,' I admitted, not looking at her while I said so. 'You may not have been concentrating on her story as you were still in shock at finding your ex-sister-in-law joining us for dinner.'

'But that necklace is just a rather decorative piece of costume jewellery of no intrinsic value whatsoever,' Eleanor protested.

I raised an eyebrow, doubting it very much. 'So where is it now? They've searched your handbag, your person, your cabin and your safe and not found it. What on Earth have you done with it?'

Eleanor gave me a strange look and reached into the pocket of her fluffy white bathrobe. 'Funny you should ask me, Meredith. You see, tonight I was planning on making a gift of it to you.' I gaped at her, not following. 'You see I know I have behaved in a rather off-hand manner towards you. It's not an easy thing to see another woman in the place of one's adored baby sister. This is not an excuse, but I hope it will suffice as an explanation of sorts. I don't think I appreciated what a good thing Tabitha had in Adam until she left him to go off gallivanting with that feckless young wine merchant of hers.' She turned to Adam, leaving me gazing at her, speechless. 'And I'm quite aware I owe a debt of gratitude to you, Adam, for saving my life. I know I never exactly welcomed you to the bosom of my family with open arms when you married Tabitha. We Hayes's are a strange lot, as I'm quite sure you discovered for yourself. I don't think I was ready to let Tabitha go; not to anyone. She was my little princess. It was nothing personal against you. You just happened to be the first man she took up with.'

'The necklace…' I said weakly. Eleanor never did anything by halves and the onslaught of her admission of fallibility, delivered with her usual hurricane-like force left me breathless.

'Yes, the necklace,' she said, drawing a flat box from the large, square pocket sewn onto the front of her bathrobe. 'It was in the safe until literally a few moments before that heathen with the snake rapped on my door. I'd just taken it out, thinking it might be a nice gesture of conciliation to give it to you. You're a pretty girl, and clearly much better suited to Adam here than my soppy sister, for all that I love her. I'd been reflecting on the whole crocodile incident and thinking I'd behaved rather badly. As tonight was party night, it seemed a perfect time to make amends. I thought I might buy Adam a bottle of his favourite tipple, offer you the necklace and give you both my blessing. I mean; I know you don't need my blessing,' she qualified, looking a bit sheepish. 'But I didn't think it would hurt to offer it regardless. It is not a pleasant characteristic to bear a grudge. I like to think I am above such things. A few little brushes with danger serve to make one reflect on things. I didn't want to appear like a wicked old witch in your eyes. So, I took the necklace from the safe. I bought it on a whim in Luxor. I'd thought to give it to Tabitha; but in all honesty she doesn't deserve it, and that new man of hers seems to be showering her with gold baubles. So, I thought it might be a nice gesture to give it to you. When that young heathen came rapping on my door, I just slipped it into my pocket. And here it is.' She held the flat box out towards me.

Poor old Honi. He'd tried hard to follow this exchange. But he didn't know the family connection, so it was all a bit beyond him. He gave a small cough. 'I do not wish to intrude upon your offer of friendship,' he said with a small formal bow, the tassel on his fez swinging forward. 'If you excuse me, I will return to my duties. Once again, Miss Hayes, please accept my most humble apologies for the most regrettable experience you have been subjected to this evening. It will be my pleasure of course to refund you the full cost of your cruise with us. I must beg of you please that you do not make a complaint of this incident.' He was ringing his hands together in appeal. It was clear he was far more terrified of Eleanor than of the deadliest of snakes. 'Here on the *Misr* we pride ourselves on giving world class service and an unforgettable experience.'

'Unforgettable certainly,' Eleanor murmured.

Honi nearly prostrated himself. 'Please, my dear lady. Our poor beleaguered country suffers enough…'

'It's alright Honi,' she said in a soft soothing caress-like voice I'd never heard her use before. It was much more appealing than her usual strident tones. 'I know it wasn't your fault that some maniac was able to gain access to my cabin with a poisonous snake in his laundry basket. I have your assurance the security has been tightened, and that is good enough for me. I won't promise never to tell the story – I'm sure with a little embellishment I could become quite the heroine of the piece. But I do promise not to retell it in a letter of complaint. Now does that satisfy you? Especially if I portray you as a hero, which of course you are!'

'It does, my dear Miss Hayes; it does!' he grinned, more monkey-featured than ever.

She gazed at him for a moment. 'And you should probably start calling me Eleanor,' she muttered. 'Since you seem to be on first name terms with just about everyone else. If it's not too late for dinner you can tell the chef, we'll be along shortly.'

'It will be my pleasure Miss… I mean Ma'am… I mean Eleanor.'

'The necklace…' I croaked again, once this lavish display of affection was out of the way and Honi had bowed himself deeply and respectfully from the room.

'Ah yes.' She handed it over to me.

Adam was sitting alongside me on the bed. I heard his sharp intake of breath as I prised open the small catch and lifted the lid. My own gasp was no less audible.

'Yes, it is a rather attractive piece, isn't it?' Eleanor said. 'I think those purple stones are supposed to be amethysts. The shopkeeper told me amethysts were mined near the Red Sea in ancient times. Apparently, they were one of Cleopatra's favourite stones, so you've chosen the right outfit tonight, Meredith – I mean Merry,' she corrected herself. 'I think those other stones are paste and glass versions of lapis lazuli, turquoise and carnelian. The setting is real gold; hence my willingness to pay what I did. It's a nicely crafted trinket, don't you think? Perhaps bluer than I'd have chosen myself with both the lapis lazuli and the turquoise…'

'Blue was the colour of royalty,' Adam said dazedly.

'Yes, so the shopkeeper told me,' Eleanor said. 'I think he was trying to ratchet up the price.'

She still didn't get it. Despite everything that had happened to her, and all her undoubted schoolmistress intelligence, she'd got it fixed in her head that it was a fake necklace she'd purchased in the Souk. So, in her eyes, a fake necklace it remained. I gaped inelegantly at her, and forcibly snapped my jaws shut.

'May I be horribly rude and ask what you paid for it?' Adam said, never once lifting his gaze from the necklace nestling in its felt-lined box.

'Well, I wouldn't usually say,' Eleanor said, shifting slightly on the stool. 'I was taught it's vulgar to talk about money. But since it seems to have created such a stir, I'll make an exception. I paid one hundred English pounds. I felt it was a fair price. But judging by the lengths those scoundrels have gone to to get it back, I imagine they decided in retrospect it was worth considerably more. Perhaps the semi-precious stones are the genuine article after all. I'll even stretch incredulity to accept those purple bits of glass are real amethysts if you say so. The looks on both your faces are a bit of a giveaway. Ah well, you can have it with my blessing, Merry. It's brought me nothing but trouble. Close encounters with bag-snatchers, muggers, crocodiles and deadly snakes were not on my list of must-do experiences when I was planning this trip to Egypt. I'll be happy if the rest of my sightseeing can pass off without incident.'

I looked up into her eyes. 'Eleanor, there's no way I can accept this. It's…'

She held up her hand in a peremptory gesture, interrupting me. 'Meredith… Merry; I will be offended if you do not. Now, I don't know about the pair of you, but I want to get on with the rest of my holiday. This time next week I will be back at school, steeling myself to stand in assembly in front of a load of gum-chewing girls. Honi promised us a whirling dervish and a belly dancer tonight. And I understand Tariq has devised a rather brain-teasing quiz just to see if we have been paying attention while he's been showing us around. I'm hungry, and tonight was billed as an Egyptian feast. I want to raise a glass to Mr Howard Carter. It is the anniversary of his discovery of Tutankhamun's tomb after all. Will you forgive me if I finish getting ready and join you in the dining room in ten minutes?'

'She has no idea what she's just given me,' I whispered to Adam a few moments later, stumbling along the corridor in a worse state of shock than either the snake or the crocodile had inflicted on me.

'It's a genuine Pharaonic necklace,' Adam said, leaning against the wall as if he might fall over if he didn't.

'It's more than genuine,' I choked. 'Don't you recognise it?'

282

Chapter 14

'The symbol you couldn't decipher means "twins",' I told Ted by satellite, mobile-to-mobile. He'd seen Adam had tried to call him and left a message for us to ring him back as soon as we returned to our cabin. We'd ducked out of the quiz, since Adam had helped devise, it so knew all the answers. But in all other ways we'd tried hard to act normal for the galabeya party. Or as normal as possible given we were both grappling with the full enormity of the necklace and all its possible implications. I gave myself a little mental shake and re-focused on what I was telling Ted which, in itself, was staggering enough. 'It solves the mystery of why Thutmosis III left it twenty years to start his campaign of destruction against the memory of Hatshepsut and her lover Senenmut.'

'You're saying Neferure had twins, a girl and a boy?' The incredulity in Ted's voice transmitted itself across a few hundred miles of Egypt from Cairo to Aswan.

'Yes; Neferamun and Djehuty; twin brother and sister, born of Neferure, daughter of Hatshepsut; and Amenmose, son of Wadjmose. Since Wadjmose was Hatshepsut's full brother, both born of Thutmosis I and his great royal wife Queen Ahmes, I'm guessing Djehuty felt he had a claim to the throne every bit as strong, if not stronger, than that of

Thutmosis's son Amenhotep. If Neferamun considered herself a hereditary princess, it's a pretty safe bet her twin brother and eventual husband considered himself a hereditary prince, for all that he was born on the wrong side of the blanket. By marrying each other they preserved the royal blood and were well positioned to stake a joint claim.'

Adam had insisted I should be the one to bring Ted up to speed. He was sitting watching me now, propped against the pillows, his eyes the deep violet colour they took on when he was in the grip of Egyptological fever or some other strong emotion. I blew him a quick kiss, gazing into his eyes as I resumed my explanation. 'Whether or not Senenmut lived long enough to see it I don't know, but I think it's pretty clear Djehuty mounted some sort of claim for the throne when he was in his early twenties, so approximately twenty years after Hatshepsut's death. I have no idea whether or not Thutmosis knew his dead wife had given birth to twins who'd been spirited away to safety. Instinctively I feel both Hatshepsut and Senenmut must have hoodwinked him; allowing him to believe any child of the union between his wife and her cousin Amenmose died at the same time Neferure did, as part of the birthing process. I couldn't tell you whether Hatshepsut and Senenmut were happy about it. It seems to me Hatshepsut went into a steady decline after her daughter died and Senenmut took the twins away. I suppose she felt she had no choice. It was a case of giving in to the need to have the babies taken to safety or stand by and watch them be slaughtered. I have no idea whether Hatshepsut or Senenmut foresaw the implications of their actions.'

'You're saying Djehuty led some kind of coup?'

'I don't really know. But it seems to me the evidence points that way. I think it's fair to say he staked a claim; yes.'

'But Thutmosis had the full force of the army behind him,' Ted said. 'He wasn't going to let some upstart from the provinces – no matter how supposedly royal – upset the apple cart. Thutmosis was the greatest warrior pharaoh Egypt ever had. He never lost a military campaign; and he fought something like fourteen of them. Djehuty really didn't stand a chance.'

'Maybe not but it helps to explain the vitriol Thutmosis felt against Hatshepsut and Senenmut,' I said. 'Even if he was able to dispatch Djehuty with barely a flicker of his military might, it must have been a pretty bitter pill to swallow to find he'd been duped quite so spectacularly. He knew Hatshepsut and Senenmut must have colluded to keep Neferure's offspring from him.'

'I wonder what happened to Amenmose,' Ted mused. 'I mean; he was the father to those twins.'

'We haven't uncovered anything,' I said. 'But if you were Thutmosis III, and you knew your wife had allowed herself to become pregnant to a man who was a cousin to you both, how do you think you might react?'

'Fair point.' Ted conceded. 'I guess Amenmose must have realised his days were numbered.'

'What's clear is that by the time Djehuty died, his twin-sister-and-wife Neferamun was either pregnant or had already given birth to their daughter, who styled herself the next hereditary princess, Neferkhare. That much we know from the stele you found, Ted. Adam and I are hazarding a guess that the hidden chamber in the Satet temple on Elephantine Island was that of Senenmut and Djehuty. But we can't be sure. The amount of damage would certainly suggest it was part of Thutmosis's bitter campaign of vengeance. He smashed the place to bits and set fire to both the coffins. It's only because they were coated in resin they weren't destroyed completely. I have a feeling that German team have years of work ahead of them to have a hope of working it out.'

There was a short silence then Ted let out a long breath. 'Merry, your ability to be on the spot when something momentous happens astonishes me.'

'And you don't know the half of it,' I murmured, looking at the flat box on the dressing table.

'Why? What else have you found?'

'It's not so much what I've found as what I've been given. I'm handing the telephone across to Adam. He can tell you all about it.'

Adam and I swapped places, and I sat in a kind of semi-daze watching him while he told the story. Even though I was sitting across the room from him, propped up against the pillows, I still heard Ted's startled *'What...!?'* when Adam told him about the necklace.

'Yes, there's no doubt about its authenticity. It's one of the finest pieces of 18th Dynasty jewellery I've ever seen. It needs a bit of cleaning up, I'll grant you. But how that shopkeeper in Luxor didn't know what he was selling is beyond me. I can only imagine he thought it was a nicely done replica, like so many of the trinkets on sale in the tourist markets; based on original artefacts and worked up by modern craftsmen. Eleanor thought she was buying a fancy piece of costume jewellery. But quite frankly Ted, I don't know how she can have mistaken it for anything other than genuine. It makes some of the most exquisite pieces in Tutankhamun's tomb look like trifling bagatelles. I can only imagine it must have been dimly lit inside that shop.'

'What's more interesting is how it found its way into the shop in the first place,' I muttered darkly. 'Just about the last place on Earth it should have been. A museum, maybe, but not a shop. It's certainly not where it was the last time we saw it.'

Adam gazed across at me, and the expression in his eyes made all the little hairs stand up on the nape of my neck. 'Ted, I hope you're sitting down. You're not going to believe what I'm about to tell you…'

I shifted forward so I was sitting on the edge of the bed. I wanted to hear Ted's reaction.

'It's not just any old 18th Dynasty necklace,' Adam said slowly, his voice throbbing with the significance of what he was about to impart. 'It's Nefertiti's necklace. Merry swears to it… Ted, are you still there…?' I could hear the far-off sound of Ted's choking fit. I reached up and took the telephone back from Adam.

'It's definitely Nefertiti's necklace Ted,' I said as his coughing subsided. 'The last time I saw it it was spilling out of the broken jewellery casket inside the tomb. Jessica commented on it, remember? While Dan was admiring the chariot, she said if she could choose one item it would be the necklace.' Ted was utterly silent now, absorbing the shock and no doubt wondering if he dared believe his ears. So, I went on, 'If you recall, I spent a lot of time in that tomb searching for a way to free us after Adam and I got trapped there and before the rest of you rescued us. I searched through most of the boxes looking for a rope. I'd spotted the necklace long before Jessica picked it out. It's an exquisite piece – absolutely stunning; full of semi-precious stones set in pure gold.' As I spoke, I lifted the lid on the square box, staring at the indescribably gorgeous piece winking darkly at me from the felt lining. Whichever way I looked at it, I just couldn't get my head around the fact I was sitting here in my cruise-boat cabin staring at a necklace that had once adorned the swan-like neck of ancient Egypt's most enigmatic queen. There was no way Adam or I dared lift it from its modern box. I was terrified to so much as touch it.

Ted sucked in a long breath. When he spoke, his voice was shaking slightly. 'You realise what this means...?'

'Yes,' I nodded, hearing the slight tremor in my own voice. It was matched by the trembling that hit my hands all of a sudden as I contemplated it. 'Either one of our friends slipped the necklace into his or her pocket, a bit like you did with the stele Ted; a single, opportunistic bit of pilfering while we were concentrating on getting two unconscious men out of the tomb. In which case I have no idea how it found its way into that shop in the Souk. Or...'

'Or someone has found a way to get inside the tomb and is systematically smuggling items out of it, intent on a spot of contraband.' Adam said chillingly, leaning his head close to mine so Ted could hear him.

'Either way, the *Misr* is steaming back to Luxor tomorrow. Once there, we intend to waste no time finding out what's going on.'

* * *

The *Misr* arrived in Luxor late in the afternoon as the sun was starting to set over the Theban hills on the western horizon. We'd spent a jittery day sunning ourselves up on deck, knowing there was nothing we could do until we got back. Every few minutes one or other of us made the trip back to our cabin to check Nefertiti's necklace was still securely stored in our safe.

The stowaway bag-snatcher-cum-mugger-cum-snake-charmer had made no attempt to come back on board. Honi had battened down the hatches to such an extent, I was thinking of renaming the *Misr* Fort Knox. I could only imagine, having failed in his mission to retrieve the necklace from Eleanor, our stowaway had gone scurrying back to Luxor empty-handed. I daresay he had a boss he had to report back to. I wondered what conclusion they might reach about Eleanor's apparent ability to make the necklace vanish into thin air.

Tonight, the *Misr* guests were due to attend the after-dark Son-et-Lumière show at Karnak. Tomorrow a full day of sightseeing in Luxor was lined up, and the day after that everyone was due to disembark at the official end of the cruise. Adam and I said our goodbyes as the *Misr* docked at the little landing platform by Luxor Bridge. We weren't staying for the last set of excursions. We'd done them all before anyway – and we didn't feel we had a moment to lose.

'Let us know if you get your dahabeeyah up and running,' Doug said jovially, slapping Adam on the back, and leaning forward to kiss my cheek. 'I daresay I can suffer another week on the Nile if you promise to feed me well and steer clear of Lake Nasser and its resident crocs.'

Francesca hugged us both. 'Yes, do let us know how you get on. I hope things settle down in Egypt, so the tourist industry picks up again. It's been a bit strange travelling on a cruise boat that's only half full. I wish you all the luck in the world with your brave venture.'

Eleanor approached us as we were bidding a fond farewell to Honi in the reception area at the foot of the carved staircase. He gave us a last monkeyish wink and turned back to his duties.

'Adam and Merry,' Eleanor said regally. 'I'm sorry you won't be joining us for the sound and light show tonight.'

'Just stick close by Doug and Francesca,' Adam advised her. 'Don't go wandering off on your own. I don't think it's likely those rogues will risk another attempt on you. Honi's going to send one of the security men from the boat along with Tariq for the rest of the sightseeing trips, just in case. They must have concluded by now that you don't have the necklace anymore – although I'll bet you've given them some sleepless nights wondering what you've done with it. But I don't want you taking any unnecessary chances. Promise me?'

She gave him a long, searching look, then leaned forward and kissed his cheek. 'I'm glad we ran into each other on this trip, Adam. It's been a pleasure.' Somehow, I don't think she was talking about his daredevil stunt to rescue her from the jaws of the crocodile. Adam blushed and gave a modest little gesture. But I was glad she'd acknowledged she'd misjudged him. I sensed a change in Eleanor. She looked softer. It might be something to do with the fact she'd dispensed with her milk-bottle-lens glasses, or perhaps that the colours she was wearing didn't clash quite so violently as before. She'd teamed the lilac blouse she'd been wearing on the first night with white linen trousers and a white headscarf. She looked quite stylish.

'You can see ok without your glasses?' I asked her as she turned towards me.

'Contact lenses,' she said shortly. 'It's sheer laziness that I don't put them in every day.' So, shortsightedness wasn't the reason she was favouring me with a similarly penetrating stare to the one she'd bestowed on Adam. 'You know, Merry, no one has ever told me I look amazing before.'

I stared at her, thinking it the saddest thing I'd ever heard. 'It's true,' I said, and gave her an awkward sort of hug. 'And thank you for the necklace. It's a very grand gesture indeed.'

'More so than she'll ever know,' Adam said as we turned away and made our way down the gangplank. 'She's not such a bad old stick, is she?'

We returned to the Jolie Ville Hotel to dump our bags before setting out on our mission to discover how Nefertiti's necklace had turned up in the Luxor tourist bazaar. 'Eleanor couldn't remember exactly which shop she bought it from in the Souk,' he remarked. 'She said they all look very much alike.'

'I'm not sure our best bet is to skulk around the Souk in any event.' I said. 'We don't want to alert anyone that we know what it is they've been trying to get back from Eleanor. I think our best bet is to stake out Hatshepsut's temple like we said and see if we can stumble across any illicit activity there.'

There's one major difference between the Egyptian desert night-time in June and in November; and that's the temperature. Back in June when Adam and I first came to Hatshepsut's temple in the dead of night to go tomb hunting it was suffocatingly hot, a bit like being wrapped in a thick black velvet cloak spangled with diamond stars. This time around the heavens were still jewel encrusted but the stars seemed pearlier, and the air temperature held a crystalline quality like pure cut glass. It was cold.

Hatshepsut's graceful temple, rising on long, pillared terraces to connect with its stark, mountainous backdrop looked especially bewitching lit by carefully angled floodlights. We knew these would be switched off soon and used their radiant illumination as a cover to skirt the dense shadows of the temple foreground and scramble into a spot in the ruined Montuhotep temple, set slightly to the south. It gave us a good view of Hatshepsut's temple and specifically the Hathor chapel on the middle terrace. Inside the chapel was a small rock-cut shrine. And there – impossibly, unbelievably - carved deep into the hillside and accessed by a concealed ancient stone doorway was our secret tomb.

I felt quite sick knowing something had been taken from it. It wasn't the same as Ted slipping the stele into his satchel. His actions were the result of scholarly fever. He'd been in the grip of the fierce thirst for historical insight and knowledge. I'd never, not for a single solitary second, doubted the purity of Ted's intentions with regard the stele, nor his promise either to return it to the tomb or hand it over to Walid at the Cairo Museum. But this was different. Whichever way I looked at it, one of our little gang had picked up Nefertiti's necklace not for its intrinsic archaeological value but for its saleability. The thought of it made my blood run cold. And if it wasn't a single, opportunistic crime carried out in the extremity of the moment, then…

But I couldn't pursue this line of thinking. Not without proof. It was too horrifying to contemplate. I pictured the faces of each member of the little rescue party who'd saved Adam and me from a slow and agonising death inside the tomb. Everything in me recoiled from accepting any one of them capable of breaching the solemn oath we'd all sworn. But there was another possibility… equally horrific… but not quite so heart breaking.

'Your hunches are usually right,' Adam said, rubbing his hands up and down his upper arms to warm up. 'So, I'm willing to go along with this one; but I can't help but hope we won't need to be here all night. Why are you so sure we stand a chance of observing some nocturnal activity?'

I wriggled closer to him and nudged under his arm. 'It's only a month until we're due to meet up to hear Walid's decision about whether to go public with the tomb. Assuming the necklace wasn't a one-off; if I were the one indulging in an illicit bit of tomb robbing, I'd want to have the portable items out of there and the place looking as untouched as possible long before then. Time's running out.'

'But it's been five months, Merry. Whoever it is has had plenty of time.'

'Not necessarily,' I shook my head slowly. 'It's no simple matter to work the ancient mechanism that opens that stone door. If someone wants to get back inside the tomb, they need the Mehet-Weret Aten discs from Tutankhamun's ritual couch…'

'… or replicas,' he reminded me. 'We used replicas to get inside.'

'Well yes; but only because we'd found out the precise weight and measurements of the originals.'

'But we're not the only ones who can figure that out.'

'Perhaps. But I still don't think it would be the work of moments, especially since the replicas you made are still languishing at the bottom of the pit shaft.'

'So, you reckon whoever-it-is has found another way inside and may still be going in at night to remove the smaller items and then – what? Make the tomb look as untouched as possible so he or she can brazen it out if and when the time comes and pretend nothing's been taken?'

I shrugged, snuggling closer to the warmth of Adam's chest. 'He or she may think it's worth the risk, since none of us was exactly in there long enough to take an inventory.'

'Except you.' I could hear the smile in his voice. 'You riffled through just about every box and casket in the place.'

'Well yes, but only because I was searching for something to help set us free. I don't think I could exactly list out all the contents item by item.'

'But you knew the necklace on sight.'

'I doubt there's a woman on the face of this earth who wouldn't. I'll bet Jessica would know it on sight too. It's the one thing she commented on.'

'So, you think Jessica is our thief?'

I snorted rather inelegantly. 'I doubt it very much.' Actually, it had never occurred to me. I took a few moments to ponder it; turning it this way and that in my mind, but dismissed it when I remembered how at home she'd made herself in Dan's bachelor pad. 'No, I think she's more than happy wrapping my ex-boyfriend around her little finger,' I said with a smile. 'It just makes me think it's rather an odd item to have chosen to take because all of us noticed it. Firstly, it suggests to me our tomb robber is a man. I don't think Shukura would make the mistake of thinking that, once seen, something like that could ever be forgotten. It also makes me wonder if, rather than brazen it out, our tomb robber – if indeed a tomb robber there is – is planning on being far away from Egypt by the time of next month's meeting, living under a forged identity and enjoying a hedonistic lifestyle.'

'Funded by the sale of priceless relics from the Amarna era onto the black market.' Adam muttered.

'Exactly. Although I'd love to hear the story he has concocted about the provenance of the pieces. I mean, I know some collectors are supposed to be pretty unscrupulous, but you'd surely want to know where to start the bargaining over price...' I stopped talking as the temple in front of us was plunged into darkness as the floodlights were turned off. Blackness engulfed us. The sudden silence was dense and eerie, disinclining us to keep talking.

It took a few moments for my eyes to adjust. But the stars were bright, and the moon was a pearly crescent dangling in the sky above the temple. If possible, the scene was even more magical in the silvery moon-and-starlight. It wasn't a view quite as old as time – arguably the pyramids hold that distinction – but I still felt as if we were looking at a little piece of eternity.

When Adam finally spoke it was to whisper, 'Are you afraid of ghosts, Merry? Because I'll bet there are a few out and about tonight.'

I stared up at the heavens. 'It's easy to see why the ancients called the stars *the imperishables*,' I whispered back, shivering. 'It's like the immortal souls of all of ancient Egypt's dead pharaohs are up there keeping watch.'

'It makes me think an individual needs to be very brave indeed to turn tomb-robber. I don't think I'd have the bottle.' He hugged me closer, and I rested my head against his shoulder. I have no idea how long we sat like that, staring at the Hathor Chapel, eyes peeled for any sign of movement. But after a while my muscles started to cramp and my bottom to protest at sitting in the same position on the hard stone floor for so long.

'Perhaps this wasn't quite such a great idea after all,' Adam said a bit bleakly. 'I'm as stiff as a board.'

I peered at my watch in the starlight. 'Maybe you're right,' I agreed. 'We're way past the witching hour and into the wee small ones. Perhaps my instincts are off beam this time. But I just have this feeling there's *something...*'

'What's that?' Suddenly I felt him go rigid, his voice a tense whisper.

'What? Where? What have you seen?'

'Up there on the hill behind the temple... look... see? Isn't that the beam of a torch?'

I craned to see where he was pointing, and finally spied it. 'If it's torchlight it's a very dim wattage,' I observed. 'Almost as if the beam's muffled in some way.'

'Perhaps that's exactly what it is. To give just enough light to see by but not enough to draw attention. I wouldn't have spotted it at all, except I just happened to look up. I was wondering how far it is to Hatshepsut's rock-cut sanctuary, and whether we should hole up there for the night like we did last time.'

'You old romantic,' I murmured, never once taking my eyes off the dim beam of light moving on the hillside.

Adam scrambled stiffly to his feet and pulled me up with him. 'Come on, we need to take a look.'

We picked our way cautiously across the tumbled remains of the ruined temple and onto the steep hillside, slipping slightly on the loose scree and avoiding the scattered chunks of fallen rock. 'I've lost sight of it,' I whispered. 'Did you see where it went?' It seemed easier to talk about the torchlight than to think about the person holding the torch.

'Over there,' Adam pointed, pulling me after him. 'There's a concrete barrier built across the back of the temple to protect it from rock-falls. I think it disappeared just the other side of that.'

We crept forward in the darkness, stepping stealthily across the rocky terrain; then dropped onto our hands and knees as the terrain became steeper and we approached the spot close by where we judged the torchlight to have vanished. Piles of boulders obscured our view along the hillside. That they'd fallen from the cliffs above I didn't doubt. I glanced up the cliff-face towering above us. It loomed menacingly in the darkness, sheer, craggy and layered with black vertical shadows. I shivered. I wouldn't want to be down here if another portion of the cliff should decide to sheer away from the bedrock and come crashing down the mountainside.

Slowly we edged around the boulders, moving silently and keeping to the shadows. The moonlight was bright enough to give us away if we moved away from the rocks.

'There…' Adam whispered, pointing.

I eased alongside him and peered through the darkness. The muffled beam of light was moving about in front of a portion of the hillside set between huge, tumbled boulders. It disappeared between them, and then emerged again, only to turn back and disappear once more.

'My God…' Adam breathed. 'The audacity of it!'

'What…? What are you talking about?'

'Whoever this is, he doesn't need the Mehet-Weret Aten discs. If I'm judging the geography correctly, I think Mr Torchbeam over there has burrowed through the hillside and into the tomb from behind. I'll bet there's a tunnel carved into the rock behind those giant boulders.'

I gaped, the blood turning to ice on my veins. 'Just like the ancient tomb robbers,' I murmured chillingly.

'We need to get a little closer,' Adam whispered, taking my hand and helping me to slip quietly from behind our rock. We hugged the rim of the cliff-face, staying deep within the shadows, and crept forward as stealthily as cats. There was a little overhang of rock above us, and we ducked underneath it, crouching behind a pile of rocks. 'I'll bet these have been excavated out of the hillside,' Adam said, pulling me close in alongside him. 'This is both a dump of the in-fill of rock, and also a handy screen should anyone happen along this way.' The moon was high above us. From here we had a much better view of the space between the massive boulders piled against the hillside, while we were hidden in deep protective shadow. 'The temple boundary is just over there,' Adam pointed. 'The concrete rock-fall barrier starts a bit further across from it. The burial chamber is probably underneath the back section but carved deep into the cliffs.'

I tried to get the layout clear in my head while Adam and I kept our gazes glued to the shadowed space between the boulders. It was weird being out here on the cliffside knowing the secret tomb was carved into the living rock within tunnelling distance.

I froze as a movement between the boulders caught my eye. Adam saw it at the same moment, and I felt him go rigid alongside me. The muted torch beam bounced towards us, and the sound of footsteps crunching on loose chippings was unmistakeable. We both held our breath.

A man was coming towards us, bent almost double in the low, narrow tunnel carved between the boulders. He stepped out onto the hillside carrying what appeared to be a long, rectangular box, a bit like an elongated shoebox. He had his back to us and appeared to be fiddling with the catch. After a moment he freed it and lifted something from inside the box. The moonlight caught on the dull gleam of gold as he held it up to inspect it. It was an exquisite golden statue. But that wasn't what made me gasp and clutch wildly at Adam's hand. As he held the statue up to the pearly moonlight, the man turned slightly.

Recognition was instantaneous and as gut-wrenching as if delivered on the end of a rapier. All my instincts shrank back, rejecting the evidence of my own two eyes. I felt the same jolt of shock then horror go though Adam. His grip on my hand was bruising.

As we watched, sick with dismay, the man carefully placed the statue back inside the box, re-secured the clasp and turned back into the tunnel. His crunching footsteps faded as he moved deep into the mountainside.

'It can't be true,' I whispered, shaking my head in stunned disbelief, and swiping ineffectually at the tears that had started trickling unbidden down my cheeks as I watched the familiar form disappear into the tunnel.

Adam's face was a frozen mask of rejection. 'Of all the possibilities… you know, I never for one minute thought… I just can't believe him capable of it…'

I collapsed sideways from my crouching position into an awkward sort of semi-recumbence against the rocks. 'Well, he is descended from the most notorious family of tomb-robbers Egypt has ever known. He told us himself, the Abd el-Rassul family were renowned for it in Howard Carter's day. He's always worn it as a badge of honour. Let's face it Adam,' I sniffed, 'tomb robbing is in his blood…'

'…But still,' Adam slumped alongside me, a dejected heap of disbelief. 'No…' he shook his head again. 'I simply refuse to believe it. There must be some other explanation.

And I'm going to find out what it is. Come on Merry…' And he leapt up, dragging me with him and made for the entrance to the rock-cut tunnel.

Chapter 15

The tunnel was perhaps thirty metres long, just over person-width wide and about three-quarters of a person high. We had to bend forward and proceed in an awkward sort of single file, but at least we were walking rather than crawling. The tunnel had been carved through the bedrock and shored up with planks of roughly nailed together wood. 'I don't like this,' Adam whispered. 'The rock's too crumbly. I can feel it breaking up under my feet. It wouldn't take too much to bring the whole lot crashing down.'

I thought of the tonnes of rock on top of us, literally the whole of the mountainside, and shuddered. I shuddered even more to think what we were going to say to Ahmed when we came across him. 'This must have taken him months to carve out.'

About halfway along, the tunnel angled to the right. We crept along it, bent at the waist. The glow of lamplight shone from the chamber at the far end. We were approaching the tomb.

Adam stepped out of the tunnel first. I was close on his heels. We both drew in a long, slow breath together. Impossible though it seemed, we were back in Nefertiti and Akhenaten's burial chamber, and the princess Neferure still lay in her anthropoid coffin in the niche set into the back wall. Nothing here had been touched. The only difference was the little oil-burning lantern that had been set on the floor in one corner, near the giant stone sarcophagus of the ancient pharaoh. It cast an eerie flickering glow across the granite and up the walls, illuminating the painted relief of Akhenaten and his queen raising their arms in worship to the Aten sun disc. The image dominated the chamber, spilling radiant sunbeams over the royal couple.

Adam and I stood stock still, staring around us, re-familiarising ourselves with the improbable and spine-tingling contents of this ancient sepulchre; then looked at each other sharing the same sense of awed wonder we'd felt the first time, and disbelief that here we were back again. The air was as dead and dusty-dry as ever. Despite the chill of the night-time air temperature outside, here in the chamber carved deep into the mountainside it remained suffocatingly hot. My skin prickled with the knowledge of how many centuries had passed since any sort of real fresh air had circulated in here. We'd come too far along the tunnel for the air of the twenty-first century to have penetrated properly. Once again, we'd stepped across the threshold of more than thirty centuries and found ourselves in a relic of 18th Dynasty imperial Egypt that still seemed to have a whisper of ancient life clinging to it.

The sound of movement reached us from the treasure chamber on the other side of the narrow opening in the wall.

Adam motioned me silently to follow him and we tiptoed around the edge of the sarcophagus. Then we crouched alongside each other, so we could see through the opening into the chamber beyond. The evidence the tomb was being looted was obvious at once. A pile of objects, wrapped in paper and bubblewrap was stacked against the nearest wall, ready to be removed. In the light of a second oil lamp on the floor just inside the chamber, I could see packing cases set alongside ancient caskets; chests and boxes ready to transport their contents away. I hadn't wanted to be right about my suspicion the tomb was being systematically robbed. But I'd never really believed the explanation that one of our little gang had simply slipped the Nefertiti necklace into his pocket in a moment of uncharacteristic kleptomania. My heart sank into my boots as I gazed at the evidence before my eyes and accepted it for what it was. There was only one saving grace – the clearance of the tomb seemed only just to have started. As Adam had said, it must have taken months to dig the tunnel through the mountainside to connect with the burial chamber. So far as a quick scan of the room was able to show me, it seemed very little had so far been removed. I caught my breath at the wonder of it all realising my memory had carried an imperfect imprint of this incredible sight all these months. To gaze once more on the contents of the tomb was like being given admittance to Akhenaten's palace in Akhet-Aten; only with all its contents displayed in one incredible chamber. Maybe there was still a hope we could save most of the treasures.

Ahmed was at the other end of the treasure chamber, dressed all in black, muttering to himself and waving his flashlight about so the beam looked like a drunken firefly. 'What's he doing?' I whispered.

'I don't know,' Adam murmured, 'but I'm going to find out.' His scan of the room had revealed something to him that I hadn't noticed. He crawled forward on his hands and knees and lifted something from the floor alongside the oil lamp. It was Ahmed's tourist-police gun.

Something about the sight of it in Adam's hands made me go shivery and weak-kneed – and not in a good way. It was of the sick-making, skin crawling variety, not the type induced by action heroes on the silver screen.

With the gun in his hands, Adam straightened and stepped forward. 'Ahmed, the evidence of my eyes is leading me to a very nasty conclusion. You have precisely thirty seconds to tell me I'm wrong.'

Ahmed lifted off as if he had rocket launchers attached to the soles of his shoes, letting out a great shout. He spun around, lost his balance and toppled sideways. He stopped himself falling by flinging his right arm out to steady himself against the wall. Even so, he didn't quite right himself in time and clattered against a tall ivory cabinet with squat feet.

Luckily it was heavier than he was – which was saying something – and it broke his fall without actually getting broken itself. I let out a gasp of relief at this minor miracle; then sucked in another one as Ahmed straightened up. 'Adam? By de holy book of Islam, you gave me de fright of my life. What do you mean, creeping up on me like dat? And what in de name of Allah are you doing here?'

'I asked you a question.' Adam said with steel in his voice. 'I don't want to believe you capable of tomb robbery, in spite of your dodgy ancestry; but I'm having a hard job coming up with any other explanation right now.'

'Dat de tomb it is being robbed is as plain as de nose on your face,' Ahmed said in a stately tone of voice, pulling himself up to his full impressive height and taking a step forward. 'But I, Ahmed Abd el-Rassul, am not de one perpetrating dis sacrilege. You forget, I am de tourist and antiquities police!' He puffed out his chest. 'I am not de poacher. I am de game-guarder, remember?'

'...keeper,' Adam said automatically. 'It's gamekeeper.' He was so used to correcting Ahmed's execrable attempts at colloquial English, he could do it even at a time like this.

'I am here to find de evidences...' Ahmed started; and then an appalled expression swept across his features. He was looking beyond Adam, closer to where I was still crouched in the narrow gap in the wall between the treasury and the burial chamber. No sooner had the thought registered than I felt myself grabbed violently from behind. I didn't even have time to scream. A hand clamped across my mouth as I was hauled up and backwards against a hard body. I felt the sharp prick of something that felt frighteningly like the pointed blade of a knife against my throat. The only thought to impress itself on my terrified brain as I felt that cold steel against my skin was that the hand over my mouth smelt of an expensive cologne-type aftershave.

'Good evening, Adam,' a male voice said from above my left shoulder. 'Or should I say good morning. Dawn will break within the next couple of hours, after all. Now, if you don't want Merry to get hurt, I suggest you hand me the bothersome police officer's gun.'

I saw Adam's eyes dilate with horror and he cast a quick panicky glance over his shoulder. But Ahmed was far away on the other side of the tomb. There was nothing he could do to help. Now the first shock was over, it only took me a moment to work out the identity of my captor. It wasn't so much the voice, smooth as butter though it was. It was the cologne that gave him away. Even though he was behind me, the image of the fastidious and immaculate Mustafa Mushhawrar rose before my eyes. Never trust a man who won't allow a speck of dust to settle on him, I thought darkly. I hadn't wanted to believe any of Adam's and my little rescue party capable of smuggling items from the tomb. In fact, another possibility had occurred to me while we were staking out Hatshepsut's temple and I'd rather imagined… Literally as the thought went through my brain the hand that wasn't holding a knife against my throat motioned someone forward. Into my line of sight stepped the malevolent form of… yes… the hideous Hussein; dressed in a filthy galabeya with an even filthier cloth wound around his head. His small black eyes leered evilly at me from his pockmarked face, and I recoiled – although not very far given the compact nature of the body I was clamped against. It was as I'd feared – and almost desperately kind of hoped – so I didn't have to accept one of our friends guilty of betrayal. There was one individual who was not of our little band of rescuers but who'd also seen inside the tomb; and he was not party to the solemn oath we'd sworn to Walid. Hussein's loathsome image had flashed through my brain when we were still outside. But I hadn't been able to rationalise the hunch then, knowing him to be in police custody, and it didn't explain what he was doing here now. And it certainly didn't account for Mustafa's deft flick of the knife at my throat. All these thoughts and more flashed through my brain in the heartbeat it took Adam to blink.

'What the…' he started, stiff with shock.

'The gun, if you please Adam,' Mustafa said politely. 'Merry is too pretty for me to wish to leave a permanent blemish on her skin. She is of the lovely complexion you call the English rose, is that right?'

Hussein gave an evil leer and held out his grubby hand for the weapon. It was not at all clear to me how two people from opposite ends of the hygiene spectrum had chosen to hook up, but if my head was not severed from my body in the next few moments, I had high hopes of finding out.

Adam darted a glance from the space above my shoulder, where I judged Mustafa's face must be, to the reaching hand of the odious Hussein, then back into my eyes. I could see him desperately searching for options, asking himself what Indiana Jones would do with or without a bullwhip, and facing down the stark reality that if he shot Hussein, as I'm sure he was itching to do, the blade Mustafa was holding would slice through my neck like a hot knife through butter. I put as much communication as I was capable of into the look of appeal I sent him. I know he was longing to be heroic; but sometimes it's worth losing a battle to stand a fighting chance of winning the war. Or so my mother taught me. He stared into my eyes, and I did my best to flash a few more signals. I set great store by Adam's ability to read my mind, and I'm pleased to say I wasn't proved wrong. With a heart-breaking look of defeat, he handed the gun to our old nemesis.

'Thank you, Adam. I always think it's best to ask nicely. Give the gun to me please, Hussein, and then I can let the lovely Merry go.'

I'm not sure if the thuggish Hussein understood the English being spoken so faultlessly, although overlaid with a pronounced Egyptian accent. It was more the gesture he responded to; I think. Whatever, he handed the gun over to Mustafa with all the obedience of a puppy completing its training.

As Mustafa lowered the knife-blade from my throat I leapt forward into Adam's arms. 'Sorry, Merry,' he muttered.

'You had no choice,' I assured him.

Mustafa smoothed an imaginary crease on the front of his linen jacket, as if I'd been inconsiderate enough to crumple it while pressed against him. I noticed his crocodile-leather shoes were dusty and wondered that he could stand it, half expecting him to whip out his handkerchief to give them a good polish. He smiled benignly at me; then turned his attention to Ahmed. 'Mr policeman, come here please,' he called across the tomb. 'You are descended from the Abd el-Rassuls I understand. That is a fine pedigree indeed. In some ways I am sorry you have turned from a life of crime to life as a crime-fighter. Your instincts remain true if your presence here tonight is anything to judge by. I daresay your skills would be of more use to me than the baser impulses of this less than fine fellow Hussein here. He seems to be a stack-'em-high-sell-'em-cheap sort. But as an antiquities thief he has contacts on the black market that I hope may prove helpful to me.'

Feeling rather wobbly-kneed, I moved to sit on one of the packing cases as Ahmed came to join us. Adam reached out and gripped his arm as soon as he was close enough, looking square into his eyes. 'Mate, I'm sorry for accusing you. I didn't want to believe it was you; God knows. Merry will tell you I said there had to be some other explanation. The only good thing right now is I can see what it is. Forgive me.'

Ahmed beamed his mega-watt smile, reminding me again how badly in need of a good dentist he was. I decided I really must make a mental note to ask Shukura to speak to her husband Selim, whom I knew to be a fine example of the profession. Crazy, the mindless thoughts that can distract you when the chips are down, and things are looking decidedly grim. With Mustafa in possession of both a knife and a gun, and with the gruesome Hussein metaphorically wagging his tail alongside him, it was hard to see how they could get much grimmer. 'Adam, my friend, you need no forgiveness,' Ahmed said formally. 'But I would still like dearly to know what it is dat you are doing here.'

Mustafa trained Ahmed's gun on us as we sat like the three wise monkeys on the packing cases in front of him. I tried to get a handle on reality, but it kept slipping from my grasp. Over there on the other side of the tomb I could see Akhenaten's golden chariot glinting in the torchlight, and alongside it the divine solar boat that was at least as long as a modern canoe. The golden model of Ahket-Aten that Mustafa had admired so much the last time we were here was still gleaming on its table. It seemed impossible these priceless relics from Egypt's ancient past – once gazed upon and handled by its most controversial king - should bear witness to the scene unfolding before them now. I had a strong sense that if I could just pinch myself hard enough, I might wake up in our resplendent cabin on the *Misr* to find this was all a crazy dream, the product of an over-active imagination and one too many glasses of wine. But the pinching just drew blood and the promise of bruised skin, so I gave it up.

'I would very much like to know what you are doing here, too.' Mustafa said musingly, fingering his narrow moustache. 'Mr Abd el-Rassul's presence I think I can account for. As soon as Hussein went missing from the high-security hospital where he was in custody I daresay he smelt a rat. I think you had already cottoned on, my friend, had you not, that Hussein here was only pretending to have lost his memory?'

I'm not sure if Ahmed knew what *cottoned on* meant, or indeed to *smell a rat* – Mustafa's grasp of idiomatic English was quite impressive – but he got the general gist.

He growled like an angry bear. 'Dis man Hussein, he kept his memory hidden for many months. But den he started looking at me with a calculating look in his eye. When he disappeared, I checked de visitor book. I saw at once dis had happened after a visit from a mysterious Mr Mushref. I have lived in Luxor all my life and I do not know of a Mr Mushref. So, I asked de receptionist to describe dis man. When she said about de narrow moustache and de shiny shoes I knew at once it must be de same Mushref as Mushhawrar. So, with my antennae alerted and aquiver, I started to stake out de tomb. I have staked it out now for almost a week. I finded de tunnel just tonight. I could see at once de signs of looting. I carried a beautiful statue out into de moonlight to breathe de pure night air and make sure I was not dreaming. But de gold was as solid and as pure outside de tomb as it was inside it. I came back and was looking for a good place to hide with my video surveillance camera when you electrocuted me with fright, Adam.'

'So was Hussein pretending to have lost his memory all along?' Adam asked.

Mustafa was still gazing at Ahmed with a look of sorrow on his face. 'Yes, I can see I underestimated you Mr Abd el-Rassul. I didn't realise you were taking the custody of Hussein here quite so literally; or that you were quite so zealous in your duties. Otherwise, I would have been more careful and rolled the boulder back into place in front of the tunnel these last few evenings. But time was of the essence. I didn't think I could spare the long, hot effort required to keep levering it in and out of place while I got on with the serious business of emptying the tomb of its choicest items. As for Hussein here and his memory loss, I don't know how genuine it was originally,' he said with a small shrug that suggested he didn't much care either. 'I remembered you'd mentioned he'd had a hand in the theft of items from the Egyptian Museum in Cairo during the tumultuous days of the revolution. You said he'd been planning on selling these items onto the black market. Well, you see, I have no contacts on the black market myself, so it dawned on me he could perhaps be of some use to me. It has taken me these many months to excavate the tunnel you have just traversed. That I did so single-handed is something in which I take some pride. I broke through into the burial chamber just over a week ago. So, you see, I knew I had only a month before that small weasel-like man from the Cairo Museum returned to deliver his verdict. I had no idea whether Hussein was in possession of his memory, but it dawned on me I needed to find out; and perhaps we could scratch each other's backs.'

'You'd break him free of his police-cum-hospital custody in return for his list of contacts,' Adam deduced.

'Yes, exactly that. He was wary at first, of course. But I crossed his palm with silver, and we reached an understanding of sorts.'

'And to think he had the damn cheek to question whether Jessica and I were to be trusted,' I muttered indignantly at Adam.

Mustafa smiled blandly. 'But that still does not explain your presence here, Adam and Merry.' He looked at us enquiringly in the lamplight.

I shrugged, deciding we really had nothing to lose. 'You may remember our friend Jessica – the tiny elfin one – commented on the exquisite beauty of one of Nefertiti's necklaces…'

I saw the stillness settle over Mustafa's chiselled features. 'But she was not the one in the jewellery shop in the Souk,' he said, damning himself in so few words. 'I was told it was a bossy and funny-featured lady wearing screaming colours and very thick glasses that made her eyes go a horrible shape.'

'Yes, well I know exactly who you're talking about as she was on the same cruise-boat as us,' I said flatly. 'And I'll say this, she didn't deserve the campaign of terror your henchman subjected her to.' I had my fingers crossed behind my back while I said this. I had a sneaking suspicion her adventures while on board the *SS Misr* may just prove to be the making of Eleanor. But all that was beside the point right now. 'I knew it was Nefertiti's necklace the moment I clapped eyes on it. What I want to know is what the hell it was doing in that shop in the Souk and how it got sold as a tourist souvenir. It's quite possible it's of more intrinsic value than Tutankhamun's golden death mask.'

Mustafa had the grace to look shamefaced. 'It is hard to legislate for idiots,' he said sadly. 'The necklace was one of the first items I removed, a little over a week ago. 'My cousin has a shop in the Souk, and it comes complete with a very solid and secure safe in which he keeps his finer items locked up overnight. He calls himself a jeweller, but it is a tragic fact he is inadequate to the task. He wouldn't know a genuine Pharaonic artefact if it reached up to slap him in the face. I asked him to look after the necklace and one or two other trinkets from Nefertiti's casket, thinking he would just keep them safe for me. I told him I had purchased them from a dealer at a good price. He decided to go one better and see if he could earn me some money. I imagine you can piece together the rest of the story. Of course, when I realised what had happened I knew I could stop at nothing to get the necklace back. It would only take the short-sighted rainbow lady to get the piece valued for insurance purposes and the lid would blow sky-high on my little enterprise, with all sorts of questions asked prematurely about how a genuine artefact from the Amarna era found its way onto the tourist market. I could not risk that. My clientele – I hope – ' he said with a quick searching and, I thought, rather doubtful look at Hussein's ugly face, 'are more discerning; willing to pay good money without asking too many awkward questions about provenance in order to add a unique piece of Pharaonic history to their private collections. So, I set my young apprentice the mission of retrieving the necklace, promising him a small reward for its return. Of course, he had no idea of its true worth. He failed of course. I imagine I have the pair of you to thank for that.'

I couldn't help it. I stared at him as if he was a slug I'd just trodden underfoot. 'You realise what you're planning to sell so ruthlessly for your own personal profit are the most magnificent treasures ever to emerge from ancient Egypt?' I leapt up from the packing case in my sudden anger and jabbed my finger towards him. 'There are only two outcomes acceptable for these priceless artefacts. You know what they are. You were there when we discussed them that morning over breakfast, looking across the Nile. The best we can hope for, in my humble opinion, is that they remain here – right here in this dead-aired, suffocating chamber where they've lain undisturbed for more than three thousand years. It's my fault they've ever seen the light of day at all. If I hadn't been locked in Howard Carter's house on that fateful night back in the spring none of this would have happened and none of us would be here now having this conversation.' I raised my voice to the rafters ... or rather the rock-cut ceiling. 'Nefertiti, Akhenaten and Neferure, if you can hear me, then I most humbly beg your forgiveness for intruding on your eternal rest. In my own defence, I never thought it would come to this; that we'd all be plagued by these despicable, unscrupulous men!'

'Merry ... please...' Adam whispered, no doubt noting the way Mustafa lowered Ahmed's gun, so it was trained on me.

But it was no good. I was on a roll. I'd come to Egypt on a simple tourist holiday, never intending any of this to happen. That it had, only for the adventure of my lifetime to be exploited so spectacularly by these selfish, self-serving, sinister men just made my flesh crawl. I decided suddenly if I had to die to prove to the ancient dead just how innocent my intentions had been, it was a price worth paying. I wanted no part of this villainy. I glared at Mustafa and gave full vent to my feelings. 'The only other outcome even vaguely acceptable is for these staggering treasures to be displayed in a museum for the wonderment of all the people of the world, now and in all the generations to come. For you to think for a single moment it's tolerable for you and that vile sidekick of yours to profit from the glory of the first and finest civilisation on earth makes me sick to my stomach. I hope all the gods of the pantheon are watching your actions tonight. In fact, I hope all the gods of all the ages of all the religions of any age past, present or future are training their sights on you and cursing you with all the divine power they have at their disposal. You're worse than the worst scum that ever walked the earth. I hope you rot in Hell, burn in the fires of Hades and walk in the pestilent plagues of purgatory forever.' I think if he'd shot me there and then I wouldn't have cared. Some people need telling. I'd have carried on cursing him, no doubt mixing my metaphors with even wilder abandon had Adam not leapt up, grabbed me and shoved me behind him while Mustafa was still removing the safety catch from the gun. (This was something Adam had omitted to do earlier when he'd had it trained on Ahmed). 'You're a louse… a termite…' I shouted as I was shoved unceremoniously backwards.

'I applaud the sentiment, Merry,' Adam grunted. 'But you don't half pick your moments.'

Ahmed leapt to his feet too. Suddenly I found myself trying to sneak a peek at Mustafa's face through a wall of protective maleness.

Mustafa fiddled with the catch for a while, and then slumped sideways. 'You don't understand,' he said, and it was in the defeated tones of one who'd sold his soul to the devil and suddenly realised what it meant. 'You just can't imagine what it was like. Those two high-ups from the Egyptian Museum pronounced their verdict and boarded a plane back to Cairo. That doddery old professor-type followed them a day or two later. You and your friends went back to England. It left just me. And my job was to keep watch, day in day out, on Hatshepsut's temple as I've done every day for nearly ten years. Only it wasn't Hatshepsut's temple anymore. I know I signed my name to that stupid oath that silly little wispy-haired man from the museum insisted upon. But he wasn't here every day, forced to stare at the temple façade knowing what treasures lay buried behind it. I have always loved our Egyptian history. But suddenly it seemed to be taunting me with all that was within reach yet beyond my grasp. I started to drive myself steadily mad with it. Perhaps you cannot imagine. But I have never had anything to offer a wife. I had an English girlfriend for some years.' Ah, I thought, that explains his perfect command of English slang. 'But she refused to marry me and left me for a British businessman. I have taken a pride in myself, in my appearance, all these years, but to no avail. I have no wife, no family of my own, and time ticks on. Every day I looked at the temple and pictured the treasures hidden behind it, and I started to imagine a different future for myself. Just one or two small items, I told myself: just enough to set myself up. I thought no one would miss a few pieces. No one was in here long enough to know every item. I thought maybe I could cover my tracks so none of you would ever suspect me – take just a few small objects and re-plaster the wall in the burial chamber so no one would suspect I'd broken through. But once I was inside...' The dark gleam in his eyes, glimpsed over Adam's broad shoulder told me exactly what he'd thought. 'If it hadn't been for that stupid necklace or, more correctly, my stupid cousin...'

'Ahmed was onto you without the necklace,' Adam said quietly.

'Yes, I see now I lack experience of how to carry this off without a hitch,' Mustafa said sorrowfully. 'I should have flown it solo. I accept I cannot now bring my full plan to fruition. Your absence and that of a Luxor police officer will be remarked upon soon enough. But I hope there is still time for me to take enough bits and pieces to keep me going; and to make my getaway before you are missed.'

'It's not too late to choose a different path,' I said rather desperately from behind Adam's shoulder. 'So far, you've removed very little. I'm sure if you repent right now, we can come to some arrangement to get you off the hook.' I'd been more touched that I liked to show by his explanation for his actions. It made him more human somehow.

His eyes met mine for a moment and I saw a deep sorrow in them. Here was someone who'd led a fundamentally decent life, turned by the glint of gold and all it might offer him. 'It is too late for that,' he said sadly. 'Perhaps if I hadn't invited our depraved friend here in on the act, it might still be possible to undo what I have done.

But he has set the wheels in motion to line up some contacts for me. Besides which, he is free now and patently in possession of his memory. There is only one way I can secure his silence. So, there can be no turning back now. I'm sorry, Merry and Adam, I think it was your fate once before to be entombed in this place? I apologise, as I fear I am about to give you a repeat of the experience. But really, I find I have no choice. With your permission I will remain here with the gun trained on you. I am afraid if I hand it across to my fiendish friend here, he may feel the compulsion to use it with or without provocation. Somehow, I don't feel he has been brought up to appreciate the finer ways of humanity.'

With a few barked orders in Arabic, he set the heinous Hussein to work carrying all the pre-packed and portable items from the tomb into the rock-cut tunnel beyond the burial chamber. All we could do was watch in an agony of helplessness as statues, precious jewels, caskets of golden diadems and other royal regalia were carried from the tomb.

'What can we do?' Ahmed asked, squirming with impotence.

'Nothing,' Adam murmured dejectedly. 'Not unless you think we can stop him with a bunch of bullet holes riddling our bodies.'

'I wonder if he'd really be brave enough to turn the gun on us in cold blood,' I mused softly. 'I mean; he didn't seem all that proficient with the safety catch. He's such a fastidious and punctilious man I wonder if he'd balk at using the weapon at all. Quite honestly, I don't suppose he could bear the bloodstains on his crisp linen suit.'

'*He* might not,' Adam said. 'But give our cruel friend Hussein a moment with the trigger at his fingertips and I suspect he'd prove himself somewhat more adept. I figure he feels he owes us one after all.'

We subsided once more into a shrinking sense of helplessness. Adam sat fingering the crocodile tooth on its boot string at his throat. Somehow, I just knew he was picturing the crocodile and the snake and thinking there must be some way to overcome this equally deadly example of the human species. At least the crocodile and snake were honest about it, never once pretending to be something they weren't.

'Ok.' Mustafa said at length. I glanced at my watch and realised dawn would be breaking outside within moments. If he and Hussein hoped to make a clean getaway, they needed to get away pretty sharpish. 'This is not as much as I had hoped to take with me from this stale-aired place. But I think it will suffice to pay off my deplorable friend here and set myself up under an assumed identity. Please do not think of following me. Your death will be assured if you do. At least I am gifting you a last few precious moments together. And when, finally, you die down here you have the solace of knowing you are keeping good company.'

In a semi-trance we followed Mustafa and Hussein into the burial chamber and watched them step into the roughly hewn tunnel. The oil lamp was burning low. Even so I think I divined Mustafa's purpose as he reached the far-off bend in his tunnel. I saw him raise the gun. 'Get back!' I screamed. 'Get back onto the treasure chamber. Now! Move! Quickly! OhmyGod!!'

The three of us scrambled backwards as quickly as our poor shocked limbs would carry us as Mustafa let off a volley of shots against the roof of his fragile tunnel. As anticipated, it brought down an avalanche of rock. I felt myself flung forward and grabbed my head with one hand, reaching out for Adam with the other as the cliffside seemed to implode on top of us.

Chapter 16

The swirling cloud of rock-smoke slowly cleared. I heard Adam beside me, pulling himself into a sitting position and spitting out a mouthful of dust. 'Pah! Merry? Are you ok?'

'Yes; I'm here,' I reassured him, reaching out and connecting with some part of him that was indecipherable but solid and unharmed.

'Oh, thank God. Ahmed? Ahmed, are you there? Can you hear me? Where the hell are you?'

A mangled groan betrayed his whereabouts. I felt Adam's hand groping for him in the darkness. Everything was pitch black and clogged with choking dust. I put my elbow over my face and tried to breathe through my sleeve. A scrabbling sound close by accompanied by a lot of huffing and puffing assured me Ahmed was pushing himself up from the floor. 'Where am I?' he asked.

'Ahmed?' I asked in alarm. 'Are you alright?'

'Who are you?' His deep voice had an unusual querulous note in it. 'Where am I?'

'Ahmed, don't you recognise our voices?' Adam asked urgently, still groping about in the dark.

'Who are you?' Ahmed repeated, sounding anxious and confused.

'Ahmed, have you lost your memory? Did one of those rocks fall and clunk you on the head?'

There was a long pause as the dust started to settle. 'No; it is just my little joke. Hello, Merry. Hello, Adam. I hope dat you are unharmed.'

Adam growled at him. 'Peculiar sense of humour you've got, mate.'

I swiped at where I imagined him to be in the darkness and connected satisfyingly with a sold mass I took to be his chest. 'I should have known by the fact you were speaking English – or what passes for it in Ahmed-speak.'

'If you can try to take things seriously for a moment,' Adam said politely, 'I think our most pressing need is to get some light on the subject. I've got a flashlight in my rucksack.' I could hear him wrestling his way out of it. His efforts were accompanied by a couple of soft grunts and a mild swearword. A small click sounded and then a beautiful beam of light penetrated the gloom. As I have had cause to note before, there really is no more wonderful a sight when all before has been stygian darkness.

The torch beam looked a bit the way car headlights do bouncing on fog, not penetrating very far. Rock dust still swirled, although thankfully the two huge granite sarcophagi formed an effective barrier, preventing the worst from entering the treasure chamber. Adam swung the flash beam over me. 'You've got a nasty gash on your forehead,' he said.

I couldn't feel it to be fair, although reaching up I felt the trickle of blood oozing down my face. I sat on the floor, propped against a packing case and watched Adam grope about in his rucksack for a packet of tissues. He applied one tenderly to my brow, wiping away a smear of blood and dust. 'Makes a change for you to be tending me,' I smiled up at him.

He leaned down and pressed a warm if rather dusty kiss against my lips. 'I hadn't realised how satisfying it is to play Florence Nightingale. Any other cuts and bruises I should know about?'

I shook my head regretfully since I was enjoying his ministrations. 'No, all things considered I think we all got off remarkably injury free.'

He held out a clean tissue for me. 'Here, hold this against the cut for a while, just to stem the flow of blood.' I did as instructed, while he groped about in his rucksack for the bottle of water we'd brought with us. 'I'm tempted to tip half of this over your head and half over my own to get rid of the dust,' he grinned. 'But I daresay taking a quick shower with it right now is not the best use we could put it to. Here, take a swig.' He uncapped it and held it out towards me. I took one long swallow, enjoying the way it cleared the dust from inside my mouth and slipped wetly down my dry throat.

Adam did the same and recapped it again, then looked around for Ahmed.

Our police chum had picked his way carefully across the treasure chamber back to where we'd first spotted him. He came back gleefully holding aloft a rucksack of his own from which he pulled a spare flashlight and another two big bottles of water. 'I wasn't sure how long I might need to remain here to stake out de joint,' he explained. 'So, I came well provisoed.'

'Provisioned,' Adam corrected with a smile.

'Look! Also, I have bananas and a some packets of biscuits!'

'You're telling us we're not going to die in the next few days at least,' I grinned at him, keeping to myself the troubling little thought that whether it would make any difference to the eventual outcome remained to be seen. Even so, it was as if Ahmed heard me.

'We will find a way to get free,' he said staunchly. 'We are de tree musketeers, no? And it is a happy thing for me to be here with you, Merry and Adam. De last two times you have been trapped inside tombs, dis one on de previous occasion and dat other one where you finded de papyrus, I have been on de outside. For me, dis is third time lucky! It seems to me if Mr Mushhawrar can burrow his way in den we can burrow our way out. We will be like a team of rabbits.'

'But it took Mustafa nearly five months to excavate his tunnel!' I declared.

Adam grinned. 'Ah, but there are three of us. And we don't have a day job to do in the meantime. We can do it in record time.'

I gazed at my two male companions; both caked in dust and grime but determined to look on the bright side and thought myself very lucky to be among such good company in my current predicament.

We shared one of Ahmed's bananas between us; then took a moment to contemplate our surroundings. The alluring glitter of gold was much dulled by the rock dust coating everything in sight. I ran my finger along the back of the golden throne swiping away a thick layer of grit and grime. 'That man needs locking up,' I muttered.

'If he survived the rock fall,' Adam said. 'He and Hussein were only halfway along that tunnel when they brought the roof crashing down.'

Ahmed and I stared at him. 'You think they might not have made it out alive?'

He shrugged. 'All I'm saying is I don't much fancy their chances. The roof of that tunnel was precarious enough already without firing a load of bullets at it.'

I remembered that long sorrowful look Mustafa had given me, as if recognising just how far from grace he'd fallen and the impossibility of turning back onto the straight and narrow. If it was indeed the case that he'd decided to do the honourable thing right at the last moment, then he and Hussein were buried under tonnes of rock and debris along with some of the loveliest of Akhenaten and Nefertiti's tomb treasures. 'We should take a look,' I decided.

We edged into the burial chamber through the narrow opening in the rock. The floor was littered with chippings, scree and loose chunks of rock. I held the tissue across my face and breathed through it to avoid inhaling even more choking dust. The two giant sarcophagi stood proud and undamaged. Thankfully they both had solid stone lids, which had survived the explosion of rock and protected their occupants. Sadly, the same couldn't be said for Nefurure's wooden anthropoid coffin. It was split in two by the huge rock sitting square in the middle of it. 'Oh no!' I breathed. 'Is the mummy damaged?'

Adam shone the beam of his flashlight into the casket. 'It's hard to tell. I think it might be a bit crushed. Hopefully the wrappings are enough to have protected the body inside.'

We crept to the gap in the wall where once the tunnel had been. Now it was a deep pile of rock, spilling into the chamber. Adam and Ahmed both shone their flashlights at it, and I felt my heart sink. Some of the boulders filling the space were massive – far too big to be manhandled out of the way. We all stared in dismay. 'Ok, I think this is going to be more difficult than we envisaged,' Adam said. He reached forward and pulled a couple of smaller stones from the pile, cutting his hand on a jagged edge. 'Ouch!' he yelped, picking a razor-sharp chipping from the wound and then sucking it clean.

Ahmed moved forward to take his place. Ahmed is a big bloke, built like a barrel and strong with it. Some of the rocks were the approximate size of beach balls, and he managed to pull a few free. He was just turning to me with a look of mingled hope and satisfaction, when a deep rumbling sounded from the tunnel.

'Get back!' I shouted, and just in time too. All Ahmed had succeeded in doing was dislodging a pile of rock so those pressing above it could come crashing down to fill the space. Another cloud of dust billowed through the chamber, coating us all in a further layer of grime as the mini rock fall thundered around us. When the dust cleared, we stared through the gloom, coughing and spluttering. The pile of fallen masonry was more impenetrable than ever.

'It's too dangerous.' Adam rasped, saying aloud what Ahmed and I were thinking. 'The rock here is just too fragile and crumbly. Remember the ancient artisans who were aiming to cut a tomb here for Hatshepsut had to give up. The original plan was for the burial chamber to lay directly underneath her temple, carved through the rock with the entrance in the Valley of the Kings. But the quality of rock wasn't good enough, so they had to abandon the plan. My guess is Senenmut did the best he could with these hidden chambers, but knew he couldn't go any further. It's a miracle Mustafa managed to tunnel his way through without causing a landslide. I think there's a very real risk we'll bring half the mountainside down on top of us if we try to burrow our way out of here.'

We stared at the barrier before us, all thinking the same thing. We could give up on the idea of being a team of rabbits. 'There's only one other way out I can think of,' I said at last.

'The Aten discs,' Adam nodded. 'We need to try to get them back from the pit shaft.'

'De Aten discs?' Ahmed queried, sneezing and blowing his nose violently on his dusty handkerchief.

We eased our way back into the treasure chamber where the air was clearer, and all took a dust-slaking swig of water. 'The replica Mehet-Weret Aten discs,' I explained. 'Adam made them to work the ancient mechanism in the wall of the Hathor Chapel. They're the "key" to the hidden door. We used them to get inside the tomb the first time we were here. Sadly, for us, we left them at the entrance, not expecting our malicious friend Hussein to follow us. He was holding them aloft when the wooden plank he was standing on over the pit shaft broke. Adam saved Hussein – an error of judgement we've both had cause to regret – but both Aten discs bounced into the pit shaft.'

'I remember dis pit shaft,' Ahmed said. 'We put down new planks from de scaffolding in the temple. We crawled across to rescue you and Adam.'

'That's right, except – tidy-minded people that we are – we put them back before we left for the hospital with Adam and Hussein. We didn't want to draw too much attention to strange goings-on in the temple via a load of missing scaffolding planks. So, sadly for us, they're not there now.'

We made our way across the treasure chamber, careful not to knock the dust-coated artefacts. The corridor was on the far side, connecting with the Hathor Chapel inside the rock-cut part of Hatshepsut's temple at the other end. With the way behind us blocked, it was our only hope of escape.

Adam and Ahmed shone the twin beams of their torches into the dark space. The light caught on the brilliant glitter of pure spun gold. 'Neferure's golden shroud,' I whispered. 'I'd forgotten about that.'

Adam and I had taken a dagger to it during our previous entrapment. Our plan had been to rip it to shreds to fashion a rope. Rescue of the Aten discs from the deadly pit shaft had been our intention back then too. I could only hope we'd prove more successful this time around. The shroud was made of pure woven gold thread. It had proved frustratingly impervious to the blade of the ancient knife I'd found among Akhenaten's grave goods. Considering the long hours we'd spent working away at it, it was remarkably undamaged. Ahmed pulled it back along the corridor and piled it alongside the chariot in the treasure chamber. 'Goodness me, it is heavy,' he puffed. Then we edged along the corridor, keeping the torchlight focused on the dark hole on the floor about halfway along: the pit shaft.

We dropped to our hands and knees as we approached and crawled forward. At the edge we lay flat out and the men shone their torches down into the blackness. It was hard to judge the depth. I guessed all three of us could stand on each other's shoulders and not be long enough to stretch from the bottom to the top. What it was *not* hard to judge was the outcome should one of us be unlucky enough to take a tumble. Not only was the pit of neck-breaking depth; its whole base was covered with up-pointing spikes ready to impale anyone who should happen to fall on them.

'Hmm,' Ahmed said with feeling. 'Nasty. And you say de discs dat will set us free are down dere?'

Adam leaned forward as far as he dared and swung his flashlight in a long sweep. 'There. You see? See that golden circle down there? It looks a bit like a flattened football. That's one of them.'

'Golden?' Ahmed raised one eyebrow.

'Yes, well, I wanted them to look authentic, so I painted them with gold paint.'

I smiled, remembering how carefully he'd worked to ensure the weight and measurements were precisely right; and his delight when he knew he'd got it just right. Crazy, to be feeling nostalgic at a time like this. 'So how are we going to get them out?' I asked prosaically, giving myself a little shake.

'Well, your idea of a rope was a good one.' Adam said. 'But you searched through just about every box and casket in the place and didn't find one.'

'I have a rope!' Ahmed shouted exuberantly.

'Trust a policeman to come prepared,' Adam grinned, slapping him on the back.

Ahmed crawled backwards then retraced his steps into the treasure chamber. Adam put one arm around me and kissed my grimy cheek. 'Here we are again,' he murmured. 'I don't know about you, but I'm having the freakiest sense of déjà vu. Of all the things I expected when we set out from the hotel last night, it never entered my head that we'd find ourselves back where we started, entombed with Akhenaten and Nefertiti.'

'Not forgetting Neferure,' I reminded him.

'No, nor Ahmed,' he acknowledged. 'Ok, so perhaps it's a little different this time around after all.'

'And without the villainous Hussein intent on causing us grievous bodily harm.' I added brightly, feeling quite upbeat. 'I'd say, all things considered, we're a lot better off this time than we were last.'

He kissed me again, then pulled back to stare into my eyes. 'If, for any reason, things don't turn out as we hope and we don't make it out of here, I want you to know I love you Merry. I love you very *very* much. I think those few days we spent with Eleanor helped me realise how different my life is now from what it used to be. I might not have chosen close encounters with killer crocodiles, deadly snakes and deadlier people, but there's not a single moment I'd undo. I know I said once before that if it all has to end prematurely and we breathe our last here in this dead-aired place, then I'd die happy. But at the risk of sounding like a broken record, I'll say it again. You're the best of me, Merry. I wouldn't have missed my time with you for the world, or for all the treasure in this tomb.'

I gazed back at him and reached over and touched my fingers against his lips. I wanted to say something similar; about how I'd met him and suddenly felt brave enough to step onto the rollercoaster when before I'd only dared venture onto the kiddie rides. But it sounded too defeatist. I wasn't ready to say any sort of farewell to Adam just yet. As far as I was concerned our life together was only just beginning. 'We're not going to breathe our last in this tomb,'

I said emphatically. 'We are most definitely going to make it out of here. You've paid a rather hefty deposit on a dahabeeyah, and I have lots of plans for how I want to furnish it. A dream like that is too good to give up on, and it's about time we got our work permits filled in and submitted. So, let's just focus on getting those Aten discs out of this pit, shall we?'

All that said, I was very happy to join him in the bruising kiss he swept me into, crushed against the hard length of him on the stone floor.

A discreet cough interrupted us. 'Merry and Adam, I have de rope. What is it dat you suggest we should secure it to?'

In the end we dragged the golden throne into the corridor. It took all three of us to shift it, grunting and sweating at the effort. The images of Nefertiti and Akhenaten were carved into the back of it with such skill, inlaid with semi-precious stones; it looked almost more like a photograph than a carving wrought in solid gold.

We pulled it as close to the edge of the shaft as we dared, then took an age securing one end of the rope around one of the back legs and pulling on it with all our combined strength to ensure the knot was tied fast. 'I suggest you sit in it, Merry,' Adam said. 'You're not very heavy, but even a little bit of extra ballast will help to counterbalance my weight. Especially if Ahmed holds onto it, too.'

I stared at him in dismay. I don't think I'd registered the bit about Adam being the one to scramble down the rope into the pit.

'It makes sense,' he said, reading my expression. 'I'm much lighter than Ahmed, and there's no way I'm letting you...' He broke off with a sudden shout as we both realised Ahmed was even now stealing a march on us, clambering over the side of the pit shaft with the rope between his big hands. 'Ahmed, no!' Adam yelled.

'It is de sensible thing for me to go,' Ahmed grunted, hoisting himself downwards. 'My job is de security of people who are not from Egypt. I will not let you take dis risk. I have no wish to be enflamed from my job.'

There was no time for Adam to correct him this time. Adam grabbed at the throne while I immediately leapt onto it. I'd thought I might baulk at sitting there, where once I imagine Akhenaten himself sat. But when the moment came, I didn't hesitate. We both pressed down with all our combined weight, so we had it as heavily rooted to the floor as possible.

'Please just be careful,' I begged as Ahmed's seal-like cap of hair disappeared beneath the edge. I felt the throne shift underneath me. 'He's too heavy,' I wailed. 'Oh, Adam, no, please...' He dropped down onto the stone floor, wedging his back up against the throne with his feet propped at the ledge of the pit shaft. 'If he pulls the throne forward, he'll take you over the edge!'

'If I don't there's every chance he'll pull the throne over, and you with it,' he gasped out.

We sat in an agony of suspense, feeling the throne shifting forwards by inches as Ahmed wriggled his way down the taut length of rope. All I could do was watch helplessly as Adam's feet slid closer and closer towards the black abyss. They had only a finger's width to go when everything went suddenly still and silent.

'Ahmed?' Adam shouted.

'De rope it is too short.' His disembodied voice floated back up to us from the depths. 'I am going to have to jump de last few feet.'

'No Ahmed, it's too dangerous. You'll fall onto the spikes. Come back up again.'

'If we don't get de discs, we will all perish in dis place,' he called back dispiritingly.

'We'll find something to make the rope longer,' Adam shouted.

'No, no; I will slide down de wall.' And with that the rope went suddenly slack as he let go of it.

'*No!*' we shouted in unison.

It sounded like more than a few feet to me. Ahmed landed with a far-off thud and a yell of pain. Adam and I darted forward. 'Ahmed?' we screamed in one voice as Adam shone the flashlight into the pit.

A groan drifted upwards. 'Can you see him?' I cried as Adam tried to get the beam to penetrate to the bottom of the shaft.

'One of de spikes it has speared my leg,' Ahmed shouted on a hollow note of pain. 'I'm sorry my friends. I have failed you.'

Those words chilled me to the bone. When I thought of him calling us the three musketeers and saying how happy he was to be trapped in here with us, how it was third time lucky for him, my heart nearly snapped clean in two. I realised how much I loved our police chum; the huge bear of a man who rushed in where angels would fear to tread and... 'Oh dear God, he'll bleed to death down there. We've got to get him out.'

Adam was already pulling up the rope. 'I need to lengthen it so I can reach him.' He shrugged out of his shirt, twisted and knotted it, then tied it onto the end of the rope. 'Yours too, Merry.'

I was already unbuttoning it. I handed it over, standing in my bra while he repeated the knotting procedure. He tugged hard on the rope and the tied together shirts. 'Ok, hopefully they'll hold.'

I put a full bottle of water in his rucksack, along with a packet of biscuits, some tissues and a flashlight. It was unspoken between us that there was no way he could hope to get Ahmed back up out of the pit. The rope was neither long enough nor strong enough to hold them both. 'You may need to use the shirts for bandages once you're down there,' I said quietly. 'Just do your best to get those Aten discs up to me so I can think about how to go for help.'

He pulled me against him in a hard hug, spared a brief glance into my eyes; then lowered the rope into the pit and levered himself over the side. I immediately leapt back onto the throne. We'd left it as close to the edge as we dared, knowing Adam needed all the precious inches he could get.

As he'd pointed out, Adam's considerably lighter than Ahmed. 'I'm nearly there,' he called up to me. 'It's still not quite long enough, but I think I've only got a short distance to fall. Ahmed? Where are you? I don't want to land on top of you.'

A groan told him Ahmed's location. I saw the rope move sideways as Adam levered himself further along the wall. Then once more it went slack. I dragged in a tortured breath, waiting for the thud and the shout of pain. I let it out again in a shuddery sigh of relief when Adam's voice called up to me. 'I'm ok Merry.' I scrambled off the throne and sprawled at the edge of the pit so I could see over the edge. Since Adam now had a flashlight with him it was far easier to see into the awful depths of the shaft.

Ahmed was huddled against the wall. I could see the deadly stake thrusting up through his leg just above the knee in a spreading pool of blood. He must have tipped sideways as he dropped from the end of the rope. A low moan escaped him as Adam reached him. I could hear Adam murmuring soothingly to him while he uncapped the water and poured it gently over the wound. 'I don't know if I dare try to break the shaft and pull it free,' he said after a long pause. 'I'm not sure I could do anything to stem the bleeding. Ahmed, mate, I think I'm going to have to leave you like this while we try and see about raising the alarm.'

I didn't hear a response. 'Adam?' I called down after a moment.

'He's passed out,' was his response. 'It's probably for the best. The pain must be agonising.'

'Can you get to the discs?'

I saw the beam of his flashlight waving in the depths. It illuminated the up-thrusting pikes of countless spears bedded into the floor. But now he was down among them rather than falling onto them from above, their potential to do him deadly harm was gone. 'Yes! One's almost within reach and the other's just over there.' I watched him ease between the spikes. 'Ok, I have them. Stand back, Merry. You don't need to catch them. It doesn't matter which side of the corridor they land. You'll need to find some way of bridging the shaft like we did with the scaffolding planks.

You can collect the Aten discs later. Ok, I'm just about to toss the first one up.'

I stood back. I had no wish to be decked by it. I heard Adam's loud grunt as he threw it upwards then, a moment later, the sickening clattering sound of it falling back between the staves at the bottom of the pit.

'Damn, it's a long way up there,' Adam groaned. 'I'm not sure I can fling it high enough.'

'We only need one.' I called back. 'Remember, we don't need both to work the mechanism. One's enough. You just need to land one of them successfully.'

It took him three more attempts to achieve it.

'Oh, thank God,' I murmured finally, jumping backwards as one of the brightly painted golden discs fell with a thud on the floor at my feet. 'I've got it,' I yelled.

'Ok. Merry I'd like to come up to join you, but I need to do what I can to stem the flow of blood from Ahmed's wound. He'll turn feverish before long. So, you need to work as quickly as you can. Just find anything that you think will bridge the gap across the pit shaft.'

I was already on my way back into the treasure chamber with our one remaining flashlight. There was only one thing I could think of, and it was already broken so I didn't have to worry about the damage I'd be inflicting. A single length of Neferure's anthropoid coffin probably wasn't long enough on its own, but if I could find a way of securing two lengths together, I thought it might just about stretch across the space.

I have no idea how long it took me to heave the fallen stone off the mangled coffin and then finish breaking it apart with my bare hands. I had a rather gruesome moment when the mummy tipped towards me and for a frozen moment, I found myself holding Neferure's three-and-a-half-thousand-year-old earthly remains in a tender embrace. With a shudder, I pushed her back into the niche. She was surprisingly heavy, but I really didn't want to think about what it was I was shoving away from me so unceremoniously.

Eventually I had the ancient wooden boards free and dragged them one by one across the treasure chamber and into the corridor. That I left a trail of destruction in my wake I don't doubt. It was simply impossible to manoeuvre the ancient coffin planks between the lovingly positioned artefacts without knocking them. I muttered a few prayers for forgiveness to Akhenaten and his queen as I went, and a few blistering imprecations to Mustafa for his selfish greed, but mostly I just focused on doing what was necessary to stand a chance of getting help for Ahmed before he bled to death.

'I'm going to have to use the rope to tie the planks together,' I shouted down to Adam. 'There's nothing else I can think of. How's Ahmed?'

'His breathing's very raggedy. I keep dribbling water into his mouth, but he hasn't regained consciousness. He's losing a lot of blood. I don't seem to be able to staunch it. I don't want to frighten you Merry. But I don't know how much longer he can last out with the blood draining out of him like this.'

I'd never heard that panicky note in Adam's voice before. I stood undecided for a moment, torn between the selfish need to beg him to shimmy back up the rope so I could have him at my side, and the heart-rending knowledge that Ahmed surely needed him more than I did. What I was also staring in the face was the stark truth that if my mission failed, I'd have robbed Adam of his one means of climbing back out of that deadly shaft, consigning the two people I loved most to a lingering death among those rearing spikes.

Biting back a frightened little whimper, I conceded to the inevitable and started hauling up the rope. I overlaid one coffin plank with the other, so they overlapped in the middle whilst giving as much length as I judged possible.

The tricky business came with wrapping the rope around the overlapping middle portion of the joined planks and securing it. I've never been taught how to tie knots and my first couple of experiments had me howling with frustration as the rope loosened and the planks swung apart.

But on my third attempt the knot held fast with the rope tightly lashing the planks together. With no time to waste I knew I didn't have the luxury of propping my makeshift bridge somewhere and loading gold on top of it to see if it could bear the weight. All I could do was lever it across the pit shaft and hope for the best.

My first shout of triumph was seeing it push out onto the other side of the corridor. I'd judged the length correctly. My second came when I lobbed the Aten disc across the space and watched it roll towards the entrance, almost as if willing me to follow it.

'For God's sake be careful, Merry,' Adam called up to me, and I could hear his heart was in his mouth. 'If for any reason you don't think it's strong enough then stop. We'll think of something else.'

The moment had come. Leaving the flashlight wedged against the wall so it could light my way I hunkered down onto my hands and knees and crawled onto the end of my coffin-plank. With painstaking slowness, I started easing my way forward. It was so silent I could almost hear Adam's fervent prayers, though he wasn't uttering them aloud. I was about halfway across when my strength gave way. My limbs were shaking so much I no longer trusted myself to move. I crouched there, motionless and terrified.

'That's my girl,' Adam called up to me. 'You're doing brilliantly, Merry. Just keep your eyes on the other side and keep going. Just a few more feet. That's all. Please… keep going.'

I forced myself to swallow. I focused on the Aten disc resting by the doorway and told myself to get a grip. But my legs refused to cooperate when I ordered them to crawl forward. So, I eased down onto my stomach and hauled myself across the remaining distance with my aching arms. I was crying with relief when my groping hands felt the stone of the corridor floor on the other side. Just in time, as, with a loud crack, the ancient wood splintered beneath me. I heard Adam's shout of horror and found the strength to propel myself forward just as the plank gave way altogether. I slumped onto the rock-hewn floor listening to the sickening sound of the coffin pieces tumbling into the pit.

'Merry…?' Adam yelled.

'I'm here,' I whimpered. 'I'm safe.' I took a moment to catch my breath; then crawled shakily towards the doorway and fumbled for the Aten disc. I'd done it! I could set us free! I could only hope the stable door between the Hathor Chapel and the outside part of the temple would be unlocked, although I didn't really suppose it would be. Then I'd need to run across the temple forecourt to raise the alarm. The oath we'd made to Walid about preserving the secrecy of the tomb just wasn't valid anymore. Ahmed's life was hanging in the balance and was more important than all the undiscovered tombs in Egypt – of which I imagine there are a few.

I lifted the disc and started to press it into the slot-like shape in the wall. A rasping sound distracted me. I recognised that sound. My poor staring eyes and my benumbed and beleaguered brain struggled in vain to make sense of it. All I could do was gaze stupidly from the wall to the Aten disc still in my hand, and back again as the stone shifted aside and the narrow entranceway opened up in front of me. I was almost blinded by the flashlight beam that shone squarely into my eyes, and nearly fainted away altogether when I recognised Dan's agitated voice behind the red splotches obscuring him from my vision.

'Pinkie, if you and Adam can't refrain from getting yourselves trapped inside this infernal place, you're just going to have to go back to England and stay there! I really can't be dashing onto flights every five minutes to come and set you free! Why aren't you wearing a top? Dear God, you're absolutely *filthy*! I say, Pinkie, are you alright?'

Too weak to respond, I collapsed limply into a heap, waved at the pit shaft behind me, and started silently to cry.

Epilogue

I'm pleased to say Ahmed is making a full recovery, although we've been told he may always walk with a limp. Hauling him up from the pit shaft was no mean feat on the makeshift stretcher we fashioned. Thankfully, Dan is fit and strong, and Adam had a resurgence of energy.

They were all there to rescue us, of course. Dan and Jessica, Ted, Shukura, and Walid. Ted raised the alarm almost as soon as we'd called him from the *Misr*. He'd suspected skulduggery from the moment we told him about the necklace. Since Shukura and Walid were visibly at work at the Museum in Cairo and Jessica and Dan were patently at home in England, it narrowed the odds somewhat about who might be the guilty party.

'Call it an old man's premonition,' he said, pushing his glasses up onto the bridge of his nose. 'I just had a feeling you were walking into a nasty situation and might find yourselves entombed once again.'

He'd entreated Dan and Jessica to come to Egypt a month earlier than planned, telling them it was urgent, and they needed to catch a flight right away. And he'd prevailed upon Walid and Shukura to perform the same miracle as before with the genuine Mehet-Weret Aten discs, temporarily removing them from safe custody in the museum to bring them here to Luxor to set us free.

Walid's dismay at the layer of rock dust coating everything in the treasure chamber was palpable. Although, let's face it, he's used to dust; he's usually covered in quantities of it himself. 'There is much work to be done here,' he said with a sad shake of his head but also with an odd little gleam in his eyes. That he relishes this challenge, he who's made a career of preserving ancient artefacts, I don't doubt.

As Adam suspected, Mustafa and Hussein's bodies were found crushed under quantities of fallen rock and rubble. Walid used the unstable nature of the mountainside above Hatshepsut's temple to close it for a few days while the excavation took place and their bodies were recovered along with the magnificent items they'd taken from the tomb (which we hastily returned to it, along with Ted's stele and Nefertiti's necklace).

I still wonder if Mustafa brought the avalanche down deliberately; or whether all the gods of all the ages did indeed train their sights on him and curse him with all the divine power they have at their disposal. I like to think for the sake of his immortal soul that he made his own decision. For the wretched Hussein's immortal soul, I couldn't give two hoots. I can quite happily spend my life without sparing him a single pitying thought. He was the third of the unsavoury triad of Said brothers to lose his life while we were on the scene, so to speak. But I am quite at ease in my conscience. Each booked his own appointment to go and meet his maker as far as I'm concerned.

Walid has let it be known that Mustafa was a fine member of Luxor's Ministry for the Preservation of Ancient Monuments, caught tragically in one of the recent numerous rock falls around Hatshepsut's temple while pursuing an escaped antiquities thief.

A quick scour of the Souk revealed a few treasures from the tomb; all confiscated with some firm words from Walid and the local police chief about trading in stolen goods. It's quite handy counting a dead antiquities thief among our acquaintances. We've been able to blame him for all manner of things. If the police chief and shop owners in the Souk have asked any awkward questions, Walid has shaken his wispy-haired head sadly and mumbled about the tragedy of the thefts from the Cairo Museum in 2011.

Ahmed meantime has been hailed as a local hero for pursuing the despicable Hussein after he broke free from his high security hospital. I think it's believed he became impaled on a stray stake while tracking down our runaway nemesis. I'm not sure anyone has thought to ask exactly how or where this happened.

So, what decision has Walid made about making public the tomb and the little rock-cut shrine to Hatshepsut and Senenmut that, in all conscience, Adam and I felt we had to reveal to him?

Well, December 2012 has not been a happy time in Egypt. The new president Mohamed Morsi has been accused by some of gifting himself almost Pharaonic powers. He made a promising start, purging a bunch of military generals from top political jobs to reclaim for civilian leaders much of the political power the Egyptian military seized after the fall of Hosni Mubarak. Then he joined forces with the United States to broker a cease-fire between Israel and Hamas after a week of fighting over the Gaza Strip. But the introduction of a new constitution for Egypt has proved fraught and divisive.

In early December, fully-fledged street battles broke out between supporters of Mr Morsi and opponents of the new constitution. Six people were killed and the army deployed tanks outside the presidential palace, taking steps to physically separate the two sides.

'This fighting is the worst clash between political factions here in Egypt since the days of President Nasser's military coup six decades ago,' Walid said, watching the television reports with shock and dismay.

Morsi put the constitution to a referendum where it has been ratified in two rounds of voting in December. But the turnout was low – just over thirty percent – suggesting widespread dissatisfaction.

'This is an experiment in Islamist democracy,' Shukura said sadly, fiddling with the numerous gold rings adorning her fingers, and staring around at us from her kohl-rimmed eyes. 'Its results will be watched across the Arab world and beyond. This remains a very unsettled time for Egypt.'

'It is not the time to make the announcement of our tomb,' Walid declared decisively. 'We must hold our pledge and wait.'

In one sense this is music to my ears and very good news indeed. I hope it means Akhenaten and Nefertiti, together with the hereditary princess Neferure, may rest in peace for a good long time to come.

On the other hand, I hope the tourist situation starts to improve soon.

I have a very good reason for this. And it is the best news of all. We have today been granted our work permits. This afternoon we plan to meet Khaled at the boatyard to take possession of our very own dahabeeyah.

THE END

Author's Note

One of the great mysteries of a study of ancient Egypt is why Thutmosis III waited twenty years to perpetrate his campaign of destruction against the memory of his aunt-stepmother Hatshepsut. That she usurped his throne while he was a small boy, shoving him unceremoniously into the background, seems undisputed. But the dramatic scenario of resentment and revenge, female usurper and bitter king, so beloved of early Egyptologists, seems overly theatrical when you consider the long delay before a single statue was smashed or temple wall defaced. Some might say vengeance is a dish best served cold. But even so, why wait twenty years? And what did Senenmut do to incur the same wrath?

So far no one has been able to come up with an explanation that is satisfactory. In truth Thutmosis' campaign against Hatshepsut was spasmodic and a bit slip shod. For so much of her reign to have survived, handed down to us across three-and-a-half thousand years suggests he was not as successful at obliterating her as he might have hoped. He left the towering achievement (excuse the pun) of her reign intact: simply walling up her obelisks rather than knocking them down. Some might say this served as an act of kindness, preserving them for posterity when they might otherwise not have survived.

One of the two most widely accepted theories seems to be that Thutmosis wished to erase the female stain from the Pharaonic line of descent. I'd be more inclined to accept this if there weren't other examples of female rulers, before and after Hatshepsut - although hers was undoubtedly the most spectacular reign of any woman and trounced that of many of the male pharaohs. She held the crook and flail firmly in her grasp for twenty years, presiding over a time of unprecedented peace and prosperity. No female rulers in Egypt ever bettered her achievement. Before the Cleopatras, other examples of female rule seem only to last for a couple of years or so. This theory also fails to explain the vitriol against Senenmut. He was still a relatively junior courtier at the time of Hatshepsut's accession and could not have been hailed or hated as the kingmaker.

The other theory that has gained credence in recent years is that Thutmosis felt no need to act against Hatshepsut until he realised his own end was near and feared his son's succession to the throne was in jeopardy. This seems strange since his son Amenhotep was a strapping young adult of approximately eighteen years of age who was certainly no wimp. Once pharaoh he went to great lengths to boast about his athletic and military prowess. And there was no question of his legitimacy. He was born of a minor queen, to be sure, but a queen none the less. This was more than could be said for his father!

The historical record gives us no clue to any rivals for the throne.

Of these two currently popular theories, I prefer the latter scenario. It's tempting to wonder about a pretender to the throne. But we have no evidence to suggest anyone came forward to stake a claim. That the princess Neferure reached a maturity of at least sixteen years of age seems likely, so it's tempting to imagine a death in childbirth for her. The evidence is unclear about whether or not she was married to her half-brother Thutmosis III before her early death.

In the absence of any solid evidence, I have presumed to imagine a set of circumstances that might fit the scanty facts as we know them, and perhaps explain the role Senenmut may have played in helping a rival to stake a claim for Egypt's royal throne.

I hope you've enjoyed this third book in my series following Meredith Pinks Adventures in Egypt. If so, please do leave me a review on Amazon. It's always a thrill to see a new review. I also read and respond to all comments on my website https://www.fionadeal.com

Fiona Deal

December 2012.

If you enjoyed Hatshepsut's Hideaway, you may also enjoy Farouk's Fancies – Book 4 of Meredith Pink's Adventures in Egypt, available to download from Amazon.

To download Farouk's Fancies from Amazon.com:
http://www.amazon.com/Farouks-Fancies-Meredith-Pinks-Adventures/dp/1482335514/ref=sr_1_1?ie=UTF8&qid=1435481796&sr=8-1&keywords=farouk%27s+fancies

Or Amazon.co.uk:
http://www.amazon.co.uk/Farouks-Fancies-Meredith-Pinks-Adventures-ebook/dp/B00HBTTTEQ/ref=sr_1_1?ie=UTF8&qid=1435481874&sr=8-1&keywords=farouk%27s+fancies

Here is Chapter One …

Farouk's Fancies

Chapter 1

Springtime 2013

'Yes!' I exclaimed with a surge of triumph. 'I just *knew* someone famous had sailed on board the *Queen Ahmes*!'

My hand stilled in the motion of reaching out to turn the thick parchment page of the antique visitors book. My fingers hovered over the entry, my gaze coming sharply into focus. I read and re-read the handwritten scrawl just in case I'd made a mistake.

Written in somewhat faded ink, it said, '*I and my party have enjoyed a splendid picnic aboard the Queen Ahmes while sailing among the antiquities of ancient Thebes.*' It was signed, '*Freddy R,*' and there, printed underneath, were the words that arrested my gaze and stilled my reaching hand. '*King Farouk of Egypt and the Sudan; Sovereign of Nubia.*' It was dated 1937.

I sat back under the canvas awning on the sundeck with a small whoop of triumph. My inkling had proved right. And, as luck would have it, King Farouk was someone who could offer not just fame but also a dash of early twentieth century royal glamour to our new venture in offering luxury Nile cruises to the discerning traveller to Egypt.

The *Queen Ahmes* is our dahabeeyah, restored to her former Victorian splendour as a Nile pleasure cruiser by Khaled, a master craftsman who specialises in renovating antique vessels at his boatyard on the Nile a little way south of Luxor. A dahabeeyah is probably best described as a kind of sailing yacht. They were the original Nile cruise boats, pioneered by Thomas Cook in Victorian times when he introduced wealthy travellers to the delights of tourism in Egypt. He took the basic design from ancient Egyptian prototypes carved onto tomb and temple walls in antiquity. Before the advent of steam ships and the modern diesel-fuelled cruisers, hiring a dahabeeyah was the only way to sail up and down the Nile.

The *Queen Ahmes* is a true vintage sailboat. She sits long and low in the water, perhaps a bit barge-like; with her narrow windows glinting darkly in the fierce sunshine, mostly looking like an ordinary houseboat. Ordinary, that is, until you see her with sails unfurled. She has two. The largest is hoisted at the front of the boat, or the prow as I'm trying to get used to calling it. The slightly smaller one is rigged on a long diagonal pole at the stern. To see the *Queen Ahmes* with both sails unfurled, billowing and snapping in the breeze never fails to raise a lump in my throat. To say Adam and I are proud owners of this beautiful antique vessel would be the understatement of the century.

I felt a slow grin spread across my face. Knowing King Farouk of Egypt sailed the Nile onboard our dahabeeyah gave me not only a deep personal thrill but also a great marketing angle. It was something I could make much of on our new website to attract would-be travellers with the lure of following in glitzy celebrity footsteps. Grinning daftly, I gazed in a kind of entranced wonder at the leather-bound tome lying lengthways across my lap. Then I lifted my gaze and let it travel across the renovated sundeck, imagining Egypt's last reigning king and his party reclining on luxurious loungers in the shade cast by the glorious unfurled sails as the *Queen Ahmes* drifted down the Nile.

Eager to share my find, I jumped up. I left the visitor book in deep shade on deck, protected from the fierce

Egyptian sunlight by a cushion, and went in search of Adam. I found him in our newly installed and gleaming stainless steel kitchen. He was brewing fresh coffee and throwing leftover lunch-scraps to the small army of stray cats who patrol the stone causeway where the *Queen Ahmes* is docked.

'What is it?' he asked, pausing mid-throw to level his gaze on my face. A sliver of chicken dangled between his fingers. 'You look like the cat that got the cream.'

'I've made a discovery!'

His lovely blue eyes narrowed on mine, darkly lashed and snapping with humour even as he groaned, 'Don't tell me, Merry. You've located an ancient papyrus that's not seen the light of day for centuries. Or perhaps you've come across a previously unknown royal tomb. No... let me guess again... You've unlocked the deepest, darkest mysteries of the pyramids in the half hour you've been out of my sight since lunchtime.'

'Stop teasing,' I grinned at him, attempting a pout that didn't quite come off. Actually I love it when he teases me, since he always does it with a smile on his face and a soft look in his eyes, and never in the hectoring tones of a certain ex-boyfriend of mine. Adam's always said I have a special talent for uncovering secrets from Egypt's ancient past. And just in case he should be accused of exaggeration, perhaps I should point out I've had all bar one of the experiences he'd just elucidated. And *should* I ever be fortunate enough to unlock the deepest, darkest mysteries of the pyramids, I'll be sure to make a careful note of all the particulars and count myself lucky. 'No, no; nothing like that,' I said airily, deciding to make him wait. 'I'll tell you all about it upstairs on deck when the others join us.'

I left him to finish brewing the coffee; grinning at the perplexed look he shot me before he turned to throw the chicken scrap through the open window to the mewing cats. I carried a tray loaded with small china cups up the spiral staircase onto the deck. Once I'd deposited them on the low coffee table in the shade, I leaned against the railing on the sundeck, letting the hot sunshine splash all over me.

The view from our licensed berth at a crumbling stone wharf just south of Luxor is truly spectacular. It's possible to glimpse the bronzed rock of the Theban hills in the distance between palm trees that nod conversationally to each other along the riverbank. Donkeys, sheep and goats stray onto the sandbars when their owners are dozing. On the opposite bank, a line of modern hotels stretches down towards the city of Luxor, soft-focused in the heat haze. The dark waters of the Nile in between are often decorated with feluccas zipping past, their triangular sails billowing in the breeze that tends to blow up in the late afternoon to take the edge off the shimmering heat.

The 'others' I'd mentioned were our friends from Cairo, Ted, Walid, Shukura, and her husband Selim. We'd invited them to spend the Easter weekend with us. This wasn't so much to celebrate the religious festival. Walid, Shukura and Selim are Muslim, after all. It was more so we could throw a kind of dahabeeyah-warming party now all the painting-and-decorating was done.

We'd taken possession of the *Queen Ahmes* from Khaled just before Christmas, and spent the time since lovingly adding all the finishing touches to transform her into a luxury cabin cruiser. We'd set aside a generous budget for décor and furnishings. Adam was more flush with cash than me, having been on the receiving end of bankers' bonuses for a number of years before disenchantment set in. I had my redundancy money to contribute, and knew my savings would see me through a lean year or two if I was careful. So with our budget burning a hole in my pocket I'd indulged in an orgy of shopping, mostly in Cairo, despite the on going troubles there. We knew we couldn't skimp on quality if we wanted to offer genuine luxury Nile cruises for discerning travellers.

My list included muslin drapes, Egyptian cotton bed linen and soft towels, iron bedsteads and antique furniture, all in white to complement the teak flooring and wooden shutters. I'd splashed out on Victorian washstands complete with porcelain pitchers and bowls in delicate designs – this despite the fact that every cabin is equipped with a luxurious modern bathroom, thanks to Khaled's skill in both design and plumbing. Now each of our six cabins (including the one Adam and I had claimed as our own) was an exquisite haven of quality and simple elegance, with a nod to the heyday of Victoriana.

We'd gone to town with no less enthusiasm in the public areas. Our semi-circular lounge bar-cum-dining room, its shape following the curve of the stern, invited weary travellers to sink onto deeply cushioned sofas upholstered in rich patterned silk, and relax with a drink in hand, perhaps dipping into one of the small library of Egyptian history and picture books we'd lined along one wall. And our pièce de résistance, the upper deck, where I was standing now, was resplendent under its canvas awning with rattan furniture, antique steamer-style recliners furnished with deeply padded cushions, potted palms in deep brass containers, and Turkish rugs scattered hither and thither across the wooden floorboards.

I gazed about me with fierce pride. Alongside all the shopping, Adam had been busy with a paintbrush. Every surface that wasn't varnished wood or polished brass gleamed with the soft calico-white of fresh paint.

It seemed we'd barely blinked and Easter was upon us. We decided it was as good an excuse as any for a launch party. So we'd invited our friends to fly down to Luxor to spend a couple of days with us.

Ahmed, our police chum, had also popped in and out as his duties allowed, although he declined to stay on board overnight saying he preferred 'de solid ground underneath me when I sleep rather dan de fishies of de Nile.'

So, all in all, we'd had something of a boat-full for a couple of days. We'd spent long, lazy hours eating the simple meals Adam and I prepared in the state-of-the-art kitchen Khaled had installed for us – talking, laughing and drinking the rather palatable Egyptian wine.

But all good things must come to an end, as the saying goes. Shukura, Selim and Walid were booked onto a flight back to Cairo this evening, and were right now in their cabins packing their overnight bags for the trip. Ted planned to spend another couple of weeks with us, and was enjoying an early-afternoon nap.

Ted was once Adam's university lecturer; a professor of Egyptology, specialising in philology at the prestigious Oriental Institute, in Oxford. He retired from England to Cairo a few years back, and we have him to thank for helping us out of various scrapes during the time Adam and I have spent in Egypt. Walid and Shukura are our good friends from the Cairo museum. They, too, have played their part in our adventures over recent months. Adam wasn't too wide of the mark when he listed escapades including finding hidden tombs and an ancient papyrus that hadn't seen the light of day for centuries. But, for the time being, and for very good reason, we were sharing a pact of silence about the discoveries we'd made. We'd agreed not to speak of them, even among ourselves on this visit.

I heard Adam call out that coffee was ready; and one by one they climbed the spiral staircase to join me up on deck.

Adam immediately spied the antique visitor book peaking out from underneath the cushion tassels. 'Aha! Is this the tantalising 'discovery' by any chance?' he asked, pulling it out as he sat down and resting it across his knees.

'What is it?' Shukura asked, settling herself into a steamer chair and tucking the colourful folds of her kaftan around her. As ever when she wasn't squeezed into the too-small navy suit she wears to work at the museum, she was swathed in gloriously flamboyant style in bright blues and greens, with a turquoise headscarf covering her hair, and quantities of chunky gold rings adorning her fingers.

I explained my find, pouring steaming coffee into the china cups from a huge silver cafetière, and motioning everyone to help themselves to sugar and milk. 'Khaled discovered it inside an ornate Victorian safe during his restoration of the *Queen Ahmes*. Somehow over the years the iron door-lock corroded and the hinges twisted. I guess the fierce Egyptian heat got to it. Khaled had to resort to a blowtorch in the end to cut through the metal. Inside he found a few old banknotes of various currencies dating to the 1930s, and this crusty-old ledger.'

'Which turns out to be a visitor book,' Ted said, leaning forward to peer at it a bit myopically. Ted is a small, dapper man in his mid-seventies, with a full head of silvery hair and a pair of wire-rimmed glasses that perpetually seem to be about to fall off the end of his nose. 'How fascinating,' he murmured.

'Adam and I glanced through it when Khaled first presented it to us. But it was just after we took possession of the dahabeeyah.' I grinned at Adam. 'We were in the first flush, or more accurately, frenzy, of painting and decorating, remember?'

Adam nodded, smiling, and I let my gaze rest on him for a moment, noting how tanned, lean and fit he looked. Actually, letting my gaze rest on Adam is a little treat I indulge in regularly. I still can't quite believe this is my life now, and how lucky I am. A year ago I was accepting redundancy from a job I'd grown horribly bored with, and plodding along in a relationship that was going nowhere. Sometimes I still have to pinch myself to believe just how much things have changed. Sitting across from me on a rattan armchair, with his dark brown hair glossed by the hot sunshine and his tanned limbs exposed by shorts and a loose t-shirt, he looked relaxed, healthy and very handsome.

I gave myself a little shake and watched him turn to the first entry. He frowned over the flowing copperplate script, the ink now faded to a pale yellowy brown. 'It's dated 1897,' he said, glancing up. 'The author signs herself Mrs Florence Merryweather of York, England.'

I grinned at him. 'Yes, I thought it a rather touching coincidence that the first guest to record her passage down the Nile on board the *Queen Ahmes* should have my name – Merry – within hers.'

He smiled into my eyes and I knew we were registering another of those odd little quirks of fate that made our ownership of the *Queen Ahmes* seem predestined. I'm not usually superstitious. But even the name of the dahabeeyah herself, *Queen Ahmes*, seemed prophetic when we first heard it. The original Queen Ahmes, an elusive ancient Egyptian queen, was closely wrapped up in how Adam and I first met, almost a year ago, on the forecourt of Hatshepsut's mortuary temple on the west bank near Luxor.

I enjoyed the little shiver of kismet that snaked down my spine, looking into Adam's blue eyes and watching them darken to violet in that strange way they have when something significant occurs to him.

'So what's the *discovery*, Merry? You were looking incredibly pleased with yourself when you poked your head into the kitchen just now.'

I looked around at them one by one, letting a slow smile spread across my face, and trying to draw out the moment of anticipation for all I was worth as my gaze finally came back to rest on his. 'Flip forwards a few pages. You're looking for an entry dated 1937.'

Adam did as directed and suddenly went very still. I love these little freeze-frame moments of his. In the same way his eyes seem to change colour, a perfect stillness will often settle over him when he's struck by something momentous.

He began to read the entry aloud. Stopped, cleared his throat, and started again. '"*I and my party have enjoyed a splendid picnic aboard the Queen Ahmes while sailing among the antiquities of ancient Thebes.*" Signed, "*Freddy R.*"' He paused and glanced up into my eyes, finishing almost in a whisper. '"*King Farouk of Egypt and the Sudan; Sovereign of Nubia. 1937*"'

I gave a little whoop, the twin of the one I'd made earlier, and repeated my earlier pronouncement for good measure. 'I just *knew* someone famous had sailed on board the *Queen Ahmes*!'

A slow smile tugged the corners of his mouth upwards, 'I'd never go into bat against your instincts, Merry. They're unswervingly accurate. So, here you are... right again! Wow! King Farouk of Egypt, no less.'

'I'm planning to make a big deal out of it on the website.' I said. 'But I'll need to find out a bit about him first. I can't honestly say I know a whole lot about King Farouk.' I'd devoted the moments not spent shopping and decorating in recent weeks to building our website to manage bookings. I was modestly pleased with the result. It marketed the *Queen Ahmes* as a dahabeeyah offering antique passage in an antique land to those drawn to Egypt by the lure of nostalgia as well as by the wonders of antiquity. This discovery was the icing on the cake.

Adam passed the visitor book around so everyone could exclaim over the hand-written entry.

'I'm with Merry,' Adam admitted. 'I know very little about our royal guest here. I know he was deposed and exiled to Europe when President Nasser came to power, but that's about it. Was he really called Freddy?'

'No,' Walid replied. 'Farouk was his first name. He picked up the nickname "Prince Freddy" when he attended the Royal Military Academy in England in 1935, the year before he became king.'

Walid is the curator of the Egyptian Museum of Antiquities in Cairo. I'd always assumed he knew more about Egypt's ancient past than its more modern history, but he was about to prove me wrong. Between them, he, Shukura and Selim painted a lavish portrait of Egypt's last reigning king.

'Farouk was born into a rather eccentric family,' Walid's wispy hair lifted in the warm breeze blowing across the deck as he studied the faded signature in the visitor book. 'He was the only son born to King Fuad, among a gaggle of girls. A fortune-teller told Fuad that 'F' was his lucky letter. So he gave each of his six children a name starting with 'F'.'

I raised my eyebrows. 'That must have been confusing at bath time.'

Walid smiled at me. 'And Farouk continued the legacy. He insisted his first wife change her name from Safinaz to Farida when they married. And he named his own four children Ferial, Fawzia, Fadia and Fuad.'

'So Freddy was certainly acceptable as a nickname,' Adam murmured.

Shukura leaned back against the cushion on her rattan armchair and gazed across the deck. Her dark brown, kohl-rimmed eyes went a bit unfocused for a moment, then snapped alert again as she sat forward and said excitedly, 'You know Farouk may have been courting his first wife while he was onboard, my dears.' To look at her, Shukura is an Egyptian lady of a certain age through and through. So when she speaks English her Home Counties accent always comes as a bit of a surprise. It's courtesy of the years she spent studying at Oxford. 'The entry in your visitors book is dated 1937, is that right?'

'Yes,' Walid answered, since he was the one still holding it across his lap.

'That was the year after he became king,' Shukura said excitedly. 'He was only seventeen. If I remember rightly, In 1937 Farouk and his family came down the Nile on a tour of Upper Egypt, followed by a grand European tour. Safinaz was the daughter of a lady-in-waiting of his mother. She was invited along to join his sisters. During the tour, Farouk fell in love with the girl, and proposed. They were married early in 1938 and she was renamed "Farida". It's said that during the first months of their marriage, Farouk took her everywhere, and gave her a present every morning. How exciting to think the teenaged king may have been in the early days of his romance when he was on board your lovely dahabeeyah, Merry and Adam. You know, he was very good-looking as a young man, unusual for having blue eyes. It's said he had an almost childlike charm and beautiful manners. To think of him here doing his courting… how romantic!' Shukura is something of a force of nature. This speech was delivered volubly and at high speed.

'So, he was only sixteen when he became king?' I asked.

Selim, Shukura's husband, sat forward and set his empty coffee cup down. Selim is a handsome man in his fifties with lively brown eyes and a thick cap of tightly curled black hair just starting to turn silver at the temples. It makes him look quite distinguished. In contrast to his wife, he speaks English softly and with a pronounced Arabic accent. 'Yes, Farouk was in England at the Royal Military Academy, finishing his education, when his father died. He came to the throne in a blaze of popularity, being the first ruler ever to speak directly to the Egyptian people in a public radio address. He was the only one of his line to speak Arabic. His predecessors in the Mohammed Ali Dynasty all spoke Turkish. So he easily endeared himself to the Egyptian people.'

'But sadly not for long,' Shukura put in with a small shake of her head that made her dangly earrings tinkle. 'He may have been a blue-eyed, charming and well-mannered gentleman, but he'd been thoroughly spoilt as a youngster and now, as king, given ultimate power, huge riches and absolutely no accountability, he set off enthusiastically on the road to ruin.'

Walid nodded. 'It's true. He was a gambler, glutton and kleptomaniac. It was said if there were seven deadly sins, Farouk would find an eighth. He had caviar for breakfast, apparently eating it directly from the can; and the quantities of oysters he ate were legendary. He liked fizzy drinks, and allegedly consumed at least thirty bottles per day! No wonder he became so fat. In later life, someone famously described him as "a stomach with a head".'

Selim sat back and crossed his legs. 'His father gave him his first car, an Austin 7, at the age of eleven; and by the time he'd been on the throne a year he owned several villas, yachts and aeroplanes as well as more than a hundred cars.'

Shukura nodded enthusiastically, setting her earrings tinkling again. 'He had all his cars sprayed red and forbade his subjects to own a red vehicle. That way he could drive recklessly without being stopped by the police. When Farouk raced by in one of his red cars, people ran for their lives. Supposedly, an ambulance followed him to pick up casualties.'

I rather wished I had a notebook with me. Whether the whole being-followed-by-an-ambulance scenario was just urban myth or not didn't matter. It would make for great marketing material on the website.

'He lost fortunes at gaming tables, despite gambling being strictly forbidden by the book of Islam,' Walid warmed to the subject. 'And he became a prodigious womaniser, often boasting of his conquests in front of Farida as their marriage started to disintegrate. He blamed her for providing him with three daughters but no son. Apparently he saw it as a slur on his masculinity. He used to go to nightclubs, and then sleep until lunchtime, and openly took several official mistresses, some of them the wives of other men, until he and Farida finally divorced in 1948. His son Fuad was born to his second wife in the early 'fifties.'

'But the kleptomania was probably the worst of his vices,' Shukura said, her kohl rimmed eyes wide with animation. 'The most famous incident was when he pickpocketed Winston Churchill's pocket watch during a meeting. The watch was an heirloom from the British monarchy.'

I felt my eyes pop.

'Whatever Farouk fancied, he took,' Walid agreed, smiling at my reaction and patting his wispy hair back into place as the breeze continued to riffle through it. 'It may just be rumour, but it's said he took lessons in pick pocketing from a professional thief. At official receptions Farouk stole watches, wallets and cigarette lighters from the other guests. I think the worst incident was when he stole the ceremonial sword, belt and medals from the coffin of the Shah of Persia when it landed in Cairo. It put a strain on relations between Egypt and Persia for years. He was nicknamed "the thief of Cairo". A great reputation for one's king to have, don't you think?'

'But a great story,' I remarked, my fingers still itching for a notepad.

'I'm not sure that was the worst incident of Farouk's thievery,' said a thoughtful voice at my elbow. 'I think we may be about to discover he stole something rather more explosive than that. Something with the potential to shake the very foundations of history.'

All heads turned at this surprising statement, coming as it did from an even more surprising source. Ted had sat quietly throughout our Egyptian friends' telling of King Farouk's biography. He'd been slowly sipping his coffee, staring out across the Nile in a rather dreamy and unfocused way. To be honest, I'd almost forgotten he was there. His pale blue eyes narrowed short-sightedly as his gaze came to meet mine. He pushed his glasses up onto the bridge of his nose. They immediately slipped forward again as they always do, back into their favourite perch right at the tip of his nose. Ted's glasses look permanently as if they're about to fall off.

'Yes,' the professor said sagely. 'There's a suggestion that one of the things he stole back in his heyday as the "thief of Cairo" was one of the famous Dead Sea Scrolls.'

I forgot my fascination with his slip-sliding glasses and stared at him open-mouthed. Judging by the sharp intakes of breath around me, I gathered the others were similarly affected.

Ted peered at us one by one, drawing out the moment as I'd done earlier. 'The suggestion seems to be that the stolen scroll may contain evidence to show some of the key figures in the Old Testament of the Bible were in actual fact ancient Egyptian pharaohs.'

Adam choked. 'Fringe revisionist historians have been spouting that nonsense for years,' he spluttered, looking at his old mentor as if he'd suddenly changed shape. 'I thought serious Egyptologists thoroughly pooh-poohed the whole idea.'

'Yes,' Ted said slowly. 'I think it's fair to say I've always scorned the idea of a direct evidential link between the Old Testament and the pharaohs of ancient Egypt. And I like to think of myself as an Egyptologist with the highest academic credentials.' His pale eyes twinkled, and I thought he might rather be enjoying the shock he'd given his favourite protégé. 'But that was before I heard about the Dead Sea Scroll King Farouk is alleged to have stolen.'

'So, where is this mysterious Dead Sea Scroll now?' Adam managed.

'That, my dear boy, is a very intriguing question, and one I hope we may be able to pursue quite soon, when your first paying guest arrives on board the *Queen Ahmes* next week.'

To read on please download Farouk's Fancies from Amazon.com: http://www.amazon.com/Farouks-Fancies-Meredith-Pinks-Adventures/dp/1482335514/ref=sr_1_1?ie=UTF8&qid=1435481796&sr=8-1&keywords=farouk%27s+fancies

Or Amazon.co.uk: http://www.amazon.co.uk/Farouks-Fancies-Meredith-Pinks-Adventures-ebook/dp/B00HBTTTEQ/ref=sr_1_1?ie=UTF8&qid=1435481874&sr=8-1&keywords=farouk%27s+fancies

About the Author

Fiona Deal fell in love with Egypt as a teenager, and has travelled extensively up and down the Nile, spending time in both Cairo and Luxor in particular. She lives in Kent, England with her two Burmese cats. Her professional life has been spent in human resources and organisational development for various companies. Writing is her passion and an absorbing hobby. Other books in the series following Meredith Pink's adventures in Egypt are available, with more planned. You can find out more about Fiona, the books and her love of Egypt by checking out her website and following her blog at www.fionadeal.com.

Other books by this author

Please visit your favourite ebook retailer to discover other books by Fiona Deal.

Meredith Pink's Adventures in Egypt

Carter's Conundrums – Book 1
Tutankhamun's Triumph – Book 2
Hatshepsut's Hideaway – Book 3
Farouk's Fancies – Book 4
Akhenaten's Alibi – Book 5
Seti's Secret – Book 6
Belzoni's Bequest – Book 7
Nefertari's Narrative – Book 8
Ramses' Riches – Book 9

More in the series planned in 2019.

Also available: Shades of Gray, a romantic family saga, written under the name Fiona Wilson.

Connect with me

Thank you for reading my book. Here are my social media coordinates:

Visit my website: http://www.fionadeal.com
Like my author page: http://facebook.com/fionadealauthor
Friend me on Facebook: http://facebook.com/fjdeal
Follow me on Twitter: http://twitter.com/dealfiona
Subscribe to my blog: http://www.fionadeal.com

Printed in Great Britain
by Amazon